STRICTLY
NO
HEROICS

B. L. RADLEY

FEIWEL AND FRIENDS

NEW YORK

A Feiwel and Friends Book
An imprint of Macmillan Publishing Group, LLC
120 Broadway, New York, NY 10271 • fiercereads.com

Our books may be purchased in bulk for promotional, educational, or business use. Please contact your local bookseller or the Macmillan Corporate and Premium Sales Department at (800) 221-7945 ext. 5442 or by email at MacmillanSpecialMarkets@macmillan.com.

Library of Congress Cataloging-in-Publication Data is available.

First edition, 2023
Book design by Samira Iravani
Feiwel and Friends logo designed by Filomena Tuosto
Printed in the United States of America

ISBN 978-1-250-81847-8 (hardcover)
10 9 8 7 6 5 4 3 2 1

*For Mum and the psychoanalysts who will read this book and
assume that you and I have a terrible relationship*

CHAPTER 1

SOME KIDS WAKE up on their thirteenth birthday with fire in their veins, ice on their fingertips, electricity chittering beneath the surface of their skin. This isn't their story.

I'm average, a normal Normie nobody. Weaker than steel, slower than a speeding bullet. Push me off a building, the only way I go is down. The day my life goes to shit is pretty average, too—with the exception of the junior hero at table three.

July spills over Sunnylake City like a warm glass of OJ, leaving everything yellowish and sticky. Me and Jav are halfway through our Saturday shift at Artie Hanson's Vegan Burger Shack, a faux-rustic diner teetering on the southern edge of the Bridgebrook district. I lean over the park-style bench I'm supposed to be cleaning, nails gouging the wood.

"He did *what*?"

"Chill, Riley," mutters Jav, tugging her hemline down to hide her knobby knees. "Don't want drama."

There won't be any, unless we make it. Bean patties sizzle in the open-plan kitchen. Flies mob the light trap while diners munch below, oblivious to slaughter and irony alike, mopping egg-free mayo from their hipster beards. No klaxons, no alarm bells. No gigantic fluorescent arrow above the junior hero's head, broadcasting what he's done.

He sits with his back to us—I can't see his face. Doesn't stop me wanting to plant my fist in it.

But no, I gotta handle this the *proper* way. Junior heroes might be the lowest-ranking members of America's spandex-snapping security force, but they're still *Supers*, A- and B-class ones, at that.

"Watch the register," I growl at Jav, pushing my peaked red Artie's cap up my forehead. "I'll get Matias."

I march into the service corridor, past the line of lockers that leads to the dumpsters and the gloopy soup masquerading as an afternoon. Matias is in the stockroom, midway through inventory (manager-ese for slacking off on his phone).

"Riley?" he asks as I storm in with all the fury of—well, a storm, I guess, if it found itself crammed in a teenage-girl-size container. Even if that girl's pushing 5'10"? "Where's the fire?"

"Got us a bun lover." I slam my shoulders against the door to the industrial freezer, arms crossed tight enough to constrict my breathing. "Not talking the whole-grain, seed-topped kind."

I relay the basics—a customer stuck his hand up Jav's skirt when she cleared his glasses. Matias's face darkens like a Beanalicious Special™ that's been left on the grill too long.

"Right." He straightens the collar of his red polo shirt. "Don't you girls worry. I'll handle this."

He barges back through the Staff Only double doors. Jav joins us for a team huddle by the napkin dispenser, wringing her cap between delicate hands.

"Told you to chill," she hisses.

I shrug. I don't see why *I'm* the one she's mad at.

Matias scans the clientele. "Point him out, Jav."

Jav dithers, suddenly fascinated by her Day-Glo–pink finger-nails. I do it for her. Our hero's a classic: white, late teens, jacked like someone stuck a pneumatic tire pump into each of his major muscle groups. Three other junior heroes share his table, bragging about their stats on the Superspotter app. Which Villain Council members they've fought, how many henchmen they've KO'd, that sort of thing. Like they're comparing baseball runs, not battles that bulldoze entire city blocks.

All model the official Sunnylake Super Squad uniform: a formfitting white costume with navy accents, a single star on the left pec. They make skintight spandex look hot rather than heinous. Something must be coded into Super genetics, keeps them all effortlessly swole. Peak performance, that's what they embody. Humanity turned up to eleven. Stronger, faster, sexier.

They're better than us. They rarely let us forget it.

The blood drains from Matias's face. "You never said he was a hero."

Hero Handsy overhears. He twists to face us, biceps bulging like they're about to pop, and flicks his honey-blond bangs from Pacific-blue eyes.

"Hey, dude." His voice is as smooth as the almond-butter caramel on the dessert menu. "Matias, right? Name's Cooper Hanson. Uncle Artie said my burger was on the house."

His uncle could be president for all I care. Restaurant policy comes down hard on creepsters. Lifetime ban incoming in five, four, three, two . . .

"Hope the food meets your satisfaction," Matias mumbles. Then he hooks me and Jav by our elbows and steers us into the staff corridor.

The fuck?

I break his grip soon as the doors swing shut. *"Hope the food meets your satisfaction?* You know there's hygiene laws about kissing ass in front of customers?"

"Obscenity laws, too," offers Jav. Quietly, though. Her heart ain't in it.

For once, Matias doesn't chew us out for lip. "Take an early break," he says. He won't meet our eyes.

Jav squeezes my wrist before I can give Matias a detailed rundown of which of his body parts I'd like to break instead. She shakes her head in silent warning. *It's not worth it.*

Matias makes like he's gonna say something else—an apology? An excuse?—but my glare dissolves whatever's left of his spine. He tugs his sweaty collar from his neck and slinks off to do more inventory.

It's warmer out here than in the restaurant. The peeling linoleum sticks to our shoes, a brick propping open the back door in the vain hope of enticing a breeze. Jav releases me, leaving me to do my usual thing where I pretend my skin doesn't hypersensitize at her touch.

"Damn, Riles," she says, shoving her cap in her locker and fluffing out her thick, bouncy 'fro. "You see why I told you to drop it?"

I wrench my own locker open, the door striking the metal frame. Who cares if I break it? That's Matias's problem, not mine. And, as I've decided, from this point forward I don't give a sticky, backed-up *crap* about Matias's problems.

"You're doing that thing again," I say. "The one where you're always right."

"Most people would see that as a positive quality."

"Most people haven't been victimized by your 'I told you so' look every day since pre-K. Yeah—see? There! That thing you're doing with your eyebrows, right now."

Jav aims those brows at the mirror taped to the inside of her door instead. She frowns at herself, digging a tube of liquid liner from her shirt pocket to touch up her faded left wing. "This is my usual face. I always look like this."

"*Exactly.*"

I earn an eye roll: another Jav specialty. "Anyway, on the subject of that Super. I actually had a kid named Cooper Hanson in my homeroom class at Ralbury. We're talking way back, though. Before . . ."

Before Cooper turned thirteen and started bench-pressing twice his weight. Before he got pulled from his regular classes to dedicate more time to the Super Squad training program.

Before.

Ralbury's the best private school this side of the river. Their uniform has a coat of arms on the blazer, like some sort of Masonic youth division. Most kids who enroll there don't *need* a summer job. They got their own Uncle Arties.

Javira Neita is the scholarship exception. We live on the same block, in the shrinking part of our district that's more projects and police sirens than Insta-friendly restaurants. We used to be in the same class, too, until she skipped a grade ahead of me in elementary. She's headed places—high as any Normie can get. Up, up, and away from Bridgebrook.

For now, though, she's stuck here: busting ass to help cover her reduced-but-still-astronomical school fees. At least she'll tip well, once she's earning six figures.

"Didn't recognize him," Jav continues as I grab my noodle cup. "Guess he looked real different out of spandex."

"He'll look different outta his skin, too, once I get it off him. I'mma peel that boy like a potato."

Jav fakes a gag. "Have some respect for lunchtime."

"Cute you think I'm joking."

"You better be." Jav's frown groove burrows deeper into her forehead. She glances at the open door, like she's scared who'll overhear. "This ain't a game, Riley. Some fights you can't win."

Don't I know it. Still, it makes me wonder *what if . . .*

I shake the noodles to ensure even powder distribution, the rattle drowning out my thoughts. "Let's tell Twitter. I'm talking full callout. Name and shame." Jav snorts like I told her to take out a hit on Cooper. Since that's my next suggestion, I switch tactics. "C'mon. If you wanna be some big-shot journalist, you gotta care about the truth."

"Journalists care about *headlines*. This ain't exactly breaking news." Jav cracks her own lunchbox. "I mean, damn, Riles. Next you'll tell me to go to the cops."

Bridgebrook girls don't do that. But Bridgebrook's been changing lately. "We *could*."

Jav laughs. She stops when I don't join in. "Shit, you for real? Don't overreact."

"How's it an overreaction?" I soak my noodles and head for the microwave. "He got to *second base* with you, and Matias did nothing."

Jav strokes the edge of her Tupperware. We get discounts on burgers, but Artie's considers itself *gourmet*, catering to the gentrifiers whose mid-rise condos creep out from the new marina like glittering glass-clad siege towers. It's cheaper to pack your own food—though Jav's five sprigs of lettuce and a chopped tomato don't exactly stoke my appetite.

"Only witnesses were his friends," she says. "They won't snitch, and the cops won't do shit." Sunlight streams through the open door, glinting off her inky skin. "He's a *hero*, Riley. They work in the same *department*."

"Okay, no cops." My noodles turn slow revolutions, the loose microwave plate bonking the door. "But *somebody*. The Super Squad won't let a junior hero initiate with sexual assault on his record." I think. I hope.

What a shame, people like to say when asswads like Cooper throw away their future. *He had so much potential.*

Good riddance, I prefer.

If Jav squeezes her fork any tighter, it'll snap. "Drop it."

"But—"

She stabs a sprig of lettuce, glaring so hard I expect it to wilt. "My ass, Riley. Not yours."

"Yeah, and if it *was* my ass, I'd make sure Cooper never did it to anyone *else's* ass, even if it meant *removing his hands*."

The microwave pings, saving us from further conversation. I stir, my back to Jav, and fork hot noodles into my mouth until my tongue's a numb, burned slug. I can't believe she wants to let Cooper get away with this. I can't believe she wants to let him *win*.

Jav's done with our conversation. She heads back on shift early. When I emerge five minutes later, she rounds one of the kitchen units too fast in her effort to avoid me and knocks a tray of uncooked patties off the edge. They clatter to the floor, loud as a pileup on the freeway.

Customers stare. Matias must feel guilty; he doesn't snap. Just mumbles for Jav to sweep the burgers into a trash bag. She does like she's told, not looking at me. Every time I glance over, she's in full customer-service mode, laughing and smiling and *yes, sir/ma'am*-ing like a windup toy.

In the end, I spend too much time looking and not enough listening. I fluff an order—first in months. Matias *does* bark at me. During cleanup, he sticks me on dumpster duty in penance. I'm too busy trying to catch Jav's gaze to shoot him the stink eye he deserves.

Okay, so maybe she has a point, much as it pisses me off to admit it. Not my ass. Not my fight. If Jav wants to lie low, dodge the drama, be the first Bridgebrook kid in a generation to aim for Harvard after graduating Ralbury with top SAT scores, then that's her choice. Not mine.

And, as I realize way late, for all the venom I spat on her behalf, I never once asked if she was okay.

God, I'm an ass. I gotta apologize. I gotta take her out for our once-a-week after-work Starbucks (one frappe shared between the two of us, measured out sip by sip from the same straw, sugar spit clinging to each other's tongues). I gotta find words for why I'm so prickly at the thought of Cooper, of anyone, hurting her.

First, though: my date with the dumpster.

I step outside, into the lukewarm sludge of a Sunnylake evening. I'm grateful our summers stay in the "boiling" range, rather than rocketing up to "instadeath" like they do farther south. Anything over sixty leaves me sweating like a politician in church.

An idling car blasts something whiny by Drake. Our radio retorts with Tim McGraw, "Humble and Kind." I hum along as I lug the stinky black sack down the steps, into the alley that snakes around Artie's redbrick backside.

The notes die when I see the hero.

He leans against the wall of the organic store opposite, vaping in cotton-candy puffs. Matias must've asked him to smoke outside. No e-cigarettes on Uncle Artie's property, but you're welcome to fondle the staff.

My stomach smolders like I've swallowed hot coals. I clench my teeth to keep the sparks locked behind them, Jav's words a reverb scratch in the base of my mind. *Some fights you can't win . . .*

I don't look at Cooper as I hurry to the dumpster. Shame he doesn't return the favor. A spandex-wrapped arm shoots past me, lifting the heavy lid.

"You're welcome." His sweetened breath strokes my cheek. "Daily act of heroism, free of charge."

I can't reply, not without cussing. My fists squeak, knotted in black plastic.

"Forgotten where to stick that?" Cooper could hold the lid up for the next three years without suffering a spasm. But he's a hero—places to be, Normies to save. This is a quick ego boost, like catching a door for a pretty lady.

I lift the bag onto the dumpster's edge. As my skirt rides up my thick thighs, Cooper's eyes drift down.

I know that look. Not attraction; just a power trip. He *knows* he's the hottest person to act like he's interested.

"Want an autograph?" His stare smears my chest like grease

from the fryer. "Some Supers have this policy against signing bare skin, but I figure, hey, if it's what the public wants . . ."

There's that handsome, cocky grin again. The one that says, *I can do anything.*

Fuck that.

I expect him to dodge—that's my excuse. Turns out, enhanced reflexes or otherwise, a surprise attack can still catch a hero off guard. Cooper's eyes have time to widen before a stinky sack of burger bits slaps him round the chops.

His jawline isn't just sharp in the figurative sense. The bag rips, dousing Cooper in a tidal wave of pureed veggies. The resultant *splat* and squeal are satisfying for all of five seconds. Then reality sinks in.

Holy shit. *What have I done?*

For Normies, our thirteenth birthdays follow the same basic pattern. Once the tears have been dried and the tantrums defused, once the kid has been consoled that no, they don't have Superpowers; no, they won't fight bad guys on TV; and yes, they're still just as unique and beautiful as everybody else, their parents sit them down for a little talk.

Not *the* talk (the one about birds, bees, flowers, trees, dingdongs, hoo-hahs, and other awkward mumbles). This talk's about *being Normie.* About what it means to grow up powerless in a world run by supermen. About how we have to pick our battles, and why those battles should never, *ever* pit us against people who can warp reality with a wave of their hand.

Hernando, my sister's dad, had that talk with me, since Mom never bothered. I boiled it down to three core rules: a Normie's guide to staying alive in Sunnylake City.

1. *Keep your head down.*

2. *Don't make enemies.*

3. *Strictly no heroics.*

Nowhere on this list does it mention beating up-and-coming heroes with a trash bag full of beans.

I stagger, torn bag slithering from my grasp. Is Cooper a Shaper? A Surger? A Summoner? I don't know—which means that right now, there are a hundred potential Ways for Riley to Die. My brain thumbs through them like a flipbook: fried by a lightning bolt, the earth opening to swallow me whole, my blood boiled out of my veins.

I stand paralyzed as Cooper stares at the trash bag bleeding mush on my thrift-store tennis shoes. The same mush cakes the left side of his face in a gooey Rorschach of beans and yam. I'm waiting for him to react. Waiting for him to *decide*. My life's in his hands. No cameras in this alley. If he says he acted in self-defense . . .

Cooper laughs. Frowns. Plucks a butter bean from his thick blond hair. As he stares at it, his expression smooths over. Like he's realizing exactly the same thing I am. Like he's running a hundred Ways for Riley to Die through his head, too.

He crushes the butter bean between his fingers, pale pulp mashing out the sides. Then he turns to me.

CHAPTER 2

"FIRED." JAV GLARES at *me*. Like this is *my* fault. "Seriously? I can't *believe* you."

I storm through Bridgebrook's new shopping quarter, shouldering aside pedestrians, slaloming between strollers and yappy teacup dogs. Jav has to jog so I don't leave her and her glare behind. Matias confiscated my cap: a ceremonial rank-stripping. Dishonorable discharge.

My stomach aches, I'm *that* furious. I hate that Cooper got me fired. More than that, I hate my relief he didn't do worse.

Artie's diner recedes into the distance, ringed by the usual congregation of Hozier lookalikes. One more kitschy eatery among all the others that sprout from the sidewalk like giant weeds. Why would I even want to keep working there? Deep down, though, I know this isn't about what I want. It's about what I need.

Anger's so much better, so much *safer* than panic. Wind whips my blonde hair into my eyes. I try to pretend that's the only reason they sting.

"What was I supposed to do?" I snap as Jav hurdles a pug and narrowly avoids trampling a mother of three. "Let him grope me, too? He's a hero! No one would've done *shit*."

"Exactly!" Jav tries to pull me around. Her weighing eighty pounds wet, it's not all that effective, but her touch thrills under my skin, and it's hard to keep powering forward at the same velocity when your knees have turned to Jell-O.

Yup, that's right. I'm the dumbass who lost her summer job, pissed off a hero, and is low-key crushing on her straight best friend. In case anyone was under the assumption that *any* part of my life is under control.

"D'you hear yourself?" Jav continues, oblivious to my suffering. "He's *a hero*! He could've seriously hurt you."

The worry in Jav's voice pours vinegar into my belly, sours all my wrath to shame. What would it have been like, for her to overhear Cooper call in a civilian casualty? To see me, mushed up like an old beanburger, tossed out with the rest of the trash?

"Look," says Jav, softer. "The world's a shitty place, and there will *always* be an asshole with a power looking for an excuse to make it a shittier one. You wanna change things? You gotta reach the top. And you reach the top by *playing their game*."

"Sorry we don't all wanna be president."

"I'm serious. You need to start thinking about the *consequences* of your actions." Her pink nails bite my wrist. "You had *plans* this summer, Riley. Now you've thrown them away. For what?"

"Uh, for landing a swing on a Super-perv? For avenging your honor—"

"Which I didn't ask you to do."

"—which you didn't ask me to do. Yeah, sorry about that. But I was also avenging my *own* honor! Not to mention *bravely martyring* myself in the face of blatant nuh . . . uh, nephewism . . ."

"Nepotism. You really think that was worth it?"

"You really think you're my therapist?"

She doesn't laugh. Shame. That crack was hilarious, since

those grand summer plans of mine revolve around actually *talking* to someone about how it's been five years since the accident, but I still wake up screaming. Only those talks rack up forty dollars per session, minimum, and that's without mentioning meds. Which means—shit.

Without this job, I can't afford therapy.

Jav must see that realization hit. She lets circulation return to my fingers. "Hit me up at the library tomorrow," she says—orders, more like. Nothing makes Jav enter drill-sergeant mode faster than research, even if it's just hunting down another dead-end summer job for her dead-weight best friend. "I've written so many essays, I spout résumé talk in my sleep."

I appreciate it. But what I want isn't me and Jav at opposite ends of a library table, the scratch of her pen filling the air with jagged lines. What I want is . . .

What?

Her and me, bumping hips all summer? Bitching about customers as we wait in line for our frappe (three shots of hazelnut and enough sugar I feel it eroding my teeth)? Listening to her locate that balance between the bougie voice she puts on at Ralbury and the voice she uses around Bridgebrook kids? Something else?

I shut my eyes. I'm not gonna cry.

Jav bobs closer. We're magnets, her proximity pulling me in and pushing me away all at once. "Riles? You up for that?"

On top of running her podcast, she has to write her personal statement for Harvard this summer: a scalpel-sharp dig into gentrification in our district. It's her ticket to the future. Which makes it way more important than babysitting me.

God, I don't want her to go. Every step she takes up in the

world is another one away from me. But I'd never forgive myself for being the thing that held her back.

I breathe her in one last time: a cocktail of citrus deodorant and coconut oil, offset by our matching *eau de bean burger*. Then I pull away. "Sorry, I . . ."

"Riley?"

I fake a smile so big it threatens to fall off both sides of my face. "I gotta head out."

Jav looks unconvinced. But she nods, gaze soft as the parting squeeze she gives my hand. "Message me, okay?"

I promise. I smile some more, though Jav's too smart to be fooled. Then I turn down a side street and study the dazzling window display of the latest department store until I can blame the moisture in my eyes on the glare.

As afternoon sinks into evening, the city ceases its impression of a microwave oven. The air no longer cooks me; the sidewalk doesn't bake through my worn-out soles. I don't know where I'm walking. I don't know what I'm doing. I don't know, I don't know, *I don't know*.

I've clocked after-school shifts at Artie's three nights per week since it was legal (plus a bit before, as Matias never bothered to check). Some kids get to worry about exams and colleges, but most days, I have money on my mind. If I do *this*, can I still afford *that*? I can't imagine what it's like to live without that question etched on my brain.

This summer was supposed to be different. Hernando's new job would cover the rent and the Super damage insurance, while my money went toward my own problems. But I guess I've never been good at dealing with those.

Fifty paces before I can control my breathing. One hundred and fifty before my heart stops pummeling my ribs. Before the adrenaline drains, before the trapped scream inside me ebbs, leaving a void that's worse than this whole day combined.

My feet carry me to a 7-Eleven. Don't know why. The other outlets on this street have cute, bright, eye-catchy logos: pastel-green circles for boba tea, red spirals for a new boutique. Their floors are squeegee-spotless, QR codes integrated into every window display. Guess the 7-Eleven vibes more with me, with its Sharpie-on-scrap-paper price signs and plastic crates piled high with newspapers and overripe fruit. It looks lost, crammed between a florist and a delicatessen. Left behind by the world. Like I'll be, if Jav gets into Harvard.

But the 7-Eleven also looks like salvation. Because there, propped in the window between lotto stickers and spatters of whitewash, sits an advertisement board.

I peer through my reflection. The board is crumbly from over-use, pinholes freckling the cork. First up: The indie phone shop wants a new techie. Pass. I can't even replace the cracked screen on my thirdhand Samsung. I could stack shelves at the mini-mart, bike take-out bags across the city, or wash dishes at the Beijing Bar, our local Chinese restaurant—but they all demand prior experience and references. Who needs references to rinse sweet-and-sour sauce off plates?

I scan the last scraps of paper clinging to the board. They want me to scrub toilets, take out trash? I'm not fussy. Hernando works eighty-hour weeks between his three jobs. I won't make him pick up a fourth; he'd never sleep again. But the only remaining offers are this crumpled thing in the corner and a fry cook position at Artie's, so the crumpled thing it is.

I can't see the job title, because of how the paper's folded. But a phone number smushes the glass with three magical words below it, at the point where the poster contorts: *We Hire Anyone.*

Sounds promising. I extract my phone from my cleavage (nature's pocket) and save the number. A few paces down the sidewalk, I duck beneath the awning of a boutique dedicated to designer handbags. After an obligatory grimace at the price tags, I hit call.

The line cuts to an automated voice. "If you're interested in hiring our services, press one. To reach reception, press two."

Guess I'm two. I poke the requisite button. Five *brrngs* later, someone picks up.

"You've reached Hench. How may I help?"

The woman's Southern drawl is dredged out of the Mississippi. She makes sticky noises between her words, like she's snapping gum. I squash the phone tighter to my ear.

"Uh, hi. I'm calling about a vacancy?"

"Sure. Congrats, you're hired."

No job's *that* easy. Horror stories bombard me: human trafficking, organ trade. Gullible young girls ground up into dog food. "Am I gonna wind up gagged in the back of a white van?"

A moist chuckle. "Not unless you *really* piss off the boss. Got a free slot on one of our summer intake courses. Swing by tomorrow; paperwork'll be waiting."

This still seems suspish. "No interview?"

"No point. Have you seen our flyers? *We Hire Anyone.* Kinda our brand."

"Yeah, but . . . hire them for what?"

A brief pause. "You don't know?"

I swallow my instinctual response of *no shit*. "'Fraid not."

"Well . . . We *are* called Hench, sweetie."

My throat closes like I've chugged from a saltshaker. Hench, as in *henchmen*. The *bad guys*.

This is Sunnylake City: hero-versus-villain central. The Super gene was first documented in a small Japanese town, near Fukuyama. They have a museum, guided tours, the whole she-bang. Even talk of a theme park. Sunnylake has the less glamorous accolade of being the birthplace of the Villain Council, where Brightspark first drove his lightning-wreathed fist into Moleman's fugly mug. Every other week, a new stand-off occurs between dorks in tights.

A- and B-class heroes are the frontliners, while C- and D-class sidekicks provide backup and cover for civilians on the ground. Then you have the henchmen. Minions who scamper after the villain of the hour—though from what I've seen, none carry the Super gene.

I've never given them much thought. They're just . . . there. In the background, part of the scenery. An army of nobodies who the heroes mow through like they're trimming the lawn.

Guess they have to recruit from somewhere. I just never expected it to be a flyer in a 7-Eleven.

I should hang up. Hernando raised me and Lyss right. *Both* of us. He didn't need to (he's not my *real* dad, as my sister loves to remind me when she's in a pissy mood). But he did it anyway. Cooked, cleaned, packed us off to school on time, grounded us when we got detention. He'd kill me if he knew I was *considering* this.

Which I'm not. Or, at least, I shouldn't be.

"Still interested?" the receptionist drawls. I open my mouth, not sure what's gonna come out of it, and—

Boom.

Fire punches the sky. I drop on instinct, same as every other Normie on the street.

I smack the sidewalk. Pain stabs. Skinned my knee. No time to cry over it. I curl, making myself small. Phone tight to my hammering heart.

The explosion swells on the far side of Bridgebrook, over by the Shadder Creek estate, where me and Mom used to live. It banishes the twilight, bright as a second sun. Windows blow on a nearby block, a bell peal of crackling glass. Screams, barks, car alarms. The wail of a baby—*wah, wah*—too small to understand that the Super Squad protects our city, that our heroes keep us safe, that it's all gonna be okay.

I wait for the flash streaks to fade from my vision. Then I stand, brush blood and grit from my stinging knee, and lift my phone.

Fucking *superheroes*.

"Sure," I tell the receptionist. "I'm in."

CHAPTER 3

HOME. PAST THE abandoned lot piled high with the skeletons of rusted cars, wildflowers winding into empty wheel arches. Past the lofts and studios, the crusty tenement houses with their graffiti-bright walls, the overflowing dumpsters, the thump of bass from a smoke-washed window.

My knee pangs at every step. I relive my words to the Hench agency receptionist, over and over: *I'm in. I'm in. I'm in.*

Why did I say that? My breath quickens at the thought of ever facing a hero again. That moment, when I knew Cooper could do whatever he wanted, that no one was coming to save me . . . It was the second-most scared I've been in my life.

At least I have the night to talk myself out of this. If I don't show for tomorrow's training session, Hench can find someone else.

My building, 26 Sloan Street, is one of those skinny three-story mid-row houses that are somehow even smaller on the inside, like a reverse TARDIS. Still, compared to Shadder Creek—Shit Creek, to locals—the row of crack dens by the sewage works where I had the dubious honor of being born, it's a palace.

More importantly, it's *home*. The first place Hernando made me chilaquiles. The first place I fell asleep feeling *safe*. Which is why it sucks so much when I punch our door code and step through, only for my foot to land on a fat, official-looking envelope. I lift my shoe and read the return address, then stomp down harder.

Blair Homes. Just what I don't wanna see.

As the elevator's out of order (it breaks whenever a Super battle occurs close enough to make the ground shake), I crumple the letter and head for the stairs. We live on the top floor. The ground floor is vacant. Mrs. Adorna, our landlady, only stays here a few months of the year since she started doing up another property on the city's far side. Which means she's missed all of Blair Homes's polite inquiries, asking to buy this lot and convert it to luxury studios. The same sort of polite inquiry as the one I intend to introduce to our garbage can.

The walls of 26 Sloan Street rise up around me, my fortress, the brickwork strengthened by the roots my family have put down over the years. But no walls stand forever, and roots mean as little to a property developer as they do to whichever Super was working through their rage issues on my walk home.

Mrs. Beauvais waves as I pass the second floor. She always leaves her door open when somebody's in. The Beauvaises are a nice family, Haitian: mom, dad, and two young kids, plus a cousin who hangs around so much he might as well move in. They've been in this building a long time—though not as long as Hernando, who jokes he'll be interred in the foundations. I return the wave, showing her the letter. The smile shrinks off her round face.

"Assholes," she says, then claps a hand over her mouth, in case her kids heard.

"Don't worry," I tell her. "I'm putting this where it belongs."

"You give it here. We got a shredder."

I fork over the letter before heaving myself up the last echoing flight. My key gums in our lock, but I lean on it until it surrenders, swinging inward to reveal my home.

Sure, our apartment isn't exactly lush. Two dinky bedrooms stand dead ahead—one for me and Lyssa, the other for Hernando and his wardrobe of work uniforms. We don't have room to swing a kitten, let alone a full-grown cat. But the damp smell is masked by lingering traces of garlic and onion, and every surface blooms with clutter. The main room is a cheery garden of thrift store ornaments and broken gadgets Hernando swears he can fix. Our apartment should feel cramped, but it doesn't. Just stuffed to overflowing with family.

Would it be *better* if our ancient peeling wallpaper was replaced with urban whitewash and quirky light fixtures? What would faux-marble countertops and parquet flooring really *improve*? If Blair Homes buys us up, they'll fix the elevator and the drafty duct-tape insulation around the windows. But will they notice what they're breaking?

Lyssa grunts hello as I relock the door. My baby sister hits thirteen in two-and-a-bit weeks and swears she'll turn Super (Wind-Type Summoner, to be precise) despite multiple assurances that our family has never seen a single occurrence of the Super gene. She sprawls on the patchwork-quilted sectional, legs poking from her boxer shorts. One is skinny and brown, the other skinnier still and made of plastic and lightweight metal below the knee.

Amputees are a semi-common sight around Sunnylake, thanks to the Villain Council. But it wasn't a Super who caused the accident that cost Lyssa an eighth of her body mass and me my ability to get in a car without hyperventilating, ribs locking down on my lungs. That one's all on Mom.

You should forgive the dead, Hernando says. It's in the Bible. But I've never read that, and if the Big Man gives out such crap advice, I don't plan to.

I return Lyssa's grunt, dump my lunchbox on the messy kitchenette counter, and start checking the dinner veggies for fur. Saturday means enchilada day—the real kind, since none of us start crying if you dice a jalapeño. I prep everything the way Hernando taught me: browning the cheap death-date beef and onions with the sauce simmering away in the corner of my eye like a cauldron of tomatoey blood.

I'll never get it tasting like he does. He claims the secret ingredient's love, and I lack that tonight.

Jav will clock in at Artie's on Monday, greeting customers like nothing's amiss. I'm pissed Matias fired me, but the thought of not spending our summer together hurts more. It's our last chance, if her Harvard app goes through.

Does that make me selfish? Maybe. All I know is that 1) the thought of not seeing her every day makes me feel like Cooper Hanson punched a hole in my chest. And 2) I can never, ever tell her. Not without ruining our friendship.

Joining Hench sounds like a surefire distraction from queer teen angst. I'm just not sure that's enough of a reason to dress head to toe in rubber and make nice with literal Supervillains.

The Villain Council gathers the biggest and baddest eggs into one evil basket. We're talking A- and B-class defectors from the Super Squad: the sort of power that makes surface-to-air missiles look like Nerf guns. The VC bond over tacky aesthetics, an abundance of eyeliner, and one common goal: take over the world.

After that? Far as I can tell, they haven't figured out much beyond *make all Normies kneel*. Possibly *make all heroes kneel*, too (they have this weird obsession with kneeling. Kinda kinky). Still, despite their growing body count, property damage bills, and new chapters in major cities around the globe, the VC hasn't taken over anything larger than Montana, and that was only for three very miserable days. (Did anyone even notice? I mean . . . Montana.)

The good guys win and the bad guys lose. That's the way it is. The way it's always been. Us Normies don't get in the middle.

After softening the tortillas, I arrange them at the bottom of the baking dish. I lose myself in it: the warm aroma of braised meat and onions, the tang of Hernando's secret sauce. After shunting my concoction into the oven, I treat my legs to a much-deserved rest, collapsing beside Lyssa and flicking on the TV.

Local news prioritizes hero activity, so it's no surprise to find the fireball from earlier topping the headlines. The screen shows a bird's-eye view of a hollowed-out building. Twisted rebar, crushed concrete. Smoke creeps skyward, a red paper lantern teetering down the street like tumbleweed. Lyssa doesn't look up, more invested in her latest TikTok compilation.

Two Super Squad members strut across the rubble, one boy and one girl. Dusk looms over the distant mountains, but our heroes shine in their angelic white spandex, all rippling muscles and flexing hair (or is it the other way around?). The villain, caught mid-monologue, waves at the laser he used to magnify his powers and level the place, touting the glories of global domination.

Yawn. I scan the crowd behind him. Sidekicks clear civilians from the area. I spot a few yellow San Fran outfits among the Sunnylake navy. They must've been vacationing here before the Super Squad alarm went off. Then you have the henchmen. Their uniform's different: a formfitting bodysuit in a green so dark it's almost black, topped off with a sock mask and black goggles. No visible skin.

I pull a face. Can't be fun, wiggling out of that after a sweaty summer night.

Suddenly—*action*. The hero tires of the villain's speech. He conjures a crackling sphere of lightning, siphoning power from overhead wires. The henchmen take aim and fire, launching glowing pulses from their oversize guns.

Can't they see he's a Surger? His mojo feeds off heat and electricity.

The hero grins. After absorbing every bolt (none of which looked primed to hit him anyway), he tosses the resultant super-charged orb back into their ranks. Henchmen fly like bowling pins. They topple to the floor, seizing before flopping limp.

I work my fingers into a knot. They're just unconscious. Right? The Super Squad always brag they keep the city's fatality count low, but do their statistics include the bad guys?

Another reason not to join that green wall of cannon fodder. I add it to my list.

Today's villain is a Summoner. Flame-Type, judging by the fluorescent-orange hairdo. Of course, he *could* be a Surger or a Shaper or even a Water-Type Summoner trying to throw everyone off—but I don't think villains are capable of that much forward thinking.

"Fools!" he cries. Fire—called it!—spurts from his fingertips. "You will never be a match for the Ferocious Flamer!"

I wince. "The *Ferocious Flamer*? Scraping the barrel much?"

Lyssa grunts. I take it as agreement.

The hero backpedals, but he can't outpace the villain in reverse. They trade blows and one-liners. Supers have great stamina—makes it easier to keep wisecracking while you're having the crap kicked out of you. But all too soon, the villain's thick fingers fasten around the hero's throat.

He doesn't see the heroine, sprinting in from stage left. Her jump gains more elevation than the best Normie gymnast (reminding us all why, after the sudden mutation of the Super gene at the end of WW2, powerless people stopped competing at the Olympics). At the peak of her parabola, she sweeps her arms up and over like a swimmer doing the butterfly.

Six snowflake prongs crackle into existence, haloing her head, so cold they steam. Frozen oxygen. Shaper, then. She can mess with the *state* of substances, converting solid to liquid, liquid to gas.

She points at the Flamer. Her javelins dart forward. A fireball intercepts, ice bursting on contact. Shards pepper them both. The Shaper heroine shakes them off, landing lithe as a lynx, crouched on the Flamer's broad back.

A clench of her fist. The air *melts*. It drenches the Flamer, hissing with hideous cold. The Flamer bites back a scream. He pits his powers against hers, fire vaporizing the liquid off his bare arms . . .

All in all, just another Saturday. I'm about to turn the TV off when—*wham!* A turquoise bolt blasts the heroine from her perch.

I only realize my ass is half off the couch when I scoot forward and wind up squatting. A henchman shot a hero? No fucking *way*.

The heroine rolls to a halt against a pile of rubble. She doesn't get up again.

The camera whips around, focusing on the henchmen. One outstretched gun glows.

I don't get a good look. The sidekicks stampede into the henchmen, and the camera returns to the central conflict, hero versus villain. It takes about ten seconds for the steaming, snarling Flamer to reinstate his grip on the Surger hero's throat.

"Pathetic!" he bellows. "Is this the best Sunnylake has to offer?"

Did he bring his own mic? Or are people with operatic lung capacity just drawn to evil? We may never know. I crane my neck at the screen like that'll help me see around the corner, to where the henchmen and the sidekicks fight.

"Hardly!" booms a new voice. Seriously—where do these guys take their projection classes? "Let's be real, though. You're not exactly A-class yourself."

A new hero mounts the debris. His white spandex glows against the drifting dust. He's a junior—only one star on his chest. Must've been helping the sidekicks shepherd pedestrians to safety.

Or, muses a cynical voice in the back of my head, *he was waiting for the right moment to swoop in and save the day.*

His mask covers his upper face and hair. I'm sure fangirls can tell who he is by his jawline, but I'm too busy following the skirmish between sidekicks and henchmen to care.

The camera crews resist me. They insist on a slow, exalting

pan up the junior hero's body. His quadriceps taper into the trim cut of his waist, with a bulge between them that rivals a medieval codpiece. He probably doesn't even have to stuff it with a sock. They say the Super gene enhances *every* part of the anatomy.

"Kneel!" shouts the Flamer, shaking his captive hero. "Unless you want your compatriot to perish!"

The new kid smirks. "Sorry. I don't put out on the first battle."

It's cheesy, but that line will still bounce around Tumblr until another hero spouts something snappier. There'll be gifsets and shippy nemeses fic (which I totally don't read, if anyone asks. Ignore my browser history).

Our hero raises his hands, palms up like he's praying. Wind plucks him into the air. *That* catches Lyssa's attention. She drops her phone on her lap and leans forward, eyes shiny.

The villain's face reddens like a burn scar. "You're a Wind-Type Summoner! You blow on a fire, it gets stronger!"

"Or," says the hero, "it goes out."

I don't care about the remainder of the battle. I just scan the background for my henchman as the hero blasts the Flamer with a jet-stream-force gust, extinguishing his flickering handful. No luck. Fleeing the sidekicks, the henchmen meld into a black-and-green sea.

The Flamer skids over smashed concrete, rolling to a halt. He snarls at the hero, struggling to stand—then shakes his head and lumbers onto the street. The henchmen pile into the rear of a waiting semi, hooking the laser in its trailer to the tow bar. Soon as the Flamer heaves himself aboard, off they *vroom*.

The sidekicks don't chase. Re-engaging endangers civilian life—that's the official line. Like we aren't in danger every minute of every day.

For now, the battle's over. Nothing more to see. With that in mind, I level the remote, intending to switch to something more interesting. Before I can punch the button, the junior hero strikes a victorious pose and rips off his mask.

The remote clatters to the floor.

"Riles?" Lyssa nudges me with her foot. "You having a stroke?"

Might as well be. My throat zips up tight from my belly to the base of my tongue. Because there, shrunk down to fit on our secondhand flat-screen, stands Cooper Hanson. Beaming, scrubbed free of bean slime. King of the whole fucking world.

CHAPTER 4

I SERVE UP our enchiladas with so little enthusiasm it's like I knew the cow personally. Even the dab of Hernando's secret sauce I suck off my fingertip tastes of dust. I remember I only have two plates to fill just before I slop a third portion down on the burner.

Cooper Hanson saved the day. That sucks major balls and so forth, but the glow of the henchman's gun is still stamped on the backs of my eyelids. I've never seen a Normie come *close* to hurting a hero before.

It meant fuck all in the greater scheme of things. The good guys still won. But with one shot, that nameless, faceless henchman changed the rules of the game.

What if my offer from Hench is a chance to do the same?

No. I hand Lyssa her plate and sag down beside her, though I wind up chewing my lip as much as my dinner. If I join Hench, it'll be for *good* reasons. Therapy! Work experience! This isn't about revenge.

I'm still awake when Hernando clomps up the stairs in his big warehouse boots. I shouldn't be, but my nerves buzz like I've downed ten espresso shots. One thing's for sure: I can't tell him what happened at Artie's. He'd only offer to pay for my therapy, on top of every other bill. And he'd do it, too, even if it meant working around the clock.

The door creaks open and he creaks in: a lanky shoelace of a man with a yawn so wide it tempts lockjaw. Hernando's always yawning. It's practically a facial feature. His eyes are bloodshot and puffy, as if exhaustion clocked him with two hard hooks. He doesn't smile often, what with being tired all the time, but he tries when he sees me.

"Morning, mija."

"Night, technically."

"One o'clock; means morning. You should be in bed."

"And miss your culinary critique?" I've already grabbed his leftovers from the fridge; I subject them to a blast in the microwave before I plate and present. "For your approval, chef."

Hernando slumps on the couch, taking his plate with him. First mouthful—his eyes bug wide. He makes this big pantomime of swallowing.

I grimace. "That bad, huh?"

"You forgot the love." He follows with a chaser of tap water. No booze in our house, not since the accident. "How's work?"

I rock on the balls of my feet, tucking my hands into my armpits. "Fine. Good. Yeah, it was good. Did I mention fine?"

Hernando narrows his eyes, contemplating further interrogation, but (thank whatever you believe in) decides he's too tired. "That makes one of us." He checks our kitchen clock, the one that hangs beneath the cross. "Five hours before I head for the Mart. You're off Sundays, yeah? Up for watching Lyssa?"

"I got you covered." I'll leave something in the fridge, say I'm out with Jav. Lyssa's twelve; she doesn't need supervision. Not that I'm biased, having latchkeyed since I could walk.

I push off the counter, shambling for my room. Hernando holds up a hand as I pass. I slap. Teamwork: the Jones-Garcia family motto. We do what it takes to keep our heads above water. I just hope Hench is a life preserver, not a shark.

CHAPTER 5

I WAKE AT eight thirty, which is a small miracle considering I spent half the night staring at the ceiling, wondering what horrors I'll face in today's training session. Obstacle courses? Combat drills? Explosives? Even (shudder) team-building exercises? At least it can't be worse than my imagination.

I sneak to the bedroom door, tiptoeing around Lyssa's arm crutches, which rest against the foot of her frameless mattress for when she needs to get up in the night. She doesn't wake. That's more a testament to her sleep apnea than my stealth skills. For a kid so small, she snores like a gummed-up hedge trimmer.

Hernando's long gone. His plate from last night leans against the drying rack, scummy with soap. Man might be a fine cook, but he never got his head around rinsing.

I flip through my messages while devouring a bowl of Krisp'n'Krunch. No milk—it smells funky, and I'm not risking it. There's one from Jav, time-stamped last night.

You, me, library tomorrow?

I can't. Not because I don't *want* to see her. I want to see Jav all the time. Too much of her, in fact, which always makes me feel grimy, because she's my *friend* and I *respect* her, and I know she doesn't look at me that way. But I'm already struggling to keep this crush under wraps. My head has room for only so many secrets, and if Jav found out about Hench, she'd go full nuclear.

watching lyss sorry

Three dots appear. No problem. Good luck with your job hunt. Period at the end of each sentence, 'cause Jav's a nerd who thinks punctuation exists online. Lmk if you need help. Sorry 'bout everything, girl.

I'm sorry, too. I shoot her a kiss emoji—in what I hope is a cool, jokey fashion, as opposed to an "I want to put my face on yours" one—and dunk Hernando's plate along with my bowl. Initiation for Hench starts in one hour. I don't want to know what'll happen if I'm late.

Wind moans between the town houses along our street. *La Llorona*, Hernando would say, one ear cocked to the sky. I resist the temptation to shut my eyes and listen. Her voice is said to bring death and destruction, and it certainly will if I wander out into the road.

I'm in my smart outfit, consisting of my least-crumpled pair of leggings and a flowery blouse that I could, in an emergency, use as a parachute. It doesn't suit me, and it sure as hell *ain't* me, but I don't have to *be* me today. I have to be a henchman. And while I doubt many of them wear floral print, I don't have a rubber suit kicking around.

My destination: the Crow Building, East Bridgebrook. Street View informs me I'm looking for a brutalist office block that dangles over the edge of the industrial district, its windows patched with plastic wrap and its walls coated in enough graffiti to add extra insulation in winter. At least it's only a two-mile walk. Not a bad commute considering there's no bus route and I refuse to Uber.

I don't do cars. Not since Mom rolled hers through the guardrail, halfway up the Andoridge peaks. Five years back now—though when the nightmares strike, they're in such high definition the crash might as well have been yesterday.

I was twelve at the time. Meaning I still hoped I was *special*. That the Super Squad would whisk me away from Mom's screaming matches with Hernando and the fake-nice mask she wore for our social workers. Actual battles seemed like an improvement on the custody kind.

Mom refused to give Lyssa and me up without a fight. Before anyone mistakes this for proof of a deeply (*deeply*) buried maternal instinct, know I once saw her yank the weave off a woman who went for the same pair of shoes on Black Friday. I'm 90 percent sure she just didn't want Hernando taking "her" stuff. Anyway, the night before the final court hearing, she drank half a liquor store and had the bright idea of smuggling her kids out of the city. Guess she knew things weren't going her way.

Most of my nightmares start like the real one: Her car meandering toward me in the lot outside my middle school. The tsunami of booze fumes when she rolled down her window. I would've walked on to Jav's house if Lyssa hadn't been in the front seat, stiff as a doll, begging me with huge, scared eyes.

I don't remember every detail. Still, the drive went as well as could be expected (for Lyssa: amputated leg. For me: a range of recurring symptoms that, according to WebMD, signify either a brain tumor or a moderate risk of PTSD. For Mom: a headstone where no one leaves flowers). Goes to show. Us Normies are plenty capable of being awful to each other without Supers getting involved.

I reach the Crow Building with fifteen minutes to spare. Whoever named it obviously doesn't specialize in bird recognition, 'cause I count only pigeons. They coo reproachfully at me from their window nooks, splattering the sidewalk with a steaming white Niagara.

The Crow Building is even more run-down than Street View let on. A three-story cuboid of concrete, it drowns the tiny bar next door in its shadow. Snot-green paint peels from its walls and one corner of the roof sags low. Posters blare out from the walls, advertising everything from long-overdue local punk concerts to the living-wage march at the start of August. Still, I'm in the right place. A placard straddles a drain cover, broadcasting its green-on-black message to either side: HENCH TRAINING DAY.

Pretty bold for a criminal organization. But Normie cops don't mess with villains, and the Super Squad won't show for anything less than a kidnapped mayor or a flattened city block. Hench can advertise all they like.

I dawdle closer. Traffic chugs by, distant sirens dissolving into honking and a pedestrian crossing's *plip-plip-plip*. Can I really take this risk? Sure, if I don't work this summer, I can't save for those eight to twelve weeks of trauma-focused cognitive behavioral therapy. But if I wind up in Sunnylake Penitentiary . . .

Will Hernando let Lyssa visit? Will Jav ever speak to me again?

"Hey! You here for Hench?"

I jump half a foot and come the closest to crapping myself I've been since I was in diapers. The man must've approached while I zoned. He looks to be in his midtwenties, with wavy black hair and acne on his chin, tall in a way that makes him look stretched. His skinny jeans only add to the impression that his legs are rubber bands, straining to snap back down to regular size. He stands at the top of the stairs, the double doors wedged open around one of his kicks.

"You coming?" he asks. "These might open into a bottomless pit, so I'd rather not go first."

At least I won't be the only henchman with a sense of humor. "Sure," I say, climbing to join him. Pigeon shit crunches under my shoes. "If you're scared."

"Psh. As if."

"But ladies first?"

He gestures me through the door. "Let it never be said that chivalry's dead."

I take the lead, swallowing my grin. The foyer's all bare concrete, like some sort of factory. "I can safely report there's no bottomless pit."

He pokes his head around the doorframe. "Continue for a few paces, would you? The floor might be holographic."

I do so, then bounce up and down. "Think you're safe." If the ground can hold my weight, it'll handle his.

The walls are nicotine yellow, veined with fluffy cobweb strings. Another board directs us through a door of clouded glass. The room beyond riffs on the same shabby theme: three elevators skulk in alcoves like they're ashamed to be spotted. The one dead ahead isn't fully closed, revealing a lightless sliver of the shaft.

A paper sign is taped to it. No words, but a green arrow points ominously down.

"Just so we're clear," I tell the man, "it's your turn to go first."

He hits the button and, once the elevator arrives, gingerly tiptoes in. I follow, holding my breath at the creak. But nothing snaps, and no anvils drop on our heads like something from Looney Tunes.

"So," he says as the doors labor most of the way shut, divided by a slice of light. It stripes his pointy pink nose. "We never did introductions."

"Right." Do I wanna get personal with another criminal? I opt for caution. "If I told you my name, I'm afraid I'd have to kill you."

He nods as if this is a regular conversation, though a smile tugs one corner of his mouth. "Of course, my mistake."

The light shrinks away. As our downward descent could lose a race against a two-toed sloth, my new coworker does the natural thing and takes out his phone. It wears a custom villain-themed case, modeled on the skimpy electric-blue leotard of Supremia the Surger. Her shapely butt graces one of the highest seats on Sunnylake's VC. That same butt is now replicated lovingly in textured plastic.

I feel kinda dirty looking. Doesn't stop me sneaking another glance.

I'm sure it's very empowering for Supremia to run around in an outfit that shows how close she shaves. No, seriously—I mean that. She has a right to wear whatever the hell she wants. I just wish she wouldn't express that right while attempting to blow up my district.

"You're a fan?" I ask.

"Yeah! You know the Superspotter app?" I nod. "I have to upload clips of battling Supers to get gilded." He flashes me his screen, filled with the app's star-spangled background. "I'll catch better footage in Hench uniform."

Ugh. I retcon my opinion of him up to this moment. *"That's why you're here?"*

His grin fades. "You don't sound pleased."

Damn right I'm not—it takes a special pucker of asshole to video Supers fighting, given the civilian casualty rates. But I'm not in the mood for smacking people with trash bags today. No matter how much they deserve it.

I press my lips together and study the wall until he shrugs and returns to his phone. After a few eons have passed, civilizations rising and falling, our elevator judders to a halt and the doors struggle open. We step out into a new building. A new *world*.

Glam doesn't cover it. Pillars rise from floor to ceiling. The carpet cushions my shoes: a deep, malevolent emerald, thick-piled and soft. I'm too busy gaping at the chandeliers to worry about leaving grubby footprints.

Yeah, *chandeliers*. They cascade from the ceiling, frozen avalanches, studded with diamonds. An IMAX-size screen fills the back wall. Upon it revolve five three-dimensional letters: *H*, *E*, *N*, *C*, and *H*.

The building up top must be a cover. This is *way* more in line with villainous chic.

The receptionist doesn't look up at our entrance, busy pouring grit into what looks like a kitty-litter tray. That's already wild, but her being in uniform adds a whole extra level of surreal. My pulse kicks. I've never seen a henchman in the flesh before—or the black-and-green suit.

The henchman—or henchwoman, I think? Henchperson? Henchfolx? Is there an accepted gender-neutral term?—is called McCarthy, according to an embossed nameplate. Wasting no time on introductions, she gestures us over. Four glowing tablets line the edge of her desk. Two get shoved into our hands.

"Terms, conditions, other boring legal stuff." McCarthy points out the relevant electronic signature boxes. "Names here, here, and here."

Her Southern accent is deep enough to drown in. Must be the gum chewer from the phone. I scroll up, scanning the small print—call me paranoid, but I like my organs where they are. Luckily, Hench doesn't ask for my blood type.

The footnotes: I'm officially an employee of the Crow Building Corporation; something something, 401(k)s, and tax forms. I may become privy to certain secret identities, which must be kept that way under pain of atomic disintegration. Lastly, I have to swear I'm over the age of eighteen.

I scratch each box with the stylus until the squiggles resemble my signature. I'm only four months off. Close enough.

Once I hit enter, McCarthy takes the tablet again. I bobble about, wondering what's supposed to happen next, until McCarthy waves us toward a plush sofa under the IMAX screen. It's green, of course. Right outta Oz. "You two sit tight and wait for the rest of your team."

I ease myself down, wincing at the leathery chirp. "How big's this team?"

"Four trainees, one captain. You'll be one of seventy-five on-call units in Hench's Bridgebrook branch—didn't you look this up on our website?"

"Hench has its own *website*?" This is wack. "So, what? Villains google 'evil minions' and you guys are top of the search results?"

McCarthy performs a big pantomime of a shrug. Exaggerated body language must come in handy when your day job involves a mask. "We have to advertise somehow. Recruitment flyers only go so far."

Superspotter guy finishes with his tablet and passes it over, stare glued to the litter tray. His constipated expression is ironic, considering. I roll my eyes. "No, it's not a holographically disguised laser. And I seriously doubt it's gonna explode."

"Funny you should say that. There was this report about kitty litter being used as a binding component in IEDs . . ."

McCarthy waits for me to size up the elevators and estimate my sprint time before cackling. "Oh, bless you, darling. Don't worry—this is exactly what it looks like. Only dangerous if the office cat's in residence. She doesn't like strangers."

I loosen my garrote grip on the arm of the couch. "Office . . . cat?"

"Yup. Goes by Mr. Bojingles, though she's actually a Mrs.—found that one out a month too late. Luckily, most villains dig the feline aesthetic, so all eight Junior Bojingleses found loving, amoral homes."

I can't tell if she's kidding. Still, Superspotter guy sits beside me, and the tension drains from my spine. I've been an employee less than five minutes, but so far, so good. No Super Squad raids, blaring alarms, or litter trays going *boom*. I classify this as a good start.

Then the elevator *dings*.

My stomach drops. Do members of the Villain Council ever swing by? I'm so not ready to meet Supremia and the Flamer in person.

Luckily, the girl who storms out is no world-conqueror wannabe. She has the athletic body type down, but she wears a sports bra/cargo pants combo, no spandex in sight. I guess that makes her our next recruit. She yanks off her motorcycle helmet to reveal a Mohawk of tight, glossy curls and enough metal in her brown face to make a TSA agent take early retirement. Every motion is vicious and shark-toothed, like she wants to take a bite out of the world.

McCarthy squints at her oddly but dispenses the next tablet and waves her to our couch. The new chick flings herself down next to me. The couch tilts in our direction, Superspotter guy not having enough weight to counterbalance. I grip the arm, praying it won't capsize, while Mohawk girl signs with stabs of the stylus.

"One more to go," says McCarthy.

And so, we wait. Silence curdles like the milk in our fridge. McCarthy creaks back on her chair, tap-tapping at her computer. My brain helpfully informs me that Mohawk girl is gorgeous, under the scowl. But between her haircut and her piercings, she looks like she can't bear to be overlooked. That sounds dangerous in our new line of work.

The final member of our squad edges past fashionably late into unforgivably. I rack my brain for icebreakers, anything to resurrect conversation, and settle for jiggling my leg. I think of Jav, alone at the library, digging into her gentrification essay with one pen in her hand and another dangling out the corner of her mouth to gnaw when she gets stuck. A selfish part of me wants her to be driven to distraction by the thought of my job-less plight, like I'm so often driven to distraction by her—but I know what she's like when she hyperfocuses. Most likely, she's forgotten the outside world exists.

Time crawls by. An old rhythmic jazz hit croons over a hidden radio. McCarthy checks the time on her monitor every ten seconds.

"Perhaps they're not coming," says Superspotter dude. That must jinx it, because the middle elevator wheezes open.

McCarthy recovers first. "Can I help you?"

She assumes the man's lost. We all do. But the old guy—*so old*—shuffles out and blinks at her masked figure through glasses so thick they make him look like a nocturnal animal.

"Is this Hench?" he quavers.

"Yes . . . ?"

"Excellent." Grandpa hobbles in. "I made it."

"You're sure?" asks McCarthy weakly.

Grandpa nods. He extracts a crumpled, familiar flyer and smooths it so it's less creased than the rest of him. "*We Hire Anyone*. Says so right there."

I hope McCarthy will put her foot down. He can volunteer at the library, or somewhere else where baggy wool cardigans with elbow patches are in vogue. But evidently, she isn't paid enough to argue. "We sure do, sir. If you could sign here, here, and here . . ."

Grandpa marks off his name before toddling toward us at a pace that'd make snails impatient. His Star of David swings from a delicate silver chain around his neck, in time with his steps. The couch is full. I stand, an unspoken offer—Hernando taught me right—but Grandpa looks grossly offended, so I awkwardly slump down again.

Mohawk girl snorts like I've committed a cardinal sin by breathing. I do my best to ignore her. Might as well get in some practice.

McCarthy lifts the landline. "Captain," she says, without punching a number. "They're ready for you."

A panel in the wall whooshes back, revealing a corridor clad in bare metal. Looks like the inside of a spaceship. A henchman bars the entrance. He's short and stocky, green-black outfit hugging him from the top of his head to his shin guards and combat boots. No skin on display, no features. No hole for a mouth. That sums up the role of a Sunnylake City henchman. Seen, not heard.

"How long were you standing there?" I blurt.

The henchman's head swivels toward me. His empty black goggles suck me in.

Grandpa comes to my rescue, while I feign immense fascination with the carpet. He hobbles up to the henchman, leaning his left hand on his cane while he offers the right. "Morning, sir—Captain, is it? Pleasure to make your acquaintance."

The Captain gives his liver-spotted palm a pump. "No name." He's British, but not the bougie sort. Less Cumberbatch, more

Stormzy. "You're a smart one." He says it like "un." "Consider this your first lesson as henchmen. *Protect your identity.* Limit what you know about each other. Surnames only. We ain't here to make friends."

"Very well," creaks Grandpa. He turns to the rest of us. "You can call me Birnbaum."

Superspotter guy raises a hand. "Turner."

My turn. "Jones."

We swivel to affix our expectant gazes to Mohawk girl.

"Sherman," she grates, like we've tortured it out of her.

The Captain freezes. "*You?*"

Sherman waggles her fingers. "Me."

"No way, I ain't dealing with this." The Captain raises his arms in an X in front of his unseen face. "Not another word. Get out."

Sherman does the exact opposite, widening her manspread until her knee bumps mine. Her Docs drag on the fluffy carpet. "You hire anyone, remember?"

"Anyone but you! Are you seriously asking for a job the day after I fire you?"

Can I risk a shade-filled side-eye without adding my name to Sherman's hit list? What sort of fuckup gets fired by *henchmen*?

She scoffs. "You can't kick me out."

"Gimme one reason?"

"I'll slash your tires."

"I'll cut *your* brakes."

"Fine. I'll kidnap Mr. Bojingles."

"Take her," says the Captain, smug. "Dogs are the superior pet."

"That makes you a narcissist," McCarthy says, leaning over her desk. "It's true, I read it in a magazine. A dog gives you mindless affection, whereas a cat makes you *work* for it."

The Captain starts to argue, then shakes his head. "Quit changing the subject. I'm not taking Sherman, McCarthy. Not again."

"Honey, you don't have a choice. Hiring everyone is our brand." McCarthy gives Birnbaum's flyer a meaningful flap. "You know how much the boss loves the *brand*."

The Captain pinches the mask over the bridge of his nose like he's staving off a migraine. "All right. But Sherm? Last warning. You shoot *one more hero*, I sink you in Clearwater River myself."

McCarthy tucks the refilled litter tray in a nook beneath her desk. "Like it needs *more* pollution."

Why's the Captain pissed? Isn't shooting heroes what henchmen do? Only—when have I ever seen one land a shot?

Last night. Sherman's the marksman from the news feature, who proved henchmen have marginally better accuracy than stormtroopers. And she's on *my team*.

Rule Number One—*keep your head down*—might be harder than I hoped.

CHAPTER 6

OUR TOUR BEGINS. We leave the main hall at walking pace—more like dawdling, thanks to Birnbaum. He's faster on his feet than I expected, but what's impressive for an eighty-year-old is a whole lot less inspiring to the people stuck behind him. I overtake at the first opportunity.

First stop: uniforms. Henchmen aren't like heroes. We're not built to perfection: girls with matchstick waists and balloon boobs; boys shaped like Doritos with legs. How do you pack us into matching costumes? You visit a tailor.

Ours is a snappily dressed no-nonsense hijabi with eyeliner so sharp it could cut you. She introduces herself as Maheen and has us wait in a narrow corridor, her assistant calling us through one by one. Turner goes first and doesn't come out again. I chew my cheek, but figure Sherman's been through this whole process once and survived. I'm not going to fall into an alligator pit. Probably.

Still, I'm nervous. I shop at the Mart, as Hernando gets a 10 percent discount on his employee card—one XL size fits all. I've never had someone take my measurements. Is stripping involved? Love my bod, bulges and all, but that doesn't mean I want to show all to a stranger.

Thankfully, Maheen drops the intimidating professional act as soon as the door closes. She chats with me about everything from where I got my blouse to whether there's a man in my life (nope) and whether I plan for there to be (pass; the thought leaves me greasy, like oil on my skin). All the while running a scanner up and down, numbers flashing on the screen. I don't even have to kick off my shoes.

"Should I tell you this?" I ask, glancing at the next door, behind which (presumably) the Captain and Turner lurk. "The Captain said . . ."

"Your captain says a lot of things. I'd advise you to ignore half of them." She winks one perfect eye; my heart flutters. "Don't worry. Your identity's safe—I make a career out of forgetting faces."

She calls fitting suggestions to her assistant, a Black girl called Shoni in a slick blue pantsuit. There's no fabric on display, no sewing kits or shears. Just some fancy computer humming against a wall, a tablet glowing blue beside it. When I ask if the rubber suits are more breathable than they look, I get two laughs in reply. The tailors don't elaborate, so I console myself that having your henchmen faint from heat exhaustion isn't a classy look.

According to Maheen, my costume will be delivered by the time I'm home this evening. I doubt it. How quickly can they cut and stitch five couture outfits? But you don't argue with women who've mastered cat eyes.

"Will it be in, like, subtle packaging?" I ask.

"The subtlest," says Shoni, and winks at Maheen.

Like that's not sketch. I thank them, warily, and head to join Turner. The underground facility is a hive of shiny metal rooms, all odd shapes and sizes, packed so tight they almost overlap. In a single step I pass from the tailors into a starkly lit armory.

Oversize guns line the walls. Each is as long as my arm, fanning into a big trombone bell at one end. As I stare down those barrels to the green-glowing filaments at each gun's core, my palms slime with chilly sweat.

Disclaimer: I'm a city girl. Plenty of pieces float around Bridgebrook. Even heard a couple of drive-bys, back when I lived up Shit Creek. But I've never held a gun before. Watching Sherman shoot that heroine was epic, but now I'm face-to-muzzle with actual weapons, and the question of lethality bounces around my mind.

Would I be able to shoot someone? Even an asshat like Cooper? What does it say about Sherman that she already did?

She's next to saunter in. "Shame you tossed my old outfit," she tells the Captain, bike helmet tucked under one arm. If she's noticed my existence, she doesn't acknowledge it. "Could've saved Maheen the hassle."

"Could save us the hassle now," says the Captain. "You know where the exit is. Feel free to use it."

Sherman pins him with a glare that, if she were a Shaper, would liquidize him and the wall behind. Speaking of Shapers, the heroine she shot falls through my mind in a smoke-swirl of glossy red hair. Unconscious? Dead? I want to ask, but that would mean getting an answer. One I'm not sure I'd like.

Birnbaum takes up the rear, peering through his magnifying specs. The Captain does a head count, ascertains that none of us have made a break for it, and claps his gloved hands. "All right. Let's get the boring shit over with."

We close ranks, forming a wonky line. Sherman winds up next to me, perma-scowl directed at her feet. The Captain leans against the giant gun rack. It's impossible to get a read on him through that blank, creepy mask.

"Welcome to your first ever Hench training day," he says in a voice flatter than most roadkill. "Which will also be your last ever Hench training day, 'cause I got better shit to do. When I first got promoted, I took this opportunity to ask the green recruits what they thought our job involved, then correct their assumptions with laminated handouts, pictograms, and charades."

I perk. I'm good at charades.

"Unfortunately, I put my youthful enthusiasm down twenty years back and forgot where I left it. So: the basics. The VC subscribes to all that Supremacy shit. Y'know . . ." Air quotes time. "*Supers are the leaders chosen by God slash fate slash evolution, and us pathetic Normies should kneel at their feet.*"

We nod (Turner a little too eagerly). Superemacists: the alt-right plus powers. Plenty of Supers climb the political tree after retiring from heroics. It helps, having the monopoly on gorgeous, camera-ready smiles. They usually downplay their abilities for the Normie vote, assuring us we're all equally important. Sometimes, you even get the sense they believe it. But there's always one who goes off on Twitter, ranting about how much *easier* life would be if us pesky Normies shut up, stopped being offended, did what we were told. A jarring reminder of how deep Superemacist ideology has spread. The VC might be the preachers, but theirs is a growing church.

The Captain nods as well. "We roll with it, so we get paid. But we ain't our clients' friends, and they ain't ours. You wanna keep breathing? You better keep your distance, and your mouth shut."

Guess that's his version of my rules. Still, I gotta know: "If they think Normies are so useless, why hire us in the first place?"

"Because Supers don't do their own laundry. Most businesses refuse to deal with our clients unless there's a gun to their head. Hench fills a gap in the market. We build super-weapons and battle sidekicks, but also tidy lairs, fetch groceries, walk the occasional giant mutated guard dog . . ." He gives a big shrug. "No guarantee of hours, but there's enough work around Bridgebrook that we get paid four or five nights a week."

Turner's hand thrusts for the ceiling. "You keep saying 'clients.' You mean villains, right?"

"We use neutral terminology. Some clients get narked if you call 'em what they are."

"If by 'narked' you mean 'pissed enough to melt your face,'" Sherman translates.

Turner's prominent Adam's apple bobs up and down his throat. "Ah."

"Always address the clients with respect," says the Captain. Seems he's testing that old theory about playground bullies, like if he ignores Sherman long enough, she might go away. "Do what they tell you, when they tell you, in a timely fucking fashion. Handle that, and you might survive the summer."

"And if a client orders us to kill?" croaks Birnbaum.

There it is. The question I've been sucking on since I saw those guns.

The Captain studies the old man (or at least I assume that's what's happening, beneath his opaque goggles). "You served?"

"Yes, sir." Birnbaum offers no further details. The Captain doesn't ask for them. Just plucks a rifle from its mount on the wall. He holds it one-handed, no visible strain. Must weigh less than it seems to.

"You know what these shoot, Birnbaum?"

"No bullet I've seen."

"Right. This dial goes up and down." The Captain demonstrates. "It charges an electrical bolt, inspired by the Surgers. Lowest setting is a static shock."

"And the highest?"

The Captain twists it all the way. The rifle buzzes like an overweight fly. He keeps it pointed at the floor as a glow builds in its muzzle, the green of Ghostbuster ectoplasm.

"Practically a Taser."

Birnbaum's pruney face concertinas around his smile. "No lethal option."

"That'll knock someone out?" asks Turner as the Captain twists the dial to its neutral setting, snuffing the glow.

"Only in films. A blast from this baby will make you lock up—like being zapped by a C-class Surger. Fun fact: Victims often piss themselves, so be sure to wear watertight shoes." Ew. I'm glad he didn't opt for a live demonstration. "But once the charge dissipates, there won't be any serious side effects. You want someone to *stay* down, you use *this*."

The Captain presses a button tucked behind the rifle's bell. A panel unfolds, revealing the glint of a hypodermic needle.

"One per rifle. Knocks anyone out for an hour, Super or otherwise." He snaps the panel shut. I get the distinct impression he's glaring at Sherman. "Let's hope you never have to use it."

I watch her, nibbling a split in my nail. I'm as glad as Birnbaum that our guns aren't deadly, but this only gives me more questions. Like: Why did Sherman waste ammo on a heroine who wasn't attacking her? Please tell me she's not carrying a flame for the Flamer. I can't handle *two* Superspotters on my team.

Five boxes span the range. The Captain assigns us one each, so we can get started on target practice. Although that is, as Jav might say, a misnomer. Because we literally have to *miss*.

Birnbaum struggles. It's hard to think of an octogenarian as a cold-blooded killer, but he nails his first target through the prefrontal cortex. The mannequin jolts on its mount, a scorched black flower blossoming between its eye sockets.

The Captain shakes his head. "Try again."

The range is a skinny tunnel, fifty feet in length. Our targets parade across the far end, propped upright on a conveyor belt. All are sculpted from a conductive mesh that shines white as Super Squad spandex, until it blackens on contact with high voltage.

I pull my own trigger. The gun hiccups in my hands, vomiting a snowball of crackling electrical light. The blast doesn't reach the targets, dissipating harmlessly against the floor. I got nothing to worry about. I couldn't hit anyone if I tried.

"Why do we miss the heroes?" I ask. "Because they're the good guys, right?"

"Wrong," says the Captain. "If you hit 'em, you'll piss 'em off."

"Won't we piss off our clients, if we're out there making three-year-olds look like sharpshooters?"

"Nah. Our clients take on A- and B-class heroes personally. We're backup dancers, Jones. We do a few twirls in our tutus, but we don't steal the spotlight."

I charge my rifle again, doing my best to put *that* image out of my head. No villain is evil enough to be subjected to my dancing. "Heroes really kill henchmen?"

"Any Super can hurt us, Jones. Don't matter which uniform they wear. They're powerful, we ain't." The Captain jerks his chin at Sherman. "Muppet here's lucky the sidekicks rushed us. If they hadn't, Windwalker might've."

"I could take him," growls Sherman. I don't believe her. The stiffness in her voice tells me she doesn't believe herself, either. She sizes up her shot—then shakes her head, slams the rifle back onto the rack, and stalks for the door.

"Oi," the Captain hollers after her. "Where you going?"

"I don't need a refresher course. Just call me when we got a job." Out she flounces. The Captain doesn't try to stop her.

I lock my rifle against my shoulder and wait for the next dummy to cross my sights. I let my eyes drift, losing focus—the Captain says that'll make our aim worse—and miss again. Just like I'm supposed to.

CHAPTER 7

OUR LESSON ROSTER for the afternoon features such highlights as How to Fall Over Without Snapping Your Ankles and How to Play Dead When Sidekicks Approach. The Captain dismisses us afterward. Apparently, over the course of a single day, we've mastered the full henching skill set.

We leave the Crow Building in the early evening, the sun doing an excellent Eye of Sauron impression in the west. After muttering goodbyes to Turner and Birnbaum, I trundle home, tapping out a message for Jav. After deleting and restarting three dozen times, I finally settle on a generic hows the research ♥ that hopefully, through its dearth of wisecracks, conveys how seriously I'm taking my supposedly jobless plight while assuring her I haven't committed seppuku with Hernando's favorite kitchen knife.

She replies five minutes later with a long line of skull emojis and a really sweet lie about how it'd be better if I was there, though we both know I'd ask constant questions and throw off her groove. Still, the selfie she sends me—her melting dramatically over a plastic library chair and squashing her chin into her neck—makes my tummy flutter.

Yeah, that's right. Her eyes-rolled-back, tongue-lolling, chinless-wonder worm impression gives me butterflies.

Teenage hormones. What even.

I'm at the age where I sometimes get red-cheeked from a) brushing shoulders with strangers, b) the fluffiest, shmoopiest G-rated fanfic, and c) the occasional inanimate object. The difference is, if I mention *those* instances, Jav will laugh and mock me for the rest of our existence on this Earth, like besties are supposed to. If I mention that *she* regularly makes the temperature of my face rival the surface of the sun; that every casual touch we share sets me alight; that when I imagine her applying today's nail paint with a grimace of such intense concentration you'd think she was performing brain surgery, my heart does three backflips and a corkscrewing somersault . . . I might fuck up something that means more to me than all the butterflies in the world.

My phone *bing*s again.

> Meet me at the library, tomorrow lunch? I can help you fill in job apps, you can listen to me whine about Neil Smith's revanchist city theory and pretend you know wtf I'm talking about.

Sounds perfect. I plan on telling her so, but more mail awaits on our front doormat. I keep my foot raised over it, just in case, but don't spot a Blair Homes logo. Just a cylinder wrapped in white paper, the size of an empty TP tube, and my name.

"Huh," I say. "Weird."

I recall Maheen's promise, but it can't be my uniform—way too small. Unless it's just the mask? Frowning at the package, I make my way upstairs, returning Mr. and Mrs. Beauvais's waves on the way.

Lyssa lounges on the sectional, nose to her phone. Each message she receives makes a *thwip* noise, like a rubber ball bouncing off a wall. She's technically too young to spend all day on Tumblr and TikTok, but Hernando's not home often enough to stop her. I mostly let Lyss do what she wants. The more time she spends arguing with trolls, the less she spends arguing with me.

We exchange our customary greeting grunts. Then Lyssa's magpie eyes latch onto my package. "What's that?"

I know from her tone she hopes it's one of her presents. No luck. Her birthday budget is negative five dollars until my first check drops from Hench.

"Mine."

"Who sent it?"

No clue. "Secret admirer."

"Who'd admire *you*?" Ass. Jav got lucky, not having siblings.

"I wish you had a twin who'd eaten you in utero," I tell Lyssa, then sashay into the bathroom and drop the latch. No black goggle eyes greet me when I tear away the packaging. Instead, I find a cylinder of plastic, cut lengthways like a sub roll, with a chip sandwiched between the halves. The chip is circular and frilled like the cap of a beer bottle. Tiny filaments waft underneath. The overall effect channels some sort of cyberpunk jellyfish. Very Lovecraft meets *Futurama*.

I borrow Hernando's mustache-trimming scissors from the windowsill. A snip along the tape seal and the cylinder cracks, chip dropping into my palm. I remove the folded black card from behind it, checking for instructions. They're printed over the crease line in Hench's noxious green block font. *STEP 1: PLACE ON NECK.*

What the hell. Today can't get any weirder.

As the chip nears my skin, my scalp tingles like I've rubbed my head on a balloon. I swear the chip *jumps* the last millimeter, clamping on like a tick.

"Holy shit!" I don't mean to blurt that out loud, but it happens anyway.

"Dad says we ain't supposed to say that unless we've had a divine bowel movement," calls Lyssa.

I'm too busy gawking at myself in the mirror to say something smart, like *You fish it out, I'll call the Pope*. Or rather, too busy gawking at the henchman who's taken my place.

A holographic rubber suit coats me head to ankle, camouflaging my billowy sleeves against the shower tiles. Who knows how *that* works. The dark green material follows the contours of my body, and I love every rounded inch. I look *badass*. I look *powerful*. For the first time, I look like someone who belongs at a Super fight.

I just don't look very much like *me*.

No hint of an identity. No hint of *Riley Jones*. Even my ratty sneakers have been replaced by big stompy boots, in the same military surplus style the Captain wears. But it's the mask I fixate on. My new face—or rather, the absence of one. No mouth. Only a faint outdent to indicate the presence of my nose. Those empty black goggles, hollowing out my eyes . . .

I reach out, watching the henchman in the mirror do the same. Our fingertips brush, cold glass between us.

This explains a lot. Always wondered how Super costumes never got ripped. Between this and the guns, Hench is packing serious tech. Our boss must keep plenty in the bank. Just, y'know, not enough to pay us over the minimum wage.

According to the card, I have to twist the disc counterclockwise twice to deactivate. First turn reveals my face, which is pink-tinged, sweaty, and unspeakably odd-looking when attached to a henchman's neck. Second turn dismisses the rest of the hologram.

There I am. Same ol' Riley Jones.

"Okay, you've been in there so long I'm starting to think you actually did find Jesus."

. . . And same ol' Lyssa Garcia.

I wash up that evening, following an insta-ramen dinner. *Dzz-dzz.* My phone rattles against the top of our fridge.

"I'll get it," chirps Lyssa.

"Like hell you will!"

Lyssa scoots to the edge of the sectional. I dredge my hands in the soapy depths and fling the sodden dishcloth in her face—to which she retaliates with a threadbare cushion. After we resolve our disagreement in a civilized manner (100 percent compliant with child safety regulations, minus yours truly yanking a fistful of my baby sister's hair), I put the phone to my ear and compose myself. This is difficult, as my new seat is composed of too many jabbing elbows for comfort, but I do my best.

"Hi there," I say, shuffling to sit cross-legged on Lyssa's back and mashing her face into the couch. "Riley Jones speaking."

"Lucky girl." A moist Mississippi accent dribbles into my ear, punctuated with a snap of gum. "You got a job."

"Right—um. What is it?"

"Does it matter?" asks McCarthy. "Active duty, conflict expected. Be outside with your uniform on in fifteen minutes if you want to get paid." She disconnects before I can stutter out an affirmation.

I release Lyssa, who shows her gratitude by attempting to bludgeon me to death with the TV remote. I disarm her and head into our room to change.

"Where are you going?" she hollers after me.

"Out. Work thing." Not a lie. Not *technically*.

"Artie's shuts up early on Sundays."

"You could learn a lesson from them. 'Bout shutting up, I mean."

Lyssa's dark eyes drill into my back. "Classic deflection. You're meeting someone, aren't you?"

"Am not." I'm meeting *several* someones, and we're gonna commit crimes of an unspecified nature.

"Is it your *secret admirer?*"

"No! Just—stay here, you goober. If Hernando gets back early, his leftovers are in the fridge."

"*My dad*, you mean?" Lyssa always says that when she wants to piss me off. I'm so jittery at the thought of our upcoming job, I don't have space in my heart for hurt.

"Yeah, your dad. Whatever."

She taps her chin. "Maybe I should text him. See what he thinks about this. Unless . . ."

Blackmail: a time-honored form of sibling bonding. I can't even be mad. Basic rule of the world. If someone wants you to do something, don't do it for free. "What do you want?"

Lyssa's demands come preprepared; she ticks them off on her fingers. "Full control of the remote every weekend. You tidy my side of our room—Dad's nagging again. *And* I'm meeting Mackenzie and Shan at the park tomorrow. I want you to take me in the chair."

That last part at least requires no persuasion; Lyssa's at the age where she needs to be regularly peeled off the couch before she puts down roots. The chair is a cheap push-along model, hospital-style, too heavy and high-backed for her to wheel herself for long. Some people get weird about her using it, like as soon as she sits down she forfeits the right to make her own coffee orders and not be touched by random strangers. But those people are asshats, and don't deserve teeth.

Take it from Lyssa: She doesn't resent her mobility aids. They don't stop her going into town. The elevator breaking every time there's a Super attack stops her. The chair doesn't stop her making more friends; people being dicks *about* her chair does. At the end of the day, she's in dire need of a prosthetic refit and the chair's comfier long-distance.

Still, I narrow my eyes. "Which park?"

"The bougie one, by the marina."

Good. Magnolia Park is closer, but that's back toward Shit Creek. I used to chase Lyssa around that square of dead grass and the ant-infested ball court, back before our lives rolled away from us in a ball of tortured aluminum and broken glass.

We haven't been to that part of town in years. I intend to keep it that way. Some things are best left buried.

"You get one weekend a month," I say, and Lyssa pretends to mull it over before sticking out her hand.

"Deal."

After we shake on it, I head for the door. I tell Lyssa I'll be back soon, but that's a lie, too. I don't know how long this'll take. Honestly, I'll be lucky to come back at all.

CHAPTER 8

AS I HEAD down the stairs and exchange waves with Mr. Beauvais, I realize I still haven't sent Jav any confirmation of our library totally-not-a-date. Guilt makes me fish out my phone again—then cramps up my thumbs before I can tell her I've got a new gig, and that I've branched out from hospitality to henching.

Jav's always been there for me. Just like how I've always made myself available for hugs when she scores less than an A-. Neither of us have dads. Hers died when she was a baby from some cancer I can't pronounce, while I have a shortlist of fifty potential candidates, each less desirable than the last. But the one thing we know we can count on is each other.

I just can't count on her to understand why I'm working for Hench.

In the end, I send a flood of heart emojis (there can never be enough) and step through the front door. Our street's never deserted, even at dusk. Two old guys swap gossip around a weathered table outside the building a few doors down, and several kids lounge on their stoops, lazily pecking at their phones.

Then there's the guy in the suit. He saunters along the road, feeding letters through one door after the next. I assume Jehovah, but when he gives us the same treatment, I spot the blue Blair Homes logo, half hidden by his hand.

Too late for me to snatch the letter and stomp on it. The guy gives me a friendly smile. It goes unreturned.

Time trickles by. Blair Homes guy makes it to the end of the block without getting decked, though I can't be the only one tempted. Ten twenty-eight. I lurk beneath the overhang, watching the digits shift on my phone.

Ten twenty-nine. I ask myself what would happen if I went back inside.

Ten thirty. A horn grunts. A stumpy black city car swings onto the street, coasting to rest against the sidewalk. It's like one of those old Western movies where an outlaw comes to town. Everyone hurries inside as the car passes, parents calling to kids, the old men's cards abandoned to the wind.

I wait until the last door slams, then twist the silver disc on my neck. Feathers tickle every inch of me. I would squirm, but the sensation vanishes as fast as it starts. My green-suited arms don't look like a part of me. I'm not entirely sure they look human.

"Get in," says the Captain through the open window.

"Hi to you, too."

"Oh, sorry. Didn't realize I was paid by the fucking pleasantry. Hurry up, Jones; we're burning night."

The crumpled figure in the passenger seat must be Birnbaum, making holographic rubber look droopy. I guess he called shotgun, pleading his arthritic knees. All six-foot-something of Turner is folded onto the back seat. He waggles his gloved fingers. The Captain must want me to slide in next to him. Not quite where I'd been during the crash, but close.

I haven't been in a car since. Judging by my locked-up legs, that won't change tonight.

I don't wanna say I have PTSD. Not without a diagnosis. I'm way better than I was in the months after the accident, when every loud noise sent my adrenal glands into overdrive. Most likely, this is some sort of residual anxiety disorder. Still, it's like someone's got a gun on me 24/7.

Some days, that gun isn't loaded. It makes me nervy, but it doesn't feel like a threat. I might go months without issues. Hell, I might forget the gun exists.

Other days, the gun's cocked. I walk on tiptoes, tense as piano wire, anticipating pain—but the finger on the trigger stays still.

Then we have the bad days. The days when the slam of a door, the squeal of brakes, the sour hint of gasoline on the breeze makes that gunman shoot. The days my mind splinters out of itself and the entire world registers only as *threat*.

And okay, *maybe* putting myself on the front lines of the ongoing hero/villain conflict isn't the best self-care choice. But things have been chill lately. I haven't had a full-scale panic attack in ages. I faced Cooper without needing a pants change, right?

But the one thing I *can't* do, the one thing my body won't let me (heart racing, head buzzing, sweat crawling down my neck), is get in the Captain's car.

I stall: "Where's Sherman?"

A motorcycle glides up behind me. Cyanide blue, purring low as a panther.

"Reporting for duty," Sherman drawls from inside the helmet, putting two fingers to her visor in a mocking salute. I don't know if it's directed at me, the Captain, or the world in general.

The Captain answers with a one-fingered salute of his own.

"Enough chat. Jones, quit acting like a spare lamppost. I'll explain our job on the way."

Turner pops the door. All I have to do is sit down. Fasten the seat belt. Breathe. Can't be that hard. Right?

"She isn't moving," says Birnbaum. The Captain groans.

"*Why* isn't she moving?" When I don't reply, he holds out his hand. "Whatever. Deactivate your hologram. Twist counter-clockwise to detach."

"You're *firing* me?" Ouch. I'd hoped to last longer than Sherman.

"No. You're quitting." His goggles are empty wells. "Aren't you?"

Yes. No. I don't know. "I'm not getting in that car."

"Then you quit."

"I wanna come! I need . . ." *I need the money.* I can't say that. Too pathetic.

Sherman kicks out her prop and folds her arms, like she expects to be here awhile. Is she wearing leathers under her uniform? Probably not—too hot. The summer night settles drowsily on my skin. I chose a basic tee to go beneath my hologram, which is a safe bet should our job carry through to the morning.

If I ever make it to this job in the first place.

"I can't deal with cars," I tell the Captain. "I'm sorry. I want to, I really do, but I . . ." I grope for words. ". . . can't."

I expect more sarcasm, but he just gives another of those expressive, two-handed shrugs. "So, hop on Sherman's bike."

"What?" says Sherman.

"What?" I echo.

The Captain hooks his elbow out the open window. "You

won't ride with me—which I take personally, by the way—and Sherman has a bike. Do the math."

"Do I get a say in this?" Sherman asks.

"Nah. Be grateful I let you take your bike out on jobs in the first place. It's way too recognizable, I told you before."

"I *offered* to bring it! Because it's way too cramped for all of us in your tiny-ass clown car!"

"My clown car has a soundproof box in the trunk, and don't you forget it." The force of the Captain's glare pierces his mask. "You've ridden with a passenger before. I've seen you."

"Yeah, a passenger who *knew what they were doing*. You ever been on a bike, Jones?"

"Nope."

"Then no," Sherman tells the Captain. "She'll get us killed."

"Not if you drive to the speed limit."

"You can stick the speed limit up your . . ."

I don't find out what anatomical explorations Sherman has planned, because the Captain rolls up his window and her voice trails away. The car putters off in a cloud of exhaust, its belly low to the road. I suspect that the Captain is smirking.

I know he didn't do this for my sake. Rather, it appears to be part of his ongoing mission to aggravate Sherman until she resigns. But if I have to choose between climbing into a car and snapping every bone in my body if I fall off Sherman's bike . . .

I pick bike.

Sherman's still fuming. Her shoulders rise and fall beneath her costume, accompanied by the whoosh of angry breath. "Should leave you here," she mutters.

"But you won't, out of the kindness of your heart?"

Sherman crosses her arms, balanced astride her seat with one boot on the sidewalk.

"Right," I correct myself. "You're a badass henchman. You don't have one of those."

I edge closer until I'm standing behind her. Waiting for her to rev and roar away. When that doesn't happen, I rest my hands on the second seat and tentatively sling over a leg.

Not my most graceful moment. Which is to say: I knee Sherman hard enough to pop a kidney. She makes a sharp, pained noise. I squeak an apology and settle to the grind of her teeth.

The passenger seat has a squishy backrest. I find myself wondering who else's been where I am. Who she *wants* where I am.

Useless thoughts. I push them away.

"Okay. What do I do?"

Sherman sits so stiff her muscles quiver. "Lean into corners with me, or we'll tip. And here." She yanks off her bike helmet and jams it over my head, almost shaving off my nose.

"Ow! What the hell?"

"You're more likely to fall."

"*That's* reassuring. What about you?"

A sulky snort. "Don't need one."

"Yeah, I think every licensed bike instructor would disagree."

"Don't need one of those, either."

"Which makes me *real* confident in your abilities." I twist from side to side, testing the shift of my weight. "This can hold both of us, yeah? Not exactly Tinker Bell here."

Sherman's blank Hench mask swings to appraise me. "*This*," she says, after an ominous pause, "is a heavily customized Harley-Davidson Low Rider."

"Good for it?"

"Hydraulic jacks, twin-cooled engine. Eighty-seven horse-power."

"You probably think that answers my question, so I'll nod along and pretend I speak your language."

Sherman blows air through her mask. "You'll be fine, Jones. Just hold on tight."

Night crawls over the skyscrapers like a swarm of black flies. Sherman kicks up her prop, guns the engine, and we're off. I grab the nearest thing. It happens to be Sherman. I crush myself to her back, a limpet unto a rock on Sunnylake's tourist-stuffed beach.

"Too tight!" she yells.

I barely hear over the roaring exhaust. Still, I relax my death grip, locking my thighs around the seat. Sherman might struggle to steer if she can't breathe.

Vibrations rattle up through my pelvis. It's weirdly okay, though. No metal box to trap me. If we crash like this, I'll die quick. Not like back then: screaming, coughing, trying to reach Lyssa and Mom, choking on the thick gasoline-stink of the fire . . .

Wind rushes against us, battering away the past. The Captain's car glows ahead, a monster with rabid red taillights for eyes. We glide in its wake, the city slipping around us like it's moving and we aren't, Sherman's body a tense line against mine.

CHAPTER 9

WHATEVER'S GOING DOWN tonight, it's big. The Captain's car chugs in front of us, joined by an armada of Ubers, all overflowing with henchmen. I count station wagons and trucks, hatchbacks and sedans, followed by a rumbling eighteen-wheeler and a limousine so dark and sleek it looks like it's carved from volcanic glass.

I clutch Sherman a little tighter. A ride that slick can only belong to a villain. Or rather, *a client*. I should get in the habit of calling them that before any face-melting occurs.

Our convoy curls off the beltway and up the moonlit mountain track, away from the city lights. The night is so thick you could stir it, hot and viscous as molten tar. The bike shakes between my legs. I squeeze Sherman's hips. She doesn't say anything, but if she did, I wouldn't hear. The wind would rip it away.

An observatory sits halfway up the nearest foothill of the Andoridges, at the highest point you can reach by vehicle. Its white dome bulges from the greenery, shining under the high, full moon. The city stretches beneath. We're too far up to see the grimy alleys, the bums on the streets, the boys who sell needles to keep their families safe and fed. From this distance, Sunnylake looks as pretty as it does in the brochures.

If I were a villain, that's why I'd crack our world open. Not to conquer it, but to make everyone take a good, hard look at the rotten bits inside.

We pull into the observatory lot. Sherman kicks out her prop. I stay right where I am, just breathing, until she shifts on her seat, slim waist flexing in my grip. "You can let go now."

"Oh. Yeah, sure." I release her, horribly aware of how sweaty my hands are. "Thanks for the ride. And the helmet! And for not getting us both killed. Or leaving me behind . . ."

"You can get off now, too."

I do so, though my wobbly legs make it difficult. Still, I manage to avoid kneeing her again. Taking that as a win.

Sherman's mask smooths her head into a flat black pebble. Has she gelled her curly Mohawk down, or does the hologram hide it? I imprisoned my blonde hair in a tight bun before I left the apartment, the loose ends clamped down with bobby pins.

"For future reference? Handle, here." Sherman points to the metal rail at the rear of the seat.

Crap. I was holding her this whole time for *no reason*? You could use my cheeks as a fire starter. Luckily, between the bike helmet and my mask, there's no way for Sherman to tell.

"No touchy. Sure! Cool. No problemo."

Sherman dismounts. Perhaps I'm a late bloomer for psychic superpowers, because somehow, I know she's rolling her eyes.

The semi is last to park, settling with a contrabass rumble and a hiss of depressurizing tires. After that, the night is almost *too* quiet. Our distance from Sunnylake reduces the roar of the freeway to a faint, dull hum. Leaves rustle, cicadas scratching like guiros in the brush. Too much nature for a city girl like me. Hope I don't break out in hives.

The Captain boots open his car door as I wrestle the helmet's chin strap. The little Ford Fiesta did well to conquer the steep road; I half expected to see it sliding back down in Sherman's wing mirror. Once I'm free, Sherman plonks the helmet on the ground beside her kickstand and we head over to huddle with our team, forty-ish other henchmen dodging around us like a dark river parting on a rock. Enough to give a squad of ten side-kicks a fair fight.

Weirdly, several henchmen pause to look at the motorcycle, then squeeze Sherman's shoulder, slap her back, and tell her it's good to see her again. Weirder, they don't cut themselves on all her edginess. In fact, Sherman *nods back*. She even gives one guy a fist bump, muttering something about a post-job meetup that earns her another back clap and a warning shush.

Highly sus, if you ask me. Not that I'm *offended* she doesn't act friendly with our team. Guess she's too cool to hang with the newbies.

I try to raise my eyebrows at her, but—masks. She doesn't notice.

"Who's our client?" Turner asks, flipping through the Super-spotter app on his phone.

"The Ferocious Flamer," says the Captain.

The loser Cooper beat on Saturday night? I snort. The Captain turns to me. His blank goggles manage to look expectant, like a teacher asking what's so funny, and whether you'd like to share with the class. Luckily, I've never had a problem with taking them up on that offer.

"That's such a bad Super name. Was 'Wildfire' taken?"

"Yeah—by an A-class Summoner, five years back. Copyrighted,

trademarked, the works. I hear he's in the third circle of the Council now. Signature move involves igniting individual carbon molecules and burning people alive from the inside out. Slowly."

Well, that's horrifying. "On second thought, the Ferocious Flamer is an awesome name and I vote we never work for any other client, ever."

"Speak for yourself." Turner turns his Supremia-clad phone around. The Superspotter app presents the Flamer's mug shot, caught mid-snarl. "Filming his battles barely earns you fifty points. He can only set, like, *three* people on fire at once!"

"Which is more than you. Shut it before he hears." The Captain glances at the limo, voice dropping low. "The Flamer's B-class, but his temper suits his powers. Don't disagree, don't argue, and *definitely* don't give sass. You won't need to worry about crematorium fees, but that's the only bonus." After that rousing speech, he pops his trunk, lifts the lid on the big metal box within, and starts handing out rifles.

Birnbaum heaves his over one shoulder, causing every joint in his body to click. "What's our job, sir?"

"Assemble a laser to destroy city hall. Maybe a school or two—I don't know the details. The Flamer didn't upload the usual brief to our app."

"A school?" I repeat. "Figured it'd be something evil, not a public service." Sherman makes a noise like a rusty hinge. I spin to her. "I'm sorry; was that a *haha, you amuse me* noise, or were you just clearing your sinuses?"

"It was a scoff. I was scoffing at you."

"Mm-hmm."

The Captain interrupts before Sherman can grind away her molars: "Sorry to disappoint, but we ain't blowing up shit. We're stalling until the Supers arrive."

"Stalling," repeats Turner, high-pitched. "You mean, like, *sabotage?*"

The Captain safety-checks the next rifle and shoves it against Turner's scrawny chest. "Nope. Sabotage's too risky. *Incompetence*, though? We can get away with that. Supers expect mediocrity from Normies. No shame using that to our advantage."

Turner's dropped jaw distorts his mask. God knows how; Maheen's a genius. "Wait. We're *not* helping our clients?"

The Captain unplugs the last rifles from the glowing charging unit in the base of the box. "We *are*. To a certain degree. Our clients want to break down society. As one of the unfortunate sods who lives in it, I'd rather they didn't succeed." He shrugs, too big and too jerky, shoulders pinching his ears. "Consider it part of the job. Mandatory pro bono."

I can't believe what I'm hearing. "You couldn't have mentioned this earlier?"

The Captain stays hunched over his charger. "Last time I brought it up on induction day, the whole squad quit."

No shit. Fighting sidekicks and avoiding heroes? That's risky, on par with Sherman's casual disregard for motorcycle safety regulations. But actively screwing the VC over? It's a wonder there's any henchmen left.

No sign of the Super Squad jet, though. If we don't do *something*, the Flamer might see this through. And jokes aside, I don't *really* want to blow up a school.

The Captain must read acceptance in my slumped posture. He hands the last guns over, holding Sherman's a beat too long. "Stay close and follow my lead. No fuckups tonight."

She yanks it away. "No promises."

The shell of the observatory is made of a thousand tessellating plastic and metal triangles. Captain leads the way to where the rest of the henchmen have gathered. As we putter after him like ugly green ducklings, I notice Sherman unlocking her phone from the corner of my eye.

"Squad selfie?"

"No," she says. I keep looking. She sighs. "I'm telling my mom to stay home."

"That's . . . actually a good idea. One sec."

I dispatch two messages of my own: saw warning online stay away from city center. Not that Hernando is likely to head downtown after his shift, or Jav to leave her bed after 11 p.m. (she's such an old woman), but it eases the tension cramp in my lower back.

Turner and Birnbaum copy us (although Birnbaum's brick can hardly be called a "phone"). As we take our positions, guns trained on the observatory door, I notice how many fingers are skittering over keypads. I hear *caught a report on the radio* and *saw a Henchman driving toward the hills*. So many messages, zipping across Sunnylake City like contrails crosshatching the sky. How long before the press intercepts one? Before they activate the Super Squad alarm? The Captain seems convinced our heroes will arrive before we do any real damage—

I don't get any more time to ruminate on the intricate mechanics of the villain alert system. A security guard stomps out of the observatory, flashlight cranked bright enough to rival the semi's high beams.

"If that's you damn kids again . . ." It clicks that the lot is chock-full of henchmen, not hooligans. His flashlight hits the ground, where it proceeds to illuminate our matching black boots. "Aw, heck."

A henchman in a chauffeur's cap slides back the limo's long panel door. The Ferocious Flamer unfolds, making the stretched car look proportional. B-class or otherwise, he's still a villain. An honest-to-God, global-domination-driven *villain*, not ten yards from me. No TV screen between us.

I'm getting light-headed. Probably because it's been half a minute since I breathed.

Above his domino mask, his red hair sprouts in devilish points. He's poured into the same black unitard he wore during his battle with Cooper, luminous fire motifs zigzagging across his pecs. Is it a hologram? If not, I hope he launders between missions. Awesome as the Super gene may be, I doubt it exempts you from underarm funk.

He prowls toward the security guard, slow as a hunting tiger, flexing one hand so fire dances above the palm. Conjuring flames with no visible fuel—total power move. The Flamer must be splitting water molecules to burn the hydrogen. Tonight's sweaty-butt-crack humidity is actually a bonus.

In truth, though, I couldn't care less about the physics. Fire is another entry on my Nope list, right under cars. I back behind Sherman, swallowing hard.

"On your knees, Normie." The Flamer's voice grates like tires over gravel. "Get some practice in."

The guard's outnumbered fifty to one. His shaking hand still treks for the walkie-talkie clipped to his belt loop. He's braver than me and more reckless by far. The Flamer can reduce him to a carbonized crisp before he can warn the people inside.

I can't watch him die. But what am I supposed to do? Thankfully, the Captain levels his gun before I have to decide. Sherman beats him to it. The guard's neck sprouts a tiny feather. Down he goes, following his flashlight to the ground.

The Flamer throws his head back and guffaws. "He fainted! My reputation precedes me!"

Sherman lowers the muzzle of her rifle. The Captain nods to her as the Flamer swaggers to the observatory door. In that moment, the pair of them seem almost like a functioning team.

"Sir?" asks a henchman in a timorous voice, waving for the Flamer's attention. "You didn't upload a plan of attack to our app or lay out any contingencies in the event of a Super Squad ambush. How should we proceed?"

The Flamer rolls his beefy shoulders. His muscles are obscene. He looks like a bag stuffed with watermelons. "There is no ambush. Our adversaries are Normie scientists; it's not like we *need* a plan."

"I suppose not, sir," says the henchman. He sounds dubious.

"Just do as I say. That's what you're here for."

Sparks eddy around the Flamer like he's conducting a colony of fireflies. It should be pretty, but it feels like we're in a forest to the south of the state, waiting for the dry brush to catch light, roar out of control.

"Let's do this," he growls, and kicks open the door.

The screams start a beat later.

"Someone should go after him," says the henchman who spoke up before.

The Captain groans, rubbing the back of his neck. "All right, you lot. Get moving."

With considerably less fanfare, we make our own entrance. The observatory rises overhead, ridged with cold blue lights. Fifteen scientists and another security guard stand frozen around a walkway halfway up the wall, the Flamer posturing before them. I stick close to the Captain, though it's hard to keep track of who's who in this swarm of holographic rubber.

"That you, Captain?" I mumble.

"Guess again," says the woman I just nudged with my gun.

"Sorry."

"Jones! Over here!" Turner makes a good landmark, being a head taller than every other henchman in the vicinity. My crew are behind me; must've walked at Birnbaum's pace. I hang back, let them catch up.

"Now what?" I ask the Captain from the corner of my mouth. He lifts the muzzle of my rifle to menace the scientists arranged on the gantry above.

"Gun up. Watch for heroes." His voice is grim. "First lesson of the day: If a client decides they're too good for our organizational app, either they have more guts than gray matter or they're about to pull some overpowered shit. Either way, stay sharp and be ready to run."

Great pep talk. Jav swears by meditation YouTube vids when she gets the pre-exam wobbles. I've never bothered. It's something I regret right now. My chakras, if I have them, are in dire need of calming.

I focus on my lungs, the way the air fills and empties me, timing my inhale and exhale until they match in length. I'm Zen. I'm chill. This is just a regular night, with a mildly increased chance of incineration.

The Flamer stomps toward a couple of lab-coat-wearing men, who cower behind the giant telescope. "Where is she?" he bellows. "*Where is Amelia Lopez?*"

"Aren't we here to build a laser?" asks Sherman, real quiet.

The Captain tightens his grip on his gun. He doesn't reply.

"Amelia Lopez!" The Flamer towers over the scientists. "You can't hide her. I know she's within this building! I know she knew we would come!"

My chakras waver further out of alignment. I don't like this.

"Who's Amelia Lopez?" whispers Turner.

The Captain elbows him. "Shut *up*."

The scientists exchange glances. Their lips remain sealed.

The Flamer cracks his knuckles. "Very well. I was going to offer you the possibility of a quick death. Now, it seems, my only option is to torture you slowly, until Miss Lopez—wherever she might be hiding—sees fit to *show herself*."

One scientist speaks. Her voice is a high, mousy quaver. I imagine I'd sound similar, if I dared open my mouth. "How do you know she's here?"

"Because the Villain Council knows *everything*."

"You're B-class! You're barely *on* the VC!"

The Flamer's features landslide into a sneer, eyebrows converging on the bridge of his nose. "Watch your tone."

"Why?" the scientist asks. "I mean, you've already threatened us with agonizing death. How much worse can it get?"

The Flamer squeezes his fists, each ringed in a heat-shimmer corona. "Perhaps you'd like to find out—"

"Sir!"

Shit. That was the Captain.

He stands as tall as he can—which isn't very. He'd be lost among the sea of identical uniforms if we hadn't all taken a unanimous step away from him.

The Flamer frowns. "Who said that?"

"Me, sir." The Captain speaks smoothly and respectfully, no hint of fear. "Alerts of our activity have been broadcast across the city. We need to start work on that laser before the heroes arrive."

"Ugh. Typical." The Flamer shoos us away. "Go on. Get to it!"

"What about them?" asks another henchman, waving his gun at the scientists.

"Tie them up, of course. Let them watch." The Flamer points back toward the entrance. "Half of you unload my laser. The other half, I want you to secure our guests before you scour every *inch* of this building for the fugitive!"

The Captain calls us over to start work on construction. I linger, watching a gang of henchmen force the scientists to their knees, guns humming on full charge. Wondering if I should do something. But . . .

Head down. Strictly no heroics.

A knot tightens in my throat. I swallow it down and turn away.

CHAPTER 10

I DIDN'T EXPECT the giant evil ray gun to come flat-packed. IKEA must've expanded their business. Unloading it is heavy, dirty work. Whichever warehouse the VC uses, the foreman must have a grudge against vacuums. Sherman and I heave the grubby boxes from the back of the truck, piling them on the observatory floor.

When our fingers graze, current snaps between us. Sherman snatches back her hand.

"Static," she explains, shaking out her fingers. "All that dust."

"Yeah, I know how chemistry works."

"Physics. We don't have chemistry."

"Duh."

I don't have chemistry with *anyone.* Definitely not Jav—only one side of that reaction's bubbling, and it's my own.

"What's the holdup?" demands the Flamer. He just completed his second lap of the telescope at the center of the room. Guess this answers that age-old question of what villains do while they wait for heroes to show: pacing with a side order of scowling, shouting at minions, and ducking outside for a quick smoke. "Why's this taking so long?"

The Captain snaps to attention beside us. "Sir, we've failed to locate the instruction manual."

"The *instructions?*"

"Yes, sir. I don't recommend building a superlaser without them."

"Well, you'd better search harder, before I start roasting you lot instead." The Flamer turns away, shaking his neon-orange head. "Honestly. *Normies.*"

Underestimation works wonders. We might actually get away with this. True to the Captain's word, the boxes I've opened hold slate-gray sheets of metal, complex-looking doohickeys and mysterious mechanical gizmos, and not one clue on how to slot any of it together. I duck to study the parts as the Flamer storms by. Turner isn't so interested in self-preservation.

"Sir," he blurts, popping to his feet from where he's been ripping bubble wrap off a convex glass lens. "It's an honor to be in your service!" He sticks out his hand for the villain to shake.

"Oh fuck," says Sherman.

I second her opinion. What happened to the Flamer being second-rate? Turner must be too starstruck to care.

The villain champs his teeth. "You dare address me? Who do you think you are?"

"A fan," says Turner. I bet his eyes have gone real shiny under his mask.

That keeps the Flamer from roasting him, at least. He actually looks a little flattered. Still, Turner's a Normie, and that makes him a gnat, not worth the Flamer's time. "Out of my way."

Turner bounds to one side, and the Flamer strides on by. Midway through my eye roll, my gaze snags on the Captain. Specifically, on the booklet he's holding one-handed behind his back.

Sherman cocks her head. "Couldn't find the instructions, huh?"

The Captain jumps. He tracks the Flamer, making sure he's

out of earshot before he tosses the booklet to Sherman. "Just hide them already."

Sherman huffs, but does as she's told. The instructions vanish beneath her hologram, as if they were never here. A few henchmen glance up at the commotion, but all quickly look away.

The Flamer stomps back toward the telescope. More henchmen scramble over it, giant green ants. They attempt to dismantle the gigantic contraption, while the zip-tied scientists curse them out and regret their career choice. Of the mysterious Amelia Lopez, there remains no sign.

"Wait." Turner spins on the Captain. "You had the instructions all along?"

"Super Squad's running late. Quit shouting about it, or everyone'll want them."

The Flamer finishes his orbit, stopping before another squadron. "Well?" he snaps. "Any progress?"

One of the henchmen—presumably their captain—offers a salute. "Sir, I believe you were talking to *those* henchmen earlier."

"How do you expect me to tell you apart? You all look exactly the same!"

Turner clears his throat. I realize what he's gonna do. "Don't—!"

Too late.

"We located the manual, sir!" Turner announces. "Didn't we, Sherman?"

Birnbaum's cane lashes out, catching Turner in the shin. "Whoops," he says as Turner hops on one leg, cussing. "Accident."

The Flamer pays little attention to our antics. "Which one of you is Sherman?"

Sherman looks at the Captain. The Captain looks at Sherman.

The Flamer circles his wrist, spinning a fireball into existence like he's gathering cotton candy on a stick.

The air dries in my mouth, tongue shriveling. His flaming handful draws my gaze, hypnotic, bright as the markings on a venomous snake. I'm paralyzed. If I look away, if I so much as *blink*, an inferno will pounce forward and engulf me.

Like I'm back in the car. Like the whole world's burning, all over again . . .

"Well?" growls the Flamer, red glow stroking his clean-shaven jaw. "Produce the manual. *Now*."

"Sherman," the Captain whispers. "Do what the nice client says."

Sherman looks up at the Flamer. Her mask hides all expression, but the stiffness of her shoulders suggests she's scowling. She better not tell him where his precious manual can be inserted. We haven't hit it off, but I don't want to watch her die.

Three seconds pass. Sherman relinquishes the booklet on the fourth. "Hope you can read Swedish."

"*Sherman*," the Captain hisses.

Thankfully, the Flamer doesn't punish her for impudence. He flips through the manual. "Here. Diagrams." He tosses it at the henchman he mistook for one of our crew. "Let's see if you're more competent than these imbeciles."

The henchman scans the manual and barks orders at her team. The Flamer storms away in search of more slackers to berate. The Captain postures at Sherman and Turner as if contemplating which to chew out first—but before he can decide, a wild-haired, wilder-eyed woman scuttles from the shadows beneath the staircase.

We freeze.

"Is that . . ." Sherman starts.

"Amelia Lopez!" Turner's voice shrills above the soundscape of laser construction: the scrape of cardboard on cardboard and the squeak of biodegradable potato-starch packing peanuts. "Are you Amelia Lopez?"

"Shut *up*," the Captain spits. Too late. The Flamer turns our way. Poor Amelia quivers from her mussed geometrical box cut to her frumpy, sensible shoes.

"Ma'am," says Birnbaum as she backs away. "It would be in your best interests to remain calm . . ."

Miss Lopez makes a noise, somewhere between a hysterical laugh and a sob. She clutches a black briefcase to her chest. Her huge eyes dance between us: me, petrified; Turner, gawking; Birnbaum, stooped; Sherman, aloof as ever; and the Captain, one hand out like he's trying to tame a deer.

"Stop!" roars the Flamer.

Amelia bolts.

The Flamer bares his teeth. He makes that stirring motion again, this time with his entire arm. The glow around him intensifies, blinding as the noonday sun. My tongue dries out again—followed swiftly by my throat, my ears, the insides of my nose. The air is desert hot, tight on my skin.

"Is this where we run?" I ask the Captain, out of the corner of my mouth. No reply. He's already hit the deck.

Before I can follow him down, the Flamer gives an animal snarl. He pitches his plasma ball at Amelia. I just happen to be in the way.

CHAPTER 11

NO TIME TO think. I dash for the exit. Flames beat my back. My legs pump so fast they almost run out from under me, panic crushing my chest. *Gonna die car's burning not gonna make it Mom—*

Whoof.

The fireball punches the narrow doorway and races up the observatory walls. The blast lifts me off my feet, hell-hot and blistering, and flings me out into the night. I collapse, choking on nothing. Cold air hits my lungs like ice water. I drown in it, gurgling, hacking.

My back's alight. I scrabble under my shirt but find no flames. Just sore skin, hot to the touch like I forgot my sunscreen. And there, pushing herself to sit, not three feet away? Amelia Lopez. The woman all this is about.

Grazed elbows, wet eyes. Briefcase clutched with clawed fingers. Why would the VC sic the Flamer on some rando Normie?

No one follows. The others must've followed the Captain's lead (at least, I *hope* they did. I can't bear the thought of walking back inside to find their charcoal husks). With the exception of the drooling security guard, Amelia and I are alone.

"Hi," I say, struggling to my feet. "This is a weird way to meet someone, but—whoa!" Amelia swings her briefcase. I dodge—just. "The *hell*, lady? What did I ever do to you?"

"You're with *them*!"

"Wait, what? Oh. *Them*." The henchmen. The villain. I glance down at my green-and-black-suited self. "Well, yeah. I guess."

She raises the briefcase for strike two.

"Hold it!" I thrust my empty palms toward her—must've dropped my gun on the way. "I don't wanna hurt you! I only took this job because my dad needs to pay rent and Super Squad damage insurance and my sister needs a new leg and I just really, *really* need therapy!"

Amelia's eyes bulge. "*What?*"

"Sorry! Too much information! I babble when I'm nervous!"

C'mon, Riley. *Think*. Only seconds before henchmen barrel out that door. Or, worse—the Flamer himself.

I make a snap decision, in flagrant disregard of Rule Three.

"Get out of here," I tell Amelia. "I'll tell him you ran to the back of the observatory, but you gotta go, now."

She waves at the packed lot. "I'm blocked in!"

"So get running!"

"No. He'll catch me. He was always going to catch me." Amelia lifts her leaky gaze to mine. "But he doesn't know all my secrets."

I check over my shoulder—still safe, for now. "Congrats?"

"He doesn't know about you."

Nope, abort. I retreat a step, toward the observatory. Judging by the yelling, the Captain and my teammates have formed a dazed human blockade—consciously or otherwise. The Flamer struggles to get past. I'm glad he hasn't taken the easy option and set them all alight. Probably doesn't have the juice, being a B-class and all. Only three people burned alive at once, right?

Which means he's saving up for Amelia. And anyone who gets caught helping her.

"I'm sorry," I hiss at Amelia. "I really am, but—"

"You tried to help me. That means you're good."

I point across the city as roaring jet engines flatten the trees at the mountain's base. Our Super Squad, here at last. "They're the good guys! Not me!"

Amelia laughs like I've said something funny. Moonlight hollows her cheeks, skin stretched tight over her skull. I can pick out the blue traceries of her veins. For all her manic energy, exhaustion is folded into each crease on this woman's forehead. Not like Hernando, worn out after his night shift and ready to topple into bed. This is a different weariness: the waking death of insomnia.

Amelia Lopez doesn't sleep because she *can't*. Whatever she's seen, whatever she's uncovered—it won't let her.

And I want nothing to do with it.

She wrenches open her suitcase. "My research. I found out too much. About all of this—about Project Zero."

Project Zero? That sounds like your classic Armageddon-inducing evil scheme. Strong pass on that.

The Flamer bursts out the main observatory door before I can say as much. "Lopez!" he yells. "Henchman—don't let her escape!"

Amelia swallows. Her eyes glimmer with tears. They paint snail-trails over her cadaverous cheeks, like she's already in the grave.

Stop, I want to yell. *You don't have to do this.* But the words glue themselves to my gullet. I can't force them free.

Amelia reaches into her suitcase. She stuffs a bunch of papers into my hands. My torso hides the motion from the Flamer. Bonus of being built like a wardrobe. "Take this. I wish I could give you more."

I try to shove it back. "Uh, no thanks." No taking candy, leaflets, or deadly secrets from strangers.

She grips my fist, forcing me to hold on. "Read it. Find the connections. After that, you'll know what to do."

I have no fucking idea. "Wait—"

Amelia swings her briefcase again. No dodging this time; it clocks me on the chin.

I stagger. Pain shoots from the point of impact, rebounding off the curve of my skull. The contents of the case scatter, more pages flying like shards of broken glass.

Amelia doesn't stay to admire her handiwork. She sprints for the road, weaving around a chicane of parked cars.

As she runs, the Super Squad plane rumbles up over the prow of the cliff, level with us. Better late than never. It's a long-nosed borzoi of a jet, its left flank emblazoned with the logo of their organization—two white S's, interlocked like snakes on the Discovery Channel. The bass *wub-wub* of the engines shakes through me, numbing my throbbing jaw, distorting my perception of the world.

Time slows. Seconds drag into minutes, hours. I float in a broad panorama, joined by the stars and the moon. Amelia's retreating figure drifts ahead of me. Running, running, running for her life.

Wind tosses her papers. Black letters crawl antlike over each page, too densely packed for my eyes to follow.

Then: fire. Gushing overhead, heat slapping my neck. The Super Squad are still in their jet; no time to save her.

I close my eyes. Doesn't mute the roar, the crackling. The agonized rip of Amelia's scream.

Fuck.

For some unfathomable reason, she thought I was one of the good guys. But a good guy would run to her, though it's too late. A good guy would try to help. A good guy would do *something* as the blazing figure crumples and lies still. Not just stand there and shake.

The Flamer wastes no time gloating. It's not like Amelia put up a fight—just a Normie, after all. Whatever led him to hunt her down, it was no more personal than an exterminator laying poison for rats. He raises his smirk to the jet, where the heroes' faces float disembodied, ghostlike behind the cockpit glass.

"Come get me," he says, and strides back into the observatory.

He doesn't spare me a glance. Why would he? I'm a henchman. Saving people isn't my job.

Bullshit. What if Amelia was Jav? Hernando? Lyssa?

I can *smell* her. Charred hair, human barbecue. The car flips and my world turns upside down and—

My last meal squirts up my throat. Tastes bitter. Sour as burned flesh. I gag and heave, clutching Amelia's papers tight to my vibrating heart.

One last retch leaves everything inside me raw like it's been rubbed down with sandpaper. My guts are water. I wipe my lips on my arm as my mind whirls in a decreasing spiral, smaller and smaller, narrowing down to this primal pinprick of focus.

I need to go. I need to get away from here.

Can't run back toward the city. I'd have to pass that scorched patch of ground. Whatever's left of Amelia—Mom—*no*. But I have to move. Have to go somewhere. Have to . . .

My eyes latch onto the nearest shelter. Beneath the shadow of the Super Squad jet, I teeter back into the observatory, following the Flamer, Amelia's last message to the world mashed in my trembling fist.

CHAPTER 12

HANDS GRASP ME, heave me in. Sweat seals the paper to my fingers.

"Jones! Hey, Jones!"

The Captain's voice crashes over me in waves. A ring fills my ears—constant, reverberating, like someone's tapping a tuning fork, never giving the note time to die. I look up, dazed. The Captain's grip on my shoulders tethers me to the world. It's all that stops me from drifting through the observatory's open skylight to join the chopper and jet. They float above us, past the glowing roof, cut from the bright white nickel of the moon.

Only—wait. Why's the roof glowing?

A hundred metal panels arc overhead, all the angry red of a stoplight. They dull as I squint at them, like they're ashamed to be caught. Frost fractals crawl across their surface instead. Real glittery, something out of a dream.

Weird.

Two specks detach from the jet. They start off tiny, like flies walking over a lens. But they grow larger, larger—

Smash.

"Take cover!" roars the Captain. It's lost beneath crashes, shrieks. Broken steel hails down, a biblical plague, shards erupting in all directions. Deafening. Disorienting. The observatory swirls like I'm in a tumble dryer.

I lose the Captain, Sherman, Birnbaum, and Turner, too. All of us divided, tossed by the churn.

Two Supers land among the cascade. I don't see them so much as I *feel* them. A charge in the air, the tang of ozone piercing through the taste of fear, sweat, and blood.

I try to run, but I stumble. I try to stand, but I fall. Can't think can't move can't *breathe*—

One of the metal panels, weakened by its overlay of frozen oxygen, strikes the floor to my left, shattering on impact. I fling up my arm. The world fills with stinging wasps, and I *scream*, and . . .

. . . Everything stops.

Is it over? Am I dead, too?

If so, why does my bruised jaw pulsate in time with the cuts on my arm?

All lights are extinguished. Beyond the bubble—I don't know how else to describe the ice-white membrane in front of my face—the observatory wallows in shadow. I can just make out the shapes of henchmen, scrabbling over one another like rats in a cage. Shooting lightning at whatever moves.

But here? It's calm. Peaceful.

I suck a deep breath. Like if I inhale enough of this cold, still air, it'll freeze my insides, stop them quaking.

Then the bubble bursts.

"C'mon, Jones! *Move!*"

Sherman. Her words are mouth sounds, meaningless. What she's saying takes several seconds to filter through the marshmallow fluff around my brain. I flinch at every boom and crash, as the heroes—one Surger, one Shaper—enthusiastically decimate our half-built laser.

Sherman loses patience. She heaves me to my feet with no visible effort.

Sidekicks rappel through the busted roof. Five, ten, more. They beeline for the scientists. A few henchmen stand in their way but quickly get out of it. Several flop over and play dead, despite not being hit.

Wise choice. My legs wobble inward. I wonder if I should copy them.

Sherman won't let me. Her shoulder wedges under my armpit. She points at the door and off we stagger, dragging each other as much as ourselves.

The worst of the downpour is over. A few broken panels cling to their frames, threatening to crash down on anyone who walks beneath. We avoid those areas, but the rest of the observatory isn't without hazards. Jagged shards carpet the floor. They stab through my shoes like I'm walking on spark plugs.

"Fuck," Sherman hisses under her breath. "Fuck, fuck, fuck . . ."

She limps, but I don't see blood. Must be hidden by her hologram. I run my hand over my arm, only to suppress a cuss of my own as I agitate a hundred tiny metal splinters, embedded in my skin.

The Flamer holds his own against the hero duo, crisping their fingers and scorching their hair. He'll go down—only B-class, after all—but not without a fight.

The smell of smoke liquefies my knees. Sherman hauls me

up, drags me on. Rotors rumble overhead. The news helicopter, angling for the best view. There's the miniature shape of the reporter, playing their audience like an MC: *The villain landed a punch! What will our heroes do?*

They won't talk about us. They never do.

The Flamer hollers for help. Henchmen open fire as the heroes advance. Their shots fly purposefully wide, crackling bright off the observatory's walls. The Surger steals electrical energy from their bolts to add to her own assault as the Shaper melts fallen metal into a red-hot tide.

A stray shot sails toward us. It's a meteorite, a falling star.

"Shit," I say.

"Shit," Sherman agrees.

Then the air solidifies again, freezing with a brittle-snap hiss. The glassy bubble trembles as the bolt strikes it, fraying at the edges.

I try to back up—the fuck *is* that? But my heel skids off the edge of a broken beam, and I'm still clinging to Sherman, and—

over

we

go.

My back smacks the ground. Sherman smacks *me*. My lungs pop like paper balloons, wind bursting from my mouth in a noisy gasp. Despite everything, I still worry about her catching a whiff of my puke breath.

Sherman couldn't give less of an obvious crap. She sprawls on top of me, groaning, legs tangled with mine. Her panting breath breaks over my collarbones. And curving over us . . .

I stare past Sherman's shoulder. Ice glimmers back at me.

Oh. *Oh.*

For once in my life, I have no idea what to say.

Sherman heaves herself up. She straddles one of my thighs, our bodies locking roughly together. Any other time, that might be distracting.

"You're a Super," I say. Each word a stone, flung in accusation. "You're a fucking *Super.*"

Sherman gulps. I see it through her mask. I assumed she toned those gorgeous shoulders at the park, doing muscle-ups on the monkey bars with the baller boys. But no. They're just a gift of her enhanced genes. Proof that she's more, better. One of *them.*

I didn't see a Normie shoot a Super on that news report. I don't know *what* I saw—but that doesn't matter. It just lost all meaning for me.

"Jones—"

"Get off me."

Her hand hovers by my cheek. "Don't—"

"Get the fuck *off.*"

Sherman's mask wags as her mouth opens and closes. She's not touching me, not quite, but the heat of her palm still caresses my face—until her fingers curl in a fist and she stands. The icy bubble (frozen air; Shaper discipline) fizzles away, leaving us exposed in the middle of the observatory.

Somehow, despite everything, I still hold Amelia's crumpled pages. I wanna fling them in Sherman's face, scream that *she's* the Super, she should deal with this—but my fingers stay clutched tight.

All around us, henchmen drag battered teammates to the

exit. The sidekicks let them. They must be uncomfortable, facing off against Normies. Not like the Flamer, incinerating Amelia as she ran. That's the difference between heroes and villains. While heroes flex on us every now and then, there's markedly less outright murder from their camp.

What a low fucking bar.

The Flamer kneels in the wreckage of his laser, defeated. Heroes pose as the freed scientists cheer. I don't look. They're the main attraction, we're the sideshow. But to me, this is about *us*. Sherman. Jones.

"Sherman! Jones!" The Captain waves from the exit. "Tactical retreat!"

I treat Sherman to one last glare. I'll deal with this revelation later. Like I'll deal with Amelia's final scream (replaying in my head on repeat), whatever secret she shoved into my hands, and the fact that I really, *really* need to brush my teeth.

We race out, hugging the walls, dark costumes melding into the shadows at the edges of the room. Our team doesn't look their best. Turner lolls against the window of the Captain's car, gripping his left arm, blood drooling around a tourniquet improvised from a belt. Birnbaum clutches his chest like he's trying to squeeze a few more beats out of his heart. They're alive, though. Considering the bloodbath behind us, that's the solidest proof of miracles I've encountered in my life so far.

I actually ponder getting into the car with them—but no. I'm not *that* mad at Sherman.

"You good to ride?" the Captain asks as I ram my head into the helmet and clamber on behind her, grasping the seat bar without prompting. Amelia's papers are now stashed in my shirt pocket. Sherman nods, but neither of us misses her wince when my leg knocks hers. The Captain cranks his ignition. "You're hurt."

"It's nothing." Her voice is doing its stiff robot thing.

"Bullshit. Follow me. Turner needs stitches; might as well get you lot patched up, too."

Sherman tilts her head. "You're taking him to the hospital?"

"No way. Last thing you kids need is medical debt. I got a guy. Just . . . don't go spreading it around." He winds up the window and starts the long reverse back down the hill.

The sidekicks' flashlights sweep the wreckage behind us. Ahead, a thread of smoke crawls into the sky from the spot where Amelia fell. I can't look. I shudder, pressing closer to Sherman's warmth despite myself. Tonight isn't the worst night of my life—but it sure comes close.

CHAPTER 13

BY THE TIME the Captain's car trundles to a halt, my heart no longer feels like it's trying to pump glue. Guess I should be glad about that. I don't know what would've happened if I'd gone full shutdown back there. If Sherman had left me.

I force that thought from my mind. The last thing I wanna feel for her is *gratitude*.

We're outside a new duplex on the edge of Bridgebrook, part of the suburban sprawl that laps at the feet of the Andoridge range. A wall of a man blocks the drive. He's big. Not like the Supers, with their triangular torsos and trim little waists. All beef, all over, like a heavyweight boxer in the off-season, milky skin and ginger beard.

Oddly, he doesn't seem fazed to see a gang of henchmen pull up in the middle of the night. In fact, he marches right over to the car and bangs on the window until the Captain rolls it down.

"We *agreed*," he says, in an upmarket voice that wouldn't seem out of place at Ralbury High. "We said the next colleague you brought to meet me *wouldn't* be bleeding."

The Captain rubs the back of his masked head. "Birnbaum ain't bleeding."

"I am," Birnbaum quavers. "Just a little."

". . . Sherman?"

"Bleeding here, too."

"Jones?"

I examine my throbbing arm. "Sorry."

"Fuck."

The big man tuts. "Language. Kids are awake. Now, who needs stitches?"

Turner burbles.

"He's not bleeding *anymore*," the Captain tries. The giant's not having it. He reaches through the Captain's door to unlock Turner's from the inside, then catches him by the shoulder to stop him flumping out. He examines the tourniquet.

"That's because you've cut off circulation to his arm. It hardly counts."

"Hi," Turner croaks. "I'm Turner."

"Good for you. I'm the sucker who took your boss as my lawfully wedded husband, for better or worse. This is, unfortunately, the latter."

"I possibly deserve that," says the Captain, while the rest of us process. He seems unconcerned by the whole *husband* revelation, and like the nice, well-adjusted closet dweller I am, I do my best not to be jealous.

"He won't appreciate me telling you that my name's Aaron," the Captain's husband continues. "But I'm going to do it anyway, because he woke our kids by calling the house at ass o'clock in the morning and is now showing up on our doorstep with a car full of injured henchmen, despite *promising* this would never happen again. Especially not when I've been on ER call for the past week and am in dire need of sleep." He sighs, rolling his big shoulders like he's shrugging off stress, and tries on a half-hearted smile. "But hi, Turner. Nice to meet you."

"Nice to meet you, too," manages Turner, with a feeble waggle of his fingers. Then his body goes slack, and he's out.

We rush Turner into the house, where the Captain shoos two kindergarten-age kids from the banister at the top of the stairs, using uncharacteristically gentle threats that don't contain a single expletive. Aaron carries Turner straight to a spare bedroom that seems to be kitted out for this purpose. I glimpse a table draped in disposable plastic sheets.

"You owe me dinner," he informs the Captain, pausing on the threshold. "Just the two of us. We can leave the kids with my mother."

The Captain slumps. "Yes, dear."

"I'm talking steak. Filet, not porterhouse."

"Yeah, yeah, whatever. Can you please stitch up this shithead before he bleeds out?"

Twin gasps from upstairs. "Swear jar!" calls one of the kids.

"That ain't sleeping!" the Captain hollers back.

Aaron frowns. "Keep your voice down, darling. The neighbors will complain again."

"The neighbors can fuck themselves!"

"Swear jar!"

"Macy, Tyler—I love you very much, but *please* go the everloving f-frick to sleep!"

"That still counts," floats down from the upper levels of the house, along with several giggles. Aaron shakes his head with a fond smile.

"Take your friends to the kitchen," he says as he shuts the door. "They can wait their turn."

That's how we wind up sitting around the Captain's kitchen,

in uniform, clutching our various injuries, staring blank-eyed at the dining table. The tablecloth is cornflower blue. A stain of what looks like old bean juice discolors one corner, and three of the four plastic mats are *Frozen*-themed. The fourth sports a shiny red fire truck. A shaggy husky lumbers up to the back window, roused from his kennel, and snorts longing clouds on the glass.

"Well," says Sherman. "This is cozy."

I can't look at her. Sherman never *claimed* to be a Normie. She just let me assume. That moment when she shot the heroine off the Flamer's back means nothing now.

I'll hate her for it in the morning. Right now, I'm too tired. Too freaked out. Too everything. No matter how hard I shake my head (Birnbaum shoots me a weird look), Amelia's screams won't fade.

"Make the most of it," says the Captain. "You ain't invited back." He sits, tapping his feet and twiddling his thumbs, before surging upright and striding for the fridge. "Nope, I gotta do something. Who wants pancakes?"

"Pancakes?" Birnbaum repeats. He's dismissed his mask, as have the rest of us. It only feels polite, like taking off your shoes when you enter someone else's house. The Captain, however, keeps his intact. No clue of the face beneath.

"Yeah, pancakes." He mimes flipping one. "You know: flat things, served on a plate? Taste real good with syrup?"

We all stare. He groans at us.

"I'm stressed; you're hungry. This solves both. Now—pancakes? Yea, nay?"

"Yea?" I try.

Five minutes later, we're watching him beat batter like a man possessed. It looks pretty cathartic. Reminds me of Hernando, before he took on more hours at the Mart and I had to step into his shoes as head chef. Perhaps he'd get along with the Captain.

Or not. The gay thing and all. Don't know how he'd deal with that. Really don't know and am *so* not ready to find out.

We munch through as many pancakes as the Captain puts in front of us. They're the miniature, fluffy, melt-in-your-mouth sort, golden and perfect. This doesn't detract from the fact that this silence—this *peace*—is worse than the insanity that preceded it.

When I was dodging falling chunks of roof, my mind couldn't wander. Now there's nothing to drown out the snapping, crackling bonfire as Amelia Lopez dies in my head, again and again and *again* . . .

I stuff my mouth with pancake. Syrup coats my tongue, metallic like blood.

Project Zero. The sheet crinkles in my shirt pocket when I breathe. Aaron returns before I get a chance to smooth it over the table, ask the Captain if he knows what the Flamer's trying to hide.

His curly auburn hair brushes the top of the doorframe as he steps through, snapping off medical gloves and pinging them for the trash can—hole in one. After informing us that Turner needs to stay under observation, he leads Birnbaum out back, who nurses a scraped shin and an asthmatic wheeze.

That leaves me alone with Sherman, since the Captain's more interested in his next batch. He can keep them coming—I spewed up yesterday's lunch *and* dinner.

He left his car keys on the table. A bunch of bronze medallions dangle off the ring. Eleven. I count them as I pick splinters out of my arm with my nails, wincing at the sting. That's an AA thing, right? For years of sobriety?

Mom was never an alcoholic. Chain-smoking was more her style. Her pre-crash bender was only, like, the third time I saw her properly wasted. That binge was just another way to run away from consequences, I guess.

Whatever the Captain might've run from, it's not my business. But I'm glad he's stopped.

Sherman's gaze ticks back to me like the needle on a metronome. Her knife scrapes her plate. We flinch in synchrony. I'm about to snap, but she beats me to it.

"Sorry."

I creak back on my chair. "Oh, you know that word?"

The Captain pours the next pancake. "Careful, girls. The thermometer just dropped ten degrees."

Sherman's eyes are hard as pebbles. "Yeah. I apologize when I'm in the wrong."

I tap the time on my phone display: quarter to three in the morning. "Well, you better start soon. I wanna be home by seven."

Her attempt to glare a hole through my head (figuratively; don't think that's included in her Superpowers) is interrupted by a ribbeting frog. We stare at the Captain's phone, which jiggles and croaks its way toward his keys, until the Captain snatches it up and squashes it to his ear, balancing his spatula on the pan.

"Yeah?" Pause. "McCarthy? Uh-huh." Pause. "Yeah. I see."

Pause. "Mm-hmm." He hangs up. Then says, very succinctly: "Balls."

"That bad?" I ask.

"Worse. Most of the laser was impounded by the Super Squad, but a few brave, overachieving sods managed to sneak components out of the observatory. They salvaged enough that our boss wants them returned to the warehouse by tomorrow night." He yawns, cracking out his spine. "Means I gotta head round the city tomorrow, collect 'em up. Could use a hand to unload, Sherm."

Sherman doesn't look at me. "Could use more. I'll bring Jones."

"Um," I say. "What?"

"Good plan," says the Captain.

"Do I get a choice in this?"

"You'll get money," says Sherman quickly. "And Captain'll buy us dinner."

"Hey, I never said—"

I narrow my eyes at Sherman. What's her game? She must know I'm not her biggest fan right now. But money is money, and I won't turn it down.

"I'm in," I say as the Captain grumbles that we only like him because he feeds us. I steal the last pancake, Amelia Lopez blazing in one corner of my mind.

By the time Aaron tweezers out the final splinter, slathers my arm in antiseptic gel, and smooths gauze over the top (surprisingly dexterous with his dinner-plate hands), it's almost four. I elect to walk home, though it's at least three miles. Less awkward than asking Sherman for a lift.

Amelia wails in my head, loud as La Llorona, as I trudge up the stairs. I pull out the papers she gave me. Lists of numbers, compiled in a table, comparing percentages from 2015, 2020, and beyond. The title is made up of several words that contain too many syllables for my post-midnight brain, plus one mention of Clearwater River.

I could muddle my way through it. I could call the Captain, ask whether he knows what the Flamer kept Amelia from revealing. Or, as soon as I'm through the door, I could stuff the papers into the trash, to join the last letter from Blair Homes.

It's the sensible option. *Strictly no heroics*, etc.

Project Zero got Amelia dead. I don't wanna wind up the same way. The rest of her precious research is being distributed over the mountains by the wind, and these pages should have followed. If she saw a hero in me, she saw wrong.

CHAPTER 14

I'M EXHAUSTED, BUT sleep won't come. I jolt between burning women and burning cars whenever I shut my eyes. Amelia's face blurs into Mom's, into my own, like I'm looking through a distorted horror-house mirror.

Luckily, Lyssa's used to me waking up screaming. She doesn't comment.

I do catch her scoping out my bandage, though, after I heave myself out of bed around ten. She raises her eyebrows and *mmhmms* at my claim it's just a bad graze. I make good on my promise to take her to the bougie park, just to shut her up.

Guarding Lyssa's vacated chair isn't my idea of a fun morning. Still, I nurse a glimmer of pride, watching her feed the ducks with her friends. She's the best shot by far. You're not supposed to give birds bread (so says animal welfare, pest control, and everyone else who hates fun), but the park sells overpriced cups of oatmeal, so stale cornflakes can't be far off the mark. Lyssa nails one duck in the noggin, and her school friends whoop so loud the sunbathing crew slide down their aviators to glare.

But I can only pretend to be okay for so long.

It happens that evening. Lyssa's vegetating in front of the TV again while I reacquaint myself with my bed and answer the barrage of checking-in texts Hernando always sends on his breaks. I slide Jav a text, too, to let her know I'm not dead and that we should meet at the library soon so she can be inspired by my presence, like one of those Ye Olde-Timey artistic muses who were paid to drape nakedly over couches and eat grapes. But then I start thinking about Amelia being, y'know, *actually* dead, and my fingers shake across my phone screen like I'm tweaking.

Usually, talking to Jav makes my chest fizzle. But this time my rib cage tightens, and tightens, and *tightens*, strangling the breath right outta me.

Not my first rodeo. I let autocorrect take care of the worst of it and repeat *in-two-three-four-five, out-two-three-four-five* until I stop feeling like I'm being crushed in an invisible fist. Still, knowing how to handle panic attacks (thanks, Mom) doesn't make them any less awful.

My most obvious trigger is getting into cars. So, duh, I don't make a habit of that. But then there's the shit I can't predict. A distant explosion that shocks me back to that crunching impact. The smell of burning gasoline. Or when I feel myself start to shake and I don't have the first clue as to *why*.

I'm not looking to be fixed. Just to feel like I have my hands on the wheel (metaphorically. Cars being my kryptonite and all). And evidently, watching a villain burn a woman to death? Not helping.

It's almost like . . . exposure therapy . . . should be conducted in controlled environments . . .

Who'da thought.

Thing is, I *knew* joining Hench was a crap idea. I guess I wanted to prove something to myself by becoming a henchman. That I could be a badass. That my mental-health bullshit doesn't have to hold me back. But it *does* hold me back. That's *why it's mental-health bullshit*. I can't just grit my teeth and muscle on through.

Lyssa comes in at some point. Doesn't say a word. I don't need her to. She's just *there*, sliding down the wall to sit, tucking an arm around me, rubbing my spine. I forget she's an obnoxious little gremlin child for long enough to hug her back.

"How come you don't get this so badly," I mutter, once I can talk again. "We were in the same crash."

The real reason: brains are weird, we're all wired differently, Lyssa got knocked out immediately and didn't have to watch that awful part in the middle that makes my mind freeze like an old computer whenever I think about it, full blue-screen-of-death.

Lyssa Garcia's reason: "Super gene, duh."

"You don't *have* the Super gene. For the last time. And I'm fairly sure 'resistance to trauma' isn't on the official powers list."

She winks at me, only she sucks at it, so it's more like a really exaggerated, staggered blink. "Two weeks to my birthday. Guess we'll find out."

She's just being a brat. *Mocosa*, Abuelita would say. No way is she getting powers.

"Stick to writing self-insert fanfic," I tell her, unfolding from my curl. My body always feels so tight and heavy after a panic attack. Like my joints have fused. I have to dig my thumbs into my thighs to stop them cramping. "That's the only way you're hanging with the Super Squad."

Unless she lies about her age and joins Hench. After last night, though, I'm never letting my little sister anywhere *near* a real hero/villain battle. I'd rather face a thousand panic attacks, every single day.

CHAPTER 15

I'M STILL TWITCHY when I finally rock up at the library. Jav must notice. She doesn't ask why I'm late, for which I'm grateful. Just gives my hand a little squeeze, for which I'm more grateful still, along with a thousand other feelings.

The library is one of those stone buildings that everyone makes a fuss about because it's stood for over two hundred years. Big whoop. Sure, the Greek pillars out front look impressive, but inside it's all drafty single-paned windows and a funky smell from where someone spilled their latte on the carpet.

Still, at this time of year, the worktables under the central skylight hit that sweet spot between "sunbaked" and "blasted by overenthusiastic AC." I'm tempted to nap. But anyone who thinks libraries are quiet has clearly never shared one with a mom-and-tots group singing "Baby Shark" at top volume. At least exhaustion gives me an excuse for smiling dopily at Jav for way too long.

She sighs, in harmony with her laptop fan. "I *said*, you look like absolute shit."

I rest my head on my folded arms. "I'm taking that as a compliment. It's an improvement on how I'm feeling."

"Seriously, Riles. Did you get *any* sleep? And what happened to your arm?"

Aaron gave me enough gauze to change the bandage for a

week. Not that I'll need it all. The cuts from the observatory weren't deep. Give it a few days and they'll scab over, itching to hell and back, like the graze on my knee.

"It's not as bad as it looks. Just fell over. Hernando said I should pound the pavement if I wanted to find work; I took it literally."

Jav squeezes my hand again, prompting palpitations. Further proof crushes are an evolutionary mistake that threatens our youth with early-onset cardiac arrest, and someone really ought to find a cure. "You'll find something. I'll help you look, I promise, I just have to . . ."

"Finish the essay."

"Finish the essay." She glares at her screen, white light glancing off her cheekbones. "There's just so *much*, you know? I got records of property acquisitions from the last five years and rising rent comparisons, everything. All the data's here. I just gotta find a *direction*. Like, obviously, *gentrification bad*. But doesn't that feel, I dunno, overdone?"

I think of handbags that cost more than a month of rent, even though that rent's rising. I think of the *thunk* of a Blair Homes letter hitting our carpet. "Maybe it's overdone in your nerd circles. But I think you have to keep talking about it, because a lot of folks around here would rather forget."

Jav always chews her pens until they snap. She slots the flattened cap of her latest victim into the gap between her front teeth. "I'll figure it out," she says, cap waggling. "Job hunting might actually be a good break. I heard a Chinese restaurant needs a new dishwasher. Szechuan Sizzler? No, they got nuked by that Flamer guy with the bad dye job . . ."

Shit. My mind buzzes like static on an old TV. "Uhhh . . ."

Tragically, me and Jav have been friends long enough to reach full fluency in each other's monosyllables. She spits out the cap. "Riley?"

"You really don't have to help. I'm good."

"Wait, you found something? And—" Her brows pinch tight. "You didn't *tell me*?"

I really am the worst friend in the world. "No—I mean, yeah. I'm sorry, I just . . ."

"Your betrayal cuts me to my core." Jav tries to sound flippant, but the hurt beneath the words is real. "Out with it. Gimme deets."

What do I tell her? That I was so sick of being pushed around by heroes I joined the group who get beaten up by them on a bi-nightly basis? Hell no. The goal's to get her to *stop* worrying about me.

"Scrubbing toilets in a condo block," I decide on. "Only temporary. Wanted to find something more glam before I shared, is all."

Pretty decent, for improv. I might be proud of my quick thinking, if it didn't feel like I just took another step away from my bestie, teased the tangled threads of our lives that little bit further apart.

True to form, Jav imparts a very woke lecture about how sanitation jobs are undervalued by our awful late-capitalist hellscape of a society. "So," she finishes, once I've made *mm*s in all the right places (because she's right, as always). "Now that we've established your new job is absolutely nothing to be ashamed of, and that you should've told me so we could *celebrate* . . ." She pushes an open book my way: *The Political Theory of Neoliberalism*. "We got an hour before I head for Artie's, so read this and tell me you agree Mr. Biebricher is talking out his ass."

It's easy to give in. To scoot my chair up, leaning shoulder to shoulder with Jav, so I can pretend I understand what a regulatory framework is and why it should be flexibilizated. To let my tired eyes sink half closed, soaking in her presence. The coffee on her breath, the little focus dent between her eyebrows, her sweet, futile attempt to explain free market expansion in a way I understand.

I don't wanna dwell on Project Zero, the Flamer, Amelia, any of it. I just have to keep moving forward with my life and follow my three rules. At the end of the day, that's all us Normies can do.

It's no Normie who buzzes our apartment that night, though. When I shunt Hernando's leftovers into the fridge and head on down, I find Sherman straddling her motorcycle, helmet held out in a peace offering.

"How's the arm?" she asks as I take the helmet and clamber aboard. Her voice is all gruff, like she wants to ask something else but can't wrestle out the words.

"How's the leg?" I retort.

Neither of us are masked—it's about eight, still daylight. Means I get to watch Sherman's mouth pucker, tight as a drawstring bag. "Fine," she growls.

I nod. "Fine." Then, in case she thinks she's gotten away with this: "Super, in fact."

Sherman stiffens like every vertebra has latched. Then twists to glare over one shoulder. There's no escaping her scowl—not when we're sharing the motorcycle seat, all up in each other's personal space. Even her *eyebrow crinkles* are perfectly symmetrical.

I can smell her, which is a weird thing to notice. Beneath her deodorant there's something sharp, like overheating electronics.

Rule Number Two: Don't make enemies flashes through my head. "Super" is shorthand for "Significantly Upped ER Risk." If the last few days have taught me anything, it's when to back down, know my place.

Then again, I've never been the fastest learner.

"Do the others know?"

"What?"

"Y'know." I mime shooting magic out of my fingertips. "Zapow! Does the Captain know? Do our *clients* know? I mean, sure, you Super types do that whole secret identity shtick. But I figured you were supposed to pick a student as your alter ego. Or a news reporter. Not a *henchman*."

Sherman's jaw grinds. She focuses on the road ahead like we're taking the freeway at 120. "Let's get one thing clear. Just because you and me wear the same uniform, that doesn't make us friends."

Right. Because she's a Super, and that makes her better than me.

"What about your *actual* friends?" I ask, burrowing into the helmet. "Those henchmen you were talking to at the observatory? They know you can freeze their eyeballs?"

If Sherman gets any tenser, she might start vibrating. "Keep your mouth shut, Jones. You need the practice."

She rolls the throttle. I get a generous point-two-five seconds to grab my handholds before we pull away from the curb.

The Hench warehouse sits at the confluence where a street spills onto the main dockland thoroughfare. Sunnylake City is built on a grid, which makes navigation easy and boring at the same time. Each block sits the same distance apart, no variation. Just a rolling, endless stream of intersections: white-striped road, red-to-green lights. Feels more like a level of *Mario Kart* than reality.

It's hard to stop myself zoning, though I make the effort, 'cause when I zone, I think of Amelia. No more panic attacks engulf me, but my brain still feels fragile, as if the rumble of the motorcycle might crack it apart.

We activate our masks as we pull up in front of a broad, hangar-shaped storage unit, surrounded by loading bays. CROW BUILDING ENTERPRISES. There are, of course, several pigeons, cooing from the arched roof. The Captain waits outside the splatter radius, leaning on his car. The vehicle hogs a full semi-size space, to the annoyance of waiting drivers. The back seats have been flattened to make room for laser components, but a kiddie sun screen remains suckered to the left rear window. Elsa's cartoon face beams out at the world.

Sherman drops her kickstand and we dismount. I rub at my holographic faux-leather suit, uncomfortably aware of the workmen taking their smoke break outside the warehouse next door. They exercise that old Sunnylake law of *don't see shit, don't say shit*, not sparing us a second glance.

"Quit acting like you're here to bury a body," says the Captain. "We're delivering property to our company warehouse. No laws broken."

As we approach, he fastballs me something. By a fluke of luck or a sudden, miraculous alteration in wind speed, I manage not to drop it on my foot. I look down at a jet-black bike helmet with a yellow smiley sticker on one side. ". . . For me?"

"No; I want Sherman to wear two at once."

"Is that sarcasm? Because her head's big enough."

Sherman folds her arms. "My head's normal-size."

"Yeah," I say. "You got *super* proportions."

She steps on my foot. "I don't need a helmet."

"And I don't give a shit." The Captain points at us, two-fingered. "You'll wear helmets, especially if you ride past my house. Aaron says he has better things to do on his day off than glue your cracked-open skulls together."

That confirms it: He doesn't know about Sherman's powers. If she can make a shield out of frozen air molecules, she can handle a tumble off the back of her Harley. And, for whatever reason, she doesn't want anyone to know.

Sherman turns toward me. I know she's glaring under her holo-gram, daring me to say something. I keep my mouth welded shut.

We stick our helmets in the Captain's car and enter the ware-house. Boxes tower above us, piled in ceiling-scraping stacks. The Captain hails the foreman, a man with granite-gray stubble who flaunts a clipboard in an authoritative sort of way. He's the first worker who doesn't either feign blindness or hurry away as we approach. Of course, if Hench owns this compound, he's probably used to folks in masks. He leads us through the forest of cardboard to a pile of flat-packed laser parts.

"I'll send some boys to help you unload," he offers. He starts yakking into his radio before the Captain can insist we got it covered.

"They'll see your plates," Sherman murmurs. "And Elsa. Your identity's compromised. No choice but to go deep cover, take the family, and run to Alaska."

"More like Australia. The farther I can get from you, the better." Still, the Captain doesn't look happy as the foreman flicks off his walkie-talkie and, not a minute later, two men jog into view. I'm less happy still.

The ground beneath my feet is suddenly very far away. I stare at Hernando as he and his work buddy swallow simultaneous yawns.

"All right," says my li'l sister's daddy, the closest thing to a father I've ever known. "Where do we start?"

CHAPTER 16

AFTER MOM DIED, I took a ride on the school counselor carousel. Didn't do much good. Mostly because they all started by telling me how *sorry* they were *for my loss*, like I'd put my abusive shitbag of an egg donor down and forgotten where I'd left her. Or like they expected me to have a grief-induced aneurysm and forget every reason why I wasn't actually sorry in the slightest.

Not that she was gone, at least. Just about the nightmares she left me with.

Still, one of the counselors—Mrs. Palmer-or-Parker; the one with the macramé necklaces and the double-stacked shelf of self-help books—told me something that stuck. There are five stages to overcoming the loss of a loved one. Denial. Anger. Bargaining. Depression. Acceptance. I hit number two for Mom, then remembered what an ass she was and skipped the rest.

For Hernando, I speed run all five in under an hour.

First, I tell myself there must be another explanation. Hernando works for another shipping company. The Hench warehouse just happened to be low on numbers tonight. His boss struck a deal, shuffling men like the little pieces on a chessboard. Hernando had no choice. When the foreman says jump, you jump; and when he tells you to go work for a criminal organization, you . . . Well, I guess you don't argue.

Hernando knows his way around, though. He breaks away

from our group to retrieve a forklift. Either this has happened before, or . . . he works for Hench, like I do. And he's been lying to his family, like I've been, too.

Next up: anger.

It claws my belly as we unload the car. How dare he lie to us. To *me*!

But that's not fair. For every reason I'm pissed at him, he has a reason to be mad, too. We're both neck-deep in the villains' business. We're both risking everything—our freedom, our lives. The only difference is that I wear a mask.

I'll stop, I plead, in the echoing cavern of my head. *I'll quit if you quit, too.*

What would I do if the Super Squad tracked the laser back to its source? If Hernando got hurt?

Nothing. Just like with Amelia. That's all us Normies *ever* do.

I feel lost as we haul the last packaged piece of laser out of the Captain's trunk. Like I'm scooping parts of myself from one life and dropping them into another. All these secrets are hollowing out what makes me *me*. Lying to Jav is awful enough. I don't *want* to—not about Hench, or the way my heart barrel-rolls whenever she brushes my bare skin. But having to look into Hernando's familiar, yawn-lined face, and pretend I don't know he's lying, too?

Drama's the only class I ever scored higher than a C in, but I'm not that good an actor. I don't *want* to be.

I know I'm not really his daughter. Hell, I only met him after Lyssa was born. I never got past calling him by his first name. I'll even accept, grudgingly, that he won't win dad of the year. Especially not this year, since we've barely seen him. When he's there, though, he's *there*. It's hard to explain. But whether he's dozing on the sectional or scarfing his leftovers at ass o'clock in the morning, I know I can tell him anything in the whole wide world, and he'll smile his sleepy smile and nod.

Except, y'know, that I like girls.

And that I work for Hench.

It never occurred to me that Hernando might have an "except," too.

The Captain slams his trunk. Hernando steers his forklift off into the towers of crates. He doesn't look back. He doesn't know who I am. I watch until my blurring eyes can't distinguish him from the stacks. We both made this choice. I can't judge Hernando for it any more than I can judge myself.

That doesn't stop this hurting, though. Somehow, that last state of grief—the acceptance—aches worst of all.

CHAPTER 17

"YOU GOOD?" SHERMAN wants to know as we leave. "You haven't made any pointless commentary in, like, half an hour."

She winces as soon as she says it, like she realizes just how dickish that came out. Thankfully, backhanded expressions of concern are my lingua franca. I don't take it personally. Or rather, I *can't*. I've burned through so many emotions this evening, I don't have any brain chemicals left for offense.

The laser has been unloaded, forms stamped and signed. By all accounts, tonight's mission was a success. All accounts except mine.

Hernando works for Hench. *Hernando works for Hench.*

"It's nothing," I mumble, in the direction of my feet.

". . . Nothing?"

I don't need a grilling. Not from *her*. "How's the Super gene treating you?"

"Point taken." Still, she shoots an over-the-shoulder glance at me as I mount up. "Jones? Talking about feelings isn't my thing . . ."

"You're telling me? I looked up 'emotional constipation' on Urban Dictionary, and they just had a picture of your face."

"The point *is*, despite that . . ." She breaks off with a shrug. "Just. Sometimes it helps, y'know?"

I count the grooves on the roof of my mouth with my tongue. "Knew you were lying," I say eventually.

"About what?"

"About us not being friends. You're giving sage life advice. That's, like, level two friendship. A couple more conversations and you'll unlock my tragic backstory."

"Ugh," mutters Sherman, in that way that means she's rolling her eyes. Our beautiful bonding moment is interrupted by the honk of the Captain's horn. He leans out his window, tapping gloved fingers on the car door.

"You ladies want dinner or not?"

Within a few minutes, we swing into the lot of Happy Burgers (Artie's budget carnist-friendly competitor). The Captain takes the drive-through lane. His emptied car rides higher on its wheels, as if in relief. I don't see whether he dismisses his hologram while he orders, but it's back in place when he returns, passing two take-out boxes through the window.

I'm not so brave. I turned my hologram off before I removed my helmet, and Sherman copied me. Costuming up at the warehouse is one thing, but we don't need a panicked citizen telling the Super Squad that a squad of henchmen are targeting a fast-food joint.

The burger's good. I know that objectively. The rich, meaty flavor bursts over my tongue. Doesn't matter. I can't taste the goddamn love.

I'm on my last bite, sucking juice from my fingertips, when my phone buzzes. I fish it out of my cleavage, waiting to swallow until I'm sure I can sink my half-chewed mouthful without choking. What if Hernando recognized me after all? What if he *knows?* It's a relief to see Jav's name on the caller ID.

"You answering that?" asks Sherman, bundling her greasy paper and lobbing it at the nearest trash can. It ricochets off the side.

"I—uh. Yeah." I pin the phone to my ear as the Captain reminds Sherman that we're henchmen, not littering delinquents, and sends her sulking off to dispose of all our trash properly. "Sup?"

It's a fight to sound chill, and not just because I'm standing in a parking lot with two other criminals, having just driven away from the criminal-owned warehouse where my sister's dad (also a criminal) works. Damn crush.

"I—I just . . ." I hear Jav swallow. "Sorry, it's a lot."

My mind snaps to hyperalert. "Was there an attack? You okay?"

"I'm fine. No attacks. Just . . . I'm still trying to figure this out myself, y'know?"

"Okay." She's not in danger. First good news I've had all day. "Wanna start at the beginning?"

"Actually, I'mma start from the end." She takes a deep breath. "Riles, I quit Artie's."

"You what now?"

"I quit!"

"*What?* Why?"

Sherman returns, rubbing sticky hands on her jeans. She quirks pierced brows at my outburst. Even the Captain sneaks a peek in his wing mirror. I sink on the motorcycle seat, twisting to one side so I don't have to look at them.

"Shit, Jav. Not because of me?" I don't want that. I don't. But I'd be flattered, all the same.

"No. I mean, not *totally*." Another deep breath. "You know Cooper—sorry, *Windwalker*—beat the Ferocious Flamer last Saturday?"

That was less than a week ago? Damn. "Still can't believe *the Ferocious Flamer* is the name he went for."

"I *know*. Well, it got Windwalker serious attention. Boy's moved up in the world. Passed initiation, got another star on his chest. He brought a bunch of heroes to Artie's earlier tonight. And—well, you were the best with parties. Took two of us to handle their orders, what with how they kept changing their minds. *Customers*."

"*Customers*," I agree. We use the sort of voice most people use when they describe roaches. I nurse a vindictive delight that Matias found me hard to replace.

"I was serving," Jav continued. "And . . . well."

I see red. "If he touched you again . . ."

"No! Lay off the potato peeler." Her sigh crackles through the speaker. "That's the thing, Riley. He *didn't*. He sat there, laughing with his friends, networking away. Even invited Brightspark, for fuck's sake."

"*Brightspark?*" Leader of the original Super Squad triad?

"Yeah! Plenty of cameras, too. Brightspark has big clout with the press—he's backing Mayor Darcy for another term."

Why our mayor would *want* to be reelected, given how many times the VC abduct her in any given month, I have no idea—but whatever. This isn't about her.

Jav's voice dips. "Cooper acted the perfect gentleman. A

woman let him hold their *baby*, Riley. He was laughing, and the other heroes were taking selfies with the staff, and they were all *so happy* . . . All I could think was how fucking *fake* it was. How any of them could do what Cooper did to me, or worse. How no one'd do *shit* about it. How no one would care, so long as they got to keep believing these heroes *protect our city* . . ."

Jav's voice strangles itself to silence. I get what she's saying. She isn't just mad at him. She's mad about *all* of it. The *us* and the *them*. The public and our so-called protectors, who justify anything, everything, with a flash of their badge. Hero patrols are supposed to make us feel safe, but they don't. Watching our Superpowered police force swagger around the streets just reminds us how powerless we are.

But Jav walked out on the summer job that was supposed to pay off her tuition bill from Ralbury. How does this fit into her five-point success plan?

"You quit," I repeat.

"Uh-huh." I picture her grin, down to the adorable bunny gap between her front teeth. "Plus, I gobbed on his burger before I carried it out to him. And when he asked for a refill, I spilled Coke all over his lap."

My heart squeezes. "I'm so proud of you."

"S'nothing," says Jav, modest. She's right. It really *is* nothing. Little, petty displays of dissatisfaction. But her glee is infectious, anyway. "Gave Matias my hat. Told him it was over, and if he didn't start defending his staff, he wouldn't have any. But since I'm down a summer job . . . Yours still hiring?"

We Hire Anyone.

"No!" The observatory, the waterfall of frozen steel—I only got out because I had a Super on my side. If Jav had been there . . .

Sherman squints. Even the Captain conveys surprise through that ever-present mask. I hunch, blocking out everything but the hush of Jav's breath.

"Sorry, you know how it is—I got lucky. Can we catch up tomorrow? I got an early start."

"Right, yeah. Should've messaged, I know, but . . ."

"You wanted to hear my voice, 'cause I'm irresistible. Later, babe."

I hang up, tucking my phone back in my bra. The fear of near-discovery fizzes inside me like I've swallowed a soluble vitamin tablet. Jav'll find work. I know it; she's smart like that. It doesn't matter what she does, where she goes—so long as she stays far away from Hench.

CHAPTER 18

SHERMAN DROPS ME off after we split with the Captain. The bike's rear light glows red. Red as Kool-Aid, as blood, as *fire* . . .

I flinch: a full-body shudder so intense it leaves me cramping. So far this week, I've had front row seats to a murder, lied to my bestie, and discovered that my sort-of dad is a borderline criminal, same as me. In short, I'm not ready to face three flights of stairs.

I slide until my ass meets our front stoop. Cobwebs gather over a mound of Mr. Beauvais's cigarette butts (he's not allowed to smoke in the house). I scratch miserably at my bandaged arm and sigh.

The bike engine cuts off. Why's Sherman still here?

"Hey," she says.

"Hey," I reply.

"You going inside?"

"Considering it. I could also sit here for the rest of my life."

Sherman taps her nails (chewed, black-painted) on the buckle of her belt. *Ting, ting, ting.* The metallic noise screws into my brain, like that tuning-fork hum from the observatory. I'm about to tell her to quit it when she climbs off her bike and plonks down next to me, knee bonking mine.

"Uh," I say. Sherman, initiating contact? Did every planet just go into retrograde? "What're you doing?"

"I can go, if you want."

I don't, despite everything. I shut my mouth. Sherman rests her helmet on the step, finger-combing her gelled-down curls.

Silence stews. I put us out of our misery. "You got questions."

She exhales, long and low. "You got more."

Damn right. "Why'd a Super join Hench? And why come back again, after you got fired?"

I can't imagine crawling back to Artie's on my knees, even if every other option fell through. Well—maybe then, but I wouldn't enjoy it, and . . . Wow. Sherman's initial shitty attitude makes way more sense.

She treats me to a brow rise. "You wanna hear my sob story?"

"That's the next level of friendship, right?" I stretch out my legs. "Actually, I wanna compare notes. Bet it can't beat mine." She snorts. I point at her. "Laugh or scoff?"

Sherman looks me over. Not in her usual scathing way, like how bougie folk eye up the graffiti that brightens Bridgebrook's concrete walls. Softer, somehow. Her gaze is sticky toffee, molten and sweet, drizzling over my curves. "Totally a scoff."

"Yeah. Totes." My heart beats double, triple time. A spark bounces beneath my skin, wanting to leap out and lick. Just physics, right? Not chemistry.

But Amelia blazes in the back of my mind, like the fire left a permanent scar on my retinas. I shiver, swallow, look away.

"Okay, question time. Superpowers. You wake up on your thirteenth birthday, and . . ."

Sherman looks disappointed. Still, she plays along, settling with her back against the step and her long legs striping the sidewalk. "Thought I was a Normie for five whole minutes. Then I tripped and fell down the stairs."

"You cast that bubble?"

Sherman nods, though she won't meet my eyes. "Surger-Shaper discipline; never presents above D-class potency. Draws on local sources of electricity and heat to freeze air molecules. Notice how everything went cold around us, back in the observatory?"

"Figured that was just me being terrified. Back to baby Sherm—what happened next?"

Her gaze drifts far away. "Well, I ran to show Mom and Pops. They couldn't believe it. Never had a Super in the family before."

"That's possible?"

"Uh-huh. Spontaneous mutation. We did a bunch of research—turns out it's real. Doesn't get talked about much, but it happens."

"Don't let my sister hear. Swears she's gonna be the next big Wind-Type Summoner." If what Sherman says is true, she might be—but I have too many other things to worry about right now. "So, you turn Super at thirteen and get fast-tracked, yeah? Usual story?"

Sherman nods. Super kids are trained for military deployment and civilian defense from the day their powers emerge. It's a stable gig and a well-paying one. Pretty much every Super tries it out. Those who don't cut it as heroes or sidekicks segue into a variety of high-flying careers, from stuntmen to bodyguards to circus performance.

You don't see 'em stacking shelves at Walmart or waiting tables at Artie's. And you certainly don't find Supers in Hench uniforms.

"What went wrong?" I ask. "Allergic to white holographic spandex?"

Sherman doesn't answer. Just tilts her face toward the slice of sky visible between the rows of tenement houses that line our end of Sloan Street. Light pollution coats the city in a greasy orange film. Our night is a constant twilight. You could forget the stars existed down here on street level, though Sherman's piercings glitter bright enough to compensate. Medusa, spider bites, nostril studs, eyebrow rings: her own tiny constellation. I wanna keep probing, but something—a fracture in her expression, a fault line in her resting bitch face—holds me back.

"It's weird," she grumbles eventually as I jiggle numbness from my butt. "Supers are . . . what? Five percent of the global population? But they make so much noise, it's like they're everywhere."

She talks about them like they're different from her. I can't figure it out. "You're still my hero."

Sherman's grip on her helmet tightens. "Don't call me that."

"Why? Scared someone'll hear? If you wanted your powers to stay a secret, you could've kept them that way."

"And watch you get zapped? No way."

That's such a Super thing to say. Does Sherman know what happened to Amelia? Does she think there was nothing I could do, or that I didn't really try?

I stood by while Amelia burned. Sherman's more of a hero than I am, that's for sure.

Silence smothers us again, until Sherman heaves a sigh. She delves into her pocket to retrieve a pair of squashed earbuds. She holds one out, not quite looking me in the eye. "Hey. Wanna . . . ?"

A diversion. One I'm glad to follow. I take the offered headphone and plug in to a funky Afrobeat. "What's this?"

"Kuduro."

"Uh-huh."

We listen for a minute, me bopping my head to the rhythm. Sherman gives my thigh a light, bro-like punch. "You have no idea what kuduro is, do you?"

"None whatsoever."

"It's Angolan dance music. Mom was born there. But Pops is Puerto Rican, and a total dork, so my library stocks plenty of Enrique Iglesias and Ricky Martin, too."

She's sharing something else with me. Something precious, about the girl behind the mask. I shut my eyes, let my ears drink it in. "I like it."

"Don't lie."

"I'm not! It's . . . It's good." I grin. "I'd share, too, but I only listen to Hayley Kiyoko and trashy pop, and something tells me that ain't your scene."

Sherman neither confirms nor denies, though the corner of her mouth does this funny twitchy thing, like her facial muscles are fighting a civil war, before curling into a slow half smile. Her music—*kuh-doo-roh*—crescendos in a thunder of percussion, then drops to silence before the next track starts. My thigh rests along hers in a hot line. This must be the longest we've spent in each other's company without throwing shade.

"Hey, Jones," she says after several minutes. I look at her, which is a mistake at this distance. I can count her long, dark eyelashes, play an imaginary game of dot-to-dot with the tiny freckles sprinkled over the bridge of her nose. Kuduro, fed into my left ear and her right, races my rattling heart. Stupid symmetrical Supers.

"Uh. Hey, yourself."

Sherman chews her lip. Then she stops the music.

"Remember how everything went wrong?" she asks. "On our job at the observatory?"

"Kinda hard to forget, what with it being literally last night."

Sherman winds her earbud wire between her fingers, over and under and over again. "Henchmen got hurt. Like, a *lot* of them. Real bad, too. This one guy from my old crew, Delmar, he had an eye out." Her expression sours. "Not every Captain has an Aaron. Del's gonna be out of action a long time."

"Sounds like the exact opposite of fun."

"Right? Missions with high body counts hit Hench at least once a month. The villains treat us like we're disposable, and this mysterious boss of ours doesn't give a fuck. Some of us . . ." She lifts one shoulder higher than the other, a stunted half shrug. "We figured it's time we did something about it."

My pulse thumps my eardrums like a wrecking ball. "Like what?"

"Like joining that big living-wage protest in the town square."

I know the one. Jav did a piece about it on her podcast, praising homegrown activism. The organizers are all Bridgebrook, born and raised. Real awesome stuff, aimed at uplifting service workers, cleaners and fry cooks and retail workers from across the city. Not criminals.

I laugh, like you're supposed to when a cute girl makes a joke. It's disconcerting when Sherman doesn't join in. "Um. You're serious?"

"Deadly."

"Sounds it! You mean you're going to tell the world that us

henchmen are mad at how we're treated by the *freaking Villain Council*? A bunch of evil Supers who are literally conspiring to take over the world?"

"Yup," says Sherman, poker-faced. "You know them?"

"You're not allowed to use sarcasm. That's *my* thing. But seriously, wouldn't we get arrested if we joined the march?"

"No law against wearing a Hench costume. Or even against being a henchman, technically. If they can prove you committed a crime, that's different, but there are plenty of loopholes." Sherman shrugs. "Delmar studied for the bar. He knows this shit."

She's actually thought this through. Sure, what happened at the observatory was messed up. Sure, knowing Normies in Hench uniform can be mutilated and killed by heroes with zero repercussions freaks me out. But making a big thing of it, publicly? For the world—and the Villain Council—to see? *Viva la revolución* and all that, but I don't want to be on the front lines.

Taking stock of my nibbled lip, Sherman averts her glare to the sidewalk. "Didn't tell you earlier because you're new. Wasn't sure I could trust you not to snitch to the Captain."

I'm not sure I trust myself. "Why can't we tell him?"

"Cap's been at Hench for, like, *ever*. He looks out for his crew and he messes with the villains' plans, but he never rocks the boat with our boss." Her fist tightens, resting on her lean, jean-clad leg. "We've been planning this for over a year, and it's getting big. Hundreds of henchmen have signed up to create a grassroots union. I don't need him trying to bust it."

Perhaps this faceless boss of ours ordered him to fire her. I wonder if the Captain told them she's back.

"You really think this'll work?" I ask.

Sherman stands, thumbs tucked in her waistband. "Someone's gotta do something, Jones. The more we let the Supers use us like we're nothing, the more they believe it."

Her wording bugs me. *She's* one of those Supers, after all. But that doesn't change the fact that she's right.

I imagine Amelia Lopez again. Skin cracked like desert mud, hair crisping to cinders. I should stay out of this. Keep my head down. But maybe I've had enough of Rule Number One.

"Well?" Sherman prompts. "You in?"

I know fuck all about marches, unions, et cetera. But henchmen can't continue like this. *Normies* can't continue like this. That I know for sure.

I stand, too, so we can make it a proper moment, the two of us bathed in the glow of the streetlight like flies caught in amber. Unfortunately, my legs are full of pins and needles, so I wind up leaning on the railing, styling it out, playing it cool. But I mean it when I tell her, "I'm in."

CHAPTER 19

SHERMAN SENDS ME a link the next day. Through DM, not the Hench crew group chat the Captain set up. No small talk, just the long blue line of a URL.

That link opens a new Twitter hashtag: #HenchMarch2K23. Enough random people like the tweets that I won't look suspicious doing the same. I'm a concerned, curious citizen, if anyone asks. Still, the multi-K heart tallies make me wonder how long this pressure has been building beneath my city's concrete skin. Beneath the rules I've taken as gospel my whole life.

Since Mayor Darcy first licensed the Sunnylake branch of the Super Squad? Since the Super gene first mutated? Or longer: Ever since we shaped our world so the people who work hardest get the least?

They're big questions. Definitely too big for 9 a.m. on a Tuesday, on only five hours' sleep.

Sunlight stabs through the chink in my curtains, bright enough to make me squint. I can't stay in bed. I slither from the sheets, leaving a damp slug track. Ew. I need five showers, stat. I'm sure I brushed my teeth at some point after waving bye to Sherman and crawling up the stairs, but my mouth still tastes like I took a bite of a urinal cake.

I find Lyssa upside down on the sectional, head dangling, legs hooked over the back of the seat as she watches cartoons, flesh and metal side by side. "You missed Dad," she tells me, without looking up.

Right. Hernando has headed out to Job Number One (which may not involve villains, but at this point, who knows?). The only indication of his presence is last night's sudsy plate.

I pick it up. After a brief hesitation, I subject it to the usual rinsing and prop it on the rack to dry.

I wanna talk to him. I do. But how do I tell him I know he works for Hench without confessing I do, too? If he gets mad, if he says I'm turning out like Mom . . . I won't just sit back and take it. Then what? I'm a freeloader in Hernando's house. He's not my *real* dad, after all.

I don't wanna think about that scenario, much less live through it. I'll worry about it when I have to and not a moment before.

I decide to worry about Amelia Lopez instead. That's still raw, not gonna lie. I mean, I watched this woman die in graphic fashion. We're talking R-rated levels of violence.

Is it grief I feel? Can you grieve a woman you knew for a little over a minute, before she hit you with her briefcase and burst into flames?

I don't know, but Amelia chose me to be her hero. *Me.* There was no one else around, but still. This woman, this entire, complex *person* of wants and needs and fears and loves, is *dead.* And I, the last person to see her breathing, know nothing more about her than her name.

I can't bear it, all of a sudden. Thankfully, there's something I can do. Because I'm an awful slug of a human, and I haven't yet changed our trash bag.

After fondling way too much mushy cereal, I find what I'm

looking for. Three crumpled sheets. All stained, all soggy, but still just about legible. I spread them on the table while Lyssa takes her shower. The prosthetic's not waterproof—she has to take it off, which means a lot of careful balancing on slippery tiles. Plus, she's made it her life goal to burn through the entire building's hot water supply every morning, so I won't be disturbed for an hour at least.

It won't be long enough. I groan, digging the heels of my hands into my eye sockets. Of course it'd be *way* too easy for Amelia to hand me a neatly typed up point-by-point report of what this "Project Zero" thing is. The tables of percentages are no more forthcoming than the last time I glanced at them. All I gather is that nitrates, phosphates, mercury, arsenic, and lead are on the rise in the local river.

That's bad, right? Arsenic, bad?

Google says yes. But I don't see why the Flamer full-on *murdered* Amelia for pointing it out. Clearwater might be the name of our river, but it's misleading. *Clear* isn't the word I'd use to describe it. Honestly, even *water* is on thin ice. Everyone knows we're destroying the environment. It's not exactly breaking news.

Searching Project Zero (on incognito, just in case) brings up a bunch of security analysts and a Greenpeace-y charity campaign. Neither seem likely to want Amelia dead. Searching her name is more forthcoming. Takes me a hot minute to locate her obituary. It's buried deep—we're talking third page of the search results. But it's there: a small entry in the *Sunnylake Times*.

The article claims she was a limnologist ("freshwater biologist," to us mere mortals). It doesn't mention family. I'm not sure if it's better to imagine there's no one who'll miss her, or worse.

I scroll through those ten lines of text again and again, thumb tapping the case of my crummy old laptop where it's held together with tape. It feels impossible that this is all Amelia has been rendered down to. There's more to Project Zero, I know it. But how did Amelia expect me to figure it out? The surname's Jones, not Holmes.

I close the laptop, folding the papers in half, then in half again. There. I tried. Didn't get anywhere, but at least I gave it a shot, so my conscience can rest. What else can I do? Post these pages to city hall? Leave flowers on her grave? I'm about to see if I can find out where Amelia will be buried (or if her ashes were decanted straight into an urn) when a notification pops up.

Jav: We still on for coffee & library?

If Jav has to ask, my whole secret-job sitch must've rattled our friendship more than she let on. Amelia can wait. I have to settle things with the living people in my life before I can worry about the dead ones.

Riley: does the Earth still spin? do the Dodgers still beat the Angels? is c. hanson still a wad of gooey gray dickcheese

I could've continued in this vein for some time, but Jav cuts me off with a graveyard's worth of skull emojis.

Jav: See you there.

CHAPTER 20

I TELL LYSSA where I'm going—not a lie, for once—and set off for the nearest Starbucks. Street level at midday is a slime of heat haze and traffic fumes. I morosely smooth my frizzy blonde bob in the window of the corner store. This humidity is a crime against hair. Why everyone portrays hell as a fiery inferno is beyond me. Spending the rest of eternity in summer's swampy armpit would be a way better deterrent from sin.

Sky fills the gaps between the buildings, flat and digital-blue, like the background on a giant laptop screen. Whenever a pigeon flaps up above the roofs, I expect it to go *splat*. I meet Jav under the green-and-white-striped veranda. First up: the good news. She must've landed the job at the Beijing Bar; she's wearing a black tee with a red double-*B* logo on one tit (which, for your information, I admire for no more than two seconds before I remember to chug that honor-and-respect-your-bestie's-tragic-straightness juice).

She's peppy, for a girl due to spend the night scrubbing plates. She trots up to me, coiled 'fro bouncing for a second after she stops, and the sight is so damn cute I almost forget how to make words.

"Hhhhiii?"

Jav gives me her patented *you're weird but I love you platonically* look. "Sup. Arm any better?"

I scratch the fresh bandages. "Yeah, way."

That's another truth. Two in one day—I'm on a roll.

We buy our frappe, pooling change for caramel pumps, then head for the library. Stale wind funnels up the street, jiggling Jav's curls. This avenue is lined with paper-leaved poplars, reaching out toward the asymmetrical black-and-white condos by the waterfront. The skeletons of buildings rise in the distance. Plastic wrap flaps from scaffolds, crane booms swinging around their axes like the necks of giant giraffes. They're always building something new here.

"You got a direction yet?" I ask. "For your essay?"

Jav sips the frappe, then passes it to me. I study the sky— better that than how a drop of coffee glitters on her pillowy bottom lip. "Sort of. Maybe studying gentrification as a knock-on effect of the Super Squad's shortcomings? I mean, they've had so many funding boosts, but . . ." She tugs her BB shirt as we head through the library's big automatic door. "Szechuan Sizzler still got flattened. The lot's been bought up by some new gastropub, and poor Mr. Wang's praying for an insurance payout. It's just not good enough, y'knooooo—oh *shit*."

I squint at her from the corner of my eye. "What?"

Jav does this hunched side shuffle around to my opposite side. "What?" she parrots.

"What?"

Jav shrinks into my shadow. "Don't make a big thing of it, God."

"I wouldn't, except you're using me as full-body cover!"

"Riley!" She tugs my arm, peering over my shoulder. "Keep it down!"

I, of course, crane in the direction she's looking. Jav meeps and yanks me toward our usual table ("Don't stare, don't stare!") but not before I catch a good long look at the boy pushing the book trolley between the aisles, against the wishes of its squeaky front wheel. Chunky-knit cardi. Black curls and an angular, statement-piece nose that he must be trying to draw attention to with his weedy attempt at a mustache. Nice smile, though, when he greets one of the old grandmas browsing the romance section by name and offers up a recommendation.

There goes my heart, melting like the whipped cream on our frappe. Slithering down between my ribs.

"Did he see?" Jav pinches my arm like she's trying to wax me. "Is he looking? Shit, my makeup . . ."

Like any high school–age boy would notice she didn't bother with mascara today. Like he'd *ever* notice her, ever *look* at her, like I do. Like—

Fuck.

I take a deep breath. Then pull out my chair and sit.

"No. No, you're good. He's, uh." Asking the old lady how her grandkids are doing. Like the decent, friendly guy he probably is. The decent, friendly guy who's undeserving of my hatred. Despite his fugly mustache. "He didn't notice."

Jav sinks onto the chair next to me, fanning herself like a Victorian lady coming out of a swoon. "Thank you, God."

This isn't a surprise. Or at least, it shouldn't be. Jav's never given any indication she's interested in anyone other than a few of the less-douchey sportsball dudes at Ralbury and Jason Momoa. Not girls. Definitely not *me*. It's just . . . something I gotta live with. The last thing I want is to give off Nice Guy vibes, like she owes me shit 'cause we're friends.

We *are* friends, though. At some point, I have to trust that, if I want us to stay that way.

It hits me then. The reality of it. What I want, what I dream of, is never going to be. That hurts. Course it does: a smack to the chest, knocking the wind out of me like my seat belt during the crash. But I'm keeping so much from her, and that hurts impossibly more.

This is one truth I can give her. I just don't know if I *should*.

I couldn't bear it if I made her uncomfortable. What if this changes everything? What if Jav starts acting nervous around me, always second-guessing her actions in case she thinks she's leading me on? Sure, I go a charming shade of lobster when she's around. But that's not *her* problem. It's mine. And maybe, if I say this out loud, if I get a confirmation that her and me won't ever be a *we*, I'll be able to stop hoping and start moving forward.

Only, how do I kick off that conversation? Do I just . . . launch in? Should I lead with some verses by Hayley Kiyoko? Are coming-out protocols sent via email newsletter to every other queer kid in Sunnylake except me?

"Earth to Riles." Jav waves her hand in front of my face. "You okay? I was gonna tell you about my new research, but you full-on spaced."

"Right. Right-right-right. Sorry. Just." I take a fortifying sip of frap. It's lukewarm by now, icy slush at the bottom of the cup. "I—I think I have something to tell you, too."

Sharing one secret won't make the others any lighter, as they dangle over my head on creaking wires. But it might stop this horrible drifting sensation, like Jav and I are being dragged by diverging currents, out of each other's reach.

Jav blinks. "Yeah?"

I twist my flip-flops into the stained gray carpet, straps chewing between my toes. "I don't want you to look at me different."

"Wow. You kill someone?"

"What? No!" I scoot the frappe over when she makes grabby hands. "Why's *that* where your mind goes?"

"Uh, you threatened to skin Cooper Hanson with a potato peeler." She grabs the frappe and takes a long slurp, eyeing me the whole while. "You better not be dealing, either."

"Again, no! Damn, Jav." I've seen too much of that. Most of us Bridgebrook kids have. There's a reason I only take Lyssa to the bougie park.

Jav pushes our frappe back. "Then why would I look at you different? Spill already."

Okay. This is it. I take a soothing sip, numbing my tongue, and say, all in a rush: "Ikindamaybedefinitelylikegirls."

". . . Come again?"

I repeat myself at normal conversational speed, then slurp crushed ice noisily enough to drown out the panic in my head. Why's it so easy to be loud about every aspect of myself except this?

A beam breaks out over Jav's face. "Riley! That's awesome, babe. Thanks for telling me." She reaches over the table, gives my hand an elated squeeze. "Dish the deets. Did you meet someone? Tell me *everything*."

The world's not crumbling. Jav hasn't accused me of being a perv for all the times we swatted each other's asses as we squeezed around the cramped Artie's storeroom. Would she, though? If I let this out?

Jav strokes my knuckles. "Riles? You okay?"

I have to. This trapped truth, one of so many—it fizzles effervescent in the gaps between my knuckle bones, where her delicate fingertips press.

"Um. Yeah. Full disclosure. I kinda like you. Like, like-like, I mean."

Jav's eyes go round. Her hand slackens, and for one horrible moment, I'm sure she'll yank it back.

"Wait, wait! I ain't getting down on one knee. I know it's not mutual. I know . . ." I wave vaguely at Mediocre Mustache. "And—and I don't, like, *mind*, or anything. That's just . . . life, I guess."

Especially for people like me. The Captain's the first out adult I've met IRL who's in a long-term, established relationship. Actually gives me hope, knowing he found Aaron. Maybe I'll find someone, too. But that someone won't be Jav. And the longer I let myself wish otherwise, the more we're both gonna get hurt.

"I'll deal with it," I say. Not wanting to blink, like my sincerity is a laser beam, concentrated by my gaze. "I'm not telling you this because I wanna pressure you into anything. Or because I'm upset you like Mediocre Mustache."

"His name's Baahir," says Jav, then flinches down into her shirt collar, peeking to make sure he didn't hear.

"Right. I'm telling you this so next time I turn red, you know

I'm not having an allergic reaction. You're my best friend, Jav. And that means more to me than screwing this up for something unrequited. I can't make what I feel go away, but I can promise I'd never do anything to make things awkward . . ." Deep breath; reassess. "More awkward than this conversation, anyway. I know it's a big ask for you to trust me on that." Especially since I'm lying to her about literally everything else. "I—I guess if this is too uncomfortable for you . . ." Another deep inhale. Any more and I might pop. "I understand. And I'm not mad if you walk away." Just, y'know. Bleeding from the tatters of my heart. "But I really, really hope you don't! Because, girl, this crush might last a month or another year, but you're *always* gonna be my bestie."

Jav needs a minute to absorb my blather. That's a minute for me to squirm on my seat, wishing I could gulp half those words back down my throat. But slowly, her beautiful smile creeps out of hiding. "Course we're always gonna be besties. I mean—*damn*, you got fine taste."

I don't realize how much tension I'm holding until it all rushes out of me. I slump over the table like I'm made from putty. "This doesn't creep you out?"

"Please! I'm flattered. Anyway, the LGBTQ-plus-whatever club at Ralbury does the best bake sales. Not that my support ever needed to be bought, but the peanut-butter cookies cinched it."

If she got any more picture-perfect Straight Bestie, I might sniffle. Which I'm totally not doing. Not one bit. Smiley-sunshine-Riley, that's me.

"Tell that to Hernando," I manage, scooting the frappe at Jav and blaming any moisture in my eyes on delayed brain freeze.

"He still hates my cooking." Thank everything I didn't see him this morning. I have no idea what I would've said, would've done.

Jav gives my hand one more stroke. It aches. Not so much her touch as the moment when she lets go. But it's a good ache, like the scabs prickling on my arm. Like something's healing over—or starting to.

"Right," I say. I have to wipe my eyes, but Jav does me a solid, letting me pretend it's dust. "Uh. Gentrification research. Over to you."

We fall back into our usual rhythm: her talking through her thought process, me alternating between listening, getting her to repeat bits, getting her to repeat bits again, pretending I understand when it still doesn't sink in, and scrolling through the socials on my phone. The pain in my chest doesn't go away. But it does fade, just a little.

Basically, Jav's interested in what progress the Super Squad has actually made toward preventing villains from destroying entire blocks of Bridgebrook at a time. The answer being: worse than none.

"Look at this," she says, turning her laptop toward me. More spreadsheets. Just what I need. "I crunched a bunch of data over the past week."

"Much data. Very numbers. Wow."

"God, that meme is *vintage*. Here." A new tab brings up a map of Sunnylake. The Bridgebrook area is so spotty it looks like it's suffering an acne outbreak. "I made this earlier. Wanted a visual. Easy, really—just checked news records, then cross-referenced on Google Maps to find the locations of every destructive Super attack from the past five years in Bridgebrook. And *here*." A new map, acne significantly reduced. Must've applied a topical cream. "Notice anything weird?"

"Other than the fact you did all this for funsies?"

"I'm being serious. Despite all the taxes that have been funneled into the Super Squad, things are getting worse, not better. And that's being taken advantage of." She taps the screen. Today's nails are the color of key lime pie. "Loads of demolished sites have been gobbled up by big property developers from downtown—especially the lots along Clearwater."

Clearwater. My brain ping-pongs between Amelia, the fire, the car crash, the Flamer's smirk, Amelia again. One big bundle of associated trauma.

"Have you looked at the records for other districts?" I ask, to distract myself. "Maybe the land value is higher there, so the pattern's different. I dunno."

Jav snaps her fingers. "Riles. Riles-Riles-Riles-Riles-*Riles*, you are a genius and I—" To her credit, she only hesitates a moment. "And I love you. Y'know. As a friend."

"As a friend," I agree. God, so awkward. Then again, the fact she's still sitting with me and I haven't melted into a mortified post-confession puddle under the desk makes this whole day a win.

Takes Jav another two hours to compile various charts. I alternate between checking Sherman's hashtag and glaring at Mediocre Mustache. Eventually, though, I can no longer ignore the groove between Jav's eyebrows, mostly because if it digs any deeper, it'll cut a canyon through to her brain.

"You'll set the laptop on fire if you keep glaring. Even without Superpowers."

146

Jav spins the screen to face me in answer. "Look at this."

I do so. "More dots."

"Not *enough* dots. Here's the last five years of villain attacks that resulted in the total demolition of a building. But—get this—a third of those totaled buildings were right here. In *Bridgebrook*."

"So what?" From the projects to the crack dens and cooking labs around Shit Creek, Bridgebrook ain't the nicest place around.

"Don't you see?" Jav's hands shake as she scrolls the mousepad, zooming out so we see the whole city in miniature. I squash down my urge to hold them tight until they stop. "It's not just that developers are buying up more lots. It's that there are *more lots to buy*. Bridgebrook is poorest of the seven main Sunnylake neighborhoods, but it ain't the biggest, not by a long shot. It doesn't make mathematical sense for a third of all property damage from villains and heroes to hit here."

"More crime?"

"Nuh-uh. Gangbangers don't fuck with the Council, and supervillains stay away from the Normie badboys in return." Jav rocks her chair onto its front legs. "So, why's the VC targeting our district? Not where I'd aim, if my goal was global domination."

The last remnants of our frappe swish around the bottom of the plastic cup. Meltwater bleeds into my cupped palms. "Got this feeling you're gonna tell me."

All four of Jav's chair legs strike the ground with a decisive *clack*. "Well, who *would* aim there? Who benefits most from putting up new houses across Bridgebrook that no one *from* Bridgebrook can actually afford?"

Blair Homes's logo—a blue wave on a white background—flashes before my eyes. "You're saying . . . No. No way."

Jav catches my wrists. Her hands are cool and damp, like she's been fished from Clearwater River. "I can't believe it, either. But—it's so *obvious*. The answer's been right in front of us this whole time. And . . . Just, *wow*. Damn, Riley. Think I found my direction."

Jav's been agonizing over her college essays since she decided she'd follow in the footsteps of Mayor Darcy: first, government at Harvard, then journalism, then politics, then (presumably) having to be rescued by the Super Squad whenever a villain decides it'd be easier to kidnap her than get her voted out. She's serious about this. She's serious about *everything*. I mean, this chick ran a politics blog when we were in *elementary*. I don't wanna crush her dreams. But, at the same time . . .

Blair Homes are a fine, upstanding sort of business (if you can call any company that when they routinely evict the poor). They're staffed and run by Normies. Am I *really* supposed to believe they're in bed with the Flamer? With the entire Villain Council? Along with every other Realtor and construction company in Sunnylake?

"Not gonna lie, this sounds like a reach."

"So did Watergate."

". . . Which one was Watergate again?"

"I'mma pretend you didn't say that, for the sake of my sanity." Jav sits back, still staring at the screen. Her eyes have started to water, it's been that long since she's blinked. "But this makes *sense*. Something's wrong in Sunnylake, Riles. Something big. I know it, you know it. We've all known it, for a long time."

Just like Amelia Lopez did.

Sweat fringes my top lip. "Okay. How does the river factor in?"

"Clearwater? I don't think it does. I know they're talking about a new marina, but—"

"No, it's nothing. Just me getting muddled. Sorry." At least this has nothing to do with Amelia and Project Zero. Still, Jav was right about there being something rotten beneath the surface of Sunnylake City. She'll chase every lead like a bloodhound, with or without my blessing.

I can't stop her. But maybe—just maybe—I can shift her focus onto something safer.

"You trust me, right?" I ask. "You, like, value my opinions? As your friend?"

"As my friend," Jav repeats. Take a shot for every time we press that point. "Yeah. When you're not making everything into a joke."

"Just mock my entire personality, why don't you."

"See?"

I shut her laptop, tracing the pug stickers stuck in ruler-straight lines down the back. "No jokes this time, Jav. This sounds like a conspiracy theory. Real QAnon stuff. You're always telling me how bullshit that is."

Jav folds her arms. "Conspiracy theories *are* bullshit. Institutions *can* benefit from below-board collusion. Two statements. Not mutually exclusive."

"Still, this all feels . . . very coincidental."

She sucks her cheeks. "I guess. I'd have to do way more research, cross-check all the facts . . ."

"Which'll take months, right? You'll miss your deadline." I

circle a particularly globular dog. "Lucky for you, I got another scoop."

"No one says 'scoop' anymore."

"Whatever. You still running your YouTube channel?"

Voices of Bridgebrook—first a podcast documentary, now with accompanying video—used to be a fun way for Jav to earn extra credit. Plus, it put her in touch with the artsy folk who endorse the big graffiti murals around the community center. They're decent people, Bridgebrookians who made it. Rich, but not disconnected. Acknowledging their roots.

Jav nods. "Hit a thousand subs before summer. Why?"

"There's this new hashtag, #HenchMarch2K23. Got a Twitter account set up and all. You probably haven't heard of it." The corners of Jav's mouth slant down. "Okay, so you *have* heard."

"Mm-hmm. Real big of the henchmen, to bitch 'bout unfair treatment while they're out there acting *villain-lite*."

I puff up. She doesn't know what she's talking about. I'd love to inform her of this, but it's hard to explain how you know the intricacies of a criminal organization while pretending you're not part of it.

Still, rattles this little voice deep inside me, *we only hide the instructions so long.*

We stall, hoping the Supers arrive before things get serious. But we don't *stop* the villains from destroying tower blocks, taking lives. Is that really enough?

"I don't think any henchman *wants* to do that job." Turner excepted.

Jav sniffs. "Yet they still do it. 'Just following orders' is never an excuse."

She has a point. Jav *always* has a point. She's better at this than me—debating and the like. Already, I can see her dipping into Politician Mode, readying a bombardment of facts to drown out my opposition. I hold up one hand. "Just . . . think about it, yeah? You could listen to their side of the story. Talk about the effects of gentrification, not hypothetical causes. Increased homelessness. People desperate to make rent however they can, even if it means joining sides with the VC."

"*Voices of Bridgebrook* always listens. Kinda the point." She checks her phone. "A'ight. Fun as this has been, I gotta head out—dishes don't wash themselves."

"They do. It's called a dishwasher."

"Ain't no room in the Beijing's tiny-ass kitchen." Jav tucks her laptop into her bag and stands (after a quick perimeter check for Mediocre Mustache). "See you, Riles."

I shouldn't be mad. Jav repeated what I used to think of henchmen, before I joined their ranks. Only one thing's changed since I slapped Cooper Hanson with raw beanburgers, and that's me. I don't know if it's for better or worse.

CHAPTER 21

I GET ANOTHER ping as soon as I leave the library. Sherman, this time.

Got something to show you. You free?

She's saved as *S* in my contacts. I'd give her a more inspired nickname (try Severe Smile Allergy, or Super-but-she-keeps-it-secret-expi-ali-docious), only Lyssa's perfected the art of snooping over my shoulder while I'm texting.

Plus, after last night . . . I've seen Sherman smile now. I'd better cross the Allergy joke off my list, or at least bump her down to Laughter Intolerant.

Right now, anything to keep me away from home is welcome. Especially if it gives me a break from worrying about Jav. I tell Sherman to meet me back at my apartment, then race her there so I can grab my helmet (hidden under my laundry pile: the one place safe from prying sisters). Sherman arrives five minutes after I do. I hear the rumble of her bike just as I'm rushing out again, past the closed bathroom door—

"Hi Lyssa, bye Lyssa!"

No reply. I find out why as we ride down the street, passing Lyssa on the way. She's coming out of Jesús's corner store, slipping her Skittles bag into her backpack. I go to wave—then remember I look like some rando in a motorcycle helmet. She doesn't look up.

Sherman pulls up outside the bar suckered onto the side of the Crow Building, above the rooms where we had initiation. I climb off the bike after she dismounts.

"Are we doing extra training or something?"

My mind helpfully supplies an image of us in the shiny silver underground range. She could, like, stand behind me, show me how to line up a shot. Position my arms and stuff. It'd be real educational—even if we're supposed to miss the heroes, it'd make me feel more confident if I knew I could send them to sleep at a squeeze of a trigger.

Sherman shakes her head. "You'll see."

There's a buzz about her today. Reminds me of those pre-eco bulbs that hum and vibrate when you turn them on. I hesitate when she leads me not toward the Crow Building but the bar beside it—only Sherman drags off her helmet to shoot me this expectant look that's probably the closest she comes to spaniel eyes, and I find myself trotting along.

The weather today is what Javira Thesaurus Neita might describe as *stultifying*. No airflow. A hummock of trash bags melts off the edge of the sidewalk, so hot the air above them wobbles like the stink lines in a cartoon. You can taste their contents from several feet away.

The bar is named Meera's, according to the unlit neon sign out front. The alley that snakes around its backside is pleasantly shady, if you can overlook the mildew crawling over the old, crumbly bricks. An extraction fan coughs humid puffs of steam. The march poster I noticed on our first day already looks mushy at the edges. By the protest, it'll have rotted away.

"Are we skipping the front entrance just to be dramatic?" I ask.

Sherman shakes her head. "Only people who use the front entrance are those we don't want in here."

"*We?*"

She slow-blinks. "Henchmen?"

Right. Because the bar sits right next to the Hench HQ, and us lackeys need our leisure time. I fiddle with my pockets (woefully devoid of ID) but no bouncer guards the gate. It should surprise precisely nobody that henchmen aren't sticklers about the legal drinking age. Sherman raps twice on a metal door beneath the extractor fan, at which point a slot shoots open and a voice rasps out:

"Password?"

"Can't remember, since you change it every day." Sherman switches to booting the door. "Lemme in, Meera."

"That's not the password."

"Lemme in before I rub Mr. Bojingles on your truck, you anaphylactic ass."

That seems to suffice. Bolts clunk and click like castanets. The door swings wide, revealing a lanky scarecrow of a woman, her bony hip cocked to bar our entrance. She's South Asian and seriously punky, with a buzz cut, a pink sari, and huge geometric earrings. No mask in sight.

When I peer past her, I see the same goes for several of the patrons. Men, women, and more sit around wooden tables that look hefty enough to tip on their sides and use as cover in a firefight. I count a few holograms, but most folk seem comfy enough to show their true faces.

And what a variety of faces there are. Every age, every skin tone, every shape. Looking from the hollow-cheeked white woman nodding off in the corner to the plump Latinx guy stimming excitedly while telling his squad about some upcoming advance in holosuit tech, it seems wild that heroes and villains treat us like we're the same cloned minion as soon as we activate our masks.

"C'mon in," says the woman—Meera? "Gang's all here."

It looks borderline derelict from the outside, but once you step through the door, her bar rocks this goofy old-fashioned diner vibe, checkerboard terrazzo and green leather seats. The building has a narrow floorplan that reminds me of a trailer home, like it could roll away one night only to pop up on the far side of the city. A *no cats* sign, hand-painted on a splintered chunk of ply, hangs over the counter.

The air tastes stale and smoky, though it hasn't been legal to light up at bars since the '90s. Boozy, too, of course. Makes my scalp prickle, my skin crawl—but my lungs have yet to start scrunching shut on themselves, so, y'know. That's nice.

"Hey, Sherman!" A holler, from the seats that barricade the front door. "Thought you got yourself fired?"

Sherman halts in front of the counter. She sinks into this parade-rest stance that they must teach all the kids on the Super Squad fast track: shoulders flat, chin up, every disc in her spine stacked. I stay a pace behind, lurking in the entranceway. Judging by the angle, Meera and I are the only ones who can see how tight her fists are clenched behind her back.

She's nervous. Why are we here again? It can't just be to hang out. Obviously, I'm awesome, and anyone would be lucky to bask in my presence, but Sherman's on a stratospheric level of cool. Not even my ego can convince me that the biker chick with Maleficent cheekbones is dragging me around for the *company*.

Sherman flexes out her fingers. Drops her hands to her sides. "It'd take more than that to scare me away." She scans the crowd. Meera's is jam-packed for such a run-down hole in the mid-afternoon. "We all know things need to change. And we all know how we can make that change happen. Only question left is, who's willing to stand up and help?"

Of course—this is about the march. Still can't quite believe I signed up for that. But when Sherman turns, studying each member of her audience, I remember why.

It's just . . . her. Something about her—the way she holds herself, that sense of *energy* humming underneath her skin. She's a glass bottle wrapped around a lightning bolt. I can't look away. Judging by the hush, neither can anyone else.

"I can't do this alone," she says, real quiet. I don't dare breathe, in case I miss a word. "None of us can. I bet you've all heard plenty of bullshit about unions: that they're a scam, they're corrupt, they're—" Here come the finger quotes. "*Anti-American*. But at the end of the day, a union is nothing to fear. It's just a way of leveling the power imbalance between us and our boss. It gives us a platform to stand on, together. You're all here because you're interested in joining, or in being a part of this protest, so, uh." A jerky shrug, a hint of a scowl. There's my Sherman. "If you got questions, now's the time, I guess. Let's hear 'em."

One of the masked henchmen at the back of the room shoots their hand up so fast it risks catching light. "We're criminals. How do we even form a union? Don't think our rights are covered in the Constitution."

That's a point. Meera saunters past me to lean on the bar, grabbing a chipped glass and subjecting it to a polish. The squeak of her cloth and jangle of her bangles provide a rhythmic backing track to Sherman's reply:

"Look at it like this. The Crow Corporation did their job of pretending to be a legit enterprise a bit too well. All of our contracts say we're some form of blue-collar worker, right? Sanitation or drivers or general miscellaneous employees. And while the guys at Teamsters don't want any association with our *actual* organization"—presumably on account of the whole "suit up after dark and commit crimes" thing—"they've been real helpful in getting our home-brewed union up and running."

I don't know what Teamsters are. Sounds worryingly like a sports club. Still, this might be the most I've heard Sherman say in one sitting, and the last thing I want her to do is to stop.

"They taught us how to do things right," Sherman continues. "So we did. We showed we had majority support, negotiated for a union contract, the works. But our boss won't listen. They know, at the end of the day, we can't demand a proper election from the city council. Not without putting ourselves under way too much scrutiny."

"So, what do we do?" calls another henchman, from the crowd.

"Well, we can't unionize Hench legally." Sherman's mouth

ticks up at one side. "But I don't think any of us have a problem going against the law. We've made an informal union, without official recognition or support."

The first henchman snorts. "Good thing we're not used to getting either."

I nod along, despite having worn a holomask for barely a week. We're the ugly secret, the zit under Sunnylake's skin. The ones who tip off the heroes, then get beaten up in thanks. No one ever looks at us. But maybe, if enough of us join the march, that'll change. Maybe everything will.

"Right," says Sherman. "We're disposable, to the VC and the Super Squad alike. But we *provide a service*. And whether our employers are CEOs or villains, if they want our labor, they need to make it worth our while to *keep* providing it."

Point. I'd like to see a villain set up their own giant laser. With or without the instructions.

"We're going to march for the money to support ourselves and our families," Sherman continues. Now the words fill her chest, projected to the back of the room. "But also to demand better treatment. Injury payment. Better organization. The incident at the observatory would never have gotten out of hand if our client had given us a detailed overview of his goals beforehand. We could've workshopped our entire operation, figured out a plan of attack . . ."

And—what? Killed Amelia sooner?

That thought jolts the pink-tinted glasses off my nose. Another henchman speaks up so I don't have to: a guy with graying cornrows. Judging by the gauze taped to his cheek, he got on the wrong side of a piece of the observatory roof. "The more efficient we get, the worse the damage."

"But that's half the problem! On every job, we stall and we mess things up and we mitigate the damage. We do the heroes' *and* the villains' jobs, for minimum wage. That can't sit right with any of you!" Sherman's voice dips; she averts her glare to the floor. Everyone leans in, holding their breath. Anticipating her next words. "I'm not pretending this is the perfect answer. But someone has to do *something*. And, like I said, I can't do it alone."

Her words reflect off the smoky windows, the array of multi-colored bottles behind the bar, and every face that's turned toward her. Echoing on and on, in all of us.

She's won me over. Even though I know she's a Super, with more in common with the villains and heroes than anyone else in this room. Would the others support her if they knew, too?

That doesn't matter. Sherman's doing something good. Something *amazing*. We all feel the electrical charge in the air, the excitement, the hope.

One henchman shuffles through the crowd, handing out leaflets, while another crosses to join Sherman. Her union buddies, I figure: the ones who helped her plan this, before she got fired. It makes my chest flutter to be counted among them. The kids at the top of the cafeteria pecking order have invited me to sit at their table.

The newcomer has a shaved head, amber skin, broad shoulders, and a yellow Etsy-looking they/them pin on their jacket. A tattoo of a purple orchid blooms on their left hand, which

I only notice because that same hand settles on Sherman's shoulder.

"So far," they tell the assembled henchmen, "every time we've passed these requests up the chain of command, we've heard radio silence. We need something far larger to catch our employer's attention. To prove we mean business."

Sherman gives their knuckles a welcoming pat. "Some of you are already part of the union," she says. "But for all the others, no matter how new . . ." Her gaze lingers on me. I have this sudden temptation to turn on my mask, if only to conceal my flush. Warm in here, with so many bodies packed together. "I'd ask you to join us, in uniform, at Sunnylake's living wage march. Henchmen need to be more visible. We need to take control of the narrative that's told about us, by media and heroes and villains alike."

I nod. Oh, yes. I am ready to control that narrative. Whatever that means.

"And if our demands aren't met?" That's the snoozy woman. Sherman's speechifying must've woken her up. I'm surprised it had the same effect on me. Politics, the sort of senate-level stuff Jav blogs about, always seems too big and far away. But this? It's close to the chest. It's personal. And, like every henchman here, I'm willing to do whatever it takes to see this through.

Sherman's mouth curls at one edge like the claw of a cat. "Simple," she says. "The henchmen go on strike."

. . . Except that.

A bubble has been swelling up within me since I stepped through Meera's back door. Puffing me out, making me larger than I am. Growing with every one of Sherman's words.

At that, it bursts.

"Wait, what?" asks the guy with the bandaged cheek. "How are we supposed to get by if we're not working? I need this money for more than Meera's shitty overpriced beer. No offense, Meera."

"Offense taken," says Meera. By now, she's powered through twenty glasses, constructing a ziggurat of squeaky-clean tumblers. They split the light into rainbows, painting the wooden counter. "But you don't have to worry. Given everything I've heard from you guys, the villains can't wipe their own asses. It'll be a week max before they beg you guys to come back."

The lumberjack takes a gulp of his drink (evidently, not shitty or overpriced enough to be off-putting). "Or they fire us all."

"Do that and they have no one. Anyway, look at me." Sherman spreads her arms. "I got fired. I walked right back in the next day."

"Some of our union organizers have contacted local food-banks," adds her buddy with the they/them pin. "They're aware of an upcoming influx in demand. We have a small fund for members—but at the end of the day, if we succeed? It'll be worth a couple days without pay."

"Max's right." Sherman tips them a nod. "Anyone know when the first strike was?"

Didn't realize there would be a pop quiz. Still, I've never been good at leaving silences to fester, so when no one offers an answer, I'm obliged to peel open my dry mouth: "The seventies?"

Sherman stares at me.

". . . I saw *Pride*, okay? If they haven't made a hit box-office film of it, I don't care."

"It was in *ancient Egypt*," says Max, leaning their shoulder against Sherman's. Obviously, the two of them have rehearsed their talking points. I find myself wondering, looking at the two of them, just how well they know each other. Is Max one of Sherman's old teammates? Something more? Not that it's any of my business. "The pyramid builders refused to work until they were fed."

That's a bit further back than expected. "Huh."

"Story old as time," says Sherman. "The little guys stand up for themselves, and the big guys cave. Otherwise, guillotines get built."

It sounds like she means it. That's the worst thing. I reblog every Eat the Rich post that crosses my Tumblr dash, but I don't keep cutlery on hand. Anyway, back then, the big guys didn't have Superpowers.

Sherman must notice the sweat sheen on my forehead. She nibbles her lip, then shrugs Max off, turning back to her crowd. "Don't you want to go to work knowing your mission objective won't change halfway through the night? Don't you want to be sure your families will get some sort of compensation if Brightspark turns you into a vegetable?"

Only that's the *problem*. Can't she see? She's pitting us against Supers far more formidable than Brightspark. It's one thing to head to city hall and chant slogans for our nonexistent rights in the hope someone in power takes notice. It's another to actively piss off the Villain Council. To walk out on work and expect them to retaliate with smiles and handshakes, not fireballs. Fireballs like the one that killed Amelia.

The burst bubble leaves a sucking singularity in my chest. It drains me of all thoughts but this distant sense of doom, like the strings holding up the sky might snap.

"Join the march," says Sherman, glaring out across the barroom floor. "Join the strike. Don't cross the picket lines. We'll get what we're owed, on the other side."

Her voice still has that resonance to it; I feel it to the core of my bones. First thought: Sherman is seriously badass. Second, third, and fourth-through-fortieth thoughts: Sherman has considerably more bicep than brain. And if she follows this strike plan through to its finish, she'll get herself killed—along with every other sucker in this bar.

CHAPTER 22

I CAN'T TELL Sherman outright that she's batshit. For purely pragmatic reasons that have everything to do with how she's my lift to work, not just because that lift has become the high point of my evenings.

It's a pretty awesome sensation. That's all.

I've learned to relax into her lead when we're together, swaying the motorcycle around corners like it's an extension of the two of us. Something, something, shared centers of gravity . . . There must be a complex physics equation that explains why it feels like I'm flying as we glide around Sunnylake on two wheels, dipping down toward the road, then back up to the sky, and I press so close to Sherman's back I can practically feel her breathe.

To me, it's magic. Magic I don't want to lose. But I don't wanna be made into sashimi by a supervillain, either.

"Heading to Meera's later," says Sherman the next night. We're installing appliances in a new villainous penthouse hideout. The utility room is bigger than my apartment. The smart fridge could fit our whole squad and keeps trying to strike up a debate on the optimal temperature for storing organic produce. "Running over logistics with my old squad. Wage pots, funds. Making sure strikers are covered for as long as possible. That sort of stuff. You, uh." She scuffs the toe of her boot along the floor. "You coming?"

I check the fridge's thermometer. My joints ache from heaving it out of the elevator, but after the observatory, I'm glad to work with anything that isn't a weapon of mass destruction. What's the AI gonna do if it turns evil? Give the villains salmonella? Tragic.

"Sorry," I say as the fridge recites tips to maintain the crunch in your asparagus. "I'm whacked. Need an early night or whatever."

Sherman looks disappointed, but she doesn't push. "Whatever," she agrees.

It feels oddly awful to watch her walk away from me (heading for the Captain, currently threatening the microwave into functionality). Like I'm in the wrong here. I glare at my shadow, cast by the dangling green glass light fixture. What do I have to feel guilty about? If Sherman told me her goal was to pick a fight with the VC, I'd have steered clear of her from the get-go.

I might still attend the march. That feels important. We deserve to be visible; we deserve to be seen. But strong-arming the VC hasn't worked for the Supers, and they've been at it for decades. Am I supposed to believe henchmen have a chance in hell?

Worst part is, I'm tempted. I can't deny that the trash-bag-swinging part of my psyche longs to stand in that picket line, at Sherman's side. I just also can't deny the *other* part, the sensible part, which has kept my ancestors alive long enough to procreate since they first climbed down from the trees.

"Did you know that you should always store bananas at room temperature?" asks the fridge. I have the weirdest sense it's judging me, so I poke around until I find the mute button and stalk over to prevent Birnbaum from carrying in the new oven solo.

Sherman can't be too mad. She waits for me at the end of our shift, and we fly together again. Her bike weaves through Bridgebrook, nimble as a kingfisher. In those moments, it's easy to let all my worries drain away and pretend the streets belong only to us and the dawn.

———

HENCH TAKES US five nights the next week. Which means five nights spent dodging Sherman's invitations to join her at Meera's, and five nights of avoiding Hernando.

There are other things to fill my time, that's all. Changing the bandage on my arm, which peels off to reveal pasty skin studded with shrinking red polka dots. Lyssa, gushing about the upcoming emergence of her nonexistent Superpowers. Tapping out message after message to Jav but wimping out before I hit send. Trying not to look like I shit bricks every time Sherman mentions her march prep: designing posters, passing word around different Hench teams. And welcoming Turner back to our crew, under Aaron's advisement to take it easy.

He seems different. Quieter. Less quick to smile, crack jokes, talk back. He's stripped the Supremia case from his phone. I should be glad about that, though I can't quite bring myself to feel it.

We lug armfuls of sweaty villainous workout gear to the laundromat. We give Supremia's signature blue convertible the full wax-and-polish treatment (Turner doesn't swoon). Good timing, as it turns out. Mayor Darcy gets bundled into the trunk a few hours later, according to Sunnylake News. At least it was vacuumed and Febrezed.

We feed several cats, tidy two basement lairs, and even loom in the background while an A-class villain—a Shaper by the name of Mercury, who must airbrush his entire body silver before each gig—interrogates a hero with some inventively applied molten metal. Luckily, the Captain sneaks out and cuts the power before any red-hot steel can drip on the hero's face. Darkness falls. We all do our best impression of headless chickens, pretending we don't know how to turn the lights back on.

Even Turner joins in. Guess he's learned his lesson. It's our side or the villains', and theirs only gets people hurt.

Mercury loses patience and stomps off to locate the light switch himself. The Super Squad bust through the roof with sidekicks in tow, giving us lowly henchmen an excuse to scramble for the exit. Out we tumble, into the night, an amorphous black blob that branches out in every direction like mold growing on fast-forward.

Mercury hid his lair under a run-down bowling alley. Asbestos walls, blacked-out windows. If it wasn't condemned before this fight, it will be after—which brings all of Jav's gentrification theories to the forefront of my mind.

I help Birnbaum across the lot and into the Captain's nearby car, so he isn't crushed by the stampede, then join the stampede myself, hightailing onto the street. I make it the entire length of the block, all the way to where Sherman's parked, before I have to fold and wheeze.

"I vote next time, we split early," I pant, bent double, hands braced on my knees. "Saving heroes is *so* not worth cardio."

Sherman snorts. She led the charge, galloping along, graceful as a gazelle. Not even out of breath. She turns off her hologram. Then, after a moment's hesitation, reaches over.

I freeze.

So does Sherman.

Until I tilt my head to one side. Letting her grasp the dial over my pulse point and twist.

The faint green shimmer dissolves from my vision. It sinks into my skin instead: this strange flickering sensation that spirals in and centers around that dial, over which Sherman's fingertips still hover without quite touching.

"Jones?" Her voice is low and velvety. My breath sticks to the inside of my lungs.

"Mm?"

"You hurt? Your heart's going real fast."

I twitch away, cover my neck with my hand. It's hot to the touch. Did I forget to slap on sunscreen this morning? "Just adrenaline. Thank our close encounter with Super-kind. And—I—wait, you can tell?"

Sherman shrugs. She shoves her hands deep into the pockets of her cargo pants, a faint pink tinge on her cheeks. Some quirk of her powers, I guess. So long as she can only *sense* the electrical impulses in my heart, not *stop* them, we're cool.

"Awesome. Free Fitbit." I point at the bike, double finger guns. "Shouldn't we vamoose?"

"Don't have to. Not yet."

Sure enough, it sounds like the Supers are keeping each other busy. Every bass boom from the bowling alley is followed by a minor earthquake. Three sidekicks guard the entrance, presumably to prevent Mercury making a dramatic escape, but they don't pursue the henchmen, and by now, Sherman and I are far enough away to pass as nosy civilians. Streetside Super battles are free entertainment in Sunnylake.

I don't actually want to hang around and watch the demolition. Might start wondering about the bowling alley's real estate value. But as Sherman and I have a moment to ourselves, I need a topic of conversation that doesn't relate to marches and strikes.

"Okay. Sherman. Sherm. While we're here, can I ask you something?"

"I doubt I can stop you."

"Oh, the mortifying ordeal of being known." I wave to the bike. "How'd you afford this on a henchman's salary?"

Sherman runs her hand over the Harley's side like she's soothing an animal. "She's my pop's," she says, more to the bike than to me.

I study the bike: the shiny chrome tubing, the details in bird-of-paradise blue. "He knows you're borrowing it, right?"

Another of her long silences. Nowadays, it seems less like she's judging me for asking, more like she's running a million and one potential answers through her head. "Yeah."

"Um, okay. You waited *way* too long. I call bull."

Sherman groans. "Yeah, he knows I use it. Just not for Hench stuff."

"For sneaking out at night, then? Like that's not suspicious." I jostle her shoulder, grinning. "Bet he thinks you've got a secret boyfriend or something."

"Or something," Sherman echoes. She glances at me from the corner of her eye.

My breath catches, like I've swallowed one of the gnats swirling around us, drawn to her glowing headlamp. Then she looks away, and I can inhale again.

Weird, that.

"He, uh. Did her up himself." Sherman runs her fingertips over the sleek leather saddle. She sounds slightly strangulated. "He likes me to take her out. Doesn't want her engine to get gummed." She picks at the stitches, catches herself, and curls her hand into a knotted little fist. "He—he doesn't leave the house much anymore. Only rode her a month before everything went to shit."

She doesn't elaborate. It must have something to do with why a D-class Super is here, rather than in sidekick uniform. I have this instinctual urge to ram my nose into other people's business—Hernando calls it my "chismosa" gene. At Sherman's words, it flares up from wherever it's lodged in my DNA. But I'm not *actually* enough of an asshole to ask.

I stand back from the bike, hands on my hips, and give it—*her?*—a once-over. "Well, look at that. The least-gummiest engine I ever did see."

"You have no clue what you're talking about."

"None whatsoever."

Sherman rewards me with her usual scoff-laugh. I'm afraid I'm starting to like it. I'm more afraid she's about to ask if I want to come to another meeting, but a *boom* from the bowling alley cuts her off.

The roof tiles flake like crust from a croissant. The streetlights flicker. Smoke plumes, pressing a thumb-shaped bruise into the sky. Whaddaya know—the one and only time I've been grateful to the Super Squad.

"Seriously," I say, before Sherman can gather her words, "can we vamoose now? We probably got half a minute before shrapnel starts flying, and I should get back to my place."

Sherman swallows whatever she was going to say. "Uh. Okay. Your place, sure."

She shoves her helmet on, not quite fast enough to disguise her frown. I subject my lip to a thorough chewing. Should I talk to her about this? Tell her that if she gets Hench to go on strike, the only jobs she'll protect are those of the Sunnylake coroners?

No. Her resolve was written all over her, back at Meera's. I could say whatever I want, but it won't matter if she doesn't want to hear. Best I say nothing at all. I could use the practice.

I slip onto the bike, grab my safety handle—"the sissy bar," according to Google, which is as rude as it's accurate—and try to lose myself in the ride. Active word: *try*. It doesn't work, and not just because of all my strike-shaped concerns.

Sherman's dad talk turns my thoughts to Hernando. I'm pissed he lied to me. I'm more pissed he spent the past eight-ish years telling me he expected more from me than my mother, declaring to the whole world that he was going to set a good example for his girls. How does Hench factor in?

But if I peel back my anger, I find only misery.

Sherman drops me in front of my house and roars off without a word. I try to decipher the tangle in my chest as I slouch up the stairs.

I miss Hernando. I miss staying up to see him home, I miss his calloused fingers catching in my fine blonde hair. I miss his low rasp of *mija*. I don't think I'm ready to talk to him yet—but then again, I'm not sure I'll ever be.

The universe takes it out of my hands. I open the door and find the man himself waiting.

"Aw, *hell*."

Hernando sits on the far side of our grotty sectional, arms crossed. "Morning to you, too, Riley Jones."

I deactivated my uniform before I hopped off the bike. Hernando knows, though. I feel it in my core, like the bad stomach cramps you get on your period that squeeze you from gullet to asshole. He knows about me, like I know about him. At least we got that in common.

I sit on the couch cushion nearest the door. I don't intend to make a break for it if this goes south, but it's nice to pretend that's an option. "You first?"

Hernando's glare contorts into confusion. "Huh?"

"I know, okay? No point pretending otherwise."

"This is about you, Riley. Not me."

He's gonna play this game? I'm not having it. "I was there that night. When you helped us unload the laser."

Hernando frowns. Does he not remember? Did I pass so close to him, under my mask, and leave no impression behind?

"You work for Hench," I say, pushing my hair aside so he can see the silver disc on my neck. "So do I."

Hernando's tired eyes widen. A moment later, the shock strikes the rest of his body and he jackknifes like I shot him with my stun gun. "Dios mío! Hench?"

"Am I wrong?"

"I thought you were seeing a boy!"

It's my turn to look dumbfounded. ". . . What?"

"Vanishing at night . . . Quitting Artie's . . . The motorcycle . . ." Hernando's hands paint angry pictures in the air while he talks, a habit he passed to me and Lyssa. "Lyss was awake when I got home. I asked where you were, and she kept *winking* at me . . ."

Wow. Guess I was right, telling Sherman her late-night adventures look suspicious.

"It'd be a girlfriend," I say faintly. "If I had one."

Hernando's eyes bug out of his head. He sags against the cushions like a deflating balloon. "Dios mío. We *really* gotta talk."

Five more *Dios míos* escape him before I'm done with my side of the tale. Cooper Hanson. Leaving Artie's. Joining Hench. Meeting the Captain, Turner, Birnbaum, Sherman . . . I tell him all of it—with the exception of Project Zero, Amelia Lopez, and the TMI stuff between me and Jav.

Even so, he must remember my line about a girlfriend, 'cause he holds up his hand once I'm done. "You . . . like girls, Riley?"

Hernando hasn't been to church, in my recent memory—fell out of the routine after picking up Sunday shifts at the hospital. He keeps the faith, though, and that scares me, just a little.

I picture Jav, sipping our frappe. Every gorgeous actress I've ever daydreamed about. Even Sherman, a million sneers and eye rolls compressed into human shape. When I think of them, that fear feels far away.

"Yeah," I say. "I do."

"You never told me. Why'd you never tell me?"

Considering we've both revealed that we work for the same villain-affiliated organization, it stings that my sexuality is the sticking point. "'Cause people assume different. People *always* assume different. Straight until proven otherwise, right?"

"Riley," Hernando says, like he's pleading. I don't know what for (me to take it back? To pretend I'm joking?) but I sure as hell ain't giving it to him.

"I get it, you know." I stand and turn away. I don't want to watch any more expressions flow over his face. "It's not something folks can see, unless I show it off. But then I'd be flaunting it. But if I keep it to myself, I'm hiding it from you. But if I tell you, I'm rubbing it in people's faces. But if I don't, I'm keeping secrets." I shrug, arms tightening over my belly like I'm holding myself together. "It's just easier, at the end of the day. To let people assume."

Those assumptions still piled on me over the years, crushing me down. They stick my teeth together whenever strangers casually ask if I have a boyfriend, or Lyssa teases me about the mysterious man who whisks me away in the night like a pudgy Cinderella.

How do I explain all that? How do I make it so Hernando will understand?

As it turns out, I don't have to.

Hernando's quiet for a long time. He taps the tips of his forefingers together, and I see his gaze skirt to the pinewood cross, which hangs above the clock on the wall. Then he stands, wincing at the pops in his knees. He crosses to the microwave and produces a steaming bowl of sopa de fideo.

"Here," he says, gruff. "Eat up, mija. You had a long night."

I didn't notice how famished I was, but hunger tears into me at his words. Only the tenets of basic courtesy prevent me from diving in face-first. The soup is a noodly olive branch, and I'm so grateful I could cry.

Hernando doesn't say he accepts me. He doesn't say he loves me. But with that one simple gesture, he doesn't really need to.

As I chew, Hernando tells me about his warehouse job. About how a gringo foreman kept making cracks about *bad hombres* sneaking over the border. How he threatened to call ICE on a woman who dropped a package because she was on medication and so exhausted she could barely stand. Still coming to work, of course, because she needed the money. She ground herself to the bone just to survive and got called lazy for her efforts.

One day, Hernando had enough.

"Please," I say, midway through my mouthful, "tell me you slapped him around the face with a bag of beanburgers."

"I didn't, and you and me are gonna talk *real soon* about the dangers of picking fights with Supers." Still, a smile nestles in the crow's-feet at the corners of his eyes, though he's too tired to re-create it on his lips. He tells me how he quit on that foreman and marched to the warehouse next door. The warehouse that was always hiring.

I nod, I munch, I swallow. Every time I take a bite, I swear I taste the love.

CHAPTER 23

THE MARCH IN City Square is scheduled for August 9. Four days beforehand, Lyssa hits the big one-three. She'll be devastated when she doesn't develop powers—but that's better than the alternative. So I keep telling myself.

Anyway, I got bigger problems on my plate. Despite my best efforts to put distance between Sherman's strike and my exceedingly squishable self, I can't avoid it entirely. March posters climb the wall of the Crow Building like urban ivy. Tags crop up on random lampposts across Bridgebrook: the black stencil of a henchman's mask, an acid-green X over where a mouth should be. #HenchMarch2K23 amasses a small army of followers on Twitter, Tumblr, and beyond.

This is a movement, and it's gaining momentum. Coasting down mountain roads at high speed. Like a car with a drunken driver, spinning toward the guardrail, out of control . . .

Don't get me wrong—I want to be happy. I want to believe we have a chance, that we can make a difference. But the low, quiet scream of Amelia Lopez scratches at my bones and the roots of my teeth: an ugly reminder of what happens to those who try.

I work. I sleep. I lie. I work again.

The night before Lyssa's birthday, Sherman and I pull up on the far side of Bridgebrook, having followed the Captain's car. Of all the places I expected to get a job, a shawarma shop wasn't one of them. We arrive in time to watch a pudgy Middle Eastern man pass a steaming bag to a Black guy with three rings on each finger and a pit bull straining on a leash.

"What's going on?" Turner hisses. I catch the tail end of his question as Sherman kills the engine. "Drug trade? Dog-fighting ring?"

The customer emerges, already digging in. He catches sight of us, all in Hench uniform. Then his eyes widen and he about-turns, dragging his dog in the opposite direction, muttering "Nope, nope, nope" under his breath.

"Way more nefarious," says the Captain, deadpan. "Zeke's selling shawarma."

"If he's such an upstanding citizen," asks Birnbaum, "why are *we* here?"

"Because while Zeke runs the least popular shawarma place in Bridgebrook, the only thing he's guilty of is a few minor health food violations."

Down the block, the man spits a mouthful of meat on the sidewalk. His pit bull snuffles at it but turns up its nose.

"And *that*," finishes the Captain, "makes him good cover."

Turner dithers behind as the Captain helps Birnbaum unfold from the passenger seat, eyeing the hurricane of flies around Zeke's meat spit. "How's this guy still in business?"

"He makes a more lucrative trade from keeping his mouth shut. This way." The Captain nods at Zeke (who pointedly looks in the other direction) through the glass. He leads us around the back and down a flight of steps, unlocking the cellar door: an iron wedge on runners, glued to its frame with rust. It takes several applications of the Captain's shoulder to break the seal.

The resultant screech sounds like someone backed over the tail of a cat.

Inside: gloom. The Captain fondles the wall for a switch. Surgical-white lights snap on, revealing long rectangular tables lined with conical flasks, their contents crystallized to their sides. Plastic tubes form a giant spiderweb, crissing and crossing, offshoots feeding into test tubes stoppered with ancient, disintegrating corks. Eight small cages line the far wall, stacked two high. Some are occupied, but only by bones.

I gulp. Those better not be descendants of Mr. Bojingles.

I've never seen so much dust. It smothers every surface, from the *hazardous substance* labels on the barrels in the corner to the floor beneath our feet. The Captain's footsteps cause miniature tornados. He leaves perfect prints, like he's walking on the surface of the moon.

Birnbaum pulls an inhaler from his pocket and takes a preemptive huff. I wish I'd brought mine, though I haven't had an attack since I was little. Turner looks entranced by all the villainous paraphernalia—until he realizes we're here to clean it, at which point he starts complaining about not being a maid.

"Suck it up" is the Captain's advice. He opens the storage closet in a billowing cloud and dislodges a stack of old dust masks. He hands Turner one, along with a brush-and-pan combo. I receive a vacuum cleaner with my dust mask, as does Birnbaum. I guess that means we're in the Captain's good books. I ain't gonna complain.

I push the vacuum back and forth, back and forth, the roar loud enough to drown the rumbles of passing cars. By the time the lab gleams, I've had to trudge upstairs to empty the vacuum seven times, shaking it into the alley out back. Zeke stuffs his nose in a baseball magazine every time I pass.

"What's our client got planned for all this?" I ask, mid-yawn, returning from my latest trip. I poke at a rack of petri dishes, the goop within wobbling in a disconcertingly fleshlike fashion.

"Don't ask questions you don't want the answer to" is the Captain's sage advice.

"My vote's on bomb, is all." Especially since there's a big sack of kitty litter in the corner. "I got five dollars on them trying to blow up city hall."

It barely counts as gallows humor. Live in any major urban area long enough in the post-Super-gene age, and this sort of thing becomes routine.

"Ten on La Caja Tunnel," offers Birnbaum, after another gulp from his inhaler. He's tackling the entranceway, where the dust is thinnest. "That would cause far more disruption."

La Caja—the cage—is one of three main routes out of the city by land. It digs directly through the Andoridge mountains, which curl around us to the east, the foothills cutting us off from the next settlement along Sunnylake's shore. You can clear the range in under ten minutes, whereas winding over the passes takes hours, especially if you trust an online map. Plenty of other tunnels puncture the mountains nowadays, but La Caja is the oldest and largest: a multilane mole hole that burrows under several million tons of rock.

Birnbaum has a point. I go cold thinking about how much devastation a villain could cause if they targeted infrastructure rather than kidnapping Mayor Darcy every week and blowing up the shabbiest parts of Bridgebrook. But thinking too hard about the VC reminds me of Jav's gentrification conspiracy, and Amelia, and everything. Easiest to focus on cleaning.

"We're done, right?" says Sherman sometime later, cracking out her spine. "If I keep polishing these tables, I'll rub through them."

The Captain checks the time on his phone. "We got thirty minutes left on our shift . . ."

We all groan.

The Captain groans right back. "All right, all right. Client won't inspect until tomorrow night. We can split."

We pack up our gear and hurry upstairs, looking forward to getting (for once) over five hours of sleep. No surprises when Zeke doesn't wave. I'm tempted to grab shawarma—we've been working all night under a cloud of warm, meaty smells, and I've produced enough saliva to dehydrate myself—but I don't want to spend my sister's birthday locked in the bathroom.

The Captain, Turner, and Birnbaum all pile into the Captain's car, after he lays trash bags on the seats to prevent the worst of the dust transfer. Off the Ford Fiesta grumbles, chugging around the first corner. Sherman taps her nails on the bike's nearest handlebar but hesitates before climbing aboard.

"Got another meeting," she says, real casual. "Drumming up a last bit of support for the march."

I discover a sudden fascination with the cracks in the sidewalk, the scrawny green weeds peeking through. "Yay. Awesome."

"Yeah." She's turned off her mask. A smudge of dust crowns the tip of her nose, the only flaw on her face. Kinda annoying. Gives me this ludicrous urge to thumb it away. "Just . . . wondering if you wanted to come this time, is all."

I wave at the Andoridge hills, backlit by a glimmer of dawn. "Sorry. Need to get home by five or I turn into a pumpkin. Then I'll be of no use to you at all."

"Really."

"Yeah, really. Feel free to hang around and watch the sunrise with me, if you want a freebie to carve for Halloween."

Sherman starts pick-pick-picking at the stitching on the bike seat. "Funny," she says, though no snort-laugh accompanies it.

"Okay, I get the feeling you're going to be disappointed when I *don't* transform." I point both fingers to the far end of the street. "Maybe I should just walk."

I don't get very far. Sherman grabs my wrist. She digs in her heels, and—

Wow. I just *stop*. Like I've run into an invisible wall.

I keep tugging, but it's a choice between my dignity and my shoulder socket, and I never had much of that first one. "Um. Sherman?"

Her jagged nails cut into my pulse point. The blue glow of Zeke's bug zapper picks out every piercing, her eyes lost to rings of shadow.

Then she whirls us around and slams me back against the shawarma-shop window.

Holy fuck. She damn near picked me up. *Me*, half a foot taller than her and twice as wide. I should snarl, get in her face. Show her I'm every bit as Bridgebrook as she is, and like hell will I be thrown around—but right now my thought processes are mostly composed of the word *guh*.

"Guh," I say.

The glass judders in its frame. Beyond it, Zeke turns another page of his magazine.

"You told me you were in," says Sherman. She's close. I mean, *close* close. *Our boobs are a breath from brushing* close. Her grip on my T-shirt collar tightens, reducing the diameter of my windpipe by another quarter inch. Her eyes are shards of brown glass. "Did you mean it? Are you really on our side?"

I squirm against the window. Overhead, the zapper crackles. Unlucky mosquito? Or Sherman, flexing her Superpowers? "Who else's side would I be on? Just—it's my sister's birthday tomorrow, y'know? I wanna be awake for it. That's all."

Sherman's eyes narrow. The zapper spits blue.

"Okay, okay! Look." I blink the bright stain from my eyes. Focusing on her, only her. "This strike . . . Sherm, you can't fight the Villain Council alone."

"We wouldn't be alone. That's the whole *point* of working together."

"And if we piss the Council off enough, we'll die together, too!"

Sherman scoffs. "You're afraid."

I grip her fists, where they're buried in the collar of my T-shirt. "You aren't?"

Keep your head down. Don't make enemies. Strictly no heroics. Any henchman who goes on strike will poke their head way aboveground, like golf balls awaiting tee-off. The VC will definitely be pissed enough to class as an enemy. I did fuck-all heroics today, but breaking two of three rules doesn't set the best track record.

Sherman scans my face. Whatever she finds must satisfy her, because she quits trying to garrote me with my own clothing.

"Yeah," she mutters, rubbing the back of her neck. "Honestly . . . Yeah. We're all scared. And—and I'm sorry."

I slump, resting my head on the glass. "This another of those moments where you apologize 'cause you're in the wrong?"

Sherman adjusts the straps of her tank top, glaring a hole in the wall a few inches to my left. "I got rules about this sort of thing. No violence, unless it's the last resort. I don't punch first." I make a disbelieving noise. "What?"

"Tell that to the Shaper chick you shot. Whatsername—Crystalis."

Sherman stiffens. "Crystalis *deserved* it."

Why? I want to ask. But that strange vulnerability shimmers in her long-lashed eyes. I can't poke this crack in her tough act. Not when I'm scared it might break her.

It's strange, standing this close. I notice all those little details: the ones that escape me usually, because I'm busy grumbling to myself about her supermodel bone structure. The tiny mole under her left eye. The chip in one of her canines. Her lips are lined with a thousand fine, dry creases. This urge to lick them smooth zaps through me, dizzying, electric. I have to clench every muscle in my body to hold myself back.

Only . . . wait, what?

I want to *kiss* her?

Kiss *Sherman?*

Sherman and Riley, sitting in a tree? *K-I-S-S-I-N-G?*

No way. It's one thing *appreciating* all that glorious bicepiness and cheekbonage. But why would I want to send my tongue on a spelunking expedition in search of her tonsils? Her: the girl at the heart of the henchmen's revolt, who wants me to keep her Superpowered secret, who just shoved me up against a window, an action that evidently rattled any remaining sense right out of my brain? Why would I want to hook my fingers in her belt loops, tug her in until her nose bumps mine? Until I go cross-eyed as I study her, memorizing every angle of her smooth brown face? Until she murmurs my name (*Jones*), a hot husk of air, and I chase it back into her mouth . . .

"Jones?"

I jump. "Huh? Wha—what?"

Sherman tugs her bottom lip with her teeth. It looks *so* very soft. "Did—did I hurt you?"

"No! No."

Not in any physical way. On the inside, though, I'm reeling. It took *so long* for me to see Jav like this. My feelings crystallized over years, slow as a stalactite, tiny granules sticking together to form something far greater. Sherman, though—she sawed through another rock formation as I walked beneath and dropped the whole thing on my head.

I'm totally blushing. Fuck.

"I'm fine. Honest. And I'm sorry if I made you doubt me, okay? This whole strike thing is just . . . a lot."

"No. You don't have to apologize." Sherman averts her gaze to our matching black holographic combat boots. "This is on me. I . . ." A lengthy pause, her jaw working silent as she searches for words. They all arrive in a rush: "Look, Jones. Not so long ago, an ex-girlfriend let me down big-time, in a big way."

Whoa, record scratch. "You . . . Ahem. Had a girlfriend? We talking gal pals, or . . . ?"

Sherman shrugs like it's no big deal. Maybe to her, it isn't. "I'm bisexual."

Oh my God.

"Me . . . me lesbian?" Did I say that in baby talk or Tarzan talk? Shit.

"Good for you. Point is, trust doesn't come easy when you've been burned before. I need folks I can rely on. Friends who've got my back."

Her grave eyes study me at point-blank range. I'm naked under that gaze. Not a bad, dreaming-I'm-in-the-middle-of-homeroom naked. The other sort.

"Are you with me?" Sherman asks, while the heat inside me dips lower, softer, caressing me from the inside. "Do you have my back?"

I remember how to talk—sort of. "I, uh, yeah. Yeah, I do."

It might be a lie. Tomorrow, I might regret it. But, I think, as Sherman nods and steps to the side, reinstating the space between us, tomorrow is a long way away.

CHAPTER 24

USUALLY, WHEN I'M tucked behind Sherman on her bike, time becomes liquid. It flows around us as we curve through Sunnylake's capillaries, the skinny back roads that feed the city's pulsing heart. Tonight, though? I'm hyperaware of how close she is, the narrow tuck of her waist, the strength in her shoulders. The ride lasts too long and not nearly long enough.

After bidding her the most awkward goodbye of my life ("Okay. So. Yeah. See you. Sometime. Around. Somewhere. Maybe. Yeah."), exhaustion overtakes my gay-crisis adrenaline rush. I don't even look at the new Blair Homes letter on the doormat. My eyes are shut before I hit the pillow.

Lyssa, gremlin that she is, wakes me up two hours later by flailing out of her bed in a burrito of blankets and whooping at the top of her lungs. I groan, roll facedown, and attempt autoasphyxiation.

"Nope. Too early for birthdays."

"You're just jealous I'm gonna get Superpowers, like you never did!"

I smack my lips and waft a fart in her direction. "Mm-hmm. You're welcome to 'em."

I'm *not* jealous. Every kid wants to be a Super, but if there's a chance of turning out like Cooper Hanson . . . hard pass on that.

Course, if Lyssa *does* develop powers, she might wind up more like Sherman. But, considering the pain in Sherman's beautiful brown eyes whenever her past comes up, I'm not sure that's a good thing, either.

A voice chimes in from the main living space: "I better not hear fighting!"

Hernando? Here in the morning? That's enough of a novelty to drag me from my bed. I hurry into the main room, while Lyssa dons her liner and prosthetic at light speed and follows close behind. We find him smearing salsa verde onto a leftover tortilla. One sniff and my saliva ducts start working on overdrive.

"Chilaquiles?"

"Had to cook breakfast for my princess," says Hernando. Lyssa sticks her head over the pan to inhale, then rests her weight against him so he can kiss her hair. I smile, watching them together. That's what a dad is. The guy you can lean on. Who leaves you in charge of his prize motorcycle, so a part of him will always be with you.

When I told Hernando about Hench, the conversation went better than I expected. We didn't yell and no plates got flung at my head, which puts it miles above the fights I got into with Mom as a kid. But Hernando didn't pull me into a hug after, like he would've done for Lyssa. I know it's wrong to expect that ('cause I'm older, and I'm not his, and so forth), but damn, if I don't want arms around me now.

I don't know how to ask for that. Guess I'll absorb his love through my taste buds, like always.

Hernando makes chilaquiles the Jalisco way (the best way)

like his mama: steeping the tortillas till they're soft as sponges. He serves Lyssa first, then me. "Enjoy, mija."

I intend to. "Not at the Mart today?"

"Don't need to be." He lowers his voice, though Lyssa's too busy stuffing her face to tune into the Adult Conversation Channel. "I got a promotion at the warehouse. Comes with a pay rise, so I cut my shift at the Mart to part-time."

I pinch my lips together. It's great that we get to see Hernando in the daytime, when we're actually awake. But what with everything that's happening at Hench . . .

Hernando must understand why I'm not whooping for joy. He opens his mouth, as if to explain himself—but having wolfed her portion, Lyssa bounces up and holds out her empty plate for more.

Hernando obediently halves his own breakfast. He spoils her so much, I swear. I tuck my own plate closer to my chest as I take my first mouthful, tomatillos bursting fresh and sour on my tongue. Birthday girl or not, no way is she getting mine.

Once breakfast's over and we've each hogged the bathroom, the three of us head to Sunnylake's prosthesis clinic. A local charity funded Lyssa's current leg, after she'd spent eleven months in a temporary, letting her residual limb find its new shape. The leg was supposed to last at least another year, but having hit her growth spurt, she's on track to catch up with me and Hernando. She had back-to-back fittings and castings in the run-up to summer vacation, and by sheer luck, her new leg should be ready today, on her birthday. It won't solve all her problems—certainly can't do shit for that attitude—but it'll make it less painful for her to climb the stairs when the elevator's out, like it is today.

I head down first. The letter from Blair Homes is right where I left it. Their squiggly blue logo sparks a chain reaction in my head: Jav, the library, her gentrification theory, the Flamer, Amelia Lopez. Project Zero. I haven't thought about that in so long. Too long. Got distracted by Sherman, the strike, everything.

Or maybe I *wanted* to be distracted. Maybe I'm still afraid to admit that, if Jav's theories hold any weight, our house might end up like the Szechuan Sizzler or the bowling alley or any one of the other mounds of rubble we pass on our way to the clinic.

I can't let that happen. I just have no clue how I'm supposed to stop it.

We take a bus into town, which is horrible, but at least I know Hernando's not judging when I spend the trip with my head between my knees. Carsick, if anyone asks.

At the clinic, a clinician aligns the new prosthesis and runs Lyssa through a series of stretches and exercises Hernando and I will have to bully her into doing every other morning. Feigned interest is an ability I honed during math class, so don't let anyone tell you algebra won't give you applicable life skills. Eventually, though, after the third time Lyssa tries and fails to conjure a miniature whirlwind in the palm of her hand, I can't stomach being in the same room a moment longer.

Hernando shoots me a disapproving glare as I stand. Yeah, yeah; I'm ditching my sister on her thirteenth birthday. Right now, though, I wanna be anywhere but here: waiting for Lyssa's heart to get broken, which would be awful, or for her to gain Superpowers, which would be so much worse.

CHAPTER 25

WHAT WOULD LYSSA'S life look like if she joined the Super Squad? Plenty of attention, that's for sure. She'd love it. And hey, maybe having a Super on my side would be helpful, if I dig any deeper into this Project Zero thing?

No. Powers or otherwise, I won't put all that weight onto my kid sister. And I happen to know a Super already.

I message Sherman to meet me at the Crow Building—not too far from the clinic, it turns out. She's waiting by the time I arrive, straddling her bike with her visor flipped to show off that silver-studded, movie-star face.

"Hey," she says.

"Hey. Uh." *Don't think about being pinned to walls; don't think about being pinned to walls.* "How'd the meeting go?"

"Good. Got another big one lined up tomorrow, if you're game." Sherman stretches, real blasé, rolling her muscular shoulders. My gaze slides down the taut line of her arms. I force it to keep moving, over her lean body and the bright blue bike, until it hits asphalt.

Don't think about being pinned to walls don't think about being pinned to walls don't think—

"Game," I manage. "Very game. Yes." I told Sherman I had her back. I can't duck out again.

"Great. So, uh. Any reason you're calling me rather than celebrating with your sister?"

There we are: right back where I don't want to be. I rub my bare arms, adjusting the straps of my tank top. "She's thirteen."

Sherman nods like she gets it, though I don't see how. "Hope that turns out okay," she says, which could mean anything, really. Then, with a kick to her bulging saddlebags: "Wanna help? Got a bunch of posters that won't stick themselves up."

"And here I joined the revolution for the glamour."

Another snort-laugh. It's baking on the street, heat radiating off every surface, so Sherman tugs off her helmet, shaking out her curly Mohawk. I have to look away before my stare gets stuck.

I'm tempted to ride along with her and leave the rest of today behind me. But I can't let Amelia's death mean nothing. Not when Blair Homes might lose patience any day now and pay the VC to evict us by force.

"Your face is doing a whole lot of strange," Sherman informs me.

Fuck it. She trusted me with her loopy, likely-to-get-us-all-dead strike plan. It's only fair that I tell her my life-threatening theories about Project Zero in exchange. We've hit, like, level five friendship.

"You remember that scientist from the observatory?" I ask. "Amelia Lopez. She spoke to me, before . . . y'know."

My explanation takes time, during which Sherman's expression becomes increasingly incredulous. Still, she lets me reach the end of my story before shaking her head.

"Hold up. Amelia Lopez told you the Flamer was behind some big evil secret called Project Zero. Your friend Jav thinks villains are destroying property so they can gentrify our side of the river. The river that is, according to Lopez's research, grossly polluted. You think the two theories are linked?"

"You got it."

". . . You realize that's, like, tinfoil-hat levels of conspiracy, right?"

"That's what I told Jav! But . . ." The cordoned-off gaps in our district where houses used to be. The roof of the bowling alley, slowly caving in. Blair Homes. "I'm starting to think she had a point."

"Uh-*huh*," says Sherman, in that slow, leading way that means she's not really *uh-huh*-ing at all. "I used to be a sidekick, Jones. If the VC pulled this many strings, the Super Squad would know."

It's a relief to hear her say so. Still, I can't fully relax. "Whatever Project Zero is, it's *real*. Amelia was killed by the Flamer, which means the VC is in on it. I gotta work this out, Sherman." For Amelia. For myself. "Please."

Skyscrapers poke bright holes in the night on the far side of Clearwater River. Downtown: a mile and a world away. Jav sees those towers as ladders to climb, but to me they've always been giant, shining middle fingers, elevated at all of us who keep our feet on the ground.

I pluck the stretched-tight fabric of my leggings. Focus, Jones. Quit wondering which villain the VC might send after me.

"Okay," says Sherman, soft. "If you're sure about this, I'm with you."

"Really?"

"Yeah." Sherman drums her fingers on the jut of her hip-bone, visible above her low-slung pants. Then her eyes widen. Must be a eureka moment; the streetlight over her head flares bright as the sun. "And if you need more intel, I know who we should talk to."

She whips out her phone, running a search. I sidle in, peering over her shoulder. The Ferocious Flamer's mug shot glares back at me, along with the headline: *B-Class Member of the Villain Council Returned Behind Bars*.

I slump, rubbing my brow bone. All this stress better not give me wrinkles. "You ain't serious."

"Yes, Jones. This is my joking face." Her mouth doesn't so much as twitch.

"Wow. That's impressive. Your deadpan has, like, rigor mortis."

She squints like she's trying to figure out if that's a compliment, blowing up the picture until I can practically see the Flamer's nostril hair. "Thanks. Look." The Flamer looks different under harsh white prison lights. Younger than I first pegged him, no more than twenty. But so what? He might be a college kid; he might have a bright shiny future ahead, moving up the VC's ranks. Amelia doesn't have a future *at all*. "He's the only person who we know *for sure* is in on your Project Zero thing. He's locked up secure as a Super can be. This might be our chance to get answers."

The thought of seeing the Flamer again ups my blood pressure until I feel it in the back of my neck. The new question that just popped into my head doesn't help. I spend ten seconds sucking the taste out of it, wondering how Sherman'll react, before I figure there's only one way to find out.

"Hey. Did you ever think about working for the VC, after your sidekick gig fell through?"

Sherman's stare is as flat as it's inscrutable. "Yeah."

"But you decided against it, right? Because they're evil peeled dicks who kill Normies for fun?"

"And they never asked. That's how it works: The council contacts you, not the other way around. Guess a D-class Shaper-derivate didn't make the grade."

Each word neutral, pared of emotion. I rock on the balls of my feet. "Right. Uh . . . No regrets?"

"No regrets."

"How sure are you? Like, out of ten?"

Sherman dismisses the app, flicking the Flamer's face up and away. "Eight." Then, before I can panic: "Only because Supremia is *really* hot."

I'll accept that. As much as I judged Turner for his crush, the lady's a walking propaganda poster for the Dark Side. Be still, my gay heart.

"Truth is, when the world screws you over, it gets real tempting to screw it back." Sherman studies the dimming horizon line, out across the Andoridge peaks. "Took me a while to realize that wouldn't help anyone, least of all me."

"That's so deep." She glares. "Sorry. I'm bad at receiving life lessons. I get this compulsive urge to ruin the moment. But seriously." I squeeze her wrist. "I'm glad. Y'know. That you don't screw back."

"Well," says Sherman.

I look at her.

She looks at me.

The San Andreas Fault busts open and a thousand new volcanoes spurt lava across California's marbled skies. At least, that's the most plausible explanation for why the temperature just rocketed two hundred degrees.

"Anyway!" I lurch back. "If we're going to visit a villain in a supermax, we should, like, do it soon? Right?"

Sherman's ears are several shades darker than normal. She looks at the blobs of chewing gum speckling the sidewalk, a nearby fire hydrant, the stripes on the road—anywhere but me— and nods way too many times. "Mm-hmm. The Flamer won't stay locked up forever."

The average sentence for a villain ranges from fifteen years to life, but the VC break their favorites out every month. A- and B-class Supers swat aside armed guards like they're gnats, which doesn't exactly boost my confidence. If I'm committed to exposing Project Zero, though, the Flamer's my only way forward.

"We need to bring Jav." I don't want her involved, but she'll hold a grudge until we get dementia if I chase her story without her. Plus: "She runs the *Voices of Bridgebrook* podcast. She can say she wants to interview the Flamer or something. They let reporters in."

"Yeah, but there's more to it than showing up at the door and saying you're writing an article." Sherman hunches, her face icing over. "My—my dad did some time."

Ah. I don't know what the right thing to say to that is. I'm not sure there is one. I just give her wrist another squeeze.

She shakes me off, glaring at her feet. "He didn't deserve it, if you were wondering. Just, y'know. Proof Supers can ruin your life in more ways than just . . . well, ending it."

Cooper Hanson, scooping butter-bean paste from his shiny blond hair. Yeah, I know something about that. "I'm sorry."

"It's over. It's past. But yeah. Between me and your friend, we might—*might*—be able to get in."

And just like that, we have a plan. A likely-to-get-us-all-incinerated plan, but still.

For now, though . . . I glance at Sherman from under my lashes. I don't like seeing her like this: wound wire-tight, jaw clenched so hard it might pop. Project Zero can take a back seat for the rest of the night.

"Thanks for listening," I say. "And for not, like, having me institutionalized."

"Still considering that last one."

"Rude."

"Part of my charm."

"Debatable. You're lucky you're cute." I almost say that last word without stuttering.

Sherman's hand slips; she accidentally rolls her throttle. We both jump when her stationary bike snarls.

"Uh," she says into the ensuing silence, a whole octave too high. "Um, posters?"

"Posters," I agree.

Sherman offers her helmet (mine's at home—don't tell the Captain) and I clamber on behind her, stomach turning giddy cartwheels. She came prepared, with a fluid ton of homemade wheatpaste spread between several mason jars. We work together to slap the posters on walls, smooth them around lampposts, and stop ourselves from sticking to them or each other (the wheatpaste is of a consistency closer to superglue). It's hard to worry about Lyssa, Project Zero, any of it, when I'm busy ignoring my urge to tremble like the dainty heroine of a Victorian novel whenever Sherman's fingers brush—or stick to—mine.

Once we've wallpapered a solid portion of Bridgebrook, Sherman takes me home. Lyssa and Hernando should be back. The sun sinks behind the high-rises on the far side of the river. Sloan Street is darker than ever; a Surger threw a tantrum down the block and half the streetlights are busted. If we lived in a better part of town, there'd be an engineer out within the hour. Here, we'll wait a week. Might have to whip up a sweepstake on which gets fixed first: the lights or the elevator in my building.

Sherman hangs around while I dismount. It's a longer process than usual, as a smear of wheatpaste has found its way to the seat of my shorts.

"Tell your sister happy birthday for me?" she asks, once I've peeled myself free.

"Yeah. Hey, wait." Call me thirsty or whatever, but I'm not ready to watch Sherman ride away. Anyway, Lyssa will be waiting upstairs with a shiny new leg and, possibly, a shiny new Superpower. I don't wanna face that alone. "Why not tell her yourself?"

I'm sure Sherman will refuse. Using me as an extra pair of hands is one thing. Hanging out together . . . She looks more nervous at that prospect than facing off against an A-class villain.

Maybe she's thinking about her ex? About whatever went down that made her so afraid to reach out again?

I don't press. Just lean back on the railing of my stoop and wait until she jerks out a nod.

Only problem is, when we reach my apartment, Lyss isn't there. No one is. If Hernando took her for dinner without me, I'm gonna be pissed. I check my phone. Two missed calls from Hernando. Probably telling me they've decided to eat out at Happy Burgers. Or . . . Or . . .

Sweat slicks the back of my neck. I redial with fumbling fingers. The call buzzes through.

"Is she with you?" snaps Hernando. No hello.

I don't need to ask who "she" is. "She's not with you?"

"*Shit.*" Hernando's swearing. *Very* not good.

Sherman keeps pulling *huh* faces, wanting to be let in on the action. A moment ago, she was my entire focus. Now that's skewed, as if whoever's steering my life just gave the wheel a sharp yank to one side. "What happened? Hernando?"

"She was supposed to go to Jesús's store for snacks! But—hell, it's been an hour. She ain't here, Jesús ain't seen her, I—" His voice breaks, and it's the most terrifying sound since Mom slammed on her brakes (too late, too late): the *crunch*, the scream, the sickening silence. "Mija, I don't know where she is."

CHAPTER 26

"JONES?" SHERMAN'S VOICE is faint, like we're miles apart.

I gotta stay calm. I can't lose it. This isn't the time to panic. This isn't the time to think of the car, the choke of thick black smoke in my lungs, dragging Lyssa—unconscious, mangled—out. Turning back for Mom (despite everything, despite the screams and the sleepless nights and the *smash* of plates striking the wall) only for the fire to get there first.

"We'll find her," I tell Hernando, because it's what he needs to hear. "You stay near Jesús's shop, I'll check the park. You called her?" Hernando makes this wretched huff of a laugh. Course he has. Probably a hundred times. But I still had to ask, and I know he's not mad at me. Not really. "Right. Lemme try, anyway."

"You call soon as you find her?"

"Course."

Neither of us says "if." This right here ain't an *if* situation. We're gonna find Lyssa, and she's gonna be fine, and we're gonna chew her out between us and give her the lowdown on why she's never, ever, *ever* running off on her own again.

Rich folks must think we're nuts for letting a thirteen-year-old saunter around Bridgebrook solo after dark. We know every soul on Sloan Street, though. Folks look out for each other around here. That's the way it *works*. But if Lyss snuck along through the shadows cast by all our broken streetlights, if no one saw which way she went . . .

That means she's someplace else. Somewhere *worse*.

I thunder down the flights, Sherman on my heels. I text as I go, thumb punching my screen.

where are you

We storm past the Beauvaises; no time to wave. Check phone; no answer. I text again.

your dad worried sick

"Bike?" asks Sherman, no-nonsense. I nod. "Which park?"

The fancy one, where Lyssa and her friends pelted ducks with stale cereal? Or Magnolia, back by Shit Creek?

Thankfully, I pick correctly. By the time we pull up, a line of text awaits.

Lyssa: magnolia park swings

I rush over. The swing chains are thick with rust. They shriek like La Llorona as my sister eases back, forth, back again, facing away from us, back as hunched as Birnbaum's. A couple of boys with their hoods up kick stones between the skeletal trees, but I don't look at them and they don't look at me. Low-level dealers, most likely—not the sort to snatch kids. But those men exist, and an avalanche of love and relief and fury crashes over me as I storm up to Lyssa and thwack the back of her head.

"The *hell* were you thinking?"

Sherman saunters behind me, thumbs in her pockets. She hangs far enough back to give us privacy.

"Ow," Lyssa whines. "Riles . . ."

"Don't you *Riles* me! Girl, you're in it so deep." I glance toward the sewage works, where a barricade of houses lists on rotting, saggy foundations, a weak defense against the stench of the city's waste. I don't know how Lyssa can stomach it, sitting here and swinging. You get used to the Shit Creek stink after a while, but I don't want either of us to reach that stage ever again.

Just like how I don't ever want to drink or drive or visit my mom's grave. You don't always *need* "closure." Some things are best left buried; some doors should always stay shut.

Lyssa fights me when I try to pull her up. "I ain't going home. Not yet."

"You go where I say you're going! In fact—y'know what? You're right. You're sitting there and calling your dad *this second* so he knows you ain't dead in a ditch. Get on that phone!"

Lyssa scowls, but does like she's told. As soon as she mutters her last sulky appeasement to Hernando—"Yeah, I'm fine, just at the park with Riley, I'm fine, Dad, I promise"—I'm back on the offensive.

"Some birthday, huh? What were you *thinking?*" She doesn't reply. Something about her slumped posture saps the fight out of me. I tilt her face up, one finger curled under her chin. "Lyss?"

Her bottom lip juts out. "I just wanted to prove I could do it. You never let me do anything!"

"Yeah, 'cause you're a kid. Suck it up. You can enjoy your crisis of independence at my age, like everyone else."

"Not just 'cause I'm a kid, though. Is it?"

I won't do her the disrespect of lying. I kneel, squeezing her knobbly knees. The sun creeps toward the downtown high-rises in the distance, running off the glass like liquid fire, casting Lyssa's face half in gold, half in shadow.

For the first time, I can't read her. It scares me how my baby sister's learning to shut herself off, act like her skin's too thick to be pierced. Lyssa's tough, but she shouldn't have to be. I don't *want* her to have to be. I want the world to do better, not for her to shield herself from the ugly parts of it.

"Hey." Our eyes play tag, chasing each other over the rust-bobbled seesaw, the ants winding through the gravel, the copse of pale, sickly trees. "What's up?"

Lyssa drags in this big shoulder-shaker of a sniff. "I'm not getting Superpowers."

"I've been telling you that for how many years?"

"You don't understand. I *need* 'em, Riles."

"You don't," mutters Sherman.

That's not for her to say. "Oh, like you can talk."

Sherman blinks. "I was just—"

"Well, you can *just* all you like, but not now." I turn back to Lyssa. "Who put that thought in your head?" She shrugs. I give her new shin a poke. "You don't hate the crutch. You don't hate the chair, and you don't hate this, either. They're your tools, right? For getting places?"

Lyssa snorts.

"Lyss?"

"Maybe I *do* hate them sometimes." She glares at me, dead on. "Maybe I *do* hate that I lost half my leg because our mom was a trash person, and I hate that I couldn't even *walk to the park alone* until I got this leg fitted, and I hate that I'm never gonna be looked at for anything but . . ." She fists the chains of the swing, lifting her new foot. "*This.*"

Oh. I shut my mouth before any more assumptions about what my sister's thinking or feeling can fall out.

I've been crafting my class clown persona since kindergarten. I make myself a joke before anyone else can, so even when people laugh at me, I'm in control. If I ever make it to therapy, I'll probably have to work on that.

But as for the parts of myself I *can't* control . . . It's easier to push them deep inside myself, tuck them away.

It sucks, hiding who I am. But Lyssa doesn't have that option. If I walked hand in hand with a girl through Bridgebrook, while most folks couldn't care less, there'd always be *some* jackass eyeballing us like we were exotic animals escaped from a local zoo. Lyssa faces those stares every time she leaves our apartment. I don't know what to say, so I try to pour all my understanding of humanity's general crappiness into another pat of her knee.

Sherman clears her throat. She glances at me, as if to ask, *Can I?* When I tip her a nod, she leans against the A-frame of the swings so she's not talking down at Lyss from on high. "Hey."

"Hey," mutters Lyss. She glances at Sherm, then at me. Then swivels to gawk at the bike, locked to the peeling railings, and back to us again. "*This* is your secret boyfriend?"

Sherman gestures down at herself. "Not exactly."

"*This,*" I say, flicking Lyssa's forehead, "is Sherman. My *girlfriend.*"

Sherman makes a startled and entirely-out-of-character *meep*.

I freeze. "Friend who's a girl! Girl who's a friend!"

"Oh," says Lyss. Then, slower, "*Ohhhhh.* I knew you liked Hayley Kiyoko for a reason. You gotta adopt, 'cause Dad wants a million grandkids."

"No, we're not . . ." I swivel my finger between Sherman and me. "We're *not*!"

"Mm-*hmm*," says Lyssa, and dips the quietly dissolving Sherman a wink.

"Oh—quit it. This's about *you*." I leave Sherman to shrink away into another dimension and pile my ass onto the rickety swing beside Lyssa. It makes a dubious squeak, but the chains don't snap and dump me in the dirt. Nice to know the *entire* universe isn't against me. "Why'd you wanna be a Super?"

"'Cause I wanna help people," Lyssa says, like she's rehearsing for her initiation.

"Not 'cause of your leg?"

"No—I dunno." She picks at the prosthetic. "I don't wanna *hide* it, but . . . It's . . . I dunno."

Her leg's baby blue, with a repeating sunflower pattern. We asked her if she wanted a color closer to her skin tone, but she refused. Said people would stare anyway, so she might as well make it pretty.

I don't get it. She *does* want them to look, but she *doesn't*?

Whatever. She doesn't *need* a fully formulated essay on her relationship to her own disability. She can take it day by day. Not my job to wrangle sense outta her, just to listen.

"You don't need to be a Super to help people," I say. "You don't have to save the world. Look, Lyss. I promise you, you're already way more awesome than any Super I know."

Sherman huffs but restrains herself to a roll of the eyes.

Lyssa smushes ants beneath the toe of her sneakers. "You're just saying that to make me feel better."

"Damn right I am. You're a total goober. But it doesn't change my point. Supers are like . . . a Band-Aid, right? Slapped over symptoms of a way bigger problem. But they don't *heal* the symptoms. Just hide 'em." Whether it's Superemacy or poverty and drugs and everything else Jav blogs about, it can't be *fixed* by *beating people up in the street*. Wild that anyone thinks that's a solution. "Lyss, you wanna be a real hero, then forget all that crime-fighting bull. Stay here, help folks who really need it. Plenty of them around Bridgebrook. Do—I dunno, social work and soup kitchens. It's not as glam, but it does way more good."

Lyssa looks dubious, but at least she isn't arguing. I stand, brushing ants off my knees.

"Speech over. We should head back."

As I flip Hernando a text, tell him we're on the way, Sherman pushes off the rusty A-frame, orange specks dappling her shoulders. She drops a hand on Lyssa's arm to deliver an awkward pat.

"Superheroes save the world on the regular." She sneaks a glance at me, like she expects me to interrupt. I feign interest in my phone. Though I don't regret telling her to shut it— where does she get off, acting like being a Super is a chore?—I'm interested in what she has to say. "They don't keep it turning, though," Sherman continues. "Normies do that."

Lyssa sniffs. "Normies don't have powers."

"They don't need them. And you don't need them, either."

"But I'd be such an awesome Summoner! Like Windwalker, y'know?" She heaves this big, dreamy sigh. "He's the *coolest*."

Seriously? I fold my arms. "He's an ass, Lyss."

Dreamy sigh número dos. "But he's got such a *nice* ass, too . . ."

"Wait, wait," says Sherman, while I feign a retch. "Windwalker? The blond pretty boy everyone ships with the Flamer?"

Lyssa still seems mopey, but she cracks her first grin of the evening when I start grilling Sherman about how she knows about *Flamewalker* (Cooper and the Flamer's super-imaginative OTP name). In a rare show of cowardice, Sherman suddenly remembers she's supposed to run chores for her mom.

As she rushes off, I holler "Thanks!" at her back. I don't just mean for the lift. I would've come alone if I had to (not a lot I *wouldn't* do for Lyss). But it meant so much, having Sherman by my side—even if she could pick her words more carefully on the Super subject.

Sherman shoots me a lopsided smile as she mounts up. She's gone before I can think of anything besides how much I want to taste it.

Me and Lyssa head out of the park. We meander back along Sloan Street. Our road is one of several threads that stitch the waterfront at one end of Bridgebrook to Shit Creek at the other, holding the two halves of our neighborhood together, over the bulge of land that tucks into the river's meander. It might just be me, but that thread feels like it's fraying. Blair Homes's SOLD! sign stands outside one of the lots farther down the road, a blue blob in the distance. Several windows are still patched with cardboard from the last time a Super battle blasted them out of their frames, and the dead streetlights leave pockets of darkness, like holes in a gap-toothed grin.

"You like her," says Lyssa, swerving around the weed-sprouting lumps in the pavement. "Don't you?"

I scuff my tennis shoes on the curb. "Yeah. She's my friend who's a girl, like I said." Lyssa snickers. I droop. "Okay. Did I make it weird, back there?"

"*So* weird. Are you, like, into girls now?"

That's the worst thing about coming out. You have to do it again, and again, and again. I glance down at her, gauging her reaction. "Always have been."

"Hey, I'm cool with it. Less competition." My glance turns to a full-on stare. "What?"

"First, you're way too young to care about competition. Second, competition for who?" She waggles her eyebrows. I groan. "Don't tell me you're serious about Windwalker."

"Serious as you are about your girl-who's-a-friend!"

Why, out of all the celebrities to crush on, did she choose the guy who thinks customer-service smiles are come-ons? "No. *No.*" I hold up both hands. "Your first boyfriend is going to be a *maximum* of one year older than you, or Hernando and I will take turns with the shotgun and the shovel. And I'm *not* being judged on my love life by a thirteen-year-old."

"Uh, yeah you are, 'cause that love life is nonexistent, and I don't wanna be a *thirty-year-old* by the time you get your act together."

I pinch her ear, lighter than she deserves. "Save the lip for Hernando. You're in for it when we get home."

"He's *my* dad," says Lyssa. "He ain't gonna be mad at me." But she doesn't sound all that sure.

Jesús waves as we pass his store, relief coloring his broad face. Mr. and Mrs. Beauvais waylay us on the staircase, thanking the Lord. Lyssa actually looks a little ashamed by the time we reach our door. Good. If she knows how many people she worried, maybe she'll think twice from now on, before running off after dark.

As I hunt for my keys, a 5'11" homing missile blasts out the apartment and barrels into Lyssa, hugging her so tightly he hoists her off her feet. "Dios mío, you scared me! Don't you *ever* do that again!"

I sidestep them as the lecture commences, intending to scoot into the apartment. But Hernando quits looming over Lyssa long enough to utter a gruff "You did good, mija" before hauling me into a cuddle of my own.

It's kinda awkward. We're not exactly well-practiced at Loving Parental Embraces. I waste several seconds standing stiff as a plus-size shop mannequin. But Hernando never gives up on me. He sticks with it until I soften, melting against his wiry shoulder, and wrap my arms around him, too.

CHAPTER 27

THE NEXT MORNING is dedicated to catching Jav up to speed. And feeling sucky about how little I've messaged her recently. I wanted to give her space after our last talk at the library, that's all—and maybe I needed space, too. Still, it means so much to open our chat and find a new message, time-stamped last night:

Happy cake day to Lyssa! Try not to strangle her, but if you do, I'll help you hide the body. xxx

Then, underneath:

Love you, Riles.

I press my phone to my heart as it contracts around a vicious pang. No fighting that pain. I let it sink all the way through me, where I'm sprawled supine on the couch, and sink out of the soles of my feet. Then I start typing.

love u too nerd x
I know this sounds buck wild but bear with . . .

I tell her all of it. Most of it. *Some* of it. The important parts, at least. I leave voids wrapped around the observatory, Amelia

Lopez, and my nighttime occupation (don't want her to get preachy). Unfortunately, this punches several holes in my reasoning for why I've gone from ridiculing her gentrification theory to being its number one devotee.

Javira: How'd you hear about this "Project Zero" thing?

It only takes a couple seconds to concoct an answer. By now, I'm stellar at this whole lying thing. If Hench doesn't work out, I could always try for law school.

Riley: just word on the street and stuff
you've been in that library too long if you haven't heard

I picture Jav glaring at her screen, cheek twitching. Her greatest fear is losing touch. Success: She doesn't dig for details. We arrange to meet at the prison mid-morning tomorrow, and I get to spend the rest of my afternoon alternating between relief at her lack of suspicion and leaden gray guilt.

HEADING OUT WITH Sherman promises to be a much-needed break. She's as forthcoming as usual with the details, but we only have three days until the march. I reckon I'm in for another lecture on how us henchfolk need to present the VC with a united front, if we want them to take us seriously and not burn us all alive. Maybe this time, I'm more inclined to listen.

By the time we reach Meera's, it's so late it's early. The night-clubs have evicted the stragglers, but golden light still shimmers through the bar's frosted windows. We enter to a low cicada hum of conversation, rising and falling, steady as breath. The bar is jam-packed, people sitting on tables and occasionally each other, asses squeezed half off the banquettes.

Three of those asses, I recognize.

"Hey!" I march over to the table that the Captain, Turner, and Birnbaum have commandeered. "What're you guys doing here?"

"Having a drink," says the Captain. "Like you're supposed to, in a bar." A lemonade, in his case. It sits beside his car keys, the little medallions all stacked. He's the only henchman who hasn't turned off his mask.

Didn't Sherman say he was against the union? I don't want to believe it—this is the guy who made me pancakes. But the other henchmen give my squad as wide a berth as they can without clambering out the windows. The Captain's table is the only one with extra space around it. I slither onto the bench beside Turner as the Captain continues: "Us three were at HQ when we noticed the commotion. Figured we should be where the action was."

Oof. Okay, so maybe holding protest planning meetings *right next door* to your place of work isn't the smartest idea. Guess it was only a matter of time before that came back to bite Sherman in the tush.

"What do you mean, you three were at HQ?" I ask. "Just, like, hanging out?"

Birnbaum and Turner look at each other and shrug.

"Yup," says the Captain, popping the *P*.

"And you didn't invite us?"

"Nup. I mean, c'mon. You two are, like, twelve."

Dick. Maybe he's a corporate plant after all. I glance at Sherman, just in case Meera granted her the authority to kick people out. Only, Sherman's not there.

While our so-called teammates dunked on us, she sauntered over to another cluster of henchmen. I recognize the one with the they/them pin and the orchid tat; they were at the last meeting. The last meeting I attended, anyway. Max, right? They give Sherman dap in this long, convoluted choreography of hand slaps, before nudging her toward a chunky middle-age Black guy with a buzz cut. His left arm is in a sling, one of his eyes bandaged over.

Must be her friend from the observatory, Derren or Declan or . . . Delmar, that's it. He sways like he's on pain meds, but his face is all business as he shows Sherman something on his phone. He believes in this, like Sherman does. Or perhaps he just believes in her.

"Ready?" he asks. His deep voice carries over the general hubbub. Sherman nods.

Turner frowns. "What's she doing?"

The Captain swigs from his lemonade like he's trying to drown himself. "Something she'll regret."

I puff up, ready to go on the defensive, but Sherman's already clambered aboard a table. "Okay," she says. "Listen up."

I couldn't ignore her if I wanted to. There's a magnetism to her voice; she doesn't speak loudly, but glasses still meet tables across the room and heads swivel in her direction.

Sherman waits until she has everyone's attention, letting the silence stretch. She stands slightly slouched, legs wide and her arms folded, like she's daring the world to mock her. The badass act would've fooled me a month back, but now I read the tension in her neck. She's nervous.

I could do something about it. Stand beside her. Hold her hand. But that's the sort of thing girlfriends do, not girls-who-are-friends. Even if they have physics. Chemistry. Whatever.

"Masks on," says Delmar. He waves his phone, the bright white camera light glinting off the rainbow of bottles lining Meera's barback. "The revolution will be televised."

I turn my neck dial, along with everyone else. Our faces vanish, taking the bar's chill vibes with them. Into the ensuing hush, Sherman clears her throat.

"Some of you know," she says, turning her masked face around the circle of henchmen. I get the sense she looks every single person in the eyes. "Some of you don't. Some of you don't want to. But this is happening, with or without you, and I'd rather it was with. For too long, we've been treated as trash, by heroes and villains alike. For too long, we've been working shit hours on a shit job for shit pay, because—well. What choice do we have?"

Plenty, for her. Pretty sure there's a whole section on Indeed dot com dedicated to low-level Supers.

That nags at me. I keep it to myself.

"That's what they"—Sherman points up, to some imaginary

boss in the sky—"want you to think. They want you to think we *have* no choice. They want you to think we're powerless. And we might be, but not in every way that matters. Stand with us, at the Sunnylake City Living Wage March."

Delmar and Max wade into the crowd. They hand out leaflets. I take one when it's pushed into my hands. It looks like it was designed using the Paint app and coughed out of the library's janky printer. But it's got all the relevant stuff. The hashtag, the date of the march, times to arrive, and the legal assurance that wearing a holographic Hench uniform in public isn't enough to get anyone arrested. Like that'd stop the Supers, if they really wanted to take us down.

I read the tagline until my eyes blur: *We Stand Together.*

The Captain raises his hand. Sherman's jaw twitches, her mask hologram stretching to accommodate.

"The question panel was weeks back. You missed it."

"Aw, c'mon. Just a quickie: Are you actively suicidal?"

Delmar crosses his arms. Or, y'know. Tries. Any menacing effect's lost, since one of them's in a sling. "Not your business, Captain."

"Leave it," Sherman says. "I can look after myself."

"Really?" The Captain slurps his lemonade. "You're doing a *great* job of showing it."

"Hey," calls Meera, from where she's pouring frothy green shots. I'm glad I'm far enough away not to smell them, although the bar's yeasty stale-beer odor is enough to shift my dinner in my guts. "You wanna get rowdy? You take it outside."

She's ignored. "Y'know, Sherm?" the Captain continues. "For someone who isn't a contortionist, you've wedged your head impressively far up your own ass. You realize you're gonna get yourself killed, along with anyone who follows you?"

Delmar and Max step up behind Sherman, joined by a couple of others, forming a masked inky wall as she stares the Captain down. The Captain doesn't spare them a glance.

"You're messing with big people, Sherm. Bigger than me."

"Not hard," says Delmar, deadpan.

Chuckles bubble. I bite my lip so I won't join in. The Captain manages to look down on Sherman, despite the logistics. "You're *replaceable*. We're all fucking replaceable. If it's easier to cut us loose than it is to *listen*, the VC are gonna cut, cut, *cut*. You ain't the first group of losers to stand up for a good cause. You won't be the first to die for that cause, either."

I gulp. Cold burns my throat like I've swallowed an ice cube. I thought I could choke my fears down for Sherman's sake, but here's the Captain, vocalizing every single one.

"Then what?" Delmar asks. "We should accept how they treat us?"

"You think *this* is bad? Wait till our boss retaliates."

Sherman's jaw squares under her mask. "He's trying to scare us."

The Captain barks a laugh. "You *oughta* be scared. The world don't owe us shit 'cause we *ain't* shit. We're Normies, for fuck's sake! And we're walking a thin line already. You give our boss a reason to look into what we actually do on our jobs and you put us all in jeopardy."

"I'm doing what's *best* for us."

"No. You're doing what you, an eighteen-year-old from Bridgebrook who wants to fight every injustice she sees, think is best for us. There's a hell of a difference." The Captain pushes up from his chair. "Look, Sherm. There are *structures* in this world. People like you and me don't have the power to change them. You can climb—but then those structures will be beneath you, holding you up."

Sherman shrugs. "Knock 'em down and rebuild."

"Great when you're the one holding the sledgehammer." He shakes his head, striding for the exit. "Harder for the brickies who have to make something out of the mess."

Sherman hollers after him: "Going somewhere?"

"Yeah. Away. I want no part in this." The Captain boots the door open. He stands silhouetted under the red neon strip, goggles black as bottomless pools. "And anyone with any sense is going to do the same. We got a *place* in this world, Sherman. Want my advice? *Remember yours, before they put you back in it.*"

I expect Sherman to say he's talking crap to scare us. I want her to. I *need* her to. Her silence speaks louder than words.

The Captain stalks away. Faint, muffled swearing floats through the window, followed by the slam of a car door. The growl of his engine recedes into the background city hum.

"Well," says Turner, "there goes our ride home."

I frown at him. "You're not leaving?"

Turner directs his goggled glare at his phone as, around us, the other henchmen nudge each other, hosting mumbled debates in their squad groups. "I quit the Superspotter app," he says.

". . . Congrats?"

"I get it, I think. Villains and heroes clash every day, but it's us Normies who get hurt. Like that poor scientist at the observatory . . ." His voice chokes off. Birnbaum's gnarly hand grips his shoulder in wordless comfort. I wonder if Turner's remembering, like I am, that he narc'd on Amelia. Perhaps I'm not the only one who thinks of fire before I shut my eyes at night.

Turner snivels, then collects himself. He still holds his stitched arm at an awkward angle, away from his side, but something solidifies in his posture: the set of his shoulders, his spine. "It's not right that everyone worships the Supers," he says, raising his voice. "We're the ones who make this city. Not just henchmen— all us Normies. The ones who clean stuff and fix things and . . . and hide the instructions."

"Well said," says Birnbaum. He looks around us. "Us Normies do more for this city than any flashy fool in tights. We don't ask for medals, or recognition. We just want to live."

We just want to live. Those words sink into me and settle somewhere deep.

Sherman doesn't let me savor the moment. Her head turns— just once—to the door, after the Captain. But when she speaks to Delmar's camera again, I hear the smile in her voice.

"Exactly," she says, nodding to our squad. "This isn't about henchmen. It's about everyone who cleans your streets, scrubs your toilets, puts food on the shelves in the shops. Everyone who's gonna march on Saturday. That's what this protest is about: making sure everyone knows who we are, and that we're not forgotten." She studies the camera, mask conforming to the high ridges of her cheekbones. "It's about time all the Supers out there realized: Normies could live in a world without you, but you would have a hard time without us."

Wait, what?

Us?

The knot in my intestines yanks tight as a noose. Sherman doesn't *get* to say that. Not when she's a Super, one of *them*.

"I'm not one for dragging out a speech," Sherman continues. Her voice is quiet, but it has that same effect as the heroes who speak on TV; a resonance that makes us shut up and listen. Everyone's drawn in, though they don't get *why*.

I chew my thumbnail, twisting the tip off between my front teeth. When I swallow, the serrated edges of Sherman's secret scrape the lining of my throat. Back at the park, with Lyssa, I called Sherman out, zero hesitation. Here, though, in front of her friends . . .

I can't do that to her. Not when I swore I had her back.

"So, let's lay this out real clear." Sherman's brown eyes narrow. "You all got two choices. Either you join the revolution, or you get out of our way."

A loud rustling follows, as a third of the patrons evacuate Meera's bar. They tramp to the exit in an unspeaking procession. The mass exodus doesn't worry me. What worries me is how many more henchmen remain.

This is it: Sherman's ultimatum to the world. And as Delmar finishes the livestream and we watch the views rocket up, I wonder how the world will answer.

CHAPTER 28

I SNEAK OUT while Sherman's distracted by Max and Delmar and Co., immersed in a crowd of laughing, back-thumping friends. The beer stink follows me up the dark-bleeding alley, as do the cheers as our video breaks the first 1K milestone, then the next. Like that's it. Like we've already won.

I walk home alone. My head hangs heavy, weighed down by Project Zero, Amelia, Sherman's secret. Should I have said something? What would've happened if I had?

If I'd spoken up, if things turned dire, if Hench's shiny new union crumbled because I revealed their founder was a Super . . . That would be seriously shitty, right? For Sherman, for me, for everyone.

Only keeping my mouth shut feels shittier still.

Next morning crawls by. Sherman and I planned to hit up the prison today. We're supposed to meet Jav there at 11 a.m. But after slithering out of bed and onto the sectional, I leave all ten of Sherman's messages (Thanks for last night. // Jones, you up? // We still on for today? // Am I being ghosted or are you dead?) on read. Quotes from her motivational talk buzz between my ears like trapped flies.

Supers would have a hard time without us . . . I'm not ready to face that argument. Because there'll be one, if I accuse her of—what? Co-opting the struggle of being a Normie? Speaking over us, like her voice—her strong, Super voice—is one of ours?

No, I tell myself, curling against the arm of the sofa, hugging my knees. *Don't get into that whole us/them crap. Don't let that ruin this.*

But there *is* an us and a them. We're reminded of it every time we flick on the TV, scan the headlines, turn our faces to the ground as the Super Squad jet thrums above Sunnylake's streets. That's the *problem*.

"Riley!" calls Lyssa, cutting through my funk. "Your girl-friend's at the door!"

Shit. She must've come to make sure the VC hasn't bumped me off. "Don't tell the block."

Hernando's ass-crack-of-dawn shift finished an hour back. At Lyssa's holler, he drops the veggies he's mutilating for tonight's bean soup and sprints past the sectional, despite my attempt to grab his legs. "No, no, no!"

Too late. Hernando unclips the chain and flings the door wide. Sherman fills the doorway, helmet tucked under one arm, uniform tag glittering on her neck.

Hernando must spot it. He crosses his arms: a lean, scowling barricade. "You work with Riley."

Sherman hesitates. She scans his expression, then presents her palm. "Sherman," she says, all proper. "Nice to meet you, sir."

"Hernando. Hernando Garcia." Hernando takes her up on the offer of a handshake. He applies pressure, to show he means business. The thin muscle stands out along his arms.

Sherman's poker face doesn't waver. Hernando's does, though, when she returns the gesture with thrice the force.

"That's—oof—some grip you got . . ."

Sherm releases his corrugated fingers. "Thanks."

Hernando manages a grin. It transmutes into a pained grimace the moment he turns away.

"Thought you wanted to give her the shovel talk?" I mutter as he slinks back to our kitchen unit.

"Yeah, but she squeezed *really hard*." He sticks his hand in his armpit, nodding to the saucepans lined up on the stove. "You kids want lunch?"

"Thanks," says Sherman, "but pass."

I peel myself from my depression in the sofa. I haven't moved from my spot all morning, and a shameful cast of my ass immortalizes my slugitude for all the world to see. I toss a couple of pillows over it, trying to make the action casual. "Yeah. I'm good."

Hernando levels a knife at us (which might be threatening if it wasn't wedged halfway through a bell pepper). "Nothing dangerous, okay? And *no* sleeping over."

I match the pepper's coloration. "Hernando!"

"You're seventeen, Riley! Rules are rules."

"No problem," says Sherman, though she sounds a little choked. "I'll have her back by ten tonight."

"Make it nine!" Hernando calls after us as I snatch my bike helmet off the top of the fridge and shuffle out the door. When I turn to glare at him, he waves his pepper in farewell.

I lead the way downstairs and out into the summer bake. I don't look at Sherman until we mount up—and then (damn it all) I find her lips doing that one-sided-quirk thing I can't get enough of.

"Hey," she says. "Your dad's kinda funny."

Curse her dimples. It takes every ounce of my negligible will-power not to be charmed. Luckily, when I burrow into my helmet (not bothering to correct her about Hernando being Lyssa's dad, not mine) those dimples vanish.

"Jones? Something wrong?"

I shrug.

"You're acting weird." She scans me like she's checking for injuries. When she finds none, she nods to my building. "Your sister okay?"

"Lyssa's fine." Making plans to hit up the bougie park with her school friends. Writing disgusting amounts of self-ship fic starring her and (gag) Windwalker. She's settling into Normie-hood, in other words. Still seems low, but she'll get over it. The rest of us did.

"Your dad?"

"Yeah, he's fine, too. You gonna work through my extended family, or do we got somewhere to be?"

I hope she'll drown any further conversation beneath the rip of her Harley's exhaust. Tragically, Sherman has this knack for doing the exact opposite of what I expect. She cuts the engine, then twists on her seat to look at me. I glimpse my reflection in her visor, the two of us wrapped in carbon fiber bubbles, shut off in our own little worlds.

"Did I piss you off?" she asks.

"You said it. Not me."

"Well, how am I supposed to *do* something about it, if you won't tell me what I did?"

I grit my teeth. I know I can't expect her to *know* why I'm mad, but . . .

No, scratch that. Maybe she *should* know. Maybe she should realize that pretending to be a Normie isn't okay. Maybe she should never have done that, and I shouldn't have had to spend my morning melting into my sofa as I figured out how to explain.

Sherman pushes up her visor. She catches my wrist. It's her gaze that holds me captive, though. Searching, hoping. Her irises shine molten, gold like they've tamed the sun. "Please, Jones," she says. "Talk to me."

I should yell, not talk. But a part of me wants *so badly* to believe this is one Super who won't let me down.

I sigh through my nose. "You spoke about being a Normie last night, but you don't know what it's like."

Sherman blinks. "You're mad about *that*?"

I knew she'd dismiss this. I knew she wouldn't *understand*. I brace my foot on the curb and clamber off, tucking my helmet under my arm with the full intention of stomping back inside. "Forget it. This was a shit idea."

"I *do* know what it's like. To be a Normie."

Sherman's outburst stops me short. "Oh yeah?" This oughta be good.

Sherman licks her dry lips. "My mom's a Normie," she tries. "My pop's a Normie, and so are my grandparents, and you. I have Normies all around me, every day."

"If this ends with 'I have Normie friends!' I'm gonna side-eye you *so hard*." I glare out across Bridgebrook, toward where the shimmery dome of our neighborhood's Super Squad hub bulges above the town houses like a crashed spaceship. "You don't *know*, Sherman. You think you do, but you don't. That power's in you, and it's always *gonna* be in you. So just . . . do me a favor, yeah? Don't act like it doesn't exist."

She scowls, strangling her handlebars, knuckles jabbing like knife tips at the underside of her skin. "Everyone'd treat me different if I told them. Delmar, Max, Meera, the Captain . . ."

"I'm not saying you have to walk around in hot pants with *Super Squad Dropout* on the ass." Though, y'know, I wouldn't be opposed. "Just . . . maybe don't impersonate a Normie? Not when you could let one of us speak."

"Didn't see you standing up to talk."

"Not the point!" I go to grab her wrist, only I miss and wind up with a handful of fingers. It'd be rude to drop them like they scalded me, so really, I have no choice but to hold on. "A lot of stuff needs saying, okay?" I give her hand a tight, furious squeeze. "But it *doesn't* need to be said by you."

Sherman glares at our feet. The streetlamp strobes overhead like the sun sensor's broken. Makes sense. Her Superpower's a weird cross between Surger and Shaper disciplines. Any nearby source of energy is a tappable battery.

The light quivers like it's afraid of her. I refuse to let myself copy it, though my brain is hardwired to correlate "Super" with "threat."

"Okay," she mutters eventually. Her hand hangs slack in mine. "I hear you. It just . . . felt good, is all. To belong. To lead, rather than follow."

My eyebrows shoot up. "Oh yeah, a Super leading Normies. No dodgy precedent there."

Sherman cringes. "Fair. Yeah. I'm sorry. I really am. But how do I take everything back?"

I don't have an answer. I'm not sure there *is* one. Mostly, I wish she'd never climbed into bed with the whole Supers-versus-Normies debate. It's fucked enough already.

"Let's just go see the Flamer."

". . . Might have to let go of me first."

I fling her hand away from me. "Right! Right."

Sherman still hesitates, bike silent beneath us even after I scramble back aboard with my usual grace and poise. "We okay, Jones?"

I weigh up a lie, but I'm sick of their taste. "Nope." Then, when Sherman shrinks in her seat: "But it could be worse. Just drive, okay? And never, ever do that again."

CHAPTER 29

SUNNYLAKE PENITENTIARY PERCHES on the edge of our district—fitting, considering the proportion of general population who are Bridgebrookian native, born and bred. You can see a corner of the roof from my high school: a distant promise of what the future holds.

Today's windier than usual. Breeze rolls off the mountains, caressing Sherman and me with the taste of earth rather than stale food and traffic fumes, billowing my oversize blouse like we're in the age of sail. After Sherman kills her engine, the bang of a flapping garbage can lid is the only break in the silence.

The apartments around the prison get reduced to rubble with above-average regularity, thanks to all the breakouts. Even so, Blair Homes and Co. haven't moved in. The pothole-pitted street is deserted. No kids kicking balls or pulling wheelies. Pinched faces peep from between faded curtains, then quickly duck away.

Everywhere I look, I find the scars of another battle. Scorched bricks, dangling power lines. Plastic wrap over empty window holes. The last VC attack could've been yesterday or last year. This part of town has the same desolate feel as the war zones you see on the TV. A place that's forgotten peace.

"This is creepy," I mutter to Sherman. "It's not just me, right?"

She's so tense she's shrunk a size. What was it like, coming here to visit her dad? I don't know how to ask. "Yeah. Is that your friend? I wanna get this over with."

She jerks her chin at a familiar petite figure, leaning against the half-demolished remnants of the prison's front wall. Jav will get us in. She has the cutest face, the sugariest customer-service voice, and none of my instinctive knack for pissing off authority. But she also has an ear for voices. Assuming she's seen the video from Meera's—everyone has by now; the viewer count just keeps climbing—there's a strong chance she'll recognize Sherman's.

Jav eyes her up as we approach. Takes her in, in all her unmasked glory: the facial piercings; the fade around her curly 'fro-hawk; her outfit (zip-loaded stonewashed jeans, a hoodie tied around her middle, scuffed boots and a belly-bar flashing sports bra). Everything about her screams *zero fucks given*, because that's the face Sherm shows the world. But I know Jav isn't judging.

She can get a bit snotty, acting like everyone from Shit Creek should shoot for the stars, but she doesn't rely on first impressions. I'll get the lowdown on whether she approves of Sherman tomorrow, after she's gotten to know her. Until then, her verdict's withheld.

"Hi," she says, trotting over. She's had her hair done in perfect box braids; they pat her shoulders with the swing of her walk. It's the sort of thing she would've messaged me about at the start of summer, along with a million selfies, but I haven't heard a word. She said we were cool after I came out, that we were still besties. Now, though, doubt tickles my throat like a half-swallowed hair. I wasn't the only one who went radio silent, after all.

"I'm Jav," she continues, while I gulp that doubt down. Jav's here; that's what matters. "You work with Riley, yeah?"

Sherman nods. "Riley says you can get us in to see the Flamer?"

I hold my breath, waiting for Jav to piece it together, to blurt *you're the henchman from that viral vid.* But though her forehead creases down the middle, she dismisses any recollections with a bright smile. "I'll try. Action plan, though: What do we actually want from the Flamer?"

I count goals off my fingers. "To confirm what Project Zero is. To learn who he's collaborating with. To make him sorry for everything he's ever done, in his entire life."

"Mm. Let's stick to one and two. A confession, and another lead. Then what?"

Me and Sherman swap matching frowns. "Uh," I venture, "we follow the lead?"

Jav makes the negative-buzzer noise, like we're on a quiz show. "Nuh-uh. We get enough information to justify taking this to someone *paid* to deal with this shit."

"The Super Squad?" The buildings are too tall—I can't see their Bridgebrook HQ. I know it's there, though, a shiny lozenge of a building crouched like a giant chrome roach in our district's heart.

"Did you miss the bit where I spent half my summer researching how much the Super Squad suck at their jobs? Nah. We find out what we can from the Flamer and present everything to the mayor's office." Jav pauses, toying with a braid. "Plus, as well as being ineffective, the Super Squad are dicks."

No arguments there. And no more putting this off. The three

of us exchange nods. Then Jav turns crisply on her heel, plasters on her best waitressing smile, and leads the way.

Sherman hesitates before following, expression unreadable, staring at the long cream-painted oblong of the prison's facade. I grasp her hand. Just, y'know, to give her a little tug in the right direction. Friendly reassurance and such. Her fingers are stiff and cold, but they soften as I hold on, curling to fit around mine.

"We got this. I promise."

Sherman has tensed her neck so much she might snap it if she nods. "I sure hope so."

We approach the gate, a classy ten-foot barbed-wire-edged number that embodies the spirit of the words *fuck off*. A guard has to buzz us through. He sits in a miniature office box, which comes complete with radio, monitor, and crusty coffee machine. The whitewashed walls peel like sunburn.

Jav code-switches like a pro, explaining our purpose in her best Ralbury accent. I don't pay attention; Sherman's grip has tightened, and I'm a little distracted by her attempt to wring the blood from my hand. Still, I catch the odd word: *school project* and *called in advance* (which, knowing Jav, she probably did).

The guard—white, steroid shoulders, army buzz cut—looks unimpressed. "What kinda school project makes kids talk to murderers?"

Jav makes her eyes real big. "The lady on the phone said you issue press passes?"

"Yeah, to actual members of the press! Damn Superspotter app. Kids these days will do anything to get gilded."

"That's not why we're here," I try.

The guard blows steam off his coffee. "Either you girls log in at the visitation office and say hello to the ladies and gents in gen pop, or you scram."

Jav stirs more sugar into her saccharine smile. She steps up to the window, pushing onto her tiptoes to make herself taller. "Well, Mr. . . . Palmer, is it? Perhaps I'll interview you for *Voices of Bridgebrook*. You can tell the world why you want to stifle the education of an aspiring young girl from the city's poorest district." She flicks her braids back from her face. "That won't go down well at your next promotion."

The guard stares her down, as if to say, *Are you seriously trying this?* "I'm doing my job—and you a favor, whether or not you believe it." He gestures to the wire fences that ring the perimeter. "This isn't a playground."

"Damn," Jav mutters. "That sort of threat always works in movies." Then, at normal volume: "Look. We just want information about Project Zero." She narrows her eyes at the guard. "You heard of it?"

She's taking one hell of a risk, saying that out loud. I'm not sure I impressed on her how dangerous this all is. Still, I can't tell her about Amelia. Not without revealing how we met.

The guard sips his coffee. "Nope. Don't much care, either. Now, back up. Last warning."

He means business. His other hand rests on the butt of his rifle, tucked to one side of his miniature desk.

Me, Sherman, and Jav share a synchronized gulp. We ain't fucking with that.

Turns out, we don't have to. As we start our defeated trudge back toward the road, a new voice rings out: "Where do you ladies think you're going?"

I freeze. We all freeze. Sherman's brows crunch in confusion, while Jav sucks her cheeks hollow as if she's tempted to spit at the newcomer's feet. Me? I curl my fist tight like I'm hefting an imaginary garbage bag, ready for my second swing.

What's a hero doing here?

And why did it have to be Cooper Hanson?

CHAPTER 30

"W-WINDWALKER?" **THE GUARD** stumbles over the code name. Guess he's not used to meeting good guys.

"The one, the only." Cooper's in full hero regalia: brilliant white suit, navy accents, gold star on the chest. His mask hugs the bridge of his nose.

Oddly, he looks less impressive than he did that day at Artie's. Sure, his spandex outlines each bulge, from biceps to crotch. His Colgate grin could induce snow blindness, and his jaw is as chiseled as if Michelangelo himself hacked at him with carpentry tools. But everything is too *exaggerated*. He's a cartoon. A caricature. Like, I'm supposed to respect the bodybuilder in the painfully constrictive tights? That's *hilarious*.

Sherman asks what we're all thinking before I can do something suicidal, like say any of this out loud. "What's he doing here?"

"Whatever he wants," says Cooper with a smarmy grin. "Perk of being a hero." He eyes her up and down. "You look familiar. Have we met?"

Sherman sucks a sharp breath. "No."

"I'm sure of it! Don't be shy; always happy to meet a fan. Was it an after-party? Autograph signing?"

I cut in before Sherman can crunch so tightly into herself that she disappears. "Like the one you tried to give me?"

Cooper's eyes widen. "Oh, no *way*!" He all but guffaws. "*Beanburger girl?*"

Of course he never learned my name. I cross my arms. "Glad I left an impression."

"Sure did! We got off on the wrong foot, huh? But hey, don't sweat it." He beams at me, real friendly. "Water under the bridge."

Hell no. He doesn't get to pretend that a Normie one-upping on a Super meant *nothing*.

Jav steps forward. "Remember me, too?"

That knocks the smile off his face. Cooper looks *nervous*. Then he remembers she's a Normie, and it's her word against his. "Just a joke, yeah? Don't make a big deal of it."

The guard interjects: "Mr. Windwalker, please. I have to ask— why *are* you here?"

"To pay my nemesis a visit, of course." Cooper looks us over: Jav fuming, Sherman withdrawn, me fervently wishing for a potato peeler. And, whether out of a misguided sense of altruism or the hope he can smooth things over, he turns back to the guard, leaning one elbow on the edge of his desk, gigawatt grin brighter than the sun. "I'll escort these girls, stop them getting into trouble. No need for you to worry."

The guard weighs it up. His gaze roves across our trio, then darts back to Cooper. I see the moment he relents, the realization of *it's not worth it* that crawls across his face. Maybe he's running his own three rules through his head.

"All right," he says, fiddling with his radio. "Go on in. You got twenty minutes."

"Perfect." Cooper waves us ahead. "Ladies first."

The Supervillain Detention Center is an underground mole run of tunnels beneath the guard towers. I don't know what to expect inside. They don't show this part of the prison on TV, in a bid to reduce the constant breakouts. Cooper plays tour guide, informing us that the walls are made of a rare metal I can't pronounce, proven to deflect Super antics.

The wire cell fronts are made from the same material (henceforth named whatever-the-fuckium). The electronics are similarly coated, so no Surger can siphon power on the sly. Summoners, being the rarest and most dangerous of the three main categories into which Supers are divided, have their own subsection, located beyond the circular door at the far end of the corridor.

Sherman walks behind me. The impact of her feet is muffled, as if she's wading through snow. Me, her, and Jav flounder along in whatever-the-fuckium-lined boiler suits, looking like old-timey divers and moving about as nimbly. Should our shells have any flaws, a malignant A-class Shaper could freeze our blood within our veins, rupture every muscle that binds us together. A Surger of similar caliber could mess with the signals in our brains, drain us like a battery.

That's the shit us Normies go up against every day of our lives. Strange, how the protective suits put that into perspective.

Cooper Hanson leads the way, spring in his step, whistle on his lips. No boiler suit necessary. He's an A-class Summoner, more than capable of self-defense. If he put his mind to it, he could tear the air from our lungs.

I'm glad he restrained himself to yelling, back when I introduced that sack of soggy vegan burgers to his face. Not *thankful*, because that implies I owe him. Just . . . glad.

Jav walks closest to Cooper, somehow resisting the urge to kick him in his shapely bubble butt. She studies the cages we pass. Five men and two women slouch inside, perfect bodies draped with loose orange scrubs. They smirk at us, like they know something we don't.

I hope so. We're counting on it.

"Why help us?" Jav asks Cooper.

He presses his palm to a space-agey access panel beside the circular door. It scans him with a radioactive-blue light. "I overheard your conversation with that guard."

"So . . . what?" She narrows her eyes. "You decided to play Good Samaritan?"

He glances at us. No more cheesy grins. As for what replaces them—well. I don't like that *at all*. If a hero's nervous, what hope do the rest of us have?

"Not exactly," he says.

The door buzzes open. Cooper ushers us into the Summoner section of the jail. In here, the defenses get a little more *inventive*. You can't keep a Wind-Type Summoner from breathing, or a Water-Type Summoner from drinking, but you can keep them immobile. Ish.

Elemental powers are harnessed through momentum. Exorbitant gesticulation and aerial high kicks indicate a trajectory along which atoms do *really weird shit* (at least, that's what they taught us during our Super Science module in seventh grade). The Ferocious Flamer won't be frolicking around Sunnylake any time soon. He floats before us, suspended in a contraption that reminds me of the gyroscopes in steampunk art. Two metal gimbals rotate inside a larger ring, while he hovers, perfectly inert, strapped to the disc at the center. Sturdy tubes of whatever-the-fuckium encase his arms to the elbow and both of his legs to the knee. They hold him in a spread eagle that'd be obscene if they'd let him keep that holographic unitard.

But the Flamer isn't here to stay. Judging by his smirk, he knows it. "If it isn't the Windwalker, my nemesis! Come to gloat?"

Cooper's scowl slashes his model-like features. "Not today."

"That's right; you did your fair share of that when they caught me." The Flamer's gaze treks to us. He must've been wearing contacts at the observatory; his actual eyes are dark, not piercing blue. His orange hair lacks its usual spikes—guess they won't let him near flammable hairspray. Brown tinges the roots, as if mud is extinguishing the flame. "What brings you and your groupies to my humble abode?"

His cell is halved. We stand on a small viewing platform, linked to the hallway behind, while he floats in his fancy bondage gear beyond yet another metal grill. This pod is significantly cooler than the rest of the prison—another effort to reduce the fire risk—but my boiler suit still gums to my sweaty back.

This man killed Amelia. The hate I feel for him is acid, eating through my stomach lining.

"I'm here for information," says Cooper.

The Flamer cracks his neck from side to side: the most motion he's permitted. "Ask away. The therapist *did* say I should liven up my daily routine."

Cooper's jaw is a diamond-cut wedge. "What's Project Zero?"

Me, Jav, and Sherman lock up.

"Uh," says the Flamer. "What?"

I emulate: "*What?* How do *you* know about Project Zero?"

Cooper doesn't look at me. "I could ask the same of you. But I'm not. I'm asking him."

"And I'm asking *you!*"

Cooper hooks his fingers through the grill, still glowering at the Flamer. "I've been investigating this for a while. No idea what you three have to do with it, but if you came to talk to him, you must be as in the know as I am."

Like hell do I trust this. I tug the sleeve of Sherman's boiler suit. "Let's go. We don't need his help."

Jav disagrees. "We think Project Zero has something to do with the new buildings going up across Bridgebrook." I kick the back of her leg. "Ow! What? Enemy of my enemy."

Cooper *is* the enemy. I fume at her as Cooper replies: "Sorry to disappoint. Project Zero involves a cover-up of the rising pollution levels in Clearwater River."

Like in Amelia's research. Sherman and I exchange eyebrow scrunches, through the grill-threaded glass of our suit visors. "Where'd you get that from?" she asks.

"You guys wouldn't know—it wasn't reported by the press." Cooper points at the Flamer. "When he attacked the Andoridge observatory, he went for one of the scientists. A limnologist. Her name was . . ."

"Amelia Lopez," I breathe. "How—how did you know that?"

His glare snaps to me. "How did *you* know that?"

"Yeah," echoes Jav. "How *did* you know that, Riley?"

"Uh . . . Word on the street?" Their expressions call bull. I scowl. "I'm not the one we're supposed to be ganging up on. The Flamer's turning us against each other!"

"Hardly," says the Flamer. "I've barely spoken. You're doing a fine job all by yourselves."

Cooper eyes me suspiciously, but I wear my Normieness like a pudgy shield. I'm no threat to him. He can tell me anything—and, judging by how quickly the words spill from him, he's been dying to talk about this for some time.

"Brightspark's teaching me to fly the Super Squad jet," he says, all in a rush. "I was in the copilot's seat, guiding us up over Andoridge, when I saw the Flamer and a henchman chasing a young woman." He shudders. "*It* happened soon after. Just thinking about it . . . God. I barely slept for a week."

Join the club. "Then what?" I ask.

"All these papers were blowing about, so we got the sidekicks to gather them. Brightspark said the woman must've been one of the Flamer's exes—"

The Flamer scoffs. We ignore him.

"—and he took the papers into evidence. Like I said, I wasn't sleeping, so I started looking into Amelia Lopez instead. Her life, her research . . ." He smacks the cage. "Nothing to do with our villain friend. She shut down her last project at Sunnylake University three months ago. All official lab results destroyed. But some of those papers had test notes on them, dated back to then. Whatever made her abandon the project, she picked it up again." His brows lower. "And the Flamer killed her for it."

Of course he has better contacts than us. Of course he has better sources, concrete proof. He's a Super. Full-on protagonist material. I'm just the NPC in his story. A quirky footnote, a punch line—*that bitch who slapped me with a trash bag*.

My fists tremble at my sides. Jav would tell me to cool it,

since we all want the same thing—like how she can overlook his wandering hands in exchange for information. Ever the opportunist. But I'm not *like her*. I can't forgive and forget just because it's convenient. I don't *like* Cooper, and I *definitely* don't like that he's sticking his fingers in Amelia's secrets.

We don't need a hero to swan in and take over. Us Normies—and Sherman—got it covered.

"Look," I say, squaring up to Cooper. "Your theory doesn't explain what's happening in Bridgebrook."

"Who *cares* what's happening in Bridgebrook?"

"Uh," says Jav, "the people who live there?"

The Flamer chuckles before Cooper can respond. "Look at you. All chasing threads. Can't stand back far enough to see the web."

"So cryptic," I snap. "So *mysterious*. How long did it take you to think of that metaphor?"

Cooper shakes the mesh wall. "And do you care to explain it?"

The Flamer treats us to a beatific smile. "Pass."

I scowl at Cooper. "Can't you beat the answer out of him? That's what you heroes do, right? At least then you'd be good for something."

"Um." Jav holds up a hand. "Maybe let's *not* violate any constitutional human rights . . ."

Cooper at least contemplates my proposal. "Tempting, but I have my career to think about. Still, let's not take it off the table."

"You could always look in the other direction while *I* beat the answer out of him," I suggest, punching my opposite palm.

Jav sighs through her nose. "No one beats answers out of *anybody*."

"You hate it when I have fun."

"I must say," says the Flamer, with another crack of his neck, "this is quite amusing. I haven't had so much entertainment since I burned Miss Lopez."

My mouth snaps shut. Jav's boiler suit squeaks as she crosses her arms. "You could repay us by telling us what we want to know," she says. "What's Project Zero? Were you the villain behind it?"

"I see no reason to acquiesce to the demands of Normies." Another neck crack; a vicious smirk. "In case you have forgotten, I *am* the Ferocious Flamer."

Sherman grimaces. "Did you seriously pick that name?"

His shoulders sink. ". . . No. Wildfire was already taken."

"Tell me about it," mumbles Cooper. "I wanted to be Typhoon."

Jav examines the Flamer over the prow of her nose. "You couldn't even choose your own code name? Damn."

The Flamer's brows lower. "Mind your words, Normie."

"Right—sorry. I should be thanking you, since you just answered my second question." Jav's smile twists into a smirk. "Whoever's actually behind this whole Project Zero thing, I bet *they* got to name themselves. Face it, Flamer. You ain't running this show. Which makes you—what? A sidekick?"

"More like a henchman," I say. I see what Jav's doing.

Steam trickles from his ears. "I am *not* . . . !"

"Maybe antagonizing him isn't the best idea?" says Cooper, but none of us are listening. Hothead with a hot temper. The Flamer really *does* fit the villainous stereotype.

"You're a distraction," I say, stepping in line with Jav. A

glint catches my eye. Her phone, half-obscured by her elbow. Is she filming? The tiny white camera light is hard to see, surrounded as we are by metallic glare. "A fall guy. You kill Dr. Lopez, get yourself arrested for some bullshit with a giant laser. Then there's a villain behind bars, so no Super bothers to look deeper."

Cooper clears his throat. I ignore him. Jav's onto something here: Whether or not Project Zero involves her theories on gentrification, the Flamer isn't the man behind it.

"Doesn't that make you mad?" I ask, trying to get a lock on the Flamer's eyes through the pinholes in the whatever-the-fuckium mesh between us. "Knowing someone else is getting away with all this, while you rot in a cell?"

The Flamer sneers. He blows a stray strand of hair from his forehead but says a grand total of fuck all.

"He won't be here long," says Sherman. "They never are."

"And I bet there's a big payout waiting." Jav studies him, nostrils flared. Breath steams and dies on the wire-threaded visor of her suit. "So, what happens if you fail? What happens if we take all that research Amelia was trying to share with the world and blast it all over the socials? If money's the carrot, what's the stick?"

The Flamer pales. "You can't do that."

"I would say 'watch me,' but you're in a jail cell with no media access." Jav pats the grill of his cage. "You'll just have to wait and see how your friends at the VC react. Unless you give us something we can use to shut Project Zero down."

"Damn." Cooper sounds impressed. "You girls are *good* at this."

"Quiet, please," says Jav sweetly. "I'm working." She returns her glare to the Flamer. "Well?"

For the first time, the Flamer looks at us with no disdain. His brown eyes widen, pleading. We might be Normies, we might be beneath him, but in this moment, we're united against something bigger. Something worse.

"I . . . I can't."

Jav turns away. "Riley, wanna send pics of those papers you got? I can start hyping this online tonight . . ."

"No!" His voice drops to an urgent husk. "You don't *understand*. This thing's too big, don't you see? Connected. What you said about the river, Bridgebrook, everything . . . It's all *connected*."

I wish I could risk opening my suit so I could take a gulp of unfiltered air. Connected. The word shatters in my head, breaking along each harsh consonant. *Con-nec-ted*. The river, the new condos . . . But how? Why?

Connect the dots. Join the lines. Take a step back, put all these disparate fragments of a story into perspective, and what do you get . . . ?

My heart beats double time. You get a whole lot of trouble.

I spin to Jav and Sherman. "Cooper—what sort of pollution are we talking? In Clearwater River?"

His nose puckers. "Untreated sewage, courtesy of the municipal works."

"Shit Creek? Gross. Look at it like this. Some property development firm—"

"Which one?" Sherman jumps in.

"Let's go with Blair Homes. Anyway, they've struck a deal with the VC."

Jav takes over the tale. "So, villains smash up uninsured properties in Bridgebrook, leaving prospective brownfield sites available for upscale building projects."

"All those big words! What she just said!" I grin at Sherman, even at Cooper. "That's enough of a conspiracy, but bear with. They've got a nice gig going on, until something goes wrong up Shit Creek."

"Stormwater," suggests Jav. "In heavy rainfall, the drains overflow. The city's crap winds up in the river."

Cooper frowns. "It's summer. It hasn't rained properly for months."

I wave a hand. "Amelia obviously picked up on something— you wanna mansplain this to the dead limno-whatever?"

"Limnologist," says Jav.

"*Whatever.* Point is, a river full of crap is bad for business! Won't appeal to all those bougie hipster types looking to rent a new condo in Bridgebrook." Possibly one that blossoms from the rubble of 26 Sloan Street. I suppress a shudder at the thought. "So they try to cover it up, right? Until they can sell all the houses. That's why Amelia's research got shut down! She must've figured out the rest of the story." I point at the Flamer. "That's where he came in."

"Makes sense," says Jav, endeavoring to stroke her chin through her visor. "Any of that sound familiar, Flamer?"

The Flamer glares at the floor. "Congratulations. Aren't you clever."

The last thing I feel for him is sympathy. The VC might hold his leash, but he's the one who sent that fireball after Amelia. He's the one who watched her *burn*.

Still, his confirmation is worth his weight in whatever-the-fuckium. This is *it*: a solid theory, and a villain's testimony on top. Do those count in court? Hell if I know—but this should be enough evidence for us to make Project Zero someone else's problem.

Preferably not someone like Cooper. He plucks distractedly at the wires of the Flamer's cage. "I don't know. Something about this doesn't add up . . ."

"Did you miss the last few minutes? Because that was me, adding. With a calculator, 'cause I'm bad at math." I nod to Jav and Sherman, triumphant. "We got what we came for. Let's split."

Cooper doesn't get to cross the finish line first. Just for once, the Normies save the day.

Out we march, leaving Cooper and the Flamer to their macho glare-off. We have to shuck our boiler suits before we exit the Supervillain Detention Center, under the supervision of a gorgeous woman less prone to smiling than Sherman. The guards in this division are all Supers—those who didn't pass the initiation trials or were deemed to be of the wrong temperament for sidekicking. They keep us under careful observation as we pack our suits into their lockers, as if we might smuggle a villain out under our clothes. I'm just glad we aren't told to bend over and cough.

You'd think sussing out the motives behind Project Zero would be something to celebrate, but Jav lapses into a silence thicker than the humid soup outside. She doesn't say a word as we sign out at the main desk, flies bopping lethargically off the reception building's dusty windowpane.

"So," I say as we saunter along the edge of the yard. I try for jovial, falling a few thousand miles short. "Windwalker's still a jerk."

Jav won't look at me. "I'm not thick, Riles."

"Please. Of the many insults I can think up for you, thick is the least accurate."

Jav glares. "You still seem to think it. You couldn't have known about Amelia unless you were at the observatory. And the only people there were scientists, heroes, villains, and *henchmen*."

Shit. She knows.

I got asthma attacks on the regular as a kid—perks of living with a chain smoker. It eased off after I moved in with Hernando, but I never forgot this sense of suffocation, the tightness in my chest, as if ashy hands reached in and gave each of my lungs a squeeze. "You forgot sidekicks."

One look at her face tells me she's not buying it. I sigh.

"Look, I meant to tell you, okay? It just got lost under coming out, and Lyss's birthday, and Project Zero, and everything else that's gone wrong this summer, and . . ."

"Bullshit," Jav decrees. "You didn't *want* to tell me. Because you knew I'd tell you what I'm telling you now, which is that you're making a terrible choice." She waves back at the prison: a vast white building, wings branching toward us like ribs from a giant's spine. "I don't wanna visit you here. Hernando and Lyssa don't, either."

"Jav . . ."

"The hell you thinking? After everything Hernando did for you? How could you throw that away?" She shakes her head, braids slapping her shoulders. "You and me, we don't got dads, Riley. But you found one anyway. I don't get it. I don't know how you could *ever* let him down!"

She doesn't know shit. "Not like I have a choice! You know I'm saving for therapy—"

"And I'm sure *watching people die* really helps. Don't give me no excuses. This is self-destructive and dangerous and *not helping in the slightest*. The hell you trying to prove?"

I jolt back. Jaw clamped. Wishing I had an answer.

"Hold up." Sherman flushes: a rose tint that clings to her bronze cheekbones and the tips of her ears. Her curls droop over her forehead, limp from being stuffed beneath the boiler suit. "We're trying to change shit here."

"*We?* Great. Of course you're a henchman, too." Jav's voice tucks low as the guard buzzes us out, then surges up like white water. "Sunnylake doesn't *need* henching to be more accessible! We need it to *stop*. All of it. No more henchmen, no more villains. *No more Normies getting hurt!*"

"You're not *listening*," I try, but Jav cuts me off.

"No, *you're* not listening. We been friends long enough for me to tell you when you're screwing up your life."

I knew she wouldn't get it. I knew she wouldn't even *try* to understand. "Oh yeah? That's what I'm doing, is it?"

"Damn right," Jav snaps. "Along with the lives of so many more people. There is *always* a choice, Riley. And you chose the summer vacation job where you go around *blowing up the houses* of people like us, so the VC's friends can move in."

That's not fair. It's not, it's *not*. "I'm trying to *stop* Project Zero, in case you haven't noticed."

"Because that absolves you from helping the villains—helping companies like Blair Homes?" Jav's glare could cut steel. "Oh, right. I forgot. Henchmen have *zero* responsibility for all the crap the VC pull in Sunnylake. They're just *following orders*."

"Jav . . ."

"Orders can be misinterpreted." Sherman crosses her arms, shoulders squared off and boxy. "We do what we can."

"While enabling the villains to cause more widespread destruction! Even if you're just doing their filing and—and vacuuming their lairs or whatever!"

Ouch. Jav doesn't know what an accurate summation of our jobs that is.

"That's the point of your protest, isn't it?" Jav continues. "That the city needs henchmen? But it doesn't. Not really. You're just one part of a broken system, and you might think you're helping, but you're just making everything *worse*."

"Yeah," I snap as we near the gates. "Says the girl who wants to go into *government*."

"That's different."

"Is it? Is it really? How come you get to dream about changing things, but I don't?" My anger usually burns fast and loud, sparks and gasoline. This is different. Frigid crystal veins branch through my body. I lean into Jav, our faces close enough to make my heart kick. "Because you're smarter than me? Better than me? Because you're going to Harvard?"

"Riley . . ." Jav's chin softens. Her eyes don't. "That's not what I—"

"Or is it because you're going to turn out *just* like everyone else when they reach the top?" I'm right up in her face now. A fleck of my spit glints back at me from her cheek. I drop my voice, real low, like it's just the two of us. "Give it another few years, Jav. Then you can start a Project Zero of your own."

It's the most cutting thing I can think to say to her. And it gouges deep. I watch those words open Jav, the scalpel slicing down her sternum and across her chest like she's laid out on an autopsy slab. I watch the hurt crack across her face like she's been slapped. And I feel really, *really* fucking powerful.

For all of a second.

Then comes the guilt. A whole landslide's worth, crushing me beneath. Making me wish I could catch every word I just said out of the air and stuff them back into my mouth.

"Yikes," mutters Sherman. Jav—she says nothing at all.

My best friend turns and walks away from me, out through the prison gates. She doesn't look back.

CHAPTER 31

THE RIDE BACK to my house feels too long and too short all at once. Sherman's bike judders over cracks in the battle-scarred road; I clutch the grip bar so tight my knuckles ache.

For once, Sherman is the talkative one. "I'll meet you here tomorrow," she says, pulling off her helmet as I wobble off on legs that feel like skin sacks filled with porridge. "We can join the protest at city hall, then tell one of the councillors about Project Zero. Sound good?"

It's what I've been working toward for the past several weeks. It's the culmination of so much effort and fear. And it's the last thing I want to think about, without Jav by my side.

She must know I didn't mean it. Jav will be the wokest Harvard grad in history. She knows it, I know it, everyone does. So what I said doesn't really matter. Right?

As if. I said what I said, and I wanted to hurt her. For once in my life, I met my goal with resounding success.

"Jones?" Shit, Sherman's staring. "Are you . . . ?"

I clear my throat. "Yeah. Fine. Tomorrow. I, uh . . ." I gesture in the direction of the prison and, no doubt, the metric shit ton of bad memories she has locked up there. "Are *you* . . . ?"

"Yeah," Sherman echoes, glaring through her reflection in her visor. "Fine."

As if. Still, us liars got to stick together.

I trudge into my building, barely waving to the Beauvaises on the stairs. Hernando is doing something miraculous involving Mexican rice, chicken, and jalapeños. He hands me a bowl as soon as I'm through the door. "Good timing, mija." *Mija.* All of it—that name; the rich smell of tomato bouillon; the *thwip* of the messages Lyssa pings to whoever she's arguing with on Discord . . . Home is too vast a concept to fit in that single word. Too vast, even, for Project Zero to take away. I know, deep down, that just this once, always-right Jav got it wrong, wrong, *wrong*.

I joined Hench for myself, but I'm gonna blow the whistle on Project Zero for everyone. For Sloan Street. For Bridgebrook. If my best friend can't see that . . . Well, I've been through a lot lately. Perhaps too much for us to be best friends anymore.

That thought stings as much as when I left Artie's behind me, along with our perfect last summer. I slump on the couch in front of the TV and try to dull all brain activity by watching the ads that play before the news.

Hernando and Lyssa join me once food is ready. No attempt at conversation, which is both gratifying and a cause for concern. We all share the chismosa gene; if I'm *not* fielding questions about my mood, my family must be feeling merciful, which means I look as shit as I feel.

The news starts on the hour. Today's broadcast kicks off with a montage of the pro-march posters that plaster every available surface in Bridgebrook. They drum up support from every industry: retail, construction, sanitation, and far more besides. Some of the Hench posters—black masks with crossed green tape over where the mouths should be—have been ripped down. More remain up, though, daring the world to keep silencing us.

"You joining?" I ask Hernando.

He sieves spiced red broth through his mustache. "Not officially. The Mart don't support this kinda thing."

"You won't go in your warehouse uniform, then?"

He blows too forcefully on his next spoonful. Red-stained rice spatters our carpet. "No. But still, I could always head down on my lunch break. Might see you there."

I get the underlying message. If I'm to attend the protest, he doesn't want me in a mask.

I've disappointed a lot of people this summer. Matias. The Captain. Jav. Yet somehow, despite everything, I've managed to avoid disappointing Hernando. Which makes the fact I fully intend to stand by Sherman tomorrow in Hench uniform really kinda suck.

"Is that your totally-not-a-girlfriend?" asks Lyssa. She waves her spoon at the TV. Sure enough, the story has changed. Now a candid shot of Sherman dominates the screen. The image must be a few years old. You can tell because she looks about fifteen—and because she's mid-battle, wrapped in a blue sidekick's uniform.

The half-chewed chicken sours in my mouth. I remember to shut my jaws before it falls out.

"Turn it up," I croak.

"Remote's in your crack."

"Lyssa!" says Hernando, scandalized. It's gonna take some getting used to, him being home.

"Sofa crack," Lyssa corrects herself. "Damn, Riles, you're dating a *sidekick*?"

No. Sherman's not that, not anymore. And if this is being dug up on TV, it can't be good.

The shake starts in the tips of my fingers. It progresses from there, swarming up my arms. I wedge my hand into the furrow between the cushions, from whence dropped change may never return. It emerges, triumphant, holding the remote. I jab the volume button and the reporter's voice swells like oncoming thunder: ". . . leader of the henchmen, revealed. Sofia Sherman is a D-class Super of a minor Surger/Shaper discipline, capable of freezing one five-by-five circle of air at a distance under twenty yards from her position."

"Sofia," I repeat. That's a pretty name. Weirdly disappointing, to learn it from TV. Guess I hoped she'd be the one to tell me.

"Until her expulsion from the Super Squad," the news anchor continues, "Miss Sherman sidekicked for Crystalis, one of our most promising A-class recruits in the junior division. Crystalis is here with us in the studio to shed further light on Sofia, as well as to discuss her motivations in orchestrating this demonstration and disguising her own identity by pretending to be a powerless citizen—or a 'Normie,' as we are colloquially known. Please, Crystalis—when did you first meet Miss Sherman?"

Our view of the studio reels back. Sherman's face shrinks into blurry insignificance behind the reporter, a fine-boned older man with backswept, graying hair. It's hard to concentrate on him with Crystalis perched on the plush sofa opposite, hands clasped over her crossed thighs.

Perfect, perfect, perfect. The bow of her lips; her long, dark lashes; her catlike green eyes. It's as if whatever created her worked down a checklist. She's even more beautiful than she seemed during that fight at the start of the summer, when Sherman shot her off the Flamer's back. Her hair cascades past her shoulders in lush ginger waves; her skin is pale as cream, smooth as silk. A formfitting yet conservative emerald dress hugs her from bust to knees.

In short, she could step on me and I would say thank you. Though that changes as soon as she opens her mouth.

"Dear Sofia—or *Shieldling*, as we knew her back then. She started training to be my sidekick when she was thirteen. They paired us up in our first class, and we were together for three years. The perfect match."

I can picture it now: Sherman combing snarls from those thick red locks, while perfectly manicured hands pinned her to a chaise longue (whatever one of those might be). The two of them wrapped around each other like cats. Pressed together, parting, pink lips cresting a smooth umber neck . . .

"And for a while," continues Crystalis, while I, overlooked by the world, hug my knees to my chest in mimicry of the hard knot inside me, "I actually believed it."

The reporter makes sympathetic noises. "What went wrong?"

Crystalis sighs, winding her hair together and draping the thick red snake over one shoulder. "It started with the little things. An earring here. A ring there. I suppose she just couldn't help herself, coming from her background."

Somewhere in Bridgebrook, in a house I have yet to visit, Sherman is watching this. What does she think? What does she feel?

I want to message her, insist I'm not listening—but I am, even if I don't believe it. Pegs pin my eyelids. Can't blink, can't move, can't look away.

"It escalated, of course," Crystalis continues. "My father did warn me—these things always do. She got bolder. More *reckless*. I caught her in the act, looting my late grandmother's jewels from my vanity."

"And how did you react?"

"Well, I was angry, of course! But I also felt sorry for the poor girl. She hadn't had the same *opportunities* as me. I gave her a chance to return everything, to apologize." Crystalis actually dabs at her eyes. "Shieldling laughed in my face. Walked out the door. Really, my only regret is that I couldn't reach her. That I couldn't convince her to do the right thing." She sniffles. "I'm a *heroine*. That's *my job*. To inspire people to do *good*. But I failed with Shieldling, and that is my cross to bear."

The knot expands until it chokes me. I want to scream like a preschooler: *Liar, liar, pants on fire!* I've never wished Amelia's fate on anyone so strongly.

Unfortunately, my glare doesn't develop the power to make people spontaneously combust. Crystalis stays right where she is, winning over the population of Sunnylake with each tremble of her underlip, each hitch of her delicate breath.

The reporter leans closer, letting the cameras get a good shot of his kindly eyes. "Was it after this that the . . . altercation happened, with Miss Sherman's father?"

"Yes. She couldn't bear to face me, so she sent him in her place. He proceeded to attack my father, unprovoked. In truth, it only makes me feel sorrier for Shieldling. Imagine what she suffered at home . . ."

This is insane. Sherm loves her dad; I see it in her eyes whenever she saddles up. I know what abused kids look like, thanks to our bathroom mirror. I can't believe he'd ever hurt her.

"My bullshit-o-meter's going off," Lyssa comments. I could bundle my sister in my arms right now and give her a slobbery kiss.

Hernando's eyebrows hurtle toward his hairline. "Come again?"

Lyssa grimaces. "Bull . . . crap?"

"Keep trying."

"*Lie* meter. Sheesh."

Hernando nods to himself, settling back against the sofa's plucked, patchy arm. "Yeah, that's what I thought."

I fumble out my phone. Lyssa's not the only one to dispute this; several tweeters demand Sherman's side of the story. However, the bulk of comments are dedicated to her own lies. Those are the ones using words like *betrayal*.

Super speaking over Normies? Jfc not surprised typical Powered Privilege
She faked being a Normie for sympathy points? Gross
Canceled. Canceled, canceled, canceled.

Shrug emojis, eye rolls. Dismissal. They shrink down everything Sherman, *my* Sherman, is. Reducing her to a single mistake.

Hernando's beautiful rice bubbles at the back of my throat. I shove my unfinished bowl to Lyssa.

"Sorry," I choke. "Gotta go."

CHAPTER 32

MINOR FLAW IN my plan: I don't know where Sherman lives. As she's not answering my messages, I suck it up and call the Crow Building. McCarthy obviously gives as little of a damn about our personal information as the average social media site, because she tells me straight away. The address is on the other side of Bridgebrook. I mutter several expletives of my own and start walking.

Strolling solo through the rougher streets in my district at night isn't an instakill like bougie folk make out, but it's not recommended, either. Luckily, I carry a portable deterrent. I activate my Hench uniform, and after that, no one dares look twice.

I stride along like I'm on a vital mission (i.e., reporting back to the VC, or fetching my client a smoked salmon and avocado on rye). It still takes an hour to reach Sherman, by which point my body is a network of sweaty canals. Rivulets gather in the creases of my armpits and my tummy rolls.

Bridgebrook delves into the darkest part of the night. The sky is a black blindfold pulled tight over the world. I double-check McCarthy's message to make sure I have the right door. Then I turn off my uniform and knock.

"Sherm! Sherman, it's Jones!"

The town houses are narrow here, made of red brick rather

than cement slabs and crammed together like Lego blocks. But it's still a whole-ass two-story end-of-row house, as opposed to our teensy apartment. Driveway out front, garage and all. This used to pass for fancy in Bridgebrook, before Project Zero showed us what rich *really* looks like.

The door opens, but Sherman isn't on the other side. I realize I've been hollering away in the middle of the night, for the whole block to gawk at—aka, not how I planned on introducing myself to my girl-who's-a-friend's dad.

The man before me must be forty plus, silver threading his curly black hair. He stares at me for a long moment, brows scrunched, before cracking a grin. An oil smudge adorns his nose; he wipes more off his hands on a stained scrap of chamois leather before easing the door farther open and gesturing me inside.

"Hi, Jones," he says in a soft, lilting accent. "You're Sofia's friend, from work?"

Sherman mentioned me to her parents? Warmth tickles my belly. "Uh, yeah. Nice to meet you. Sorry for showing up so late . . ."

"No need to apologize. Beatriz is working night shift at the hospital; not like anyone was asleep."

I shuffle over the threshold. Sherman's house is narrow and neat—except for the garage, visible through the open-propped side door, which doubles as an automobile graveyard. The rear wall is made up of tool racks, subdivided by masking tape. Disemboweled engine parts leak black slime onto the concrete floor, while an orange bike stands on a lift, the concertina crossbars extended, elevating it two feet into the air. A radio pumps out a bop in Spanish, resting on a rollable mechanic's cart. The caustic smell of oil and varnish shoots up my nose like I've eaten a spoonful of wasabi.

"Glad to hear it, sir."

Sherman's dad waves a hand. "Please, call me Luis." He must notice me snooping, because he nods to the familiar blue Harley, snoozing just inside the garage door. "You've already met the third great love of my life, yes? After my beautiful wife and my beautiful daughter?"

Aw. That's cute. I guess he doesn't know his beautiful daughter just became Normie Enemy Number One. "Yeah. Sherman—Sofia—said you guys fixed the bike up?"

Luis's smile goes a little dreamy. "Soon, I'll be allowed to ride her as far as I like again. Until then, I trust Sofia with her as much as I trust her with Sofia." He tosses his greasy rag over his shoulder. "And yes, we fixed her—you should've seen her when I first got my hands on her! Had to tear down the transmission and engine completely. Rust in the fuel tank—hell, all over. Needed a full-body sand-down, and new chain and sprockets, of course; plus Sofia and I had to drain out the brakes, refill and bleed . . ."

Oh God, the bike gobbledygook is hereditary. I slip off my shoes, lining them beside Sherman's Docs on the mat. "Great father-daughter bonding time, huh?"

Luis cuts himself off with a chuckle. "Sorry. No workshop talk with new people—Beatriz has to keep reminding me."

"Fight-or-flight instinct kicks in if I have to make conversation about mechanics or sportsball. Nothing personal."

Luis beams. "You're funny, eh? Just as Sofia says." Then, while I'm reeling from the fact that Sherman doesn't just *talk* about me with her dad but apparently *compliments my sense of humor*—"It's like learning a second language. Like Spanish. You ever want to become conversational, you swing by one weekend. I have an old Yamaha to tune up—easy stuff, good for beginners."

"Wow. That's really kind, but . . ." I stop myself. I don't actually want to turn him down. This whole bike business obviously means a lot to Sherman. And I can't deny the appeal of the idea: us working on a project together, building something rather than helping the villains blast it apart. "I'd like that? I think." I glance again at the garage, like Sherman might materialize from a stack of old mufflers. "But right now, I need to talk to Sofia."

Luis must pick up from my tone that this isn't a social visit. He doesn't launch an inquisition, just steps around me to lock up, calling through the house. My Spanish is garbage, despite Hernando's best efforts, but I still catch a few words—*tu amiga*—before Luis nods me up the stairs. "Top hall then, Jones. Last door."

"Yes, sir. Luis. Thank you."

I hurry to the top landing, tap my knuckles on Sherman's door, then edge it open when I hear no reply. It sticks on a sports bra, discarded on the threadbare carpet, which might fit around one of my arms. I toe it out the way. "Sherm?"

If I had to picture Sherman's room, I'd envision something neat but gloomy, like the aesthetic posts you get when you type "gray" into Pinterest. Reality is way more colorful. Her walls are stenciled with faded flower patterns and plushies jostle for space on her bed. A cape-size red-and-black flag—Angolan, I guess—hangs from the back of the door, and a little santo figurine props up the books on her shelf. A seven-horned papier-mâché carnival mask leers down from the top of the wardrobe. The floor is a soup of discarded outfits: all variations on the theme of ab-flashing crops and baggy, zipper-laden pants.

I pad farther into the room—only to trip on a snake nest of discarded belts. "Girl, you need to welcome our Lord and Savior Marie Kondo into your life."

Sherman doesn't respond. She sits cross-legged on her bed, facing away from me. I step closer, frowning. Her earphones are jammed deep. The bops and bounces of music—kuduro?—must be battering her brain like a swarm of angry bees. She must not have heard Luis yell.

I don't wanna startle her, so I creep along the wall until she can see me—whereupon her eyes widen and she rips out both buds at once. "Jones? Why're you here?"

"Was in the neighborhood." I pull at my sticky collar. "Okay, I lie. I power-walked over from Sloan Street, which is why I'm currently drowning in my own sweat. You're welcome, by the way." She continues to stare. I resist the urge to scratch like a monkey, though the moisture under my arms is drying to a tacky crust. "Did you, uh, see?"

The beam of a passing car streaks through the gash in her curtains, illuminating her face in a ghostly flash of light. Her tear-streaked face.

I slowly slump beside her. "Well, damn."

Sherman hugs a pillow to her chest, tight enough that her forearm muscles bunch. I didn't know girls *got* forearm muscles. Might be a bad time to appreciate that, as Sherm isn't embracing so much as *crushing* the pillow. Seriously, she squeezes any tighter, it's gonna pop.

"Why're you here?" she asks again.

"I came to see if you were okay. If you needed anything, if I could help."

Her red-rimmed eyes won't latch onto me. "What can *you* do, huh?"

Why's she gotta say it like that? "I dunno."

"Then maybe you shouldn't be here at all."

Ouch. She can't mean that. She's just hurting. Lashing out. That's all. Her music pounds away, quiet but relentless, shaking apart my thoughts. When she pauses the Spotify playlist, the gaping silence is worse.

I have to break it: "Sherm . . ."

"Tell me you didn't believe her," mumbles Sherman, into her pillowcase.

"What?"

"Crystalis." Sherman spits her name like it scalds her mouth. "Tell me you didn't believe the crap she said about me."

"Not a word." When I touch her, running my nails feather-light up the back of her arm, she leans into the contact, not away. "What happened between you and her? I mean, you don't have to tell me, but . . ." I remember a night not too long ago, after I saw Hernando at the warehouse and had the bottom ripped out of my world. "Talking about your feelings—sometimes it helps."

I figure Sherman won't take me up on the offer. But then she rubs under her nose, makes this wet slurp of a snort. "We were like, fifteen, right? And Crystalis could always be cruel. But one time, a week before our initiation, I saw her . . ."

The words trail away. I jostle her arm. "Sherman, what?"

"It was a night job." Sherman stares straight at her carnival mask, though I get the sense she doesn't really see it. "We were shadowing a bunch of heroes, but we got separated. The two of us were first on the scene after Supremia shorted a substation. She'd already run off, along with another villain—some B-class Shaper, can't remember his name. If Crystalis and I could chase them down, it'd look real good for us."

I nod. Sounds like the sort of chance all pre-initiation Supers snap at: the opportunity to prove themselves before the world in the most dramatic way possible.

"Only problem was our witness. Some old Normie off the streets. He wasn't being helpful. He kept swearing at us, asking whether we were gonna turn the lights back on, and I . . ." She shuts her eyes. "I guess Crystalis got tired of it."

A part of me doesn't want to know. But I have to. "What did she do?"

"She froze his leg." Sherman's nails dig into the pillowcase. "Like, the blood *inside* it. He hadn't done anything—he was just being rude, y'know? And she did *that* . . . And I could tell, just from how she was smiling, that she thought it was justified."

Holy *shit*. "That's fucked."

Sherman continues like she didn't hear. Like she's back there, on a midnight street, blown bulbs on every streetlamp, broken wires sparking in the dark. "Of course, the guy started screaming. Didn't take long for Crystalis to realize how badly she'd screwed up." She gives this wrecked little laugh. "Or how scared I was. Last I heard before I got the hell away, she was offering the dude a thousand dollars to blame it on the villain. She must've sold some jewelry to pay him off. Because when her parents found out and got pissed . . ." She hunches around her pillow like she's winded, a blow to the solar plexus from years past. "Crystalis knew I was freaking out, that I might snitch on her. So she told them I'd been stealing."

For every sentence, she hammers a new crack into my heart. "She lied."

"Not according to the world. She's daddy's precious darling. Only her daddy started on mine when we went around to get my stuff. I'd been staying for the weekend. Me and her . . ."

She trails. I don't push. A part of me, however selfishly, doesn't want that confirmation. I don't want to know that her last girlfriend was a Super: so much more powerful, more beautiful than I'll ever be.

Still, I only *daydream* about skinning assholes with potato peelers. I'd never actually *do* it. Guess I got that going for me.

"I should've gone alone," Sherman says. "I *wish* I'd gone alone. But I was seriously freaked out, after what I saw. My dad insisted. He was trying to protect me. He's *always* trying to protect me." Her voice quakes. Even with all her union talks, I guess she's not used to saying so much in one sitting. When she scrubs under her nose again, she leaves a shiny streak on her arm. "He told Crystalis's dad exactly what his daughter did. Crystalis's dad called him a liar, reminded Pops he was a police officer. Said he'd press charges if he kept talking. He—he accused my pops of being a crappy father and worse. Called him every name in the book, trying to antagonize him. But Pops didn't punch him. He was too smart for that." She chokes, just a little, on her next words: "He didn't punch him till he started threatening me."

"Damn," I croak.

"I used to try so hard, y'know?" She rams her knuckles into her mattress, grinding there like she's picturing Crystalis's face. "I wanted to be the *good girl*. The Sidekick who set an example for Bridgebrook. Who proved we could all make it, if we followed the rules, smiled pretty, and *tried*." Mopping her eyes on the back of her hand is about as useful as approaching a busted hydrant armed with a Kleenex. "But after the shit Crystalis got away with? I realized. No matter how good my grades, or how well I *enunciated* my *fucking consonants*, I was always gonna be expendable to people like *her*."

Just like a henchman. Suddenly, her job switch makes a lot more sense.

I wonder what Jav'd say if she was here. Probably something about how she still thinks you can change the world if you reach the top of it, even if you gotta crawl the whole way. I want to believe that, too, but I recall the Captain's words about using the structures of society as your climbing apparatus. Once you're up there, once you've made it, you're stuck. If you dismantle that scaffold, it all comes crashing down, burying you alive. Maybe we'd have more chance of changing shit if we burned it all from the bottom.

Silly thought. It'd make a cute Twitter post, but it doesn't hold an answer.

"I'm sorry," I whisper.

"Why?" Sherman's snort sounds dangerously wet. "You weren't there."

It's true. I didn't know her then and couldn't have helped if I did. Just a normal Normie. Nothing more.

But, I figure, as I shuffle through her stew of unwashed sheets, a Normie can still slide her hand up to cradle Sherman's clammy cheek. A Normie can still press our foreheads together, Sherman's springy curls tangling into my bangs.

A Normie can hold her there, as her deep breaths fracture into heaving sobs, hitching gasps, silence. And, once it's all over, a Normie can close the distance between our damp, quivering lips.

For the next five seconds, I know nothing but that pressure. Sherman's face is 80 percent tears and snot right now, but I couldn't care less. Not with her lips on mine—lips I've been dreaming about for weeks. I've stared at them enough to know their shape, their tapered edges and full bow, the ease with which they form a frown. But that's nothing compared to this: to discovering how soft they are, how every little chap catches like it's trying to hold me close . . .

She flinches away. I stay frozen, heart thumping. But after that first shocked moment, Sherman lets out this low, *agonized* whimper and throws herself against me like she's starving, arms locked tight around my neck.

My mind circles every point of contact with a pink glitter gel pen and surrounds them with love hearts, one for each of the butterflies in my belly. A series of snapshots: Sherman's tongue painting a slick signature, tagging her name on my lips. Her shaky grunt of approval when I part them, let her in. Her legs, split around my broad waist. Her lean weight on my lap, anchoring me down.

What's time? What's Sunnylake City? What's the world?

Softness slides through me like I've swallowed velvet. So long as I'm kissing Sherman, I don't know the answer to those questions, and I sure as hell don't care. So long as she cards my hair—a little lank and in need of a wash—while my thumb draws circles at that crux where her thigh joins her body, gentle at first but with increasing desperation. So long as—

Sherman pulls away. Disentangles, disengages, scooting to the far side of the bed.

"I'm sorry," she says.

I reach after her. My fingers curl on air. "Kinda copying me, from when I said I was sorry earlier."

"Jones." She swings her legs over the side of the bed and sits, slouched so even her flat tummy pooches over the band of her jeans. "I can't do this."

"What?" Kiss me?

"The strike," Sherman elaborates. "The march. Delmar and Max, they're right." They must've left her a message. She sniffles like she's succumbed to a summer cold (impossible; Supers don't get sick). "I'm not the leader the henchmen need."

I can't lick my lips in case I clean the taste of her away. That lovely velvet in my lungs chokes me, just a little. "Anyone with functioning eyeballs can see Crystalis lied—"

"It's not about Crystalis. It's about *me*. Who I am. *What* I am." Tears shimmer on her lashes, and it's unfair how even at her lowest, she's beautiful. "I told the other henchmen to join the revolution or get out of the way. Now it's my turn. I'm getting out of the way."

I can't believe I'm hearing this. "Yeah, you messed up, bigtime. But sitting on your ass and feeling guilty? How does that help *anyone*?"

"Not sitting on my ass. *Staying in my lane.*" Sherman's nails dig into her clasped hands. "I won't be another asshole Super who steals the spotlight. If I show my face tomorrow, it'll get us attention for all the wrong reasons. I gotta stay here, stay quiet. So I can't hold you back."

She sounds so sure; that's the worst thing. "I'm not letting you abandon everything you've worked for, just because some trolls on Twitter—"

"They're not trolls. They're people. Angry people, who I did wrong by." Sherman's eyes are bright as the studs in her brows and nose. "Nobody wants me at that protest. I'm done with Hench. With the protest, the strike, everything."

This is wild. I get freaking out over the Twitter dogpiling, but quitting entirely? She poured so much into this demonstration. Giving up over backlash from her fuckup makes it seem like . . .

Well, like her support was conditional on all of us looking up to her. Like it never mattered that much to begin with.

"You can still come with me," I try. "To city hall. To expose Project Zero."

"And pass the protest? I don't think I can." More like her pride won't let her. She wipes her face with trembling hands. "I'm sorry for letting you down, Jones. Really."

That apology strikes me square in the chest. Not because she doesn't mean it (I know she always does). But because it's so. Fucking. *Useless.*

After everything we've gone through—the battle at the observatory, facing off against the Flamer—Sherman wants to walk away. Like she doesn't care about my home, or *every other* home with a target on it.

So, she screwed up and people are pissed. Boo-hoo. She can lie low, wait for it to blow over. They're not gonna hunt her down, sic a villain on her or destroy her house. But I don't get the choice to ignore what's happening to poor Normies in my district, on account of being one. And I think—hope—I wouldn't take that option, even if I could.

I point between us, fighting to keep a steady voice. "What about *this*?" Surely our kiss counted for something?

Sherman makes saying fuck all into an art form. Guess that's a no.

I shove to my feet. "How can you talk like that? Like this isn't important?"

She has the audacity to look wounded. "Jones?"

"Did it ever matter? Any of it—you telling me to stand by you, the protest, Project Zero? Or did you only ever care about proving you weren't just some heroine's sidekick? About *getting back at your ex?*"

Sherman winces like my words are bullets, ripping her apart. Maybe they are—especially after that news report. But just because Crystalis massaged salt into Sherman's old wounds, it doesn't make Sherman any less wrong. She shouldn't look the other way. Not while my city, *our* city, burns.

When I lick my lips, I can't taste our kiss. Just my own stale spit.

It aches to leave her there, cheeks frosted with tears. But not nearly as much as it would to stay. I storm away from Sherman, down the stairs, past Luis, out into the night.

CHAPTER 33

I TURN ON my hologram as soon as I round the corner. Hiding my face, my hot, stinging eyes. Melding into the shadows. Anger pulses against the shell of my skull like it's trying to hatch. Our broken kiss burns my tongue. My first ever. Perhaps my last, since no other volunteers have made themselves known, and Project Zero has already gotten one associated Normie murdered.

I can't even celebrate that I finally made out with a girl. Even if I felt anything other than numb, who would I tell? Jav?

I want to, I need to. But she's left me, too.

Fuck this entire summer. The earth keeps crumbling out from under me. Every time I think I've found a stable patch of ground—Hernando's apartment, my summer job, my best friend, *Sherman*—it gets wrenched away. I'm running out of places to put my next step.

I keep walking anyway, but my ribs are barbed wire. Each breath tears deeper into my lungs. The sidewalk wobbles under my feet like it's about to cave in, and my chest hurts and my stomach hurts and my eyes are blurring over and everything blurs like I'm seeing through smoke haze—

In-two-three-four-five, I repeat to myself. *Out.*

I glare at the sky. Bridgebrook's backstreets bleed shadow. The skyline is a snaggletoothed smile of terraces and towers, new builds rearing high above the old.

In-two-three-four-five. Out.

I walk. Timing my breath to the steps:

In-two-three-four-five. Out.

No thoughts about where I'm headed. No thoughts of what I've left behind me.

I pass cleaners heading out for the night shift, construction workers in high-vis jackets, clubbers, randos on the street. All give me a wide berth. Let them. I'm walking the city. Breathing it in.

In-two-three-four-five. Hold.

I stop before a yellow-and-black line of tape that cordons off a pile of rubble. A pile of rubble that used to be the Szechuan Sizzler. I'm near Artie's, where the main Bridgebrook shopping quadrangle sheds its poverty-pitted past like flakes of old skin. The demolition site is floodlit, ringed in mesh fencing. A glossy sign rests against the scorched remnants of the restaurant's front wall. It shows a diverse family of diners, grinning like they're paid by the smile. They're seated in a chic bistro, pendulous lighting and chevron-patterned linoleum on the walls.

TO BRIGHTER FUTURES, the sign reads. MELBA DEVELOPMENTS. The dad is raising a toast.

I release my breath when my head starts to spin, tucking into a ball, crouched on the sidewalk where I first saw Cooper pose for the cameras. I stare up at that sign. Absorbing every detail. The crisp edges of the font. The wine in the uplifted glass (too red, like blood in a Tarantino movie). I wonder how many letters Melba Developments bothered to send before they hired the Flamer.

How can Sherman turn her back on this? I want to be

furious on behalf of every henchman she's disappointed and the hundred-thousand-odd residents of Bridgebrook beside. But my thoughts boil down to a singular point: *How can she turn her back on* me?

In-two-three-four-five. When you feel a panic attack coming on, you're supposed to remind yourself it's a temporary state of existence; that this cramp of your diaphragm, the crush of your rib cage around your organs, will pass. You're supposed to sit back and relax, assured that life will continue on the far side.

But I don't want a life that villains might smash up at any moment, just so someone far richer than I'll ever be can add another zero to their savings account. I deserve better than that. We all do.

I uncurl slowly and stand slower still. I glare through the faint sepia tint of my projected mask until the streetlights blur. Until the smashed bricks and snapped wires meld into a river of destruction, dark as Clearwater.

Just one Normie, versus a bunch of villains in suits as well as spandex. I don't know if I can do this without Sherman. Without Jav. I don't know if I can beat Blair Homes and the Villain Council and everyone else who thought it was *easier* to kill Amelia than fix one of the thousand things wrong with my city. But I'll never, ever forgive myself if I don't try.

CHAPTER 34

THE PLAN: CATCH the bus to city hall tomorrow morning, present my case to whoever will listen. Don't think about Sherman.

Listen to demonstration outside. Keep not thinking about Sherman.

Have Mayor Darcy congratulate me on my investigative skills, not thinking about Sherman the whole while.

Sit for interviews, receive a medal (that might be a bit farfetched, but hey, I can dream). Continue to not think about Sherman, ad infinitum.

The reality: Get waylaid by Lyssa as I unlock the door—while thinking about Sherman.

"Where you going?"

"Out."

She clasps her hands, flutters her eyelashes. "With your giiiiiiirlfriend?"

Any other day, I'd groan and elbow her. Any other day, Sherman wouldn't have summoned her hissing, bitter ice shield on the inside of my chest.

"No," I mutter, wrenching the door chain from its latch.

"Hey." Lyssa pokes my shoulder. "Riles. Monosyllables are my thing. Quit copying me."

"No," I say again, just to be an ass. When I step into the

hallway, Lyssa trails after me. "*No*. Get back inside. You're not coming."

Lyssa pays me as much attention as usual. "Last night, on the news . . . Was that really her? She's really a sidekick?"

"*Was*," I correct her. "Still not coming, Lyss."

Lyssa only looks like Mom when she smirks. It's in the way her nose wrinkles up. Makes my guts twist, though I try not to let on. She leans against the whitewashed bricks, legs crossed, sunflower shin over brown. "You know I'm just gonna follow you, right?"

"Which is very sweet and noble and sisterly of you, but *like hell*."

"I'm not trying to be sweet and noble and sisterly! I've just never been to a protest before." She locks up after us. Her key fob has a plastic Windwalker charm, complete with teeny blond quiff. "That *is* where you're going. Right?"

I don't want to put Lyssa in danger. But equally, I can't worry about where she is and what she's doing. Not today, not with so much at stake.

I groan, running my fingers through my lank hair, scraping it back from my face. ". . . Stay close." She beams, wrenching her key out before grabbing my arm, tucking against my side. "Yeah, not that close. I don't want folks to know I'm babysitting."

"Ass."

"Goober." I shove her. She shoves back, then stamps on my foot with her prosthetic foot ("Ow, ow!") and, for a while at least, life returns to a semblance of normal.

We reach the bus stop in record time. No sign of Sherman.

That pangs, the knife in my back twisting deeper. I cover my nose to block the worst of the diesel fumes as I pay our fare. Hopefully, the driver isn't offended. Buses are *tolerable* on the vehicles-likely-to-cause-panic-attacks scale, but that don't make it a happy experience. It becomes less happy still when I spot an unexpected face among the passengers.

Jav is perched on the big back seat. Her dark eyes clock me, then widen to match my own. Guess neither of us thought the other would show.

Awkward. My choices range between confronting her like a sensible, mature seventeen-year-old or sulking by myself on the front seats. I'm veering toward the second option, but Lyssa hurries up the aisle, flowery leg collecting stares from several passengers. I follow at a slower pace, glaring at anyone who doesn't look away.

Both of us jump when the engine starts. Jav scoots so Lyssa can plop down beside her rather than on top. A duffel hangs off her skinny shoulder, the outline of a rectangular folder inside.

"Hey," I mutter, squeezing past to flump on Lyssa's far side, as far from Jav as I can get.

"Wow," whispers Lyssa, when Jav doesn't reply. "Cold."

Jav folds her arms, hugging her bag to her chest. "Why you here, Lyssa?"

"To annoy Riley, mostly."

Jav still won't look at me. "Yeah, I respect that."

They pause, like this is a sitcom and they're waiting for my laugh track. I just press my cheek to the warm, fly-splattered window, gazing along the street as the bus door seals in a gush of sticky summer air.

I could tell Jav to get off again, that I don't want her help. But there's a difference between *want* and *need*. And pissed as I am, bristling from last night's stand-off with Sherman, I know I'd regret it.

Jav's good at pitching an argument. She can persuade everyone at city hall that our theories aren't the result of a night spent huffing whippits from empty whipped-cream tins. I meant what I told Sherman, about Project Zero being the most important thing right now. How hypocritical would it be if I let beef with my ex-bestie get in the way?

That beef's still there, though. Whole bull's worth.

I should apologize, I know, but Jav owes me something, too. Why can't she admit it? That just this once, she was wrong?

Our bus climbs the humpbacked suspension bridge, over the marina with its bright white sails and the constant chime of tackle.

"I'm sorry," Jav blurts as we rumble over Clearwater's stinking expanse. Then, before I can hope—"'Bout your friend, I mean. Sofia Sherman."

Not the sorry I'm after. I slouch, folding my arms. "You retweet every callout post you see."

"Yeah, well." Jav winds her thick braids between her fingers. "Feels different, when you know the person. Don't think we got the whole story, is all."

She's right—but that's not my tale to tell. Anyway, after last night, pitying Sherman's at the bottom of my to-do list.

We go back to glaring out the window. If I focus on the passing city, the seat rumbling under my ass, I can almost pretend I'm on a moving massage chair. Or back on Sherman's bike.

Downtown bulges up in a forest of glass and steel. The bus cuts between the towers, sunbeams pinging around us like balls in an old arcade game. It seems like every stop lets on a new load of tourists fresh from the lakefront. My nostrils clog with the oily odor of sunscreen and patent leather sandal.

Lyssa's savvy enough to suss out that Jav isn't in my good books. She abides by the age-old laws of sisterly loyalty and doesn't force conversation. The three of us scowl at our phones in silence until the bus pulls up outside city hall.

While Bridgebrook gets carved up like a jacked car in the chop shop, a patchwork of old and new, this is the sector of Sunnylake everyone wants to immortalize. A monument to Mayor Darcy's vision for our city, a shiny edifice that oozes dollar bills. Souvenir shops jostle on all sides. Selfie sticks bristle like masts at the marina. City hall—a long box striped with pillars—multiplies across a million batch-printed postcards and I <3 SUNNYLAKE tees.

But though a few tour groups amble around, they're not the majority. I'm terrible at guesstimation, but I'd say over five hundred protesters have gathered, though the demonstration won't kick off for an hour. They wear familiar uniforms: red tabards from a local mini-mart, the high-vis jackets of garbage men. As we walk toward city hall, I spot the deep green of a Hench suit, hear the scratch of markers over a makeshift cardboard sign. The heady reek of Sharpies mingles with cheap coffee and anticipation. The thrill of making a change.

I hope to make a bigger one. I elbow my way through the crowd, Jav and Lyssa close behind.

We reach the steps with minimal casualties, although my feet have been trodden on so often they're practically two-dimensional. Arrows direct wheelchair users along a dank side alley. I guess the planning office decided a ramp out front was too much of an eyesore. Lyssa bounds up the stairs, the casing of her new shin catching the sun.

"Aren't you guys joining the protest?" she asks once we're at the top, thumbing back over her shoulder.

I make accidental eye contact with Jav. "Nope. We got other business."

A row of Normie cops stand sentinel under the pillars of the hall, watching the protestors prepare. I expect them to stop us, or at least ask what we're doing—but they move aside, letting us pass.

Weird. Growing up in Bridgebrook has given me an instinctive freeze-or-flight reaction to flashing blue lights. Still, I ain't complaining.

The foyer smacks us with conditioned air. Jav adjusts her braids, straightens her skirt, and struts to the reception desk. She uses her Ralbury voice to address the guy behind the counter. From their conversation, she must've called ahead, set up a meeting with some environment-department official called Mr. Caluna.

She's handling this sensibly as ever. Fondness bubbles through me, until I remember we're mad at each other.

The receptionist rattles off a floor number and an office, buzzing us past security without bothering to search our bags. We thank him and head off to save our city. No heroes required.

First thing that strikes me about city hall? It's *nice*. Walls lined with gleaming russet wood like an old colonial house, fancy lights that remind me of the chandeliers in the Crow Building's basement. Maybe they shop at the same department stores.

Second thing: It's *empty*.

"Not just me," whispers Lyss as we step out of the elevator, onto the third floor. We have yet to pass a single person. "This is creepy, right?"

"Everyone's at lunch," says Jav. "Got off early, before the protest starts."

We pass the security office—also abandoned, though the guard's coffee cup steams on the edge of his desk. A long line of identical doors later, we arrive at one whose placard reads MR. JOHANNES CALUNA // DEPARTMENT OF ENVIRONMENTAL HEALTH.

I take opening duties upon myself, as Jav's engaged in a last-minute dress rehearsal, mumbling her key points under her breath. The door is the sealable fireproof sort that makes you picture what'd happen to your fingers if they got caught in the hinge. The underside drags on the fluffy carpet.

Mr. Caluna's office seems designed to muffle his visitors. The carpet eats the sound of our steps, while abstract canvases blare from the wall (one of which I swear is a blown-up version of my first potato painting from kindergarten). The black, cycloptic eye of a camera keeps watch from above.

It doesn't seem like the sort of place you come to be heard. Which makes it surprising that Mr. Caluna isn't sitting behind the desk.

Mayor June Darcy is.

CHAPTER 35

I'VE NEVER SEEN her in person. Like the Super Squad, our mayor stays on the other side of the TV screen. Most of the time, her appearances feature her getting dragged off screaming by the VC or returned, ruffled and rumpled, in the arms of a beaming hero. Having all five-three-in-two-inch-heels of her sitting within poking distance? Quite the trip.

I do the natural thing and blurt, "Holy shit!"

Mayor Darcy takes my unorthodox salutation in stride. She stands, presenting me with a soft hand that smells of lavender moisturizer. She's a plump white woman, about forty, with wavy, shoulder-length blonde hair and cheeks a chipmunk would die for. Another girl might call her motherly, but from me, that's hardly a compliment.

"Good morning," she says. I half expect her to break out the milk and cookies. Or for Supremia to bust through the wall and take all of us hostage. Honestly, this could go either way. "You must be Javira."

"Uh . . . Riley Jones. Here for emotional support." I wave at Jav. "She's Javira, aka the mastermind."

Mayor Darcy diverts her hand accordingly. "Well, Miss Mastermind, it's a pleasure to meet you. Mr. Caluna can't be with us, but I was fascinated by what you had to say to him."

Me and Jav exchange glances. I see my own confusion

reflected in her eyes. I'm flattered the mayor would take time to talk to us about Project Zero, but I figured she'd be busy stopping world hunger or whatever. Still, we *have* uncovered a conspiracy at the heart of her city. Who knows? Maybe my fantasy about medals isn't so far off the mark.

Lyssa slings herself on one of the two free office chairs and digs out her phone. Mayor Darcy's eyes widen. "I'm sorry, but I'll need to confiscate that for the duration of our meeting."

Jav sits, too, frowning. "I have evidence on mine. Caught our whole conversation with the Flamer. Plus, I was hoping to record your comments for my podcast . . ."

"I'm sorry—I'd rather hear what you have to say first. Don't worry, Javira; you can be my nine o'clock tomorrow morning. Official interview, everything on the record."

Jav's eyes glitter like we're at the Academy Awards and her directorial debut documentary is up for nomination. Lyssa isn't such an easy sell.

"Can I go outside, then?" she asks, pushing up, careful to center her mass over both legs. "I ain't sitting here while you talk about boring shit. Not without my phone."

I can't believe her sometimes. "You realize this boring shit's important?"

"You realize I don't care?"

Ugh. She'll only be a liability, asking endless questions about what's going on. I warn her to stay near city hall and describe what I'll do to her if she doesn't (censored slightly, for Mayor Darcy's delicate ears). We wait for the door to oh-so-slowly swish shut behind her.

The mayor leans back on Mr. Caluna's plush leather chair. Her smile is smaller now. Cozier. Like we're painting each other's nails on a girl's night out. Makes me feel more at home in this big fancy room, in this big fancy building where girls like us don't belong.

"Your friend isn't involved in this?" she asks.

"Nope. And she's, uh, my sister, actually."

The mayor doesn't trip on the "but you look nothing alike!" trap. "Well, I envy her carefree attitude." She extracts Mr. Caluna's in-box tray from its wire frame. "Your phones, please?"

Evidently, when villains abduct you every other week, you get obsessive about security. Me and Jav's phones join the mayor's snazzy custom model. Then Jav opens her file and scoots the first grainy diagram of Bridgebrook—courtesy of the dodgy library printer—across the desk.

"We have reason to believe," she starts, in her best Ralbury voice, "that the Villain Council is colluding with several of the city's leading real estate agents . . ."

And away she goes, explaining how her district, our district, is under siege.

The mayor doesn't interrupt or tell us we're paranoid. She just nods, gasping at the appropriate moments, studying the charts and statistics Jav provides with as much earnestness as Jav herself.

Jav likes being listened to. She draws herself up straighter, raising her voice. "And then we have Dr. Lopez."

I shut my eyes. It's been almost a month since Amelia died, and it simultaneously feels like forever ago and yesterday.

I hope I'm doing what she wanted. I hope this is enough. And whatever my doubts regarding God, Jesus, and the life ever after, I hope that somewhere, somehow, she's at peace.

"I'm sorry," says Mayor Darcy. "Who?"

"Dr. Amelia Lopez." Jav smooths the printed obituary on the desk, a tiny portrait of Amelia beaming at us from the top left corner. Her eyes look so much brighter than when I met her. Before Project Zero ate her alive. "A limnologist, killed during the Flamer's attack on Andoridge Observatory. We managed to visit the Flamer in prison. He revealed that he was hired to take her out because of her research into rising pollution levels in Clearwater River." She nods to her phone. "I, uh, kept it recording during our conversation. Everything's a bit muffled, but you can hear the incriminating bits."

I grin. That's my bestie for you.

Y'know. If that's something she still wants to be, after this. If I still want her to be.

The mayor scoots to the edge of her seat. "What about Miss Lopez's research? Do you have this with you?"

Jav rummages through her duffel. "'Fraid not. It's hard to piece everything together: Sunnylake University dropped the project and all records were wiped. But I believe some files are at the Super Squad HQ. We've spoken to Windwalker, who has reason to believe Dr. Lopez's study focused on pollution from the Bridgebrook sewage works—I'm sure he'll corroborate our story. For now . . ." Jav slaps a folder down on the desk. "Here's my cross-comparison of VC attacks in Bridgebrook, as compared to other districts in the city, along with the concurrent increase of new, more expensive housing and retail units that take their place. Obviously, this could be coincidental. Two sets of statistics rising in tandem doesn't necessitate a correlation."

She's using loads of big words. She does that when she's nervous. I give up on trying to follow what she's saying. It's easier to squeeze her knee, over her leggings. Jav inhales like she just remembered oxygen's a thing bodies need, every once in a while.

"*But* several of these development companies put in rejected offers to buildings that were later demolished by villainous activity. That gives them a motive. Connecting this to the murder of Dr. Lopez is a simple matter of following the money. If her report were to be released, property prices would fall across Bridgebrook. The firms involved want to sell off their new builds *before* the revelation. When Dr. Lopez refused to stay silent, they ensured she couldn't blow the whistle early."

Jav stabs one of her Excel charts. Blair Homes's name is listed beside one of the color-key squares at the side. Not like I hadn't guessed. Still, that confirmation—*my home is a target*—slams me with the force of a roundhouse kick.

"Individuals on the directorial boards of these companies are colluding with the VC," Jav says. "They've ended countless lives and endangered way more. Amelia Lopez is the most obvious victim, but we can't forget everyone who's had their home and livelihood destroyed by villains and henchmen." She studiously doesn't look my way. "If you want to clean up Bridgebrook, ma'am, I'd suggest you start here."

And she sits back, triumphant, and waits for the applause.

It doesn't come.

The mayor's smile widens, but it's no expression. More like

two pegs are stretching the skin back from her face. "That's *very* good."

My forehead scrunches. "We're not joking."

"Neither am I." Mayor Darcy switches the cross on her legs, smoothing her pencil skirt over her lap. "What a pity. For such smart girls, you fail to appreciate the *larger* picture."

Kill Bill sirens. I hold up both hands. "Is . . . is this the start of a villainous monologue?"

The mayor looks shocked. "How reductive of you. Good, bad . . . Kindergarten concepts. We pretend we believe in them, dressing our heroes in white and our villains in black—but in truth, morality is a human construct. It only exists in so far as we *convince ourselves* it does."

"Yup," mutters Jav. She snatches back the chart. "Villainous monologue alert."

Fuck. I throttle the arms of my chair. Outside the window, someone—Delmar?—shouts instructions to the crowd. The whole point of this demonstration is to show our city that Normies aren't powerless, but I don't think becoming a villain is what the protestors had in mind.

Mayor Darcy takes her phone from the tray, taps twice at the screen, then puts it down again. Like *that's* not suspicious. I scope the exit. The heavy fire door would take us a minute to open, and I don't fancy a three-story dive from the window. All in all? Prospects: not great. "Uh, what did you just do?"

"Nothing to concern yourself with. Now, if I'm delivering a 'villainous monologue,' this is the part where I regale you with my motives, correct?"

"And we foil your plot, last minute," says Jav as I reluctantly dismiss my thoughts of self-defenestration. She's pressed against her chair like she wants to phase through it. "We've all seen heroes-versus-villains play out on TV."

The mayor nods along. "Such a shame real life doesn't work like that."

"Duh. You'd have to be thick not to realize those battles are exaggerated for entertainment value." Jav flips her braids over her shoulder. "Right, Riley?"

"Right," I say, a beat too late. My brain spins soggily, doing a great impression of a flushed toilet-paper roll. The battles are *staged*? I figured theatrics were part of the Super-gene parcel. "Totally, one-hundred-percent guessed that, yup. Knew all along."

The mayor makes the understandable assumption that I'm a dumbass and returns her attention to Jav. "You were surprisingly close, you know. Just a little overzealous. Not every clue leads back to gentrification."

Jav shakes her head. "The Flamer told us we were right. Our theory makes sense!"

Outside, the protestors set up a chant: "*We want to live! We want to live!*"

The mayor's smirk turns patronizing. "That doesn't make it *true*. The *truth* is that while multiple housing companies profit from this arrangement, I laid down the terms. Sunnylake's sewage system is old and faulty—the works, the pipe network, everything. If the scale of the problem was known, a complete overhaul would be our only option, resulting in a considerable tax hike."

She mentioned the T word. My brain switches off. I can't

help it; it's a knee-jerk defense mechanism to ward off impending adulthood.

Jav isn't so afflicted. "And you're starting your reelection campaign."

The mayor nods. "No PR manager wants to work with 'sewers down, taxes up' as a slogan! I'm supposed to clean up Bridgebrook—that's my *brand*. Not make the city—excuse my French—*shittier*."

"So you need to keep all reports on the water quality of Clearwater on the DL," Jav continues. She crumples her files as if she can mash this entire day into a ball and lob it at the nearest trash can. "Long enough to secure your next term in office."

Mayor Darcy beams. "I knew you'd figure it out."

This is all so wild. But while I struggle to compute what she's saying, I know one fact for sure, and it's that I want nothing more than to punch her upturned button of a nose until it's concave.

"You don't *deserve* to be mayor," I spit. "You've done fuck all for Sunnylake."

"Really?" She gestures to the disc on the side of my neck. "What about Hench—my little employment scheme?"

No *way*. "*You're* our boss?"

A modest shrug. "Only of the local branch. Hench outfits have been operating in most cities since the VC spread beyond Sunnylake. They provide low-skilled labor opportunities to the impoverished, who would otherwise be lost to drugs and petty crime. Sunnylake has one of the largest agencies, you know? As a result, our employment rates are excellent, and we have a phenomenal hero response time, thanks to henchmen setting off the early warning system. It's quite ingenious, really."

"*We want to live!*" scream the protestors outside. "*We want to live!*"

"They don't sound grateful," says Jav.

"Yeah." My nails dig into the foam arms of my chair, the windows in the observatory crashing down around me once again. "Try doing a hero's job without Superpowers, for minimum wage."

The mayor's milk-and-cookies smile curdles. "You'd have nothing at all, if not for Hench." She pivots toward the window, sunlight bathing her face. No dramatic shadows here. "Listen to me, girls. I'm not the villain of your story."

"Really? You're sure acting like it. Lemme guess: The only way we leave here is in a body bag?"

Jav elbows me. "Don't give her ideas!"

The mayor rolls her eyes. "Such *melodrama*. I have no intention of killing you. I simply want to help you *see*."

"See what?" Jav's still wringing her file, knuckles bloodless. "That anyone who stands in your way disappears?"

"We *did* offer Miss Lopez—"

"*Doctor*," I snap.

"—a generous sum to move her sampling station a short ways upstream, to the other side of the sewage plant. A shame she refused to see reason."

"A shame she did the right thing, you mean?"

The mayor looks genuinely disappointed. "I told you to *listen*. Right, wrong . . . They're not *applicable* to adult life, dear."

"But they make for good distractions." Bitter realization in Jav's tone. She's miles ahead of me; I'm still reeling over the fact that Mayor Darcy, Sunnylake's most-kidnapped, isn't the victim here. "Villains are an *obvious* enemy. They're easy to hate. So long as we're looking at them, we don't pay any attention to you."

The mayor golf-claps. "Very good! The Villain Council want to promote their slogans and gain publicity—but at the same time, the radical Superemacists among them could cause immense harm, if left unchecked. Thankfully, our Super Squad needs villains to justify their state funding, and I find it *far* easier to run a campaign when my constituents have something to fear. Nothing brings people together like a common enemy."

"So that's it?" I ask. Adrenaline is ice water, inundating my veins. More pushes through me with every pump of my pulse. "Everyone running this city is privately scratching each other's backs, heroes and villains and everyone between? That's the secret behind Project Zero?"

Mayor Darcy rolls her shoulders under the elegant blue princess neck of her dress. "I *did* suggest a far less dramatic name for our . . . mutually beneficial collusions. But—well. When working with Supers. You know how it is."

"Oh, I got *plenty* of alternative names. Like . . . big evil circle jerk."

The mayor sighs. She looks me over, adjusting her designer specs on the bobble halfway up her nose. "I once sat in your chair, Riley. I could've chosen to reveal everything—but I didn't. Perhaps you can tell me why?"

". . . Because you're a shitty person?"

"No. Because it *wouldn't change anything.*" Her smile is syrup, though I taste poison beneath. "You can't fight the world. I'm only one part of this, Riley. The same as the VC, the Super Squad, the companies buying up Bridgebrook. We all have a role to play.

There is no single enemy for you girls to take down. There is no mastermind. So." She leans forward. "When you discover how deep-rooted the suffering in our world is, do you dig it out, destabilizing all that grows above? Or do you let it grow?"

I push up from my chair. "That's a really nice metaphor, and I appreciate the work you put into it, but I can't think of a snappy way to say 'no thank you' right now."

Jav rises, too, wiping her eyes. "I get out my spade," she tells the mayor.

"There! What she said. C'mon, we're outta here."

Jav's words from the prison still fester. But as we turn for the door, united, it almost feels like things are back to normal again. Jav and Riley, Riley and Jav. We got each other's backs, 'cause no one else does.

Then Mayor Darcy tuts. "Really, Riley? What about Blair Homes?"

Fuck. I stop dead.

"It would take a word," Mayor Darcy continues, cheek pillowed on her soft, pale palm. "Just one word. Then Blair Homes diverts their attentions from 26 Sloan Street to . . . Say . . . 42." A crinkle of those kindly blue eyes. "How would you like that, dear?"

My throat closes. If she can save my home with a word, she can destroy it with one, too.

"And you." The mayor swivels on her chair, beam pinning Jav in place. "You have ambition—a trait I admire. How much easier would it be to climb to the top, if a hand reached down to pull you up?"

"That's bribery," Jav tries, but her voice lacks its razor edge.

"No, no. A leveling of the playing field—affirmative action." The mayor sneers out the window, at the protest's lurid heave. I hear the shrill peeps of whistles, the thud of speakers. Someone's brought an air horn, which they blast with no regard for anyone's hearing. I hope Lyssa stayed on the steps, where the crowd isn't so thick. "So many children start this life halfway up the stairs to success. They have friends in high places, legacy parents—but you weren't so lucky. Why not accept help when it's offered?"

Jav falters, eyes covetous like she's just seen a new shade of nail polish. But she shakes her head. "Affirmative action don't come with a price tag."

She's right (as always). I wanna save my home. Course I do. But could I live with the cost? Could I wave at the Beauvaises every day and eat Hernando's cooking, while another family came home to find a smoldering bomb site taped off by the Super Squad?

Fear of what the mayor might do to my little world still batters me, a cyclone trapped beneath my skin. But my world's not the only one at stake.

"We pass," I tell the mayor. "You're not giving us a way out. Just a way to become *you*."

The mayor doesn't hurdle the desk and brain me with Mr. Caluna's stapler. She squeaks back on her plush chair, still smiling, observing us from under pale lashes. "I hoped you wouldn't say that. Still, your sister seems resilient. I'm sure she'll overcome the grief."

Blood drains from my face. "Uh, no. You said you *weren't* going to kill us."

"I also said I wasn't going to explain my entire plan to you—but it made for *such* a good distraction." Mayor Darcy checks her phone again. "Would you look at that?" She turns the screen to us, revealing the scrolling headline banner and the severe-faced reporter who ran the interview with Crystalis. "Breaking news! The Flamer escaped the supermax. And I bet he's *so* eager for vengeance against the mayor who put him there."

Jav pulls the shoestring fastening of her duffel bag tight as a garrote. "What does he have to do with this?"

"Tragic, really," the mayor continues, like she can't hear. She snaps her phone case shut, sliding it into her pocket. "Two young girls, dying in a villainous attack at the very heart of our city . . . I daresay you'll become poster children for the Super Squad's next funding campaign."

I haven't blinked in so long my eyes itch. "Wait, wait, wait. The Flamer's coming here? To kill us?"

"Oh gosh, no! He's screwed up enough lately. I'm not leaving this to chance." Her sweet smile never wavers. "The bomb a couple rooms down should take care of things."

"Bomb?" Jav whispers as I struggle to work my way around the enormity of the fact that we are "things," and "take care of" is apparently code for "blow into itty-bitty pieces."

"You're *framing* the Flamer?"

Mayor Darcy shrugs. "He shouldn't have told you anything. Perhaps this will be a good lesson for him."

I don't want to be a lesson or a victim or a fucking *ad campaign*. And I really, *really* don't want to die. Bile climbs in my throat. Projectile vomiting on your enemy isn't the most effective defensive tactic, but it would still be mighty satisfying.

Outside: the bass beat of helicopter rotors. Indecipherable

chants from the crowd. And above it all: the roar of the Super Squad jet. Its engines drown out the protestors; its wings blot out the sun. Our heroes have arrived—but not to save the day.

"Everyone has three choices," the mayor continues, tapping her nails on the desk's beveled edge. "To join Project Zero. To look away. Or to be crushed. I made mine, and you made yours. Really, when you think of it like that . . ." She flashes us that bright, shiny, camera-ready smile. "I'm not going to kill you, girls. *You* are."

CHAPTER 36

JAV DARTS FOR the door. The mayor pulls the pistol from Mr. Caluna's drawer. "I wouldn't do that if I were you."

"That's a gun," I say as Jav's footsteps stutter to a halt. An *actual* gun. I bet it doesn't shoot electrical bolts.

"Very astute." Mayor Darcy scoops our phones into her handbag and loops the chain strap over her shoulder. Patent leather, crocodile-effect. Think I saw that same overpriced model in a boutique, back when I first found the Hench flyer, a summer and a lifetime ago. "Now, once I leave the building, all it will take is one phone call to set off the bomb." She uses her spare hand—you know, the one *not* holding the pistol—to rumple her hair out of its neat waves. "You'll perish in the explosion, destroying a beloved monument of our city and generating the perfect sob story to demonstrate why this city needs increased Super-Squad support—and my strong leadership. Life returns to normal, and after the next scheduled villain attack, Sunnylake forgets you ever existed." She beams at us, dabbing her mouth on a tissue to smear her makeup. "Project Zero in full operation. Magnificent, no?"

Jav gazes at me, beautiful brown eyes pleading. For what, I don't know. I'm welded to the spot. The world shrinks until it fits the pistol's mouth: a lightless O; a soundless scream.

After five harrowing seconds, Jav sits. I copy her.

"There," purrs the mayor. "That wasn't so hard." She keeps her pistol trained on us as she trots to the door. It takes some effort to wrestle it open one-handed, but she manages. "I'm sorry, girls. I didn't want it to end this way, but you left me no choice."

Only once the door swings shut again, locking with a loud *clunk*, does Jav whip around in her chair and scowl.

"What the hell! Why didn't you *do* something?"

"Like *what*?"

"Dive on her while she was distracted? Or while she was fighting the door?"

"Did you not notice the *gun*? Sorry for not being Bruce Willis!"

Jav shakes her head, pulling fretfully on her braids. "Why're we arguing? We're locked in city hall with a freaking *bomb*."

"*I* didn't start the argument."

"Sorry, sorry. I'm just." Her voice dips. "Fuck. I'm scared, Riley."

Scared doesn't begin to cover it. The mayor had us from the moment we walked in. We never stood a chance.

"I can't believe this," I whisper.

Jav mops her puffy eyes. "I know. It's like an episode of *Scooby-Doo*. The real bad guy wasn't the monster; it was the businessman wearing the mask."

"At least you're Velma. I'm just . . ." I wave up and down at myself. "Scooby."

She sniffles. "Give yourself some credit. You're at least a Fred."

"But nobody *likes* Fred . . ."

This is ridiculous. We're talking about *Scooby-Doo*. It's the sort of filler conversation you have on your lunch break, not when you're about to get turned into human hamburger.

I look at Jav, straight on. "I don't wanna die."

Her chin trembles. "Neither do I."

"What do we do?"

"I don't know."

Her admittance—because Jav never, *ever* doesn't have a plan—is the final straw. Time slows. This is it: breaking point. Either I succumb to the panic . . . or I tame it. I survive.

"Okay," I whisper. A crack in the silence. "What do we know about bombs?"

Jav plucks at the sleeve of her Ralbury blouse. *Pick-pick, pick-pick*; today's peacock-blue nails pinch loops into the hem-stitches. "Mayor Darcy said it's phone activated. And she'll have left it in one of the nearest rooms. To . . . to *take care of things*."

I eye up the scissors in the monogrammed stationery pot on Mr. Caluna's desk. "If we found it, we might be able to do something. Like . . . like snip the wires or whatever."

"Which wires?"

"I don't know! You're the genius!"

"I wanna do *government* at Harvard! Not fucking *bomb disposal*!"

"Fair. If there's a red one, we can cross it off our list; I've seen enough movies to know that's a bad idea."

"Excuse me if I don't trust you to do this based on your *pop culture knowledge*!" Jav stares at the stack of files on Caluna's desk. Then up to the camera in the corner. I imagine the cogs and wheels whirring in that gorgeous, marvelous brain. "No.

Forget finding the bomb. Too much of a risk of setting it off. We need to get outta here and use that CCTV footage to bring the mayor down." She opens a folder, tugging a hefty paper clip loose. "Can you pick a lock?"

I cross my arms. "Are you insinuating that because I grew up in Shit Creek, I know how to pick locks?"

"Well, can you?"

I snatch the paper clip. "Duh. Gonna need another of these, though."

Jav obliges. I drop to my knees in front of the door. At least here, focused on the keyhole in front of me, I don't have to dwell on whether they'll be able to scoop up enough of my remains to justify a coffin.

"Why bother with footage?" I ask, scraping the tumblers. The key (haha) thing when you're lock-picking is visualization. You gotta *see* the mechanism in your head, know how it all fits together, how all those tiny teeth interlock. Luckily, I've always had a vivid imagination. "Camera might not even be on. Why not just split?"

"Escape without any evidence, we have less than when we arrived. We need that footage, or there's no point surviving at all."

Sounds a bit over the top. I'd rather run for the border and camp out with Lyssa's abuelita than risk explodey death. And— holy shit; I'm thinking of *fleeing the country*. And I'm not *freaking out of my head*.

I know it's because I haven't acknowledged the depth of the shit pit we've landed ourselves in. Once I do, I'll be useless. I gotta ward the panic off, concentrate on the here and now.

I shut my eyes. Force them open again. Keep picking. The soft scritch of it, the tension and release, the scrape of metal on metal is all that keeps me sane.

"Where would we even find the footage?"

Jav bounces on the balls of her feet, looking everywhere but the bomb. "I vote the room with all the monitors we passed on the way up."

"And if you're wrong?"

"And if you can't get us out of here?"

Either way, we're fucked. Thankfully, the universe has mercy, because the lock takes that moment to pop.

I huff sweaty hair off my forehead. "You were saying?"

We don't talk about the obvious stuff, like how the mayor's gonna leave city hall before us, or how our lives hinge on the chance she dials the wrong number the first time. We don't talk about whether it'll hurt, or whether it'll all be over so fast, our lives snuffed out like candle flames, we won't notice.

We definitely don't talk about who we'll leave behind. But I think of them as we race along that corridor, empty offices on every side, silent as tombs in a mausoleum. Hernando. Lyssa. Sherman, and that last kiss that never got to be more. Her thick curls between my fingers, her lips parting for my tongue. The perfect yin-yang of our clasped hands.

"Here," pants Jav. "Security room."

I dash in after her. We face an array of screens, each showing an identical office. If I was alone, I'd give up and sprint for the elevators, but Jav's never been good at admitting defeat. She scans along until she finds Caluna's room, recognizable by the open drawer and the still-shutting door.

"There! And—yes, the files have audio!"

We're not dead yet. Why aren't we dead? I picture Mayor Darcy pausing in a ladies' restroom to perfect her act. Untuck her blouse, apply dark eye shadow to her cheeks for bruises. Make it look like *she's* the one running for her life.

"Okay, seriously," I say as Jav slides into the computer chair. "We're wasting time. I'd rather be alive without evidence than dead with it."

Jav's eyebrows are scrunched so tight they almost touch. The monitor highlights the curves of her face in blue. "You think the mayor will stop? We'll just delay the inevitable. She'll come after us. The Super Squad, the villains, they all will."

I cast a mournful glance for the door, but I hear what Jav's saying. Running might save our lives, but it won't save my home, or Bridgebrook.

"Just another minute." Jav's fingers fly over the keys. "That's all I need. One minute, please."

"You talking to me or God?"

"Whichever will save me from death-by-explosion." Jav's fingers keep gliding over the keys. "Grab that thumb drive from my bag."

I hand it over. It sports a bright orange sticker with *Baahir* Sharpied on the side. Wonder who lent her *that*. I raise my eyebrows at Jav, only for her to snatch it out of my hand. "Stay focused!"

She jams the stick into the port under one of the monitors. We watch the green bar creep across the miniature control screen. The dull whine of a computer fan grinds down the bulges on my brain. I'm staring down the barrel of a gun again. Waiting for that pull of the trigger. Skin prickling. Armpits sticky. Gulp in my throat too huge to swallow.

I'm not safe, I'm not safe, I'm not safe . . .

Usually, that's all in my head. Usually, I'll do the breathing exercises I found online and try to logic my way back to sanity, reminding myself that I'm not dangling upside down in a car, held by the cutting cradle of my seat belt, vision spinning, head a swirl of gasoline fumes.

Usually, I don't have a bomb approximately one hundred feet to my left.

The USB flashes. Jav yanks it loose. Nothing explodes. I concentrate on that, over the rapid-fire rat-a-tat of my pulse: *We're still alive.* All we gotta do is stay that way.

The elevator pings. And my hope falls away, along with the inner lining of my stomach.

Me and Jav meet each other's eyes. "Hero," I whisper. "Come to finish the job."

"Flamer," she counters. "Come to start it."

I clutch my paper clip. May not be the most effective weapon, but so help me, I'm gouging out an eye before he takes me down.

"Riley!" Sherman screams. "Where are you?"

I drop the clip.

Jav tilts her head to one side. "Are you . . . *blushing?*"

I wrench open the door of the security office. Fighting to keep the grin off my mug. "Sherm—"

Sometimes, when you gamble, you hit jackpot. Other times . . . Well, you win some, you lose some. Sometimes, no matter how many dimes you push into the arcade game, you don't get the prize.

Or, as in this situation, sometimes the bomb goes off.

CHAPTER 37

HEROES ALWAYS STROLL away from explosions on TV. Just saunter along, not looking back. I'm starting to think that's all CGI.

We're far away, in the last room before the elevators. The percussive force still picks us up and tosses us like balls at the Super Bowl.

White stabs my eyes. The *boom* blasts out a second later (loud, so loud, can't *think see hear* . . .).

I strike something. Solid, soft; I can't tell. I hit it hard enough that it doesn't matter. My scream's punched out of me before it can sound.

Ears ringing. Eyes burning. Every nerve screeching *pain-pain-pain*.

Mom's car rolls again, seat belt slicing my stomach. My skull is a balloon, swollen tight around that pressure, that terror, that wordless, primitive certainty that *this is how I die* . . .

Wait. Not a seat belt. *Arms.* Pulling me close, holding me safe.

Vision swims back, crosshatched with fire. I feel myself scream. It's a full-body exercise: muscles tensing, throat blazing as I push sound past my vocal cords. I can't hear it. Nothing but tinnitus: a mosquito drilling into my brain.

Chunks of debris hurtle around us. I brace for impact—*gonna die, gonna die.* But the boulders burst open, shattering off Sherman's shield. Its surface glimmers, alive with dashes of lightning-bright brilliance. We curl together in the eye of the storm.

Jav, I plead, mouth moving clumsy around the word. But she's here, too, collapsed against Sherman's side.

I'm so grateful I could kiss her. I don't know *which* her—possibly both. But now's not the time—especially as the far end of the corridor caves away, darkness gaping beneath.

Sherman's eyes widen. She yells something. The arm over my chest tightens (mmm . . . biceps . . .). The other hooks Jav. I don't know what she's saying, but I get the gist.

Hold on tight.

I cling like my life depends on it. Right now, it probably does.

Tremors shake the ceiling, cracks spider up the walls. Time for one last thought. I make it a resounding *FUCK*. Then the floor buckles, and down we go.

CHAPTER 38

THE WHOLE ORDEAL can't last more than thirty seconds, as the three of us batter against Sherman's shield like hamsters in a dropped ball, clothes and skin and hair frosting over wherever they touch. Doesn't stop it *feeling* like thirty days and thirty nights, or some other form of biblical torture.

Sherman forms the shield beneath us to slow our descent. Banishing it again just as fast, again and again, before the cold burns.

We still smack down hard, but it's only brain-*rattling*, not brain-*splattering*. I spend another small eternity sprawled flat out on the rubble. Only once the room quits spinning do I push to sit. My ears ring so hard they hurt. Sherm's words—*"Let's all agree to never, ever do this again"*—drift to me from afar.

The skeleton of city hall rises above us. Hollowed, blackened, innards gouged out by a red-hot melon baller. The blast burst the floor we were on and punched holes in both below. One of them, we fell through.

The ceiling droops like an overstuffed hammock. Cracks braid the plasterwork. Sherman re-forms the shield over us and dust soon coats it, gray and heavy as volcanic ash.

That's just background scenery. As I blink the residual flashes from my eyes, all I see is Sofia Sherman. Gorgeous. Grumpy. Dressed in—of all things—a navy-blue Sunnylake sidekick uniform.

"You came back," I croak, though I can barely hear myself speak. Then, just to be a shit: "My hero."

Sherman doesn't waste time snorting. She shouts something loud enough for my busted eardrums to catch: "We need to move!"

Threads of sunlight pierce the billowing dust. When this cloud clears, we'll be left in the reception area of the building the Flamer allegedly blew up, heroes charging in to rescue us from all sides. Or not, given who they work for.

How could this happen? Would the mayor really go this far to shut us up?

Perhaps, whispers something at the back of my dazed mind, *we're more of a threat than she wants to admit.*

I try to stand, but my legs won't obey me. It takes several attempts, and when I manage a tenuous vertical I still have to stabilize myself on Sherman's arm.

Jav, though? Jav doesn't try at all.

"Jav?" I whisper. Then louder, since I can't hear myself— "*Jav!*"

Sherman says something muffled. Telling me to stay quiet. The sidekicks will arrive soon, sweeping for survivors.

I don't listen. I crouch beside Jav, cataloging my own aches on the way. Raw and tender all over, skin prickling from heat and cold. Feels kinda like I've had a full-body exfoliation session with a cheese grater. A phantom echo of the blast still rattles around my head.

Jav looks *worse*.

I thumb dirt and blood off her slack cheek. "Jav. Jav, please. Jav, you gotta open your eyes—*Jav!*"

Her lashes quiver apart. I could sob with relief. Then I see how mismatched her pupils are, one bulging like she's high while the other shrinks down to a pinprick. How she struggles to focus on my face.

"Rile . . . Riley?"

Jav's never confused. Jav's never out of it. Jav's needle-sharp and cleverer than anyone I know, and she always, *always* knows what to do. This isn't right. This isn't *her*.

Jav reaches up, the backs of her shaky fingers brushing my chin. Her nail polish is chipped, her hands grazed and ice-speckled.

"Did we . . . did we . . . do it?" Her voice is so faint, it could come from the far side of City Square.

"Yeah. We sure did."

She flumps back. "This is all your fault."

"What? *How?*"

"I'll work it out later."

Ass. Still, I can't bite back my grin.

Sherm jostles my shoulder. Her voice sounds a little louder than it did a minute ago but still nowhere near its usual volume. I have this sudden, sickening fear it'll never come back, that I'll never fully hear her say all the things I want her to—but then her words sink in, and I realize we got bigger problems. "Sidekicks incoming. Go, *now*. Grab her feet."

We're lucky Jav's such a twig. I'm still jellified from shock, so Sherman handles most of her weight, hooking her under the armpits. As the beams from the sidekicks' flashlights pour over the rubble around us, the roof bowing dangerously overhead, Sherman dismisses her shield in a whirl of ash and hot, itchy dust.

We run. Over the hammer of my heart, I wonder if we'll ever stop.

CHAPTER 39

ADMITTEDLY, TO CALL it "running" is generous. We hobble, stagger, and trip to the exit, dodging chunks of plaster and hooded specters of gray-black smoke. A fire door stands at the rear of the foyer. My hearing has recovered to the point where I can tell people are yelling beyond it, just not what they're saying.

"Shit," mutters Sherm. "We're surrounded." She nods to my uniform capsule. "Activate your mask."

I do so, letting Jav's legs drop. "What about her?"

Sherman slaps a silver disc onto Jav's bare neck. The familiar Hench mask rushes out, hiding Jav's lax features and the blood glossing the right side of her face. Sherman shoulders open the door, and we burst out, into the light.

We dive into the throng, using poor Jav as a battering ram as much as an excuse to shove people out of our way. Thankfully, there are enough henchmen and sidekicks around us that we don't stick out.

I take a moment to ponder how Sherman arrived on time, since the bus takes at least half an hour to reach the city center. She must've donned her old sidekick uniform and hopped on the Super Squad jet as soon as the mayor's alert went out. Wild—her face is probably one of the most broadcast in Sunnylake right now. But she did it anyway, and it *worked*, because sometimes the world is wild, too.

Jav isn't the only victim. Collapsed bodies cover city hall's front steps, tended to by first aiders in the crowd. Their blood is bright, plastic red, the color of my old Artie's cap. It looks artificial, too liquid somehow. I've never seen so much of it before.

God. Everyone's gonna think we're dead. Hernando. Lyssa.

Lyssa.

I drop Jav's feet. "I'll catch up. Gotta grab my sister."

Sherman doesn't argue. She lays Jav down, then wrenches off her own Hench tag and hands it over. Another remains on her neck; must be projecting her sidekick gear. "Put this on her. We meet around the back of city hall."

Though I can't see her eyes beneath the lenses of her half-face mask, the curve of her lips looks way too kissable. I lean toward her. "I always complain when the leads start making out at the worst possible moment in action movies. But right now, I kinda understand the urge . . ."

"Thought you were going to get your sister."

"Right—yeah! Sister. See you. Stay safe; don't get dead!"

Those lips quirk on both sides, poking adorable dimples into her cheeks. "Same to you."

I battle to the front of the building. Takes me all of ten seconds to spot Lyssa. The air in my lungs is hot and gritty, like I inhaled too much ash. It smolders inside me as I see my baby sister curled on the front steps of city hall, her dirty face streaked with tears. Seeing her cry makes me want to strangle the world.

Or, better yet, the dumpy blonde woman who kneels beside my sister, gathering her to her bosom for a cuddle while the cameras flash. Mayor Darcy. Her makeup smeared, her hair a golden briar patch. She looks bruised and delicate, a jewel that needs to be protected from us rough and scary Bridgebrook girls.

A mustache of sweat fringes my top lip. It takes every fucking *ounce* of self-control not to march over there and scream *get away from my sister*.

Luckily, I only wind up waiting a minute. That's how long it takes a first-aid responder to triage Lyssa and declare her low urgency. My sister shuffles off to one side, with the mayor's help. Expression vacant. Slack as when I pulled her, unconscious, from Mom's car.

Cameras flash, capturing the perfect simulacra of sympathy on Mayor Darcy's face as she helps her sit. The fuzzy mics prove too much of a distraction. She steps away, accepting the foil shock blanket a paramedic drapes over her shoulders, and plasters on a brave smile for the reporters.

I take the opportunity, sneaking in and grabbing Lyssa's hand. "C'mon."

She yanks free. "Who're you?"

Ears still buzzing. I half hear the words, half read them off her lips. "Nice to know you listened all those times I told you not to talk to strangers."

Her eyes pop wide. "*Riley?* Why're you a henchman?" Like that's the zaniest thing about today.

"Long story." Long as this summer, in fact.

She glances back at city hall's droopy facade, quivering all along the line of her back. "You're okay? You weren't—the explosion—"

I think that's what she's saying, anyway. Might've missed a few words. I crouch before her. Cup her cheeks, smearing the dusty tears away. "Yes," I tell her. "I'm one-hundred-percent dead. I decided to use my last seconds of existence on this plane to come here and tell you you're a goober, one final time."

Lyssa's chin trembles. She doesn't laugh. Just flings her arms around me and holds on tight.

Gross, gross, gross. She's getting snot on my T-shirt. But I'm so thankful she's safe, I'd let her use me as a body pillow/tissue for the next hour, if we didn't have to move.

"C'mon. I'm fine. I got you, Lyss."

I heave her upright, leaning on my side. It's as we stumble off, away from the smoking husk of our town hall, that I check on Mayor Darcy.

False tears glisten on her ash-smeared face. My murderous intent must broadcast through the news crew surrounding her. She glances at the step where she left Lyssa. Finding it vacant, she scans the crowds. Her soggy gaze snags on the two of us, and I know *she knows*.

Good. I *want* her to fear us.

I look directly at Mayor Darcy and give her a one-fingered salute.

CHAPTER 40

I CATCH UP with Sherman and Jav, two blocks down from city hall. It should be a safe distance, but news crews buzz about, unloading camera rigs and mics from their vans, while reporters prep their makeup and practice Serious Faces in the wing mirrors.

I slap the spare disc on Lyssa's neck and turn on her hologram, both of us hiding bruises beneath fake rubber. As we walk past the reporters, tension climbs my vertebrae like the rungs of a ladder. We look like henchmen, fleeing the scene of the latest VC attack. Any moment, someone's gonna freak out. *Any moment.* But the shouts don't start and the accusations don't fly, and no heroes wrestle us into headlocks.

I internally thank Delmar and Max and the other protestors. Even if the explosion at city hall will hog the news, they've shown Sunnylake that henchmen are more than lackeys. They proved we have a voice. If I want my own voice to be heard, I have to survive. Something tells me my chances will rise once I'm no longer so close to the hovering Super Squad jet that its engine wobbles my soft tissues.

"What's our next move?" I ask Sherman as we approach. My ears are so woolly, I can barely hear myself speak.

Sherman sucks on her bottom lip. "I don't know."

Her grip on Jav's arm is all that keeps her upright. Her eyes are open, but she's limp like her ligaments have been cut.

Will she be okay? If I'd spent today on the couch, eating my feelings, Jav would've come to city hall alone. She might not have made it out of the office. My bestie would be *dead*, and I'd never know why. This morning, I could barely look at her, but the thought of her being gone is so awful it flushes the anger right out of me.

I duck under Jav's other arm, taking her weight. It's the least I can do, after everything.

There's so much I want to tell her—*I'm sorry, I should've kept my mouth shut, you're nothing like the mayor*. It'll have to wait until she stops staring like the whole city's spinning. Still, it warms my chest when she rests her head on my shoulder, long braids patting my back.

"Call an Uber," I tell Sherman, after guiding Jav around the next street corner, far from the camera crews. "We have to get her to the Captain and Aaron."

Sherman's gonna suck her lip right off, if she's not careful. "You think the Captain'll help us?"

"You know him better than I do."

Sherman taps her fingers on her unseen belt buckle, one-two-three-four, one-two-three-four. Then nods. "Captain it is." Still, she hesitates, before digging out her phone. Must be a pocket *somewhere*, under that hologram. "You gonna be okay with this? The car, I mean?"

"My vehicle phobia is the least of our worries."

Five minutes later, an Uber pulls up. I steel myself. This is it. My big, transformative finale, where I muscle through my fears. Where I grab every nightmare by the throat, look 'em dead in the eyes, and growl that I won't be beaten. I got this. *I got this.*

My stomach jiggles like jelly. I swing myself into shotgun, playing it cool, and—

"Nope. Nope, nope, nope." As soon as ass brushes chair, my brain starts barfing up bad memories. I lurch out onto the sidewalk, breathing like a weightlifter. Exorcising the scent of sandalwood Yankee Candle Car Jar from my lungs. "I'll—I'll walk."

Sherman eases Jav into the back. She smiles weakly at me, lolling against the window. Blood from her cut forehead smears the glass. I'll worry about her later. I'll worry about all of it—the video, how many brain cells Jav lost and whether it'll damage her chances at Harvard—once we're safe.

"It's five miles to the Captain's," says Sherman. "At least."

"Guess I'll see you there. Splitting up's safer anyway, right?"

Lyssa pokes my side. She's been quiet these past few minutes—staring between me, Sherman, and Jav, taking in the holographic uniforms, everything. I almost forgot she's here. "Have you *ever* seen a horror movie?"

"Have you ever seen me puke on floor mats? Because that's guaranteed."

"Ew. Fair." Lyssa contemplates the open car door, then backs up with a shake of her head. "I'll come with. Dad's always on me about how I need more fresh air."

A smile squirms onto my face. She's pretty cool sometimes. For a goober.

We should get moving before the mayor sends her Super search party further afield. Still, I snag Sherman's wrist before she can slip into the seat beside Jav.

"Hey, uh. You came back. For me. Guess I owe you one for that."

Sherman rolls her sidekick mask up all the way. So that *isn't* holographic? Makes sense; heroes love to rip them off and dramatically reveal their identities. Dismissing a hologram doesn't have quite the same vibes. Sherman's curls are pasted to her forehead with sweat. She gives this jerky shrug, one shoulder rising higher than the other.

"I came back for everyone."

". . . But mostly me."

"For the *city*. Like you said—Project Zero's big." Bigger than any of us imagined.

"The city screwed you over," I point out.

"Yeah. Because I screwed up."

"Big-time," mutters Lyss.

"But," Sherman continues, glaring past me at the speed bumps that bulge from the road, "that doesn't *matter*. I still gotta fight for what's right. Some things are more important than my hurt feelings."

She listened to me. Beneath my mask, my smile grows until it threatens to split my head in two.

My head's a hive of things I want to tell her. The mayor. The Super Squad. The real culprits behind the Flamer's so-called attack. Mostly, though, I just want to hold her hand.

Maybe I'll get the chance, once this is over. Assuming we both survive.

"You still, like, ninety percent came back for me, though, right?"

Sherman rolls her eyes. But she's smiling, too.

CHAPTER 41

LYSSA AND I walk in silence. Unsurprising. What are you supposed to say to the revelation that your big sister is a henchman? Still, though she could easily overtake me, now she's sleeve-suctioned into her new model—she spent enough time on her old prosthetic to stop her muscles weakening—she matches my limping, slowpoke pace. Even as that pace keeps slowing.

Turns out, five miles is a long-ass way. Especially when an explosion is ringing in your ears, trapped in the jar of your skull. I wobble all over the sidewalk like I'm failing a police sobriety test. Two blocks—that's how far I make it before my legs buckle. I wind up ass-to-the-curb, turning off my hologram, finger-combing mortar dust from my hair and ignoring every stare from passersby. Lyssa lends me her phone, along with several threats of what she'll do to me if I look through her stuff, so I can message Sherman.

"I'm not gonna be the best passenger," I warn her when she pulls up some indeterminable amount of time later—however long it took the Captain to drop her off at her place, so she could grab her Harley. Then it clicks that motorcycles don't spontaneously grow giant chrome tumors. "Wait. Is that a sidecar?"

Sherman tosses her helmet underarm to Lyssa. Something inside me unclenches at the sight of her face. That half smile.

Those long-lashed brown eyes. Ash caught in her curls like summer snow. "My dad's. Get in."

I do so, with the creaks and groans of someone five times my age. Lyssa hangs back, moodily kicking pebbles into the street, but the temptation of the ride must trump whatever grudge she's holding, because she piles in beside me and away we roll. I brace my head in my hands—still feels wobbly, like it might fall off if we corner too fast—and project gratitude in the direction of Luis Sherman.

We hit the 'burbs, bike and car rolling to a halt outside a familiar duplex. The door opens before I can knock. There stands the Captain, in costume, arms crossed. Might be menacing, if not for the tiny boy koalaed around his shin.

"Fuck you, Jones" is the Captain's opening line.

Kiddo sends his finger on an exploratory expedition through his nasal cavity. "Swear jar," he says.

"The fuck were you thinking, bringing this shit to my front door?"

Kiddo extracts a booger. "Swear jar *twice*."

The Captain takes a step forward. He drags the kid onto the bristly welcome mat. "I said I wanted nothing to do with this," he growls, jabbing a finger at me. "I *said* you'd just get yourself hurt. I told you *and* your girlfriend. And did you listen?"

Yeah, up until he dropped the g-bomb. Behind me, I think I hear Sherman choking. I can't look at her. "Um. What?"

The Captain levels a Look.

I cough into my fist. "We ain't . . ."

The Look continues, capital letter included. How's he *do* that, through his mask? Special dad powers or something. "Look,

314

Jones. I would say *I hate to say I told you so*, but it'd be a lie. Gloating is all that gives me serotonin. Of *course* you muppets had to go one beyond pissing off the VC. Of *course* you brought in the heroes. Because one gang of angry Supers ain't enough."

Jav must've filled him in on Project Zero, which means she's both conscious and coherent. That's reassuring. Or it should be. I'm almost too tired to feel it. My hair smells scorched. Every joint throbs like . . . Well, like I got hurled about by an explosion, then fell through three stories of a building inside a giant hamster ball. I'm broken glass in a bag of skin.

"Cool," I say. "Can we come in?"

The Captain huffs some more, postures some more, then shuffles to one side, leg warmer in tow. "Yeah. Had Aaron prep for houseguests soon as downtown started exploding. Figured someone might swing by."

I still have to concentrate, to pick apart his words. The ring in my ears might be fainter now, but it hasn't gone, and a full-face mask isn't exactly conducive to lipreading.

I prod Lyssa inside ahead of me, glancing down the street. No one follows. No one looks. It's sleepy Saturday suburbia, all around. The only sound is the slap of water as a kid hoses off a semi two driveways down, and the *kch, kch, kch* of a sprinkler, pirouetting slowly over a frazzled brown lawn. Doesn't feel *safe*, though. Nothing does, after the mayor's revelation. If my ribs squeeze any tighter, my organs will pulp out between them.

"You knew we were involved?" I ask.

The Captain's laugh is rough as sandpaper. "My SOS sense was tingling."

"Save Our Souls?"

"Sherman Offends Someone."

"Hey," mutters Sherman. She squeezes past me, into the house, studiously avoiding eye contact, while I try to think about anything but the point where her back presses, briefly, to my front. "This one's on Jones. I can't take credit."

"Mutual effort," I tell her, because I'm feeling generous. Then, glancing around—"Where's Jav?"

"Your friend's with Daddy." The second of the Captain's kids—Macy?—traipses out of the kitchen, spatula in hand, painting the floor with creamy batter. She's about six, with cute flower clips in her curly black hair. "She's real pretty."

And smart and sweet and still okay. Jav has to be okay. I shoot the kid a smile. "Yeah. Yeah, she sure is."

"Macy . . ." The Captain dislodges Tyler, rescuing the spatula before his big fluffy husky—panting in the midday heat—can lick up the drippage. The dog collapses in front of the fridge, thwarted. His tail thumps the ground and he cranes his head for pets as Lyssa, Sherman, and I trudge after the Captain.

The Captain makes a beeline for the sink, spatula still in hand. He rummages for a cloth. The floor gets a wipedown before he stands to assess the sizzling pan on the stove. "Right. Should be hot enough. Pancakes?"

I melt onto the chair beside Sherman, Lyssa taking the one beside me. "Yeah. As many as you can make."

A QUARTER HOUR passes before Jav wobbles in. Aaron has to help her to her seat—hopefully that has less to do with her head wound and more to do with the compression sock on her ankle. I didn't even notice she'd twisted it.

"Are you okay?" is the first thing I ask, around my mouthful of pancake. Mmm, the Captain makes 'em good. Thick and fluffy. They sit heavy in my gut—not that I'm complaining. I need to feel weighed down, so I don't drift out of my head into our gaping lack of a plan. "Bad question. Obvs not. But, y'know. Surviving?"

If we all look as tired as we feel, Jav must be dead on her feet. Still, she nods.

"Yeah, surviving." Sherman nudges a steaming plate in her direction, chewing noisily at a peanut-butter-covered pancake (all about that protein). Jav pushes it away. "No thank you. My head's too full to eat."

"Your head is also badly bruised," says Aaron, hovering at her shoulder. "I really think you should go to the hospital. There's only so much I can do here. I don't have any scanning equipment, and I'm not a head trauma specialist—"

"Not until this is over." Jav slaps the USB stick down in the middle of the blue plastic tablecloth. "We have to get this video online."

"Nuh-uh," says the Captain. He's multitasking furiously, helping Macy stir the final batter batch while keeping an eye on the pan. I'd offer to help, but there's a manic edge to the way he flits around the kitchen, keeping himself busy, like if he slows down he might have to actually *think* about what he's landed his family in. "Soon as you upload that, it gets traced to my house. Next thing you know, the Super Squad come knocking."

"I'll use a VPN."

"Great! Good for you! I'm sure you will, but not on one of my computers." The last glug of mixture slaps the pan. "Send it to your phone. I'll drive you out of the city, and we can splatter this all over socials once we find a nice garage with Wi-Fi."

"No can do," I say. "The mayor added phone theft to her long list of crimes."

The Captain rolls the pan until it's covered in batter. "That might be for the best," he says, after a solid minute of listening to the oil hiss. "Means you won't be followed."

"She didn't get mine." Lyssa plonks it facedown on the table. Her Windwalker charm bounces off the nearest Elsa mat. "We can use that."

I use my forkful of pancake to sponge up spilled syrup. "We'll have to dump it after."

Lyssa wavers, stroking the chipped edge of her phone case. But eventually, she nods. "You told me I didn't have to be a Super to do good stuff," she mutters. "And whatever's going on here . . . it's important. Right?"

I reach over the table to pat her fingers. "Right."

"And people are getting hurt, and this is the only way to stop it?"

"Right."

She tugs her hand from under mine. The phone, too. "Then I'm coming with."

"What? No, that isn't—"

"It's my phone." She glares, squeezing the Windwalker charm like she's strangling a voodoo doll. I wish. "You don't know how to unlock it, anyway."

"I can see the pattern in the grease prints. Which, gross, by the way."

Lyssa slips the phone back into the pocket of her shorts. Her eyes are still bloodshot, though it's been hours since we walked away from the dust and smoke around city hall. "I'm coming, too, Riley. Let me do this."

No help from the Captain, Sherman, Aaron, or Jav. They alternatively watch and pick at their pancakes. Right. My sister, my rules.

My sister, who I want as far from this as geographically possible.

My sister, who's as stubborn as I am, and will follow anyway.

I roll my tongue against the smooth, hard backs of my front teeth. "We're just going to upload the video and ditch the phone, right? No danger there." No more than on any night I've worked for Hench.

The Captain nods. "It's settled, then. We leave tonight."

"What's the rush?" Sherman wants to know. "They all think Jav and Riley are dead."

Her voice is clearer, but still distant. I dig a finger in my ear as if I can pry an obstruction loose. "Uh. About that."

I explain my glare-off with the mayor. The Captain isn't impressed.

"You *flipped her the bird?* What possessed you to do *that?*"

"It was a spur-of-the-moment kinda thing."

"You were in *disguise*! She had no proof it was you!"

"Yeah, well. It felt really badass at the time."

Sherman rolls her eyes, but I see her smirking.

The Captain tosses his final pancake, catching it without looking. "Nope. Not badass. Just *bad*. I would say I can't believe you were such a twit—but then again, I know you."

I creak back on my chair, patting my pancake-puffed stomach. "You still let us into your house."

A poke with the spatula, to stop the batter sticking. "Yeah, yeah. I've trained a lot of henchmen, but you and Sherm have a special place in my heart."

"Aw."

"As well as in hell."

"Swear jar!" chorus Tyler and Macy. They share the final seat at the table, Tyler a wriggle away from falling off. The Captain scoops the last pancake onto their plate. Since we *did* rope them into this whole mess when they're too young to spell "citywide conspiracy," I can't hold a grudge.

***

TWENTY MINUTES LATER, we're ready to roll. Jav was permitted access to the Captain's laptop on the solemn promise she'd only email Lyssa the video, not upload it. Hopefully, that won't cause any red flags. She donates log-in deets for her Tumblr and Instagram accounts, while Sherman forks over her Twitter. She's gained influencer levels of followers. Most seem to be there to call her variations on "shitbag Super" and—oh, lovely, tell her to kill herself. That's a fun new escalation.

But if people wanna be angry, we can use that. Let's put all that mindless dogpiling to use.

I grab Sherman's hand when I catch her staring at the screen, pulling gentle but firm until she looks away. If every person currently shitting on her for Wokepoints really gives a damn about Sunnylake, our vid will be trending by the time we get home.

Home.

Hernando.

He must've seen the news about city hall. Will he have raced over? Has the mayor issued statements yet, incriminating the Flamer for my and Jav's deaths? All while my phone is buzzing away in her handbag, with each of Hernando's increasingly panicked texts?

The Harley revs outside. We have to move, and fast.

"Ready?" asks the Captain. He shakes his keys at us, all nine bronze chips rattling. I catch Lyssa's arm as she follows him out the door.

"You should message your dad, yeah? Let him know we're alive."

She jerks away. "You sure that's a good idea?"

"Why not? You can stick your phone on airplane mode straight after."

"That won't stop government-level GPS tracing," says Jav. Aaron helps her fold into shotgun. She rests her bruised head on the Ford Fiesta's half-unrolled window, raising bloodshot eyes to me. "It'll take someone with the mayor's clout ages to access that sort of surveillance. But since she has friends in the Super Squad, that shrinks our timeline."

"Meaning what?" Sherman asks.

Jav treats her temples to a fingertip massage. "Meaning we need to hurry. We have to upload this video and ditch Lyssa's phone before they get a fix on our location."

And hope the fallout is large enough to stop the mayor coming after us. And hope the world listens. And hope Project Zero ends.

Sometimes, hope is all you have. It's enough. It has to be.

The Captain swings into the driver's seat, slamming the car door. He glances back—just once—at his family. Aaron, stethoscope dangling from his broad neck. Face unreadable, expression crawling down into his ginger beard to hide. Macy and Tyler, whining that they don't wanna stay behind, that they don't like it when Dad wears a mask.

Then he cranks the ignition. "Let's hustle. We make for the La Caja Tunnel, do what needs to be done, and get back to Sunnylake in time to watch the shit meet the fan."

"Swear jar," mutters Tyler, but his heart hardly seems in it.

Aaron hefts him onto his hip. "Stay safe," he says.

The Captain won't look at him. "Yeah, yeah. I owe you dinner out again."

"Mm-hmm. Tonight. Which means you'd better be home by seven."

"I'll do my best."

That's hardly a promise. I don't know what to make of that. Judging by how his shoulders slump, Aaron doesn't, either. He carries Tyler back into the house, scooting Macy ahead of him. She shoots pouty faces at her other dad, all the way.

"No goodbye?" asks Lyssa quietly as she takes the rear seat—she'd probably rather be in the sidecar with me, but with only one helmet between us, I won't risk it again. I watch to make sure she latches her belt.

The Captain picks at the stitching on his steering wheel. "We don't say that to each other."

"C'mon, Jones." Sherman activates her sidekick costume. The geometric white-and-blue design flickers into existence, masking her sports bra and tattered black jeans. "Let's finish this."

I nod. But as I flop into the sidecar, I can't help but think of how much easier it'd be for Project Zero to finish *us*.

WE DAWDLE THROUGH Sunnylake, well within the limit. Last thing we need is to be pulled over for speeding. But the buzz of the motorcycle engine is enough to make me sweat. We might as well be careening around the tight downtown streets at ninety.

Our route to La Caja Tunnel is peppered with ambulances and police cars. Steady streams roll past in both directions. By now, I bet the Flamer has been apprehended—if he was ever truly released in the first place. Minus two Normie victims, the Super Squad has everything under control.

Mid-afternoon on the weekend, La Caja is quiet as it gets—which isn't very. A line of traffic snakes ahead of us, red bumper lights receding into the distance. None of us had time to shower. I still smell like I'm burning. That, combined with fumes filling my nose as cars choke the close-packed tunnel with gray smears of exhaust . . .

I wish I was behind Sherman, so I could hold on to her. I cling to the lip of the sidecar instead as she draws up next to the Captain's car. He drums his steering wheel like a woodpecker.

"C'mon," he mutters, while I try to breathe as shallowly as possible, one hand cupped over my nose. He keeps checking his mirrors. His voice is a faint scratch, just audible above the grind of engines and the ring the bomb put in my ears, the one that has yet to die away. The one which might never leave. "C'mon, c'mon, *c'mon*."

We've gotta hurry. Anyone involved in Project Zero will ensure the next time we die, it sticks. We're the villains of this story. We intend to destroy our city as we know it. Topple the skyscrapers, bulldoze the banks, condemn those who let Project Zero grow. The heroes are just doing their job, thwarting our plans. Like every villain before us, *we're going to lose*. And between the time we spent at the Captain's and whatever funky spy tech the Super Squad can use to sweep for Lyssa's phone, they should be arriving right around—

"Uh," croaks Lyssa. She points out the open car window. At the slick silver jet that mounts the skyline behind us, blinding us with the glare off its reflective wings. "That's not good. That's not good, right?"

Now.

CHAPTER 42

THE LED-STUDDED SPEED limits wink out. They're replaced by a hundred stop signs. The cars ahead trundle to a halt. The Captain smacks his horn, shocking the tinnitus back into my ears. "No! Keep moving!"

But the authority of the lights overrules one angry guy in a Ford Fiesta. We get dirty looks from the drivers in front. Those looks only get filthier as the Captain locks the parking brake and kicks open his door. He darts to his trunk, popping the silver box within, muttering "fuck-fuck-fuck" all the way.

He passes two bell-nosed rifles out. One for Sherman, one for me. His hands only shake a little. "Jones? Remember everything I taught you about shooting to miss?"

"Yeah?"

"Be a darling and forget it?"

I'm not sure I *can*. But I have to try. I wobble out of the sidecar after Sherman cuts the engine. When I cock my rifle, the hum of the charge is lost to my damaged ears. Just gotta trust the Captain plugged these babies in before he set off this morning.

"Jav, Lyssa?" I say. "Stay in the car."

It'd be quite the badass moment, if my head wasn't swimming from the concentrated diesel fumes. I have to lean on the hood until my knees remember how to hold me up. Lyssa tries the door, but luckily, the Captain keeps the child locks engaged, and she'd have to crawl over Jav to reach the front seats.

"Plan?" Sherman asks the Captain.

"Don't die," he says, swinging his rifle up to lock against his shoulder.

"Real motivational."

Around us, cars swerve into the highway's outer lanes as the jet descends to a low hover, its shadow darkening to pitch. A panel whooshes open on the plane's glossy underside, and two white-clad Supers leap from within.

Even at a distance, I recognize them. Tornadoes funnel around the Windwalker's legs. They carry him to the earth, Crystalis clasped to his side. Her hair swirls, a nest of red snakes.

Sherman drags down her sidekick mask. It hides her eyes but not the daggers she's glaring.

Car doors open, car doors slam. Civilians know better than to hang around, unless they're looking to get gilded on the Superspotter app. A smart car demonstrates its small turning circle, chugging out the same way we came in, but most folks just abandon their vehicles and sprint for the emergency exit signs.

We don't bother. We can't run, not with Jav's busted ankle—and no way are we leaving anyone behind.

"We could always leave your friend behind," says the Captain. Sherman thumps his arm so I don't have to. "Ow! What? They'll chase you guys, who'll be running in the opposite direction to *me*." Despite his words, the Captain twists the dial on the side of his gun all the way up to full. Ghostly turquoise charge builds in the barrel.

We're three hundred yards into the tunnel. The exit floats ahead of us, a glowing doorway in the dark. A gash in the fabric of space that leads to a world of sunlight and lies. Windwalker and Crystalis look minuscule from this distance. No news crews; they must've stayed at the bomb site. Our heroes stroll toward us, real leisurely, as if they have all the time in the world.

"Cooper!" I call. "We found out about Project Zero—you won't *believe* what's going down!"

"Oh, I know." Cooper's voice rumbles off the arched ceiling. "Brightspark told me everything, after I left the prison. The difference is that I saw the benefit in keeping my mouth shut."

I grimace. So much for that.

When the Windwalker lifts his hands, the wind lifts, too. Fingers of hot, stale tunnel air pluck at my shirt, beneath my holographic uniform. "Last chance, henchmen. Put the guns down and surrender. This doesn't have to end badly."

"I'm afraid it does," says Crystalis. "We can't risk them talking."

Windwalker's chin does a wobbly thing. "Can't we just bribe them?"

"Nope. Orders from above—they've caused too much trouble." She smirks. "Don't worry. I'll take care of them if you're squeamish."

I pray that Windwalker's gonna stand up to her. Tell her this is wrong, that they're supposed to lower Sunnylake City's homicide rate, not add to it. But he touches his chest, where a third star spangles, announcing his promotion to Team Leader.

Quite the feat. He'll be the youngest in decades—history books will remember his name. They always remember the names of men like him.

"I'm *not* squeamish," he insists.

A tiny cyclone lifts Crystalis's red locks, making them float around her head like she's underwater. She pats his nearest muscle. "Feel free to prove it. You take the Normies." She smirks at Sherman: standing at the head of our triad, between me and the Captain. "The Super's mine."

"Not anymore," Sherman snarls, and dashes forward.

We all know how this goes. One no-holds-barred Superpowered slugfest, coming up. Crystalis emits a laugh as high as my tinnitus, summoning a broadside of frozen oxygen spears to greet Sherman's mad charge. Sherman bellows a war cry, her shield bursting out between them, the tunnel lights pinging and sparking above. We're talking IMAX levels of awesome—until I intervene.

"Stop!"

Icicles shatter to nothing. Sherman turns to me, as do Crystalis, Windwalker, and the Captain.

"What?" asks Windwalker, a little peevishly.

I point to the car. "My sister's got nothing to do with this. She doesn't know what's going on!"

"Damn right I don't!" comes Lyssa's weedy voice, floating through the open window.

I raise my hands, gun pointing at the ceiling. "Don't kill her for my mistakes. *Please.*"

Windwalker and Crystalis engage in a brief, silent conversation. It utilizes only their eyebrows, which waggle furiously, distorting the lines of their masks.

"It's too much of a risk," Crystalis says, after Windwalker shakes his head. He shakes it harder. "The mayor said no survivors. You *heard* her."

"I don't care. I'm not killing some Normie kid."

"But you will kill my *sister?*" Lyssa yells. "Ugh! I can't believe I liked you!"

Windwalker sighs. "Get out and get moving."

I have to open the door, thanks to the child lock. Jav cowers in the footwell, having propped her swollen ankle on the seat in a contorted yoga pose. Lyssa clambers over her. She emerges from the car, slow and shaky. The dial of her Hench mask catches the gleam of the overhead lights. She must've been scratching at it; her neck's a crosshatch of raised red stripes. "Come with me, Riley."

"I can't."

"I'm not leaving you!"

"Yeah, you are." Still, I pull her in. Wrap myself around her like a crash cushion that puffs up to protect her from the slamming weight of the world. "You *have* to."

"That's enough," Crystalis snaps. "The kid goes now or not at all."

We're out of time. I breathe instructions into Lyssa's ear and draw back from her, cupping her little face. "You're gonna make your daddy so proud."

"Uh, no; he's gonna kill me. And you. So you gotta promise me, okay, Riley? Promise me you won't die here. Dad's got dibs." Her voice is a Velcro scratch. She scrubs her damp cheeks, breath hitched on a sob.

Windwalker rubs the back of his neck, averting his eyes. I

don't care if this will keep him up at night. I don't care if he'll need therapy. We're still gonna be dead, and I'm still gonna break my promise to my sister.

Crystalis could cut our throats with no remorse, but that just makes her a monster. Cooper's a rational guy. He weighed up the pros and cons of joining Project Zero, and decided that the Captain, Sherman, Jav, and I are expendable collateral. He'll kill us so he can nail that pay rise, rub elbows with Brightspark, boast about the shiny new star on his chest. Nothing I do, say, scream, will ever change his mind—so I don't bother. I just kiss Lyssa's forehead and lie.

"Course I promise. I'll see you real soon." Lyssa nods. I smooth her hair back from her face, tuck it behind her little brown ears. "You remember what I told you?" She nods again. "Good girl."

"Love you, Riley."

"Love you, too, goober."

I turn back to Windwalker. I might not be able to square off against him in a fair fight. I might be nothing more than a Normie with a nonlethal gun I was never taught to shoot straight. That doesn't matter. This is one battle he'll remember for the rest of his days. I'm gonna put a scar on that pretty face.

"Lyss?" I call.

She pauses. "Yeah?"

"Tell your dad I'm sorry."

Lyssa's sniffle echoes around us. "He's your dad, too, dumbass. Tell him yourself."

Then she's gone, aiming for that slice of blue sky, her phone in her overalls' pocket. Strength bursts inside me as I watch her trudge toward the light. The Captain moves to flank me, Sherman standing ahead. This is us, saying yes, we are nothing. We are dust. But we're the dust this city is built on, and we're taking it back.

Or, more likely, we're gonna die trying.

CHAPTER 43

I BRACE MY rifle against my shoulder. "Interlude over. As we were."

"Finally," says Crystalis. She flings a volley of steaming glass at Sherman, transformed from the grit canisters on either side of the road.

Sherman throws up a new shield—just. The lights go haywire. Rainbows glance off in every direction, prismatic. We stand in a massive disco ball. Shards shatter around us, peppering the cars to either side of Sherman before dissolving back into sand.

For a moment, it's like being in the observatory again. No time to freak out, though. I got my own Super to fight.

Me and the Captain squeeze our triggers. The difference is, he had the sense to let his rifle gather power, whereas I'm blasting my gun dry. It releases a pathetic puff of light that doesn't even reach Windwalker. The Captain's lightning bolt, on the other hand, whizzes past his left shoulder.

Windwalker laughs. "Shame you henchmen can't shoot!"

I charge my rifle in the meantime, sending another shot his way. Another miss. Dammit.

"That's it," mutters the Captain, under his breath. Does he think I'm doing this on purpose?

Perhaps he has a plan. I hope he has a plan. I sure as hell don't.

I miss again, backing up on shaky legs. Windwalker could toss us into the walls, snap our necks, finish this quick. But for whatever reason—theatricality? Lingering regret?—he drags it out.

The Captain fires again, with marginally more accuracy. A gale bats the glowing ball at me. I duck—barely. The bolt sails overhead, static lifting the hairs from my head. It dissipates against an abandoned car, arcs zigzagging over the metal shell, leaving a black scorch mark, as if it's been struck by lightning.

I take another potshot in the meantime. Windwalker doesn't bother to smack mine off course—doesn't need to. But he still turns toward it, to be sure.

It's the distraction the Captain's been waiting on. He squares his stance, and, with suddenly improved marksmanship, squeezes the secondary trigger beneath the rifle's black flare of a snout. Away zooms the tiny feathered bead of a knock-out dart, swooping toward Windwalker's neck.

It should strike him. Not the film of ice that crusts the air an inch from his pulse point.

"I'm wise to that trick," purrs Crystalis. "Come on, Windwalker. You're facing off against Normies! Don't embarrass yourself."

Windwalker's cheeks redden beneath the edge of his mask. "All right," he snarls, rounding on us. "Playtime's over."

He jabs one hand forward, toward the Captain. Then he squeezes his fist and *pulls*.

That's all it takes. The Captain isn't punched back into his car or whirled like a turbine. In fact, there's no visible change at all. The only hint that something's wrong is the *crack* as his rifle meets the floor, audible even to me.

The Captain drops, scrabbling at his throat. *Crap.* He can't breathe.

Windwalker grabs another handful of air and drags it out in the same direction as the first. "I could create a vacuum inside you," he muses. Another handful. "Rupture your lungs . . ."

He sounds sickly fascinated by his own words. Perhaps he's never killed anyone before.

The Captain arches. His spine's a flexed bow, head thrown all the way back. I know he'd be screaming, if he could.

"Captain!" calls Sherman. Crystalis hammers her with a salvo of steaming ice shards before she can run over.

The Captain's mouth opens and shuts uselessly under his mask. He's dying in front of me. Like Mom. Like Amelia Lopez.

This time, I refuse to watch.

The knock-out dart is my only real weapon, and I don't trust my aim enough to waste it. I need to get closer. Windwalker targeted the Captain. Perhaps that means he can only focus an attack this intense on one person at once?

I have to try. I lower my head and *charge.*

Windwalker raises his other arm. I halt—or rather, I'm *halted.* Hurricane-force wind blasts me in the face. It's the exact opposite of the Captain's predicament, though it achieves much the same effect. My cheeks fill like when a dog sticks his head out a car window. Wind squashes my tongue back down my throat, my eyeballs into their sockets.

Another gust rips the gun out of my hand. It dashes it against the asphalt, the cartridge of tranquilizer shattering. Noxious green goop puddles on the road.

Panic scratches my mind. Oh God. We're dead. We're so absolutely, completely *dead*.

The Windwalker certainly seems to think so. "This," he sneers, "is why you Normies should keep your heads down."

Then the ignition starts.

We all peer around the fume-clogged tunnel, trying to pin-point the source of the growl, before 2,831 pounds of Ford Fiesta slam into Windwalker from behind.

The wind drops; I crash to my knees. The car powers on, smooshing Windwalker into the road. Then it slips into park and reverses (and scoots back and forth twice more, just to make sure).

The driver's window rolls down. *Fzzzz.* A faint noise, made quieter by my malfunctioning ears, like gas escaping around the cap of a carbonated drink. Jav pokes her head out.

"What?" she calls defensively. "I stayed in the car!"

The Captain curls where he fell. He slurps huge, painful-looking gulps of air. Windwalker mirrors him—the difference being that he has a car using him as a parking space. He moans. I don't care. I pound over to the Captain as Crystalis surveys the results of our battle with a withering sneer.

"Do I have to do everything myself around here?"

She waves her hand. The temperature plummets. Breath plumes from my nostrils. The air shimmers, and the sweat on my skin *prickles*, solidifying, glossing me in a hard rime shell—even as my feet heat, sinking into the melting road . . .

"Not her," snarls Sherman. She hurls a shield forward, block-ing Crystalis's assault, and—

I think back to that news report (*she can freeze one circle of air at a time, just one*) and—

Oh hell. Crystalis grins.

"No!" I yell. "Don't!"

Too late. I'm too late. The shield quivers between us. I can't see through the crackled ice, but I still hear the scream.

"God," breathes Jav.

I don't believe in him. But as the ice crumbles away, leaving me staring at Sherman, my Sherman, speared on a spike of road tar that Crystalis melted and re-formed with a wave of her hand, I'm willing to make an exception.

Please, no, I pray. *Please God, don't let this be real.*

As usual, the Big Man doesn't listen. The tar melts, sloughing back into the road. Sherman follows it down. Limp as a rag doll, heavy as lead.

"Sherman!" I rip my sneakers out of the half-molten asphalt, dashing back toward her. Crystalis doesn't look, just waggles her fingers in my direction. I stagger to a halt before I skewer my neck on a steaming line of ice needles.

Hot tar laps Sherman's legs. Crystalis raises her hand, and the road swarms up and over. It devours Sherman's feet, her ankles, her calves. She could be eaten entirely, mummified—but Crystalis stops at the knees. I doubt it's out of mercy.

"There," she says, clapping like a happy kid. "That's so you can't run away!"

Sherman doesn't reply. Blood leaks through her hologram, slicking the road. There's a hole in her back. I can't see it, but I know it's there. The spike didn't go all the way through, but there's lots of important stuff it could've punctured. Spine. Kidneys. Liver, perhaps—I didn't do well in biology.

Crystalis hunkers down beside her. "I intend to freeze the blood of your Normie friends. All I have to do is work out who to start with. Maybe you could point out your favorite?"

Sherman gurgles something.

Crystalis cups a hand to her ear. "What's that? Didn't quite hear."

I take a sneaky step to the side, hoping to skulk around the ice needles. They swing with me, ten tiny daggers, ready to run me through.

Sherm makes a sound like she's dying. Which she might be. No, don't think about that.

"The big one it is," says Crystalis, emerald gaze flicking toward me. There and gone again, dismissive, cruel. This isn't about hurting me. This is all about hurting *Sherman*—but that doesn't blunt the sting of her words. "Ugh. *Please* tell me you're not hooking up with that pachyderm. I take it as an insult."

Sherman tries to spit at her, but the wet string flops back on her chin. Crystalis laughs, while I do my best not to imagine what frozen blood feels like. She cups Sherman's cheek, mock tender.

"How about a kiss, for old time's sake? A reminder of everything you're missing out on?"

She doesn't give Sherman the chance to refuse. Just dives in and plants one on her. It's long, passionate, and (in my humble opinion) unnecessarily wet. Then, all of a sudden, it's over.

Crystalis jerks away. She sits, putting those perfectly toned buttocks to use. One hand flies to her mouth. The other remains trapped in Sherman's grip.

"I said," snarls Sherman, so hoarse I have to read the words off her lips. "*Go. To. Hell.*"

Crystalis's eyes roll. Not in a sarcastic way. She clutches her throat. Her mouth gapes, tongue curling. Ice glistens in her throat. A tiny bubble of a shield. A kernel, a seed of death, germinating inside her.

She shakes; she struggles. Then her fox-green gaze narrows, and she points at me.

Agony. It blazes out from my fingertips, swarming up my arm. Voracious, feeding on my heat like it's eating me alive. Cold, so *cold* . . .

"No!" shouts someone. Sherman, I think. Then there's a *splat*, and the agony fades.

I blink back tears, clutching my pulsating wrist. Crystalis smiles cruelly up at me. That's unnerving, since the rest of her slouches by Sherman, drooping to rest on the malformed road. An ice shield covers the stump of her neck. Must've expanded inside her. Blood drains in gentle glugs, like a tomato juice carton tipped on one side.

Oh no. *Hell* no. I can't see this. I can't deal with it right now.

I stare at my hand instead. It's twice the usual size, puffy and discolored. Bruises spread beneath my skin like inkblots on paper. It hurts. It hurts so damn much. But it'll heal. I think. Then it'll be as if Crystalis never touched me.

"Uh," wheezes the Captain, pushing up on his elbows and pointing at the decapitated head. "You never told me you could do that."

Sherman looks as shocked as the rest of us. "I didn't *know* I could do that." At least, I think that's what she says. Her voice is so frail I can no longer tell.

The pain in my hand is nothing in comparison. I stagger over, hurdling the majority of Crystalis. I wipe her blood off Sherman's cheek on my sleeve—have to stop myself before I keep scrubbing. I want the stain of her gone, forgotten. Out of our lives.

"You saved me," I whisper. "Again."

Sherman grins—a proper one, not her usual half smile. There's more blood on her teeth, I don't know whose. "I'm . . . just that good . . ."

"Shut up. Don't talk, okay? Just lie here a bit. Think you can handle that?"

She flops her head on my lap in answer. The Captain heaves himself upright, using the nearest bumper. He trudges to his car, hissing at the new dents.

"Shit. My insurance don't cover running heroes over."

"You're welcome," says Jav, hooking her arm through the window. "I thought it was damn good parking."

Spoke too soon. Windwalker surges back to life. He rears up, taking the Fiesta with him, heaving it high above his head like a circus muscleman. Typhoons swirl around his fists.

The Captain flies backward. He slams into a dented hood, bowls over it, and flumps gracelessly down the other side. Jav sways on the driver's seat, screeching.

Windwalker bares his teeth. "You Normies *dare*—"

That's as far as he gets. His knees sag in. His brows beetle beneath his torn mask: a final look of perplexed rage. Then he keels, the car smashing back down on top of him with a satisfying *crunch*.

Two darts bristle from his neck.

"Cavalry's arrived," growls Birnbaum. He and Turner stand at the mouth of the tunnel, in Hench uniforms, pistols raised. "Nice shot, kid."

"Fluke," says Turner. "I was aiming for his chest—bigger target."

How many points would a twofer fight win him on Superspotter? I don't care, and he doesn't seem to, either. He came to help us. They both did. If I weren't supporting Sherman's head right now, I'd run over and give them the biggest tackle hug known outside of football. Even if it threw Birnbaum's back.

"You're late," grumbles the Captain. He peels himself up—again—and limps to his car for the second time. Jav clings to the steering wheel, glass-eyed and shaking. The Captain ignores her, retrieving a crowbar from the trunk and tossing his rifle back in. He makes his wincing way back to us, whereupon he plonks down and starts levering the road off Sherman's legs.

"Can I help?" I ask, running fingers through her curls, combing out the snags. I'm still breathing too fast and too shallow. Every inhale tastes of blood and tar.

The Captain shakes his head. "You're helping plenty."

Sure enough, Sherman appreciates my pillow services. At least, that's what I assume she's conveying, through her vise grip on my bruised hand. Birnbaum approaches, splashing through Crystalis's leakage with no aversion. Behind him, Turner gags.

"Oh, that's a headless body. She's dead. Very, *very* dead . . ." He stumbles away, ashy pale. Lyssa takes his place, inching around the abandoned vehicles in the tunnel's mouth, eyes huge. And—crap. That's a whole-ass corpse my baby sister's staring at.

"Lyss, look away!"

For once, she does what I tell her. She doesn't want to see.

"Took us a while to figure out where you were," Birnbaum explains, creaking into a crouch beside Sherman. Captain must've called for backup before we set off. "Young 'un here figured you were either underground or dead if none of our emails got through."

"Texts," Turner manages from where he's bent over, undulating around a dry retch.

"Yes, those. Thought you might need a medical assist, so an ambulance is on its way." Birnbaum assesses Sherman, wrinkly mouth tight. "Let's see what I can do in the meantime. Patched up plenty of our boys, back in Nam."

The Captain budges aside, giving him space to work. He wiggles the crowbar into Sherman's new asphalt leg warmers. "Fuck, that's hot. Doesn't it hurt?"

Sherman nuzzles my thigh. She says nothing at all. Her nails dig into my defrosting, bruise-puffed knuckles. It stings, but whatever. I'd take that pain any day over the moment her grip limpens.

The red pool under her spreads and spreads. Soaking through my pants, sticking to my skin.

CHAPTER 44

WE WAIT FOR the ambulance inside the tunnel's gaping concrete jaws. Forever, it feels like. Then a few minutes on top.

My mind is brittle porcelain. I'm webbed over with cracks, one tap away from shattering. At least there's no smoke. Not like the last time I sat on a bloodstained road, waiting for blue lights to crest the hill.

Because this time isn't like that time. Because my memory of the crash is fuzzy, like I'm looking through bubble wrap, whereas I recall every millisecond of our fight with Crystalis and Windwalker. Because I have friends all around me, and whatever comes next, we'll face it together.

Because this time, the body on my lap isn't past saving.

Birnbaum at least has the decency to heave Crystalis off to one side. The Captain (with considerably less respect for the deceased) treats her head to a hearty kick. Means I don't have to worry about my sister seeing any more stuff that's liable to leave her as messed up as me.

"Did you do it?" I ask her. Sensation dribbles from my legs. I itch to shift, reintroduce a little blood flow to my backside, but that would mean jostling Sherman.

"Upload the video?" Lyssa won't look at me, for some reason. "Yeah. Every account I have. Yours and Jav's and Sherman's, too."

"You turned thirteen three days ago. How many accounts *do* you have?"

". . . Let's not talk about that right now. Point is, it's out there. No taking it back."

Here, cushioned by the warm-lit walls of the tunnel, the weight of a mountain suspended over our heads, it doesn't feel like my life is changing. But once I step outside, there'll be no escape. Will Sunnylake break under this revelation? Or worse, will nobody care?

I wind Sherman's limp fingers through my own. I guess we'll find out, soon enough.

A wail of sirens, the screech of brakes. Paramedics haul ass to Sherman and Cooper (who, since none of us have volunteered to free him, is still being smushed by a couple tons of car). As they lift Sherman onto a stretcher, the numbness in my legs snakes upward, winding around my organs. I have to use the nearest car hood to crawl upright. My hands leave sweaty prints.

Sherman will be fine. She has to be. *She has to be.* But that doesn't change how fucked we are. We killed a Super. We gave another one a solid decade of physical therapy to look forward to. No way do we get away with this.

I can't stomach watching the paramedics work on Sherman's slack form. I trail Lyssa to the end of the tunnel instead. Neither of us needs to explain why we hate the smell of blood and exhaust.

"So," I say, squinting at the lowering sun. "Long day, huh?"

She doesn't reply. I figure she's overwhelmed—I certainly am. But when we step out from under the lip of the tunnel, daylight soaking our skin, I realize she's scowling.

"You *lied* to me, Riley. About working as a henchman. About *everything*. And now again. You didn't know you'd survive, so you lied about that, too!"

The highway ahead is deserted. The sidekicks must've set up a roadblock. The mayor wouldn't have wanted any unnecessary witnesses to our execution. Very considerate; it means traffic hasn't bottlenecked around the tunnel mouth. The ambulance must've used medical creds to wheedle their way through.

Won't be long before the Super Squad realize they last swapped communications with Crystalis and Windwalker ten minutes ago: more than enough time for them to dispose of two Normies and a D-class sidekick. But for now, at least, since every other driver in the tunnel made a beeline for the nearest exit, the busiest road in Sunnylake City is the most peaceful. Even with my misbehaving ears, me and Lyssa can hear each other speak.

Shame I can't think of anything to say.

I go to touch her cheek. She shoves me back. "Fuck off. Why'd I care if you die, anyway? You're an ass."

I can't argue. Just like I can't expect her to be cool with every mistake I've made this summer. "I'm sorry."

She sniffs. "Is that a lie, too?" But when I tuck my arm around her, she lets me hold her for all of five seconds before ducking to one side.

I leave her to sit on the empty hard shoulder, murdering ants as they crawl from fissures in the asphalt. Jav rests against the edge of the tunnel, weight off her bandaged ankle. She holds an ice pack to her temple with one hand, courtesy of the ambulance guys, and browses Lyssa's phone with the other. Aaron said something about her not looking at screens for a while—suspected concussion and all—but it'd take more than a medical emergency to cure Jav's FOMO. Her frown weighs heavier the longer I watch, so I sidle in, bump our hips.

"Sup?"

"Everyone's passing blame like it's a hot potato. Mayor Darcy claims deepfake. Says we set her up, used a double, manipulated the footage—but ain't nobody fooled."

I lean on the steep embankment, dry grass stabbing my back. I didn't realize how sore I was until the adrenaline ebbed, but new aches pulse out from my bones, like how Mrs. Beauvais's arthritic knuckles can foretell the rain. *There be storms ahead.*

"You think shit's gonna change?" I ask.

"I hope so." A notification pings; her face lights up. "Hey, one of the henchmen involved in organizing the protest agreed to do an interview for my podcast! Delmar or something. Says he wants to keep the focus on the protest."

"He'll have a good audience."

"Uh-huh. My subscriber count's way up."

That's my Jav—riding this tsunami to fame and fortune, leaving us all behind.

Still, despite the pride on her face, she looks nervous.

"That's a lot of responsibility," I say. Even for a seventeen-year-old who might've just saved Bridgebrook.

Jav droops. "I'll deal with it tomorrow." She clicks the log-out button on her Twitter and passes the phone back to Lyssa, before leaning against me and smooshing her cheek on my shoulder, like she used to when we were kids. "Riles?"

"Yeah?"

"I'm sorry." I wait for the clarification. This time it's the one I want. "For that shit I said at the prison. I don't understand why you joined Hench, but I should've tried. You're my bestie, Riles. And you're nothing like them villains."

"And you're nothing like Mayor Darcy." I toss one arm around her shoulders. "I'm sorry, too."

Guess I should get used to saying that. Between her and Lyssa, I'll be repeating it for years to come. Sherman has a point, though, about apologies. Feels good to own your fuckups.

Sherman. If I let myself worry about her, the constant simmer of panic in my brain will jet up like a waterspout. I catch one last glimpse as the paramedics load her into the back of the ambulance. Sealed into an oxygen mask. Beautiful brown eyes shut. I want to call out, but she won't hear me. She'll be fine. I just have to keep telling myself that, over and over, until it comes true.

The Super Squad jet makes another low pass. Scanning the area? Calling for reinforcements? This was always gonna end badly. You can't outrun the law when the law can fly, command the elements, shoot lasers from assorted orifices, etc. Still, our annihilation at the hands of every registered hero and heroine in Sunnylake feels like a distant threat. A problem for future Riley.

Jav and I support each other's weight. Jav has a harder job of it, but she doesn't complain. "You think I should do it, Riley?" she asks. "Harvard, journalism, politics? Can I do all that, and still be me?"

"Assuming we survive the next hour, I think you're gonna do whatever the hell you want. And you're gonna do it awesomely."

Her dark eyes pour into mine. "But what if I screw up?"

"You got me here to hold you accountable." I unpeel from her, parking my ass on the weed-speckled panel that stops the embankment slumping over the hard shoulder. Grainy concrete scrapes my thighs. "I solemnly swear to take you down before you go full evil monologue."

Jav fidgets with her braids. "Head shot?"

I ditched my rifle when Sherman dropped, so I mime taking aim. "Yup."

"Double tap? Zombie style?"

"You betcha."

She flicks the braids over her shoulder. "Then I won't pitch my global takeover till you hit up the range. Seriously, I know henchmen got this thing about not shooting straight. But that shit was *embarrassing*."

I turn my pretend rifle into two middle fingers, but I'm grinning. That fades as empty cars growl to life all around us, high beams pinning us in place. Every hair on my body prickles upright like I'm about to be at the center of a lightning strike. There's a Surger nearby. A *powerful* one.

I lift my arms, squinting into the bright white lights. As Jav and Lyssa do the same, I step sideways, subtle as I can, keeping my sister in my shadow.

"Well," says a voice I know from the TV, from advertisements, from every "So There's a Villain Attacking Your School" PSA they make us watch in homeroom. "Isn't this interesting?"

The leader of the Super Squad strides between the empty cars. They roll away from him, clearing his path. Brightspark's in good shape for a guy pushing fifty. *Super* shape, really. He looks like Cooper Hanson with the addition of three decades, silver-fox streaks, two post-fistfight nose jobs, and a whole other level of superiority complex. The lines of his Purex-white costume guide my eyes to the trio of stars on his chest, and he smiles like he has a long-lens paparazzi camera trained on him.

Two sidekicks flank him, V formation. Their outfits match Sherman's, though the holographic specs look better fitted. They give us brief once-overs. Brightspark doesn't look at us at all.

"You," he says as he saunters past. "Stay right where you are."

"Does he mean us?" whispers Lyssa. All the surrounding cars grumble a warning when I take another step in front of her. Guess that's a yes.

Jav clears her throat. "We're not resisting," she says. Real chill—though her raised hands tremble. She nods to Lyssa, who holds her phone aloft. "You've seen the video, right? It's blowing up everywhere. That's us in it, me and her." Nod to me this time. "We're not dead. We're not victims. And we're sure as hell not the bad guys."

Brightspark surveys the tunnel. Cooper, the trashed cars, our dropped rifles. Crystalis's head. His Ken-doll smile drops.

My ears buzz. I hope it's that lingering tone from the explosion. If an A-class Surger can amp car lights until they fritz, he can do the same to our brains. Still, if Brightspark's fucking with anyone's neurological signals, he has the decency not to gloat about it.

"Heroes down," he says. A blue dot winks on an earpiece that curls, larvae-like, around the shell of his ear. "One deceased, one injured." The buzz becomes a whine. I fight the urge to shake it out of my head—no sudden movements. "We have suspects on scene . . ."

"Stop."

Even with a car on his back, Cooper Hanson's voice carries.

"Stop," he repeats. Coughing wetly. Chest rattling on every inhale.

I can barely see him: prone beneath the car, past the arch of sunlight that extends into the tunnel. He's spotlighted by the fluorescent overheads, shiny sweat coating the over-tensed muscle in his single free arm. A paramedic kneels at his side, needle in hand. She must've jabbed him with pure adrenaline to get him conscious again. I wish she hadn't bothered—until Cooper raises his face to Brightspark.

His red-soaked bangs coagulate to his forehead, and his neck's a bulging mass of veins. But his blue eyes are clear as the sky.

"It was self-defense, Brightspark. You know it was. We—Crystalis and I—were dispatched on . . ." He has to pause. Draw a shuddering, red-flecked gasp. "On orders to kill these Normies. On behalf of the mayor. The Normies, they just . . . just defended themselves . . ."

"Stop talking," the paramedic says. "That pain you're feeling right now? More busted ribs than I can handle."

Cooper keeps glaring at Brightspark. Jaw square like he's facing down a villain. Perhaps, in his own way, he finally is. "I'll testify and everything. I'll make sure the world knows the truth."

Is he for real? Is Cooper Hanson doing the right thing?

Brightspark looks at us for the first time. Jav, me, Lyssa. His pale eyes narrow, each pupil haloed by lightning.

I'd look away, only this is my nth near-death experience today, and I have no more fear to give. I meet Brightspark's gaze, expression empty as the rest of me. He wants to lobotomize us via electroshock? He can start with me.

The high beams flare, then fade. That brain buzz dies, too, melding into the hush of dried grass stalks rippling over one another on the median. Hairs settle all over my body, as Cooper makes a groan of what could be relief or "there goes another rib."

We're off the hook? Just like that? Damn. I guess that's what friends in high places can do.

Only Cooper's not a friend to us. No way near.

He'll always be the boy who squeezed Jav's ass, because she was his waitress and his uncle owned the burger chain and he knew he'd get away with it. If he's decided to be a better person, I wish him the best of luck, but his heel-face-turn doesn't make me like him. It just makes me hate him a little less.

I'm sure he'll live with it.

"Sir!" One of Brightspark's sidekicks gestures to Crystalis. The remains of her, anyway. Ew, ew, ew. "You can't be serious. Windwalker is clearly not in a fit state to make such declarations. If these Normies truly helped murder a heroine..." He sounds skeptical. "Surely we should remand them to custody?"

"No. We're to escort them to the hospital." Brightspark mutters something too low for me to catch, and the distant silver dart of the Super Squad jet hairpins around a downtown spire and hurtles back toward us. "I daresay they could all use a visit to the nearest emergency room. The police can question them there, as witnesses to Mayor Darcy's crimes."

"Which you knew nothing about, of course." I regret the words as soon as I say them. Filter—what filter?

Brightspark reapplies his smile. He turns a slow circle, hands on his hips, beaming at the paramedics, Cooper, the Captain, me. "Well, we had our suspicions. As Windwalker here can demonstrate, with his research into Dr. Amelia Lopez."

Windwalker snorts. But he doesn't call Brightspark out on his bullshit. And, biting my tongue, neither do I.

Perhaps Darcy will push the investigation back in Brightspark's direction. Perhaps he'll pin all this on her. But the eyes of the world are on them now. I've done my bit. I'm fucking *tired*, and I just want to go home.

CHAPTER 45

I STAND OVER the grave.

Isn't fancy. Just a lump of granite, carved in that classic tombstone arch. Like a little doorway. Funny, right? When we die, they stick a stone door above our heads, as if we've got anywhere else to be.

Sunset streaks the sky, feathers of fire. I take a deep whiff of my lilies. They smell like Mom's funeral. Waxy, sweet, just a little nauseating.

There's a lot I could say. For once, I choose not to. I just stand there. The breeze lifts my hair from my neck and exposes the faint red circle where a uniform tag once sat.

Then I lay the lilies down.

It's taken me a while to visit. Two whole months—which feels shitty, except my life has spun into a whirlwind of interviews with Supers and police officers, hospital visits, shopping around for a decent therapist. The days whiz by, too fast for me to grasp. I've barely had time to exist, let alone buy flowers.

By now, I've told the truth, the whole truth, and nothing but the truth, again and again and again. I've watched our video from city hall so many times it replays when I sleep. I've talked on Jav's podcast, on the Sunnylake news, to strangers in the street. And I've told everyone who asks and several who don't that no, I'm not the one who uncovered Project Zero.

If they want to meet her, they'd have to follow me here. Through the gate of Sunnylake cemetery, to a gray stone ringed in lilies.

"Think she'll like them?" Sherman asks. We pooled funds to buy a decent bouquet from a stand at the open-air market. She suggested lighting candles, too, but I don't want open flames anywhere near.

"Dunno," I say. "We didn't exactly talk about our taste in flowers."

Sherman takes my hand, interlacing our fingers. Both of us look down at Dr. Amelia Lopez's name, inscribed in stone. Remembered, as she should be.

Sherman isn't doing so bad. She's down one kidney, but if anyone thought that'd bench her, I want to try what they're tripping on. She's even riding her bike again, despite protests from her dad, mom, Aaron, every doctor she's spoken to, and anyone else with common sense.

I'm not in that last category. I trust her when she says Supers heal faster than us Normie types.

I squeeze her hand. My fingers are stiff and sore. Unsurprising, given how many minor blood vessels Crystalis popped. The ringing in my ears faded ages ago, but the world's still a little muffled. Maybe it always will be.

Doesn't seem so awful, really. Not when I know my family, my house, and my neighborhood are safe.

"Where to?" Sherman asks as we leave the cemetery through the spiky black iron gates. Her motorcycle rests on its prop, tilted away from the curb. It fills the space between us when Sherman steps into the road, crossing to the bike's far side.

The city reeks (as always) of garbage and traffic and melting tar, but when Sherman leans closer, over the saddle, my senses swirl with *her* instead: sun-warmed leather and electricity. Way down the street, where the houses begin, the splinters of a smashed Blair Homes sign reach up like fingers grasping futile at the sky.

"Thought you had work." I lean closer, too. My thigh nudges the motorcycle's side, right against the bulgy silver circular bit that pokes out of the engine. I have this vague suspicion it's called an "air filter" and a vaguer horror that Luis might yet make me fluent in gearhead. "Don't want the Captain to fire you again."

"I'd like to see him try."

Masks aren't allowed when you're being grilled by the authorities, so it goes without saying that I've seen the Captain's face—not that I'm telling you what he looks like. He's busy as ever, rebranding Hench as an independent operation. McCarthy has suggested a bunch of alternatives to lackeying for villains. Rubble clearance after Super attacks, construction of affordable housing, cat breeding. Not sure if she's serious about that last one. Hench will never compete with the big boys from downtown. But perhaps they can buy a few lots, make a big difference to small people.

"Okay, token protest over," I say. "I ain't gonna turn down free taxi service."

Sherman hangs her helmet off the handlebars so she can fold her arms and remind me yet again that she has serious biceps, and I am seriously gay. "Who said anything about free? I got fares, Jones, and you're racking up the meter."

"Right, right. What's the exchange rate for, uh . . ." I check the tiny, pointless fashion pocket on my shorts. "Three balls of lint?"

"I was thinking more like a kiss." Sherman quirks one corner of her lips in that way she knows I can't resist. I swat her.

"Quit abusing your dimple powers."

The dimple deepens. "Is that a yes?"

I don't bother answering. Just lean over the bike, cup her face between my palms, and pay up.

It's amazing. Slow and soft, smooth as silk. Her tongue dips into my mouth, mine into hers. She tastes of warmth and spit and, faintly, coffee, and my lips tingle like I've licked a battery, and *God*, I wanna feel this same glittering sparkle all over.

I can't help but deepen it. Slow to urgent, soft to firm, my hands sliding down to her hips, over the bare, solid warmth of her muscular sides. Not caring who might see.

Sherman grunts in what can only be approval. She buries one hand in my hair, her other arm wound around my neck, and crushes herself against the bike between us like she wishes it were me. Forget leaving room for Jesus; her Harley is plenty wide enough to appease our parents. Still, I'm tall enough to tilt her back a little, and she trusts me enough to let me, making this sweet, breathy noise that means more than I have words to describe. I kiss it off her lips as the world narrows to the points where we touch.

Tragically, a buzz interrupts our canoodling. I extract myself, grimace an apology at Sherman, and check my phone—only to groan at Hernando's caller ID.

Changed it to *Dad* on a whim, couple weeks back. Then *Hernandad*, because I got weirdly nervous about it, and puns make him pull a face like he just bit a lemon. It's currently just *Dad* again. We'll see how that goes. But today? Feels kinda good.

Until I put the phone to my ear.

"Hi, mija."

"Hey."

"Y'know what's funny?"

"Uhhh . . ."

"I'm home. Lyssa's home. But neither of us can see *you*."

I check the time, and—shit. Past curfew. Hardly my fault, though. I mean, *8 p.m.?* Exceptions only for evening therapy sessions? Brutal.

"You're awful at jokes," I tell Hernando. "That's not funny at all."

"Wait until you hear the punch line. Grounded for a week, unless you get back here as fast as humanly possible—put me on speaker—*without* breaking speed limits, please, Sofia. Super reflexes or not."

Sherman jams on her helmet, curls spilling through the open visor. "Yes, sir."

"Still not funny," I tell Hernando as I wedge my own helmet over my head and slot onto the bike behind her, tucking an arm around her waist.

A faint crackle—Lyssa, laughing maniacally in the background. "Is to me!"

Goober.

"Home it is?" asks Sherman as I hang up.

I tuck my phone into nature's pocket. "Home it is."

Hernando's cracking down so hard on me. Almost like I nearly got myself blown up while uncovering a conspiracy to gentrify our district. Still, every time he ruffles my hair, cooks me breakfast, calls me mija, I see the pride in his eyes.

Sherman doesn't break any speed limits. Cuts one red light mighty fine, though—then, once we arrive, bribes me out of telling Hernando with another kiss. I pull back before she dissolves all thoughts of curfew, melts me down like a bath bomb, leaves me full of nothing but sweet, thick foam. Still, as she sails around the corner, away into the night, her warmth stays with me. A glittering tingle, just a little electric. Diamond dust on my lips.

I don't quite know where we're going, me and her. But I sure can't wait to find out.

Four texts from Jav arrived at the same time I did. I check my phone as the elevator—functional, for now—creaks up to the top floor.

Finally. The essay has been defeated, at dire cost to sanity and soul.
Need hugs to revive me.
Possibly chocolate.
Definitely chocolate.

"Dinner's getting cold!" Hernando calls—must've heard the elevator. His voice carries through the paper-thin walls. "It's gonna lose the love!"

I pick up the pace, shooting off a reply before I bash through the door and toe off my sneakers and grunt hi to Lyssa and sink into the perfect, warm embrace of home.

Riley: emergency chocolate and hugs delivery due on your doorstep first thing tomorrow
Jav: You're my hero.

That's the last thing I see before I send my phone to sleep, in accordance with Hernando's new rules for family dinner. Then there's just me and my reflection in the black screen. Smiling.

It's small, this life I've built with my family and friends. But it's enough. We're Normies, after all. We can't run around saving the world.

ACKNOWLEDGMENTS

A CONFESSION: I have never been to the US.

My goal was to develop a fantasy version of this country, informed by the IV-line of US pop culture I've been hooked up to since childhood. Obviously, all mistakes are 100% intentional, and are actually a clever illumination of how the US has established a worldwide cultural hegemony, which has shaped a flawed simulacra of the country within my imagination, and . . .

Have I covered my arse yet? Anyway.

There aren't enough words in the English language to express my gratitude to the brilliant Beth Marshea at Ladderbird Lit. I wouldn't want anyone else to be my guide as I venture into the world of authorship. Thank you—and Annalise!—for encouraging me to take the secateurs to this novel, and for (gently) slapping my wrists when I tried to snip away too much. You guys are hereby dubbed the Sherman Defense Squad.

To my editor, Holly, at Feiwel & Friends—thanks for the wonderful conversations about cats and cosplay and everything in between. Working through your suggestions helped me see the true potential of this novel, and your enthusiasm made me fall in love with Riley's character all over again! My thanks to Brittany, too, for your marvelous insight—and thanks to Avia Perez and Jessica White for wrestling the time line into shape.

My sensitivity readers have asked not to be named publicly, but I remain eternally grateful to them. Thank you for the effort you poured into educating me. This story shines so much brighter for your input. My especial gratitude to the wonderful writer of that letter. Your kind, insightful words resonated deeply.

I holler appreciation across the Channel and the Atlantic at my entire beta crew. You guys caught the most heinous of my Britishisms and liberally showered me in memes. This is for you, Linked (speed-reader extraordinaire; French, but I'll forgive you), Christina (my love to the Peep!), Ally, Max, Callista, Audrey, and Dahlia. Special shout-out to Lisa—the best friendships are built on bones. May our skull collections continue to grow. And another shout to Jess, my nemesis— you listened to my gripes and groans, teased me for going to bed disgustingly early, and reminded me of my awesomeness whenever I started to doubt. Stay villainous.

Thanks, Mum and Dad, for smiling and nodding as I blathered to you about this project. For popping the bubbly before I'd even signed the contract. For always loving me, even when you didn't understand. Especially then, I think. You guys are my rocks.

It takes a village to raise a kid, and a megalopolis to write a book. For my brother, John, the SheSizzles girls, the ACC crew, the Avosquado, and the Fourth Legion; for those who helped me through my own Mental & Physical Health Bullshit (you know who you are) and all those I've forgotten—you guys make me who I am. I don't know if the world should thank you or flip you off for that. Let's find out together.